MORE PRAISE FOR AWARD-WINNING

Emma Holly

AND HER SIZZLING NOVELS

"[A] potent combination of heady sexuality and intriguing characterization."   —*Publishers Weekly*

"Emma Holly is a name to look out for!"
                                —Bestselling author Robin Schone

"A deliciously steamy read. This is how erotica must be written!"
                                —Michele Hauf, author of *Flawless*

"Fun, sexy, romantic."   —*All About Romance*

"A sensual feast."   —*Midwest Book Review*

"She creates tantalizing tales."   —*Rendezvous*

"A wonderfully passionate read."   —*Escape to Romance*

"Deeply sensual and emotional."   —*Booklist*

"Holly's gift for sensual detail is absolutely stunning!"
                                —Award-winning author Susan Sizemore

"A treat . . . moves seamlessly from one hot and sexy situation to the next . . . More from Ms. Holly, please."
                                —Elizabeth Coldwell, *Forum*

"A story of sex, romance, and intrigue that goes beyond the norm."
                                —*Affaire de Coeur*

"I CAN'T WAIT FOR THE NEXT EMMA HOLLY STORY."
—Thea Devine

Berkley Sensation books by Emma Holly

HUNTING MIDNIGHT

PERSONAL ASSETS

STRANGE ATTRACTIONS

THE DEMON'S DAUGHTER

COURTING MIDNIGHT

BEYOND DESIRE

ALL U CAN EAT

MIDNIGHT DESIRE

HOT BLOODED

(with Christine Feehan, Maggie Shayne, and Angela Knight)

HOT SPELL

(with Lora Leigh, Shiloh Walker, and Meljean Brook)

Midnight Desire

EMMA HOLLY

BERKLEY SENSATION, NEW YORK

THE BERKLEY PUBLISHING GROUP
Published by the Penguin Group
Penguin Group (USA) Inc.
375 Hudson Street, New York, New York 10014, USA
Penguin Group (Canada), 90 Eglinton Avenue East, Suite 700, Toronto, Ontario M4P 2Y3, Canada
(a division of Pearson Penguin Canada Inc.)
Penguin Books Ltd., 80 Strand, London WC2R 0RL, England
Penguin Group Ireland, 25 St. Stephen's Green, Dublin 2, Ireland (a division of Penguin Books Ltd.)
Penguin Group (Australia), 250 Camberwell Road, Camberwell, Victoria 3124, Australia
(a division of Pearson Australia Group Pty. Ltd.)
Penguin Books India Pvt. Ltd., 11 Community Centre, Panchsheel Park, New Delhi—110 017, India
Penguin Group (NZ), Cnr. Airborne and Rosedale Roads, Albany, Auckland 1310, New Zealand
(a division of Pearson New Zealand Ltd.)
Penguin Books (South Africa) (Pty.) Ltd., 24 Sturdee Avenue, Rosebank, Johannesburg 2196,
South Africa

Penguin Books Ltd., Registered Offices: 80 Strand, London WC2R 0RL, England

MIDNIGHT DESIRE

PRINTING HISTORY
Catching Midnight: Jove mass market edition / May 2003
"Luisa's Desire" from *Fantasy*: Jove mass market edition / April 2002
Berkley Sensation trade paperback omnibus edition / August 2006

Berkley Sensation trade paperback ISBN: 0-425-21014-6

An application to register this book for cataloging has been submitted to the Library of Congress.

PRINTED IN THE UNITED STATES OF AMERICA

10 9 8 7 6 5 4 3 2 1

CONTENTS

Catching Midnight

GET out!" cried Gillian's mother, hoarse from days of weeping. She pulled one hand from cradling the baby's head so she could point. "Get out before it is too late!"

"Mama?" said Gillian. She hovered inside the threshold of their crooked wood-framed house, afraid to enter but even more afraid to leave. She was only ten, far too young to face the horror in the streets.

But that, it seemed, was what her mother wished.

Her mother coughed into her hand, then cuddled the baby closer to her breast. His dimpled little arms hung limp. Beneath the left was a blackened swelling, the pestilence's telltale bubo. Gillian shifted her glance from it to her mother's face.

Her cheeks had not looked fevered the night before.

"You *must* leave," her mother said. "You are the only one of us who might survive."

She sounded angry. Watching her, Gillian tried not to wish her mother had ever stroked her hair the way she was stroking Col's. Col was the boy and he was sick. Her mother had borne other babies, boys both, who had not lived to see their swaddling. Naturally she wanted to save the one who had.

"Wh-where shall I go?" she asked, the question squeaking.

For a moment she thought her mother would not answer. She looked so weary, even wearier than when Papa had gone to France with the soldiers to seek his fortune. Her eyes were shut, her cheeks roughened by drying tears. She coughed again, then turned her reddened gaze to meet her daughter's.

"Go to the forest," she said. "You know you love playing in the woods."

By myself? Gillian thought. I should go into the forest by myself? But she did not say the words, no more than she asked when she might come back. Instead, biting her lip, she moved to gather the loaf that sat on their splintered table. Else she would have no food at all. The bread was almost white. A luxury bought with hoarded coin.

"No!" snapped her mother before she could touch the crust. Chin aquiver, Gillian snatched back her hand. Her mother softened her tone. "It might be tainted, Gill. I do not want you to take sick."

Gillian stared at her. Sometimes she sensed things other people could not, secrets hidden behind the masks they wore for the world. Her mother would scold her if she spoke of what she saw, telling her such nonsense was the devil's work. The devil's work it might be, but Gillian was not sure it was nonsense. She knew when shop-keepers meant to cheat them, knew when the butcher's daughter feared the back of her father's hand. Now a suspicion dawned at the awkward look on her mother's face. Her mother did not believe the loaf was tainted. She was saving that fine white bread for Col: Col, who would probably die before he got the good of it.

When her mother dropped her eyes, Gillian knew the guess was true.

She backed away, blinded until her pooling tears spilled down. "Good-bye," she said unsurely and then, because she could not help it: "I love you, Mama."

Her mother made a sound like a hinge in need of oiling. Still rocking the baby, she pressed one fist to her mouth. "You live," she said fiercely. "You live."

Gillian would rather her mother say she loved her back. For the last time, she looked around the room where she had been born: at the chickens scratching listlessly in the corner, at Col's battered cradle, at the stool by the fire where her papa had liked to whittle fancy spoon handles out of wood. He had been able to make them look like anything, like animals or trees or even people's faces. She remembered how he had leaned over his knees while he worked. Had he loved her? She could not recall the feeling if he had, only the pile of shavings between his feet.

He was dead now, fallen somewhere in France. Though Gillian knew this, leaving the place where he had been felt like losing the last tiny piece of him she possessed.

Swallowing hard, she nodded at her mother, then turned to stumble into the narrow, sloping lane off which they lived.

The city she found outside was changed.

Gone was the noise and color she was used to. Fog had swept in from the Thames and a silence like a pall enshrouded London, broken only by eerie moans. The churches had ceased to ring the death knell. Perhaps no one was left to pull the ropes. Perhaps no one was left at all. Waxed cloth sealed the windows, hiding whoever might cower inside. Even on Cheapside, the widest of the city's streets, it seemed by every stoop a body lay, some covered hastily, some simply left to rot. Gillian hurried past the unmoving forms, trying not to see who they were, trying—so far as she was able—not to breathe their putrid stench.

A figure appeared through the swirling mist. In front of the shuttered chandler's a woman garbed all in black rocked on her knees on the paving stone. Gillian knew her. Mama bought candles from her shop. Once, she had given Gillian an oatcake slathered with summer honey. She had called her a wild little raven for her dark curls.

The chandler's wife did not recognize Gillian today. "Where is the priest?" she keened to no one as she swayed. "Where are all the priests?"

Gillian's nerve abruptly failed. She broke into a run, her tough bare feet pounding the frosty ground. Her footfalls echoed off the half-timbered building walls. To her jangled imagination, the rhythm did not quite match. Ghosts, she thought, following her out of town. A cat streaked out from an empty alehouse and she shrieked. Just a cat, she told herself with her hand pressed to her heart. And at least it was alive.

Though her mind was full of terror, she remembered to turn on Foster Lane where the goldsmiths had their shops. More people moved here. They did not seem to see her as she pelted past, shuffling along as though caught in treacle, muttering to themselves or staring into space.

"End of the world," cackled one young, bearded man. "Wages of sin for Jews and witches. And there, there behind you, comes the Queen of the Dead!"

His manic laughter frightened her more than his words.

To her relief, Aldersgate appeared ahead of her in the gloom. The air sweetened almost as soon as she darted beneath its arch. She was outside London's wall but still she ran as if demons chased her, her breath coming in gasps, her sweat like ice beneath her ragged kirtle. Past Moorfield's bog she flew, past the last stubbled fields. The fog was thinner here, like ribbons of drifting silver. The ribbons shredded as she crossed them. She saw a cart abandoned in the ditch, half turned on its side. She did not look to see what was in it, did not look anywhere but straight ahead until the bare tall woods closed round her.

As they did, a vine as thick as a snake caught her ankle. Exhausted by her flight, she fell headlong into the bracken and lay there winded, unable to move except to crush a dried brown oak leaf in her fist. With bitter understanding, she realized how pointless her mother's advice had been. Not a soul stirred in the woods. No one to help her. No one to hold her. No one to keep her from harm. Col and her mother had each other. Gillian would die alone.

I do not care if I die, she thought, defiance in it. Shadows flickered like phantoms as a wind rattled the branches above her head. Care if I die, they seemed to whisper.

Then, like the dead men she feared and envied, she fell asleep.

SHE woke at twilight to the sound of grown-up voices, voices so vibrant, so rich, her blood thrilled in her veins. One voice was a woman's, the other a man's. They stood close by and she heard them well.

"You are breaking the rules you set," said the woman. "By the terms of our agreement, the folk of the cities and towns are mine."

"I see no walls here," said the man. "All I see are trees and earth."

"She is mine. I watched her. I chose her. Even you can see her heart is filled with what I love."

"Her heart is good, Nim Wei. She will not suit your brood."

"That certain, are you, Auriclus? That I and mine are evil and that you and your 'noble savages' are pure? Faugh. Living apart from humans does not make you good. Refusing to drink their blood or interfere in their fates merely proves that you are lazy. Power will not go away because you ignore it. But why do I waste my breath? You understand me no better than you did when I was your student, no better than you understand any of those you sire."

This conversation was so inexplicable, Gillian opened her eyes to peer through her hair. From where she lay with her head on her folded arms, she could only see to the strangers' knees. The man wore a peasant's rough boots and baggy woollen hose, but the woman had robes fit for a queen. Their silk was as red as berries, with embroidery of shining gold. The thread, used so generously the cloth was stiff, formed a pattern of castles and crowns. Beneath the hem the woman's feet were encased in slippers of emerald satin bedecked in pearls.

Gillian felt a pang of envy just to see them. Only princesses wore shoes like that. To her amazement, the slippers bore not the slightest smudge of dirt. Even the ox-hide soles looked as if they had come straight from their maker. Gillian could not imagine how the woman had performed this feat unless she had flown into the woods.

Apparently unaware they were being watched, the man responded to his companion. His voice sounded to Gillian like an angel's. It rang with authority, with a sweet and virtuous depth.

"I refuse," he said, "to allow you to corrupt an innocent."

The woman snorted. "Believe me, there is no need to corrupt her. What she is her nature already holds. All I shall do is bring it to fruition."

"It does not matter what you believe. I say you shall not—"

The woman's satin slipper stomped a twig so hard it exploded beneath her heel. "Claim this girl and the truce between us ends."

With this vow, an invisible force shimmered in the air, thickening and building until the atmosphere pulsed with danger, like waking at night and knowing a monster lurks in the dark. The hair on Gillian's nape prickled as she held her breath.

The man's answer was a growl. "I know you do not wish to pit your children against mine."

"Mayhap I do not, but I trust you know I will. Come, Auriclus." The woman's manner turned coaxing. "What can this mean to you? One small girl who has already tasted the delights of civilized living. She will never be content to live in some moldering cave. You do her no favor by claiming her for your pack."

A strange realization took hold of Gillian's mind, a sense as strong as any she had known. These two adults were fighting over her. She, who had never been valued by anyone, was the prize they both desired, the child whose goodness seemed a matter of debate. Before she could decide whether to be flattered or insulted, Auriclus spoke again.

"If you are so sure of her, Nim Wei," he said, "why not ask her whom she prefers."

Nim Wei stiffened. "She hears us?"

Without waiting for an answer, she turned and knelt before Gillian in the leaves. Anyone else would have been awkward, but Nim Wei's movements flowed like a dance. Her skirts twirled outward and settled gracefully down. A scent came with them, of parchment and dust—peculiarly pleasant to the nose. When her hands slipped beneath Gillian's elbows to help her stand, a fiery tingle moved through her skin.

Until she felt it, Gillian had not known how cold she was.

The woman set her on her feet as if she weighed no more than a bubble.

Gillian's gaze found the woman's face. "Mother Mary," she breathed, gaping in amazement. The woman was beautiful beyond believing, her skin so fine and white it shone like a beacon through the mist. Tiny sparkles of color danced in its nimbus, dazzling Gillian's senses. Her hair, which fell to her hips, resembled a moonless night spun into silk. Her eyes were exotic, slanting almonds of onyx black. As for her lips, the loveliest rose would hang its head in shame against their pink perfection.

Gillian was more convinced than ever these two were angels. No mere mortal could be this fair.

"No," said the woman with a husky laugh, "the last thing we are is angels."

Gillian could not wonder that the woman had read her mind. If a girl like her could do it, even a little, why not this beauteous vision?

As the woman stroked the line of Gillian's jaw, the man squatted down as well. When he tossed back his hood, his looks were also extraordinary, but in a rougher, more earthy way. Though his hair was dark, it was not as dark as Nim Wei's. His eyes were the color of moss, his smell like a forest in the rain.

"You must choose," he said gently, and Gillian thought she had never heard anyone sound that kind. He made her think of being cuddled by a fire, of dozing off in protective arms.

"Auriclus," the woman warned sharply enough to cut through Gillian's haze. "None of your tricks or I swear I shall carry out my threat. She must choose on her own."

Gillian shook herself. "What am I choosing?"

"Life," said the woman. The word vibrated so forcefully color rose in her companion's cheeks. The way she said it was like a call to battle no warrior can resist. Though the man frowned at her, she was not chastened. "One of us shall make you what we are and you shall taste life in its fullness."

"Make me what you are?" Gillian repeated. "But why?"

"Because you are what we love: a creature whose passions are too big to contain. A creature with a seeking mind. Think of all the things you have desired. To have your hunger sated. To rule over those who slight you. To be brave and strong and beautiful all your days. Long days, during which you shall never be sick or helpless or ignored. You will be loved, Gillian, as a goddess."

Gillian looked from one otherworldly face to the other. They were, in their way, like husband and wife. "Why may I not choose you both?"

"Because *he*"—the woman shot a look of scorn at her companion—"wants you to be good. He wants you to forgive those who have hurt you, wants you to live like a monk in a little cave, away from humans and all their delightful toys. Away from books and wine and music. Away from ships and jewels and dancing boys. I want you to be a queen, Gillian. He believes you should be a beast."

Gillian turned her gaze to the man. His eyes seemed to hold all the sadness in the world. He reminded her of a painting of a saint.

"Think," he said quietly. "Who do you want to be? The girl who secretly wished her brother dead? Or the girl who kissed his forehead while he slept?"

The woman laughed. "As if it were that simple! As if she could deny what she is inside! Always she will want more. Always she will be greedy."

The man did not contradict her, nor draw seductive pictures of what choosing him would mean. With a flush of shame, Gillian recalled the sermons of the traveling friars. Lucifer's snares were sweet, they warned. He would promise your heart's desire to steal your soul.

Just like the one called Nim Wei.

"Hah!" barked the woman. "If I am a devil, so is he."

The man ignored her. "Think," he said again. "If Nim Wei is the one to change you, her nature will color yours. You shall partake of her powers, but also of her weakness. You will find it that much harder to be good."

Gillian already knew she was not good, not like her mother, not like Col. *Why must you misbehave?* was the question she knew best. All the same she did not think she *wanted* to be bad. Bad people went to Hell. Gillian did not wish to burn.

"What if I cannot choose?" she asked.

"Then you will die," said the man. "Perhaps not from the pestilence but from starvation. No child could survive in these woods alone."

Gillian thought back to the fine white bread her mother had saved for Col. She looked at the woman's darkly shining eyes. Why should she be good when in the end she was still abandoned? She could be a queen herself: beautiful, beloved, dressed in gorgeous robes and shod in satin shoes.

The woman seemed to see her daydreams clearly. She smiled with such understanding, Gillian thought her ten-year-old heart would break. What would it be like, she wondered, to be a creature this strong and free?

With a deep, regretful sigh, she turned to the man. He did not smile, but in his face she read approval.

"You," she said. "I choose you."

One

Scotland, February 1370

THE cave was hidden in the ancient forest, a quiet place with a mouth like a gash in the hard gray stone. No one knew how long it had been a den, not even the pack, and they were centuries old at the least. Ulric, their leader, claimed to remember fighting William the Conqueror's men at Hastings, but when Gillian pressed him for details he simply said his side had had no horses and were soon defeated. His human life was gone, he said: dust. He could not fathom why she was interested in the past.

The pack did not like to count their years, even by implication. They lived in the moment, in the hunt, in the playful mating of flesh and fur.

Auriclus would have known the history of their home. Auriclus was many years Ulric's senior. He was an elder, one who kept the secrets of their kind—the greatest of which being how to change human into *upyr*. Sadly, as soon as the transformation was complete, he removed the memory from their minds—and offered precious little to replace it. Gillian had learned their race could not bear children. Their ranks, small as they were, could only be swelled by mortal kind. Once changed, the sun became their enemy, the sweet, seductive song of death. A few *upyr* succumbed, like drunkards to wine, but most learned to avoid its light. These paltry facts she had gleaned in the time it took her sire to bring her to this spot.

He had not stayed even one day longer.

"Live well," he had said as he faded into the trees. "Live well and free."

His departure stunned her. She had been newly changed, confused by the swift alterations to her form. Not only had she traveled the length of England within a week; she had grown from child to woman. Auriclus had warned her *upyr* always shift to their perfect age, whether eighteen or thirty-nine. When he explained, she had thought it would be fun. She had not dreamt how lost it would make her feel.

Her childhood was gone forever.

And he had left her, *left her* with these strange adults who could turn themselves into wolves, who lived on blood and ran in the dark and tried to teach her to do the same.

But she was not an animal. She was a human being.

For months she refused to have any more to do with them than she must, though they knew enough to treat her as a child—whatever her outward appearance. Snuffling her gently, leading her kindly, they let her drink from prey they caught. During the day, while she slept, they curled around her in their wolf forms, sensing she would find that most reassuring.

She did, though she was damned if she would let them see it.

She had been betrayed. She was determined not to trust again. Rather than join their nightly hunts, she explored her odd new home, taking weeks to clear debris from entrances to tunnels that wound for miles through the pine-topped ridge.

Most of what she found was rubbish: half-gnawed bones, broken bits of this and that. Sometimes, though, the treasures she encountered were perfectly preserved. Brass-bound coffers would open on clothes so outlandish she knew they must come from foreign lands. And the books! Great piles of them lay in forgotten corners, with illuminations as fresh as if the monks had daubed them the day before. Whole nights could pass while she ran wondering fingers over the text, wishing desperately for someone to teach her the words.

"Leave those," Ulric would say when he sniffed her out. "Life is about the chase. You will learn nothing you need from those dusty tomes."

She begged him finally, abandoning her pride, but he no more knew how to read than she. None of them did. They had forgotten their human ways.

"Run with us," they said in answer. "We will teach you to read the wind."

Though she would not come as a wolf, Gillian came, and learned, and grew to like their company in the end. It was not in her nature to be alone. But the books always lured her back. Their scent reminded her of Nim Wei. Maybe Gillian would have known more if she had chosen her. As shameful as it was to admit, maybe the risk to her soul would have been worthwhile.

One thing she knew for certain. *Upyr* more powerful than the cave's current inhabitants had owned these volumes. Magic buzzed along their bindings like dozing bees. From the night of her transformation, Gillian could protect any garment she wore from soil or age, but to preserve one's possessions for millennia—how could that be done? Had those responsible been killed or had they left the cave of their own free will? Was Auriclus as great as they were, or was he perhaps their child?

Tonight the questions stung like nettles. Restless, she went where she always did when frustration overcame her, a high, round chamber deep within the rock. The chamber was not natural. Men had carved and polished and decorated it with pictures. In its center, a fountain bubbled from the earth. Its ice-blue water cast a glow that dappled the mosaics ringing the walls. Three twisting columns divided them into scenes.

Like a ritual, Gillian passed them one by one, her fingers trailing the surface behind her. In the first scene, *upyr* in man form flew like arrows among the stars. In the second, the sea was swallowing a volcano while tiny inhabitants fled in boats. Finally came a scene of wolves chasing prey, with this very cave in the background. The pictures stirred her old guessing-sense, making her feel as if all that kept her from reading their secrets was knowing how to unstop her ears.

This is our past, she thought. We came from those stars, and escaped that cataclysm, and took refuge in this cave. But which of us? And how many eons ago?

She sat on the fountain's rim to ponder. Being kept from the answer should not have been the torment that it was. The pack had been good to her. She had healed in their care and grown strong— stronger, in fact, than the other *upyr* had expected in one so young. Physically, none of the females could overwhelm her. Mentally, she was willing—if not always able—to match wits with them all. Because of this, she would never have to live as the least among them. She should have been ready to take the final step in becoming pack. She had lived beyond her apparent years. By mortal standards she was an adult.

But she could not choose, could not take her wolf soul and be forever bound.

Nim Wei had spoken true. Gillian always wanted more.

Wolf song drifted up the night-dark passage, warning her an end to her solitude was near. The throaty howl of Ulric, their leader, was the easiest to pick out. A human would have heard one note, but Gillian's more sensitive ears discerned a haunting three-part chord. She could not prevent a thrill from moving through her as the howling rose and fell. When the other wolves joined in, the scrap of human in her quailed. The *upyr* simply exulted.

Their hunt had been successful. They had taken down something large, a bear from the honey-bright smell of the blood.

Her mouth filled with saliva and her pulse pattered in her veins. Though she was not wolf, her heart still beat with theirs. This was pack magic, a reaction so ingrained she could no more control it than she could the sudden aching between her legs.

Ulric was coming. From the day she joined them, she had been his favorite, though he loved her then as a pup in need of spoiling. Years would pass before she noticed the bridled hunger in his gaze.

He had been waiting for her to grow up.

A blur of furry bodies tumbled into the fountain chamber—six gray wolves as tall as her waist. They yipped with excitement, shedding the last of the winter's snow, growling in mock displays of dominance. Not even bothering to change form, Stephen pinned pretty Ingrith to the floor and began to mount her. The pack was never shy, but this was mating season and their wolf natures drove them hard. In moments, Stephen's and Ingrith's yips turned to guttural pants.

Gillian's body seemed to contract as she caught the resonance of their lust. Stephen's black-pointed tail was waving madly, his nails scrabbling on the stone. Gytha, the senior female, barked in disapproval but the coupling pair merely wriggled together with more zeal.

As their bodies reached the point of utmost pleasure, Helewis, the largest but most submissive of the pack, set up an involuntary howl. She shimmered out of wolf form almost before the sound had faded, clearly embarrassed to have been caught losing control. Head hanging, she joined Gytha—also wearing her human shape—in drinking deeply from the fountain. Water they could imbibe, as long as it was pure. As Helewis knelt, she shot Gillian a nervous glance. Gytha, who had been Gillian's rival from the start, pretended she was not there.

This, too, was a function of the season. As a rule, the pack controlled their animal halves. When the real wolves came into heat, however, competition among their *upyr* brethren heightened—though they had no breeding status to win or lose. Even in wolf form, *upyr* could not bear young.

Without intending to, Gillian came to her feet. Her attention sharpened on what had drawn her. Not the women. She had bested them in too many fights to be much on her guard. Only a male could have tightened her nerves: the male who was stalking toward her across the room.

She did not need to see Ulric clearly to know that it was he. Though he walked as a man, his wolf imbued his every gesture. The way he moved, the way he held his head and curled his lip, declared he was their king. His naked body was lean with muscle, his eyes like golden fire. The only sign he wore of their recent hunt was a light mantling of sweat. An ability to shed impurities was a useful *upyr* gift, but he bore other tokens of his nature. The glossy blond hair that fell to his shoulders was a little too thick for human, a little too soft for wolf. His flawless skin glowed in the dimness like moon-kissed pearls.

"Little one," he said, halting a step before her. He smelled of sweat and musk, ambrosia to her *upyr* nose. More than that, though, he stank of lordship.

She met his gaze, taut, fighting her instinctive drive to submit. Her resolution wavered as she glanced past the sheen of exertion that painted his perfect chest. His manhood was flaccid but thick—and just flushed enough to tell her he was not completely at rest. As if her attention were a touch, he began to rise, swelling, hardening, until he had reached a state of arousal only the strongest could control.

The reminder was not just for her but for them all. Ulric was superior. Unlike Stephen, their leader ruled his needs. Gillian found herself unable to look away. Blood stained his thrumming shaft in the shape of a handprint. The mark could only be intentional, kept on his skin by effort of will. Gillian recognized it as an invitation to lick him clean.

"You killed tonight," she said, stating the obvious, resisting the urge.

Ulric's eyes narrowed with his smile. "Always you fight me, little one. Why can you not give in?"

"I have a name."

"You have the name I give you." He stroked her lips with the pad of his thumb. "If you want to play queen with me, you had better be prepared to be one."

Hearing the interplay, Gytha snorted, but at Ulric's bare-toothed challenge she backed away. Even if she disapproved of their leader's desire to make a younger *upyr* his queen, Gytha had too much sense to interfere. The pack supported Ulric, not her, however she tried to cow them.

As if the interruption had not occurred, Ulric drew his hand

down Gillian's neck. He shook his head at her gown—one of her
finds—but for once did not tease her for donning clothes. This garment had a single shoulder and a band of gold embroidery to gather
the ivory samite beneath her breasts. The long slit up its skirt made
the delicate material whisper pleasantly when she walked.

But Ulric did not appreciate the subtleties of ancient fashion. As
his hand cupped her breast, his thumb found the swell of her nipple
through the silk, circling it gently, drawing its center ever tighter.
Stubborn to the last, Gillian refused to flinch away or sigh.

"We saw a new female wolf today," he said casually, watching
her eyes, watching the helpless flush that crept up her cheek. Gillian
knew he meant a real wolf, not an *upyr*. They were the only *upyr*
here. "She was white, Gillian, a yearling bitch with silver markings.
She joined the pack that dens in the valley. She is small yet, but I
suspect she will be the breeder before next season. She was quick
and scrappy. Playful. Fearless. She would make you a fine familiar."

Gillian's hands clenched. Though part of her craved what he
described, the rest could not be content. The rest wanted more out
of eternity than Stephen and Ingrith's grunting bliss. "I told you I
have not decided what I want."

Ulric's laugh rumbled like a growl. "You do not have to tell me
what you want. My body already knows. You reek of your lust for
me, your hunger for my blood. Here—" With the edge of one nail
he cut a line of red across his chest. "Take what you need. See how
easy giving in can be."

Her teeth sharpened before she could stop them, stinging
within her gums. Gillian could not look away from the wound. His
blood welled slowly, as if reluctant to leave his flesh. His life was
there, his strength. No gift was more intimate among the pack, and
yet she did not want to accept, did not want to need to. Tired of her
resistance, Ulric cupped the back of her neck and pulled. His scent
swirled in her head. Moaning softly, she let him win.

His taste was sweet and wild and potent. Her body tightened,
then grew heavy with desire.

It was always thus, for all *upyr*. One hunger fed another until it swelled beyond reining in.

Ulric felt it, too. He did not wait for her to finish before he took her—not that she was in any state to stop him once his blood flowed past her tongue. A taste was enough to madden them both. Grabbing the back of her hair, he pulled her away.

"Robe," he ordered hoarsely.

She did not hesitate. She pulled the cloth out of his way.

He lifted her as if she weighed no more than a pup, urging her thighs around him, finding her tender entrance with his crown. There he held, jaw bunched, eyes burning, as he teased her secret flesh with his erection. *I can control myself,* the action said. *Can you?*

He was astonishingly hard. Gillian could not restrain her response. Wetness flowed from deep within her. Feeling it, the tip of him trembled. Then he drove inside.

His head fell back on a silent scream of bliss. Clasped now by her sheath, the blood on his phallic skin pulsed like a brand. The feel of it made her whimper. For a moment, she thought he would howl at her sudden convulsive grip, but he managed to swallow the outcry back. Instead, already starting to pump, he strode to the wall, slammed her against it, and braced her there with his weight.

"Bitch," he snarled, and he did not mean it fondly. Sounds caught in his throat—half wolf's whines, half man's—as he worked her hard. All she could do was tighten her legs and cling to his shoulders. His thrusts were too quick to count, too forceful to oppose. They made a storm of blows, a pounding, relentless hail. He could not last at this pace. Indeed, he did not try. In seconds, he achieved a groaning peak.

As always, she was moved to see it. From the day she reached womanhood in truth, he had taken her like this, like a starving man at a feast. The first time he plunged inside her, tears had sprung to his eyes. When she touched him back—tentative, curious—his skin had flushed like a rose.

He had said her name then, over and over: *Gillian, my Gillian.*

His want was unmistakable, but in all these years he had never convinced her she truly was the wanted thing. Maybe she was close to some image in his mind of a perfect mate. Maybe, on some level, even he knew the match was flawed. If this was so, it would explain why he seemed to feel he could only hold her by force.

Now, spasming hard, his hands clenched on her hips and his eyeteeth slid sharply out. "Gillian," he growled and opened his golden eyes.

His chest was still bleeding but their position was such that she could not reach the wound with her mouth. He stared at her, angry, though he did not move away. His organ throbbed insistently inside her. In this, too, he differed from mortal men. *Upyr* appetites took time to quench.

His anger told her he knew he had not quenched hers.

"You want this," he panted as if expecting her to contradict him. "You need it more than breath."

The rolling pressure of his hips told her which "this" he meant. She did not answer but bent to lick his neck. Ulric shivered, then turned his head just enough to ease her way. It was a grudging but clear surrender. His groan when she bit him was one of pleasured pain.

He came again from that alone, his organ jerking, his breath catching in a gasp. She knew her little victory annoyed him. He preferred that she succumb before himself.

"Enough," he said when he finished shuddering.

She released him and licked her lips.

Eyes slitted, he did not ask if she had drunk her fill but carried her down the passage to his private chamber. The room was roughly square, with chisel marks on the stone. It held two wooden stools, a tapestry of men hunting stags that she had found on her explorations, and a strange glass lamp whose oil never burned away. The shelf that held his bed was a niche dug from one side. Reaching it, he tossed her onto the furs. Gillian expected him to follow and he did. Resenting her own desire, she stared at the micaflecked roof while he crawled over her, pulled off her gown, and entered her with a grunt.

Her body did not fight him any more than it had the first time. Instead, it quivered and held him tight.

Ulric grinned in anticipation. "This time," he swore, "I shall make you beg."

She wished he would not say such gloating things. They tainted her pleasure even as she took it. And there was pleasure, sweet as honey, dangerous as the sun. Again and again, he made her body sing with delight. She did beg then, but only so he would stop. Her *upyr* flesh could bear whatever he gave her, but her too-human heart was tired.

"There," he said, pulling free of her one last time. He was breathing hard but his eyes glowed with satisfaction. Yet again he had proved he was her king. Now he would be indulgent. Now he would cradle her to him and let her rest.

"You see," he said, "I know you better than you know yourself."

In a way this was true, but—sadly—he only knew part of her. The rest, the part that wanted more than life in this cave, he pretended did not exist.

Rising up on her elbow, she gazed at his drowsy face. "You will never understand, will you? Why I want to read those books I found. Why I care where we came from. Why I want to travel in the human world."

Ulric opened one eye precisely the way his wolf self would. "Humans have their fates and we have ours. To us their world is forbidden."

"Forbidden by whom?" she demanded, her voice rising with exasperation. "The man who dropped me here like a kitten?"

"Auriclus is an elder. We cannot know why he acts as he does. Besides"—he circled her navel with one finger—"we took good care of you."

"Yes, you did, the very best care. For that I shall always be grateful. You and the others have been my family. But sometimes I feel like a child the fairies left: a changeling. I do not truly belong here."

"Do not be foolish. Of course you belong. Auriclus made you. You are pack."

"Maybe Auriclus made a mistake."

His snort told her how ridiculous he considered that. Gillian sighed. "Do you question nothing?"

He sat up, taller than she now, a frown puckering his silken forehead. "What is there to question? Our life is good, little one."

"Do not call me that!" She scrambled out of the furs before he could stop her, grabbed her discarded gown and yanked it on. "My name is Gillian. Gillian! I am not your private pet!"

Her outburst surprised them both. She had not intended to fight. His face reddened and he crossed his arms—more to keep his temper in check, she suspected, than to demonstrate it was there. "Is it Stephen you want then? I know he is pretty, but he can barely beat you in a fight."

"No-o," she crooned, going down on one knee as she read his hurt. "I have never wanted any of the pack but you."

"He could not make you queen," he said, obviously unconvinced.

Gillian laid both hands on his muscled thigh. His skin was warm and smooth, rosy still from gorging on the bear. Queen of what? she thought, but did not utter the words out loud.

"I would rather be nothing and no one," she said, "and have the whole world to explore. My hunger to learn is as deep as that for blood."

She saw she had gotten through to him, at least a little. His brows drew together above his nose and his eyes pinched up with worry. She knew he was trying to understand, but after a moment the effort proved too much. He shook himself as if shedding water.

"You will not feel this way once you have taken your wolf soul. That will make you calmer. That will teach you your proper place. Tomorrow night I shall lead you to the valley and you will choose your familiar. We cannot have you upset like this anymore."

Rather than argue with his pronouncement, Gillian inclined her head and backed away.

"Wait," he called. "Do you not wish to spend the night?"

She paused. "Are you ordering me to?"

The flash of pain in his eyes tempted her to relent. "Little one," he said. "Gillian. Do you not know how much I love you?"

Her throat was almost too thick to speak. "I know you believe you love me," she said with another bow. "And you honor me with your words."

His need tugged at her, and his will. Everything in her that was pack strove to obey. Only her instinct that his kind of love was not enough firmed her resolve to go.

—————

KNOWING she had little time to spare, Gillian slipped past the others' chambers and up one of the smaller tunnels. She was careful to make no noise. Dawn was hours away and her packmates would not be sleeping. Luckily, as far as she knew, only Ulric had the gift of reading minds. Compared to Auriclus and Nim Wei, his skill was crude. If she focused on calming her thoughts, she could shield them without his knowledge, could betray him without his knowledge.

Shaking off a twist of guilt, she focused on moving swiftly through the lightless passages of the cave. As she did, her senses adapted to perceive with more than her eyes. Memory guided her, but sometimes she thought her very skin could see. The tiny hairs on her arms seemed to feel the walls when they drew close.

She could do this, she told her quaking spirit. She had prepared. She had the skills she needed to succeed.

From a crevice that lay hidden behind a fall of rock, she retrieved a pile of clothes and a chamois sack. The clothes were a tunic and leggings of black silk, a hooded black velvet mantle, and a pair of black kidskin boots. The tunic and mantle fell to her shins in billows of cloth. They were relics of an older time, preserved by elder magic. Putting them on made her feel both daring and apart.

Though she had been planning this escape for months, she had not quite believed she would go through with it until now.

Dressed for travel, she continued up the passage. A turn to the right at a waterworn column and a crawl through a chimney almost too small to let her pass led her to the last rocky stretch before the exit. A wisp of chill night air stirred her curls against her cheek. She knew she was almost there.

To her dismay, a shadow blocked her path to freedom. Someone leaned his back against one side of the narrow slit.

It was Lucius, the oldest male among the pack. At any rate, he looked the oldest. His hair, which he wore cropped short in the manner of a Roman coin, was completely silver. Along with his dark gray eyes, it glistened softly in the starlight.

Too late she remembered he had not accompanied the others back from the hunt.

"Lucius!" she exclaimed. "I was coming to take the air."

"You were not," he said bluntly, but without ire. His reserve was a matter of jest among the pack. In truth, he was so controlled she sometimes wondered if he had emotions.

Rather than try to sustain the lie, she moved to face him. The outlet opened onto a ledge high above the forest floor, a ledge only an *upyr* or a mountain goat could attain.

"You are leaving us," he said after a silence.

If his mind had brushed hers, the touch was too subtle to mark. Ulric often claimed that Lucius was their best tracker. Perhaps she had unwittingly left him signs.

If this was the case, she could not undo it now. Matching his pose, she braced her back against the icy rock. Her foot bumped his but she did not move it. Fear was not a weakness an *upyr* should show. "Are you going to try to stop me?"

Lucius shrugged, impassive as always. "Wolves sometimes leave their pack."

"But I am not wolf."

His eyes flashed in the dimness. "You will always be wolf. You have loved us and we have loved you. That is not a stain you can wash away. Wherever you go, our mark will be upon you."

This was the most impassioned speech Gillian had ever heard him make. He rubbed his forehead as if he had surprised himself. Gillian's eyes stung with feeling. At that moment, she did not know how she could leave.

But Lucius had other ideas. "You will need this," he said brusquely and handed her a scroll that was wrapped in a leather tie. "No, do not try to read it. Just put it away."

Gillian tucked the offering into her sack. "What is it?"

"A map through the forest, to the places of the humans."

"The humans." She stared at him, wanting to be sure he was saying what she believed.

"I know you have decided to leave and I know why. I find—" He hesitated, then went on in a strangely belligerent tone. "I find I do not wish you to fail. The feeling is illogical, perhaps, but I . . . I am fond of you. That being so, I must advise you to seek the humans. Our kind are territorial. If there are elders, or even other *upyr* whose path you cross, they will either flee or try to hurt you. Humans will do neither if you are careful to hide what you are. Some of the things you wish to learn they know how to teach."

"You sound as though you could teach me."

An odd expression came onto his handsome, weathered face, as if he were listening to distant music he was not certain he wished to hear.

"Once," he said, his brow furrowing, "once I knew things. I allowed myself to forget. It was easier not to remember, not to care. But I know you should not trust the elders. They are unpredictable."

Gillian shifted against the wall. "It is forbidden to associate with humans." She said this even though she had not ruled the prospect out. She wanted to hear what he would say.

Lucius must have sensed she was testing him. His lips curled in a small, dry smile. "Auriclus has forbidden it because few *upyr* have the judgment to pass unseen. This has always been a problem for Nim Wei. Living as she does in the cities, she has lost many broods to the humans' fires. Some children she has had to kill herself for their indiscretions. Ruthless though she is, even she does not want a war." Without warning, his eyes locked onto hers, causing her spine to prickle in heated waves. "I am surprised she let Auriclus take you without a fight. Your mind is the sort she likes."

"You knew," Gillian breathed. "You knew she chose me."

"Guessed," he said and propped the sole of one bare foot against the rock. The crescent moon chose then to appear between two pines, silvering his naked body in its light. He seemed more alien at that instant than any of the pack as wolves, a creature of polished metal instead of flesh. If he judged her for being Nim Wei's chosen, he hid it well.

"I have met her," he said, "in passing. She struck me as no more evil than others of our kind. I do not think her interest a badge of shame. I tell you this, though: You cannot afford niceties of conscience among the humans. You must use every advantage, every subterfuge in your power. Our kind are not well known, nor much believed in, but those who do believe have learned to kill us. You would bring danger to all *upyr* if more were to be convinced. They outnumber us by too many times to count. Trust me, you do not want to be the object of their next crusade."

"I shall be careful," she promised, close to tears. The fact of her departure was suddenly very real.

Lucius nodded, then looked out over the valley of snow-capped trees. "You should go. You must be far from here by dawn. Ulric will set me to track you but when I fail, he will come after you himself. His heart is unwise where you are concerned."

Gillian's heart was almost too full to speak. "Keep him safe," she said, the words a raspy whisper.

"So far as I may," he agreed.

She wanted to fling herself into his arms and beg for comfort—
or at least ask why he cared enough to help. His face was blank as
stone. He did not want her emotion any more than he wanted his
own. Instead, swallowing her tears, she swung her weight over the
ledge for the long descent.

Two

GILLIAN did not dare stop traveling just because dawn had
broken. Like most *upyr*, she could tolerate the sun as long as
her skin was completely covered.

But not without cost. The pleasure of its sparkle made her
giddy, then slightly sick. As the hours passed, she weakened and
grew tired. The dozenth time she fell into the stream she was following to mask her scent, she knew she had to rest.

With a mind as bleary as a drunkard, she could not trust her
own decisions.

Later, as she dozed beneath a blanket of leaves and boughs, she
thought she heard the baying of a hunt but was too heavy-limbed to
rise. The pursuit soon passed. If she had been the quarry, Lucius
had managed to lead them away.

Lucius, she thought, missing him, missing all of them—even
Gytha—as if she had lost an arm. She might not have fit their way
of life, and they might have squabbled endlessly over precedence
and control, but the pack had been her companions.

She woke again just past sunset, alone but for a pair of ill-
tempered squirrels.

In reward for their scold, they broke her fast, after which she continued south and east through the forest, taking Lucius's map as her guide. Tiny castles marked what she assumed were established towns. Surely one of them would suit her needs.

On the second day of her journey, she surprised a white-tailed stag. She must have smelled harmless, because it did not flee. Catching it by the neck, she drank lightly enough to leave it tottering but alive. Her restraint was due to more than its beauty. Somewhere in the recesses of her mind she knew the creature's life belonged to the king not of wolves but of human men. This was the royal forest and that was a royal deer.

A name came to her: Edward. When she was young, her king had been called Edward.

The memory unsettled her. Until that moment, she had not realized how far behind she had left the human realm. She wondered if she had forgotten as much of her life as the pack.

On the third night she entered open land. Her first sight of the sky, so wide, so deep, made her stumble and catch her breath. The last of the snow lay in glowing patches among the low, rugged hills. Lights twinkled on their slopes, not stars but shepherd's fires. Her mouth filled at the thought of lambs who would soon be born.

Distrusting the temptation, she gave the shepherds a generous berth.

She wanted no suspicious two-cart village; she wanted a bustling town where a stranger might, if not be welcome, at least find a way to pass unremarked.

Her desire to avoid too-simple folk must have thrown her off her course. What she found at the end of the fourth night was not a town, but the endless sweep of the sea.

Gillian had never seen the sea. She did not know enough about the land of her birth to guess at this one's name.

Whatever it was called, its ceaseless breath inspired the odd perception that it was alive: moody, surly, the restlessness of its depths only hinted at by the churn and hiss of its waves. The water was gray in the darkness, echoing the ominous sky. Clouds piled atop one another on the horizon, their bottoms black as ash, their tops a radiant white in the waxing moon.

A shiver of pleasure moved through her veins. This, she thought, was a setting for adventure.

Unable to resist, she picked her way down the rocky beach. At the edge of the water she dropped her sack, removed her boots, and ran knee deep into the foamy surf. The water was so cold it stole even her breath. Laughing softly, she splashed the nearest spume.

"Hello, sea," she whispered, and tried not to mind that it could not answer.

Taking the opportunity to look around, she saw she stood in a natural harbor. A spit of broken rock, barely rising above the waves, curved around to connect an equally craggy island to the shore. At the island's summit perched what appeared to be a church. Her *upyr* eyes could just make out a line of Roman arches.

The shape of the island curled even more to protect the bay. At its far end, where it almost touched the mainland, it faced a cliff beneath which lay a row of small upturned boats. The smell of fish drifted from them, even stronger than from the sea.

Curious, Gillian collected her belongings and walked in that direction. Maybe she had reached a good-sized settlement after all. To her disappointment, she found a mere handful of hulls when she drew near. No town then. She would have to retrace her steps on the map.

By this time, a line of sunrise pink was glimmering beneath the clouds. Gillian needed to find shelter. She squinted at the cliffs. She had seen shadows on their upper reaches that probably meant caves. Happily, after a hasty scramble, she found one near the top. The fit was cramped, but it would keep her safe for the day.

If she shed a few tears before she slumbered, she gave the weakness no more weight than it deserved. She was a free *upyr* now. She would grow used to being alone.

WHEN she opened her eyes at dusk she nearly screamed. A hideous imp crouched inches from her nose with glaring black eyes and a gaping maw and bony yellow claws for feet.

Her stolen life was over.

The devil had sent his minion for her at last.

Then the imp cheeped plaintively and Gillian was forced to laugh at her fears. Her intruder was a baby bird, an extremely ugly baby bird, but certainly no servant of the fiend.

"What are you doing here?" she asked as she tickled its fat, downy belly. Not yet properly feathered, the creature spread bony wings. The skin beneath was as bumpy and pink as a fresh-plucked chicken. Seeming impatient, it shifted from claw to claw. Gillian smiled. "Run away from home, have you?"

As if in emphatic agreement, the bird plopped on its bum with its legs splayed out before it. It looked like an angry snowball with wings and eyes.

Then she felt it: the tiny brush of alien thought. She sensed what she heard was not precisely words, but her mind turned whatever it was into spoken language. *Food,* the creature almost said, picturing strips of bloody flesh dropped in its craw.

Gillian was instantly enchanted. *Yes,* she thought back, *I understand you!*

Less delighted, the bird repeated its imperious demand. *Hungry, hungry, hungry!*

Oh, for goodness sake, thought Gillian. *Let me send you back to your mother.* Wherever this baby had wandered from, it could not have been very far. It looked as if it could barely waddle, much less fly. No doubt her cave had an unsuspected neighbor.

She peered out to check, catching the dying sun full in her face. It stung for a moment before she was able to grab her hood and pull it forward.

To her left lay what could have been a nest, a simple hollow scraped in the dirt between two rocks. Grass and moss grew around it, providing—along with some clumps of down—a bit of padding for the two scraggly youngsters who sat more patiently than their sibling.

At the sight of Gillian's apparently monstrous head, they stuck their legs in the air, opened their beaks and squalled.

Gillian was trying fruitlessly to hush them when a different cry drew her attention upward. At first she could not see what had made the sound. Then, silhouetted against the orange and scarlet clouds, she spied a spiraling brown cross.

Round and round it swooped, mounting higher with every turn. Its wings were outstretched, its tail fanned to make the most of a column of rising air. Each motion seemed effortless, each adjustment of feather and joint precise.

Beautiful, Gillian thought, and heard an echo of something similar from her small companion, something that also seemed to mean *mother*. The baby tensed on its black-taloned yellow feet and stretched its useless wings—no doubt dreaming of the day when it would ride the wind.

Intent on her business, the mother bird paid her audience no mind. Her blunt black head sought something in the sea below.

Suddenly, without a flicker of warning, she folded her wings and dove. Down she plummeted, a straight-line blur of speed with the wind whistling in her wake as if for a crossbow's bolt.

Gillian's heart lodged in her throat. *No,* she thought, certain the beautiful, reckless creature would dash itself on the rocks.

Food! exulted her downy companion.

An instant later, Gillian saw the object of the dive, a fat, white seabird bobbing placidly on the waves.

Out shot the huntress's wings. Out shot her taloned feet. Without even dampening her feathered legs, she stalled her dive and grasped her meal in the selfsame motion. Stunned by the lightning blow, the seabird did not struggle as her captor bore her up to the ledge where Gillian and the baby watched in awe.

She landed on a tall, besmuttered rock, obviously a plucking post of long standing. Then, with her victim held firmly in one claw, the mother bird broke its neck with a single twist of her steel-blue beak.

Still breathless, Gillian's heart pounded with excitement. Never in all her days with the pack had she seen anything to match this hunt!

If wolves were kings of the forest, this bird was the empress of the air.

Come, invited the baby, with the friendly innocence of the well-fed young. *Eat.*

Gillian laughed. That seabird's blood would scarcely make her a mouthful. Then she stopped. The baby waited at her elbow, homely head cocked halfway round, eyes bright with what Gillian suspected was more than the usual intelligence of its race.

Strong, thought the bird, still not moving toward its meal.

Gillian knew the bird meant her. She was strong. Like the mother's spectacular flight, Gillian's vitality was worthy of admiration. A shiver of prescience rippled along her skin. She did not know the ritual of bonding. Ulric had never taught her. She knew, though, as surely as she knew her name, that this was how her kind found their familiars.

If she had paused to think, she might have questioned the wisdom of her next actions, might have doubted if they would work. But instinct drove her, an instinct that must have been bred into her with her transformation to *upyr.*

Would you like to be strong with me? she asked the funny black-eyed chick. *Would you like to join your life with mine?*

She never knew if the baby understood. A rush of noise dissolved her perception of her surroundings, her perception of herself. Pain wrenched like gnashing teeth, then disappeared. Stars spun round a void of black. *Love,* said a hollow, silver whisper, as clear and fickle as a mountain stream. *Love is the center of all flesh.*

Gillian was the whisper. Gillian was the stars and the void and the two fragile hearts that beat faster and faster and then as one. Their blood roared like the wind.

Food, thought the bird.

And the bird was her.

Three

AIMERY Fitz Clare, younger brother to the baron of Bridesmere, lay on his stomach atop a sandstone cliff with his nephew Robin. Spring it might be, but the weather was chill and dreary, a nasty, gusting drizzle that swiftly soaked through their woollen cloaks.

Discomfort aside, it was perfect weather for catching hawks.

"Do you think they finished eating those ducks we dropped them?" Robin whispered.

"Not yet," Aimery murmured back, amused at just how loud his nephew could make a whisper. If it had not been too wet for their prize to fly, they would have lost it.

Robin wriggled with impatience but held his tongue. He was eight and towheaded like his father, all birdlike bones and big, round eyes. This two-day journey to the coast, his first with his beloved uncle, had filled him with more than his usual bounce. Always before he had been left at home while his older brother, Thomas, served Aimery as assistant. This year, however, Thomas was fostering at Alnwick with the Percies. Robin had leapt at the chance to replace him. Despite his youth, he had gamely risen to every challenge his uncle set to test him.

Satisfied he had done all that was possible to prepare, Aimery squinted across the white-capped sea at Lindisfarne Island and its priory. Hundreds of years earlier, on that very rock, Vikings had poured from their dragon boats to take their first significant English plunder. Descendants of Vikings themselves, the Fitz Clares' main concern these days was the Scots. Once victims, their neighbors to the north had turned raiders, too.

But the ironies of war, past or present, were not on young Robin's mind. "I could stick my head over the edge," he volunteered. "See how they have got on."

Aimery grabbed the back of his belt before the boy could put his words into action. "I shall take the rope down," he corrected, "and you shall wait up here."

Robin grumbled under his breath but stilled at the warning lift of his uncle's brow.

Sometimes, being thought a crazed berserker was a boon.

"No pouting," Aimery chided, observing his nephew's lower lip. "Lady Fitz Clare would have my hide if I let you fall off this cliff."

"Would not, either," Robin disputed. "Mother only pretends to care what I do when you can see."

"I am sure that is not—" *True,* he began to say, then shut his mouth. His sister-in-law was a strange one, given to fits of drama as well as an occasionally jaw-dropping indifference to her sons. She had taken an intense and—as far as Aimery was concerned—futile liking to him the minute she laid eyes on him at her betrothal to his brother. The situation made life at Bridesmere a good deal less comfortable than it might have been.

"Thomas says she only let Father breed her again because you have a soft spot for babies."

This bit of intelligence left Aimery speechless. Surely even Claris would not do something so extreme. The lord of Bridesmere was accounted a handsome man. He could win his way into his marital bed on his own merits. Aimery shifted on the matted sea grass. "Horses 'breed'," he said, "not people. And you and your brother should not gossip about your parents."

"Huh," said Robin. "If something is true, how can it be gossip?"

His sharp little face was harder than a child's should be, though his eyes betrayed a shimmer of youthful tears. Aimery cupped the back of his head, pricked by a memory of when this skull had barely filled his palm. His nephew had been a scrawny, wrinkle-faced runt with a peeping cry. When Aimery held him for the first time, the urge to protect the bundle of life had been so overpowering, he had scarcely noticed when Claris caressed his hand.

Babies called to the very bedrock of who he was and Claris certainly knew it.

"All the same," he said aloud, "a respect for one's elders is a virtue."

"I respect you," said Robin. "Everyone respects you."

Aimery sighed. "Some respect me. Others are just afraid."

"Stupid *bougres*," Robin muttered with a bravado that said he had been afraid once or twice himself.

"Be that as it may," said Aimery, "a true knight treats even those he does not completely approve of with courtesy. And he does not call them stupid *bougres*."

Robin pulled a face, but Aimery could tell he was considering what he had said. Like most boys his age, he was mad for chivalrous tales.

Would that his mother had outgrown them—or at least refrained from trying to cast Aimery as her Lancelot.

With a frown, he shook off the thought. "Now," he said, "let us see if our future huntress is ready to be caught."

Together, they anchored the rope around a half-buried boulder, securing the other end to Aimery's waist. Aimery allowed Robin to double-check the knot. He was not going far. A few meters descent would take him to the falcons' ledge.

Despite his size, arms hardened by swordplay allowed him to land as softly as a cat. Edging closer to the place he had seen the nest, he loosened the drawstrings on the linen sock in which he would bag his bird. His height above the beach was dizzying, but he knew better than to dwell on that. Many a task was best accomplished without much thought.

He stilled as the nest came into view.

As expected, the heavy meal he had dropped the birds, grounded today by the rain, had left them dozy. The parents perched, feathers puffed against the cold, on a stunted pine that grew from a crack in the rock. Fortunately, their three offspring huddled within easy reach.

One of the birds, a female, he was certain, was appreciably larger than the rest. Where her brothers were puffs of white with dark pin feathers poking through, she was nearly fledged. At once he knew she was the one he would take. Her color was the rich, deep brown falconers preferred, with a tawny golden speckling to mark her breast. The fullness of her crop told him she had eaten heartily. Greed notwithstanding, the way her nestmates snuggled against her sides told him her temper must not be bad.

He was glad for that. He preferred his birds competitive but not cruel.

His chosen seemed to glare at him, but he knew the expression was due more to digestion than to wrath. Under normal circumstances, none of the birds would have let him get this close. Lowering his head to lessen the peregrine's fabled aversion to the human face, he grasped a crevice in the wall, leaned toward her, and slipped the sock over her head.

As soon as she felt it, she cacked in alarm and struggled wildly. The sleeve of cloth was designed to let her feet and head stick out. This immobilized her wings but not her claws. To keep her from injuring herself, he cradled her against his chest, cupping her head so she could not see.

She calmed at that, enough to permit him to tuck her between his chain mail and his cotehardie. He had no choice but to confine her. He needed both hands for climbing. Nonetheless, he regretted the panic he must have caused.

She was stiff with it by the time he hauled himself over the cliff. Only the hammering of her heart let him know she was alive. His own heart pounded as well, and he wondered if she could feel it, if it made her think of him as more of a fellow soul.

I am flesh and blood, he thought as he stroked her trembling form. Just flesh and blood like you.

She was warm beneath his hand. Vital. Vulnerable. Awe swept

him as it had not for years: that even this furiously frightened creature would come to view him with trust. God had sent Aimery challenges to be sure, but this was a gift to beat them all.

As new to this drama as the bird, Robin waited by the rock with eyes like saucers. "Have you got her?" he asked. "Have you?"

"I do," Aimery answered, fighting a smile. "Have you fetched my tools?"

Too excited to speak, Robin pointed to a well-worn leather satchel.

"Good man. Are you prepared to hold her as we practiced?"

"Yes," Robin gasped and this time Aimery did smile.

"Breathe now," he reminded the boy as he handed over the bundled bird. "Fingers on her breast. Thumbs around her wings. Do not squash her but hold her firmly. She may be a baby yet but she is strong."

"Why does she not move?"

"She is too scared to move, but we shall make her better soon."

From a clean wrapping of silk he retrieved his sharpest needle and a length of linen thread. The peregrine stared at him with black and shining eyes, her beak gaping as she panted out her terror. Robin was biting his lip hard enough to turn it white. To Aimery's relief, he held their captive steady.

"Good lad," Aimery praised. With the dexterity and speed that made him the envy of other falconers, he pierced the bird's left lower lid, drawing the needle outward from the eye so as not to scratch the cornea. The falcon squirmed frantically at the pain but Robin was able to subdue her.

"That's a girl," Aimery said and just as swiftly performed the procedure on her other eye.

At this second insult she uttered a mournful cheep, repeating the plaint as he tied the threads' four ends behind her crown. The pressure drew her lower lids over her eyes. She was blinded then, a change that immediately relaxed her.

The transformation was one he had witnessed many times but

today, again, it filled him with wonder. Something about this bird was different, something about this day. But maybe Robin's presence made him see the mystery anew.

To Aimery's surprise, when he looked up, tears streaked his nephew's face. He supposed he should have anticipated the reaction. His brother's youngest had a tender heart.

"You hurt her," Robin said, a tentative accusation.

"Yes, I did," Aimery admitted, because he did not believe in lying. "Had I not seeled her, her nature would have compelled her to keep fighting. By the time we fitted her for a hood, she would have battered herself to bits. She does not know we mean her no harm. That she will learn with time."

Blinking back tears, Robin gave him a shaky nod.

"She needs a name," Aimery pointed out, hoping to distract him.

"P-p-princess," Robin stammered, and Aimery ruffled his flaxen hair.

The boy would come up with a name like that. He was probably spinning stories of dire enchantment as they spoke. But let him have his dreams. Aimery had lost his young enough. He would spare Robin that disillusionment while he could.

"Think you can hold her steady while I cope her talons and put on her jesses?"

Robin squared his shoulders and sniffed hard. "Yes," he said, "I can."

GILLIAN had not known what madness was until the man dropped his bag over her head and snatched her from the nest. Fear like a bottomless pit had engulfed her every thought. The actual moment of sewing her eyes shut she could not recall.

The bird had borne it alone.

Only gradually did sanity return. When it did, she found herself still blinded but free of the sack and clutching the man's gloved fist as he swayed with the motion of a giant horse. Above the jingle of the harness, she heard him singing softly beneath his breath, a rough but tuneful sound.

To her amazement, the bird listened to it as in a thrall. Her familiar seemed to think this man was her new best friend.

Some friend, thought Gillian, more than a little annoyed by her lack of sight. Her claws, too, were not as sharp as they had been. On the other hand, the way the man stroked her breast feathers was rather nice. And she had been tiring of life in the eyrie, especially since her wings were not yet reliable. Playing kill the twig with her nestlings had been fun, along with sunshine and solid food. As long as she was in bird form, both those luxuries could be enjoyed. Unfortunately, much as she dreaded being on her own, it was hard to feel mothered by a creature to whom she could not truly talk.

Gillian supposed she would have to let that musty old daydream go.

She was back to her first plan, to make a home among the humans. Certainly she could not have asked for a better disguise until she found her bearings.

She would be damned, however, if she was going to do it blind.

───※───

AIMERY braced himself before entering the inn. Even as a boy, he had not relished meeting strangers. Achieving his full growth had made the ordeal worse. Once he became a supposed hero, it was intolerable. Blowing his breath out slowly, he stepped inside.

The proprietor stood by a crackling fire, a smile beginning to lift his face as he dried his palms on his greasy apron. The smile faltered, then pasted itself back on, when Aimery and Robin entered the light.

The serving girl, probably his daughter, crossed herself and muttered a prayer. As if ruled by a different intelligence than her hands, her gaze slid from his face. Across his shoulders it drifted, then down his chest. It halted wide-eyed at his crotch. Aimery gritted his teeth. At least her eyes could not measure him through his mail.

"Well," said the innkeeper, his palms now rubbing nervously together. "Ye'll be wanting lodgings."

"And a meal," Robin added, his challenging tone a clear defense of his uncle.

"We shall eat in chambers," Aimery assured their blanching host. "Our companion"—here he stroked Princess's head—"is not fond of crowds."

Already the other guests had begun to stir, hands leaving tankards to find the pommels of their knives. They did not appear to be brigands, merely merchants and pilgrims pausing on a journey. Aimery knew their reaction was instinctive; few would actually challenge a man who looked like him. He did not bother to grasp his dagger. That would only increase their fear. Nevertheless, their actions tightened the skin behind his neck.

One man's whisper rose above the others. "It is he," he said, "the Butcher of Bridesmere."

When Aimery smiled, with deliberate insincerity, the man turned pale as milk.

To no one's surprise, Aimery and Robin were shown a room without delay. Equally predictable, all its inhabitants decided they would sleep somewhere else.

"*Bougres,*" Robin muttered.

"Never mind," Aimery soothed. "We shall have the place to ourselves."

He hid his amusement in searching the room for a likely perch. Wrapping Princess's jesses around the back of a chair seemed good enough for the time Aimery would take to remove his hauberk and wash up. For the next few days, until their bond was firm, this bird and he would be inseparable.

Clearly fascinated by the way her blinded head turned back and forth, Robin sidled closer. All in all, Aimery was pleased with how calmly their prize was taking her captivity.

His instincts had not misled him. This bird was unique.

"Is she trying to see?" Robin asked.

"Probably. But she may also sense a bit of her surroundings through her feathers."

"Through her feathers?"

"She can feel the stirring of the air."

Robin stood on tiptoe. "Can she tell that I am near?"

"I imagine so," Aimery chuckled, "since she is not deaf."

As if she understood, the falcon's head swiveled toward Robin and stopped. Robin nearly fell over as he tried to freeze. The bird ruffled her wings but did not bate from the chair.

"Can I help you when you train her?" Robin whispered, his body trembling with pent-up excitement.

"If you like," said Aimery.

His nephew's mile-wide, blinding grin more than made up for the ignorance of strangers.

⸻

GILLIAN waited to work free of her jesses until she heard her captors' snores. Amusingly, the boy's were louder than the man's.

But humor could not obliterate her fear. She was not sure how many weeks had passed since she had worn human form. Four at least, and possibly five. Until now it had not seemed important, but what if she had forgotten how to change? What if she was trapped in this bird shape? No one had instructed her in these secrets. She might have done something wrong.

Inexplicably, her thoughts turned to the man: to the steadiness of his wrist, to the low, rough sweetness of his song.

I would like to talk to him, she thought. I would like to know what goes on in his human mind.

The change was on her before she knew it. She experienced a lurch of oddness as her physical self went from something to nothing to something altogether different from what it had been. Her ears roared and sensation twisted her heart. A moment later, it was done. She checked herself: face, body, fingers. She felt too tall for a moment, too naked and earthbound. And then she was Gillian again, the runaway *upyr*.

Too impatient to wait, she tore the bothersome stitches from her eyes. The tiny wounds healed in a heartbeat. No matter. She would replace the threads before she changed back. She knew where the man kept his tools and had the strength of will to use them.

Far better, after all, to make her captor cut them off.

Intrigued to be once more in the abode of men, she gazed about. The inn was a simple cruck-frame construction, built in adjoining bays. Wattle and plaster filled the space between the beams and somewhat stinky rushes covered the floor. One small shuttered window let in a welcome breath of air. A bed took up most of the space, its hangings threadbare but untorn.

Gillian had never slept in a proper bed.

To her puzzlement, the snoring boy lay curled on a pallet in the corner. Blankets were piled atop him, along with the man's wool cloak. Unless she had misremembered, humans were as apt as wolves to share their warmth.

She stood over the boy looking down, thinking how small he was, how innocent and full of dreams. With a start, she realized she could hear his dreams. Like a knight from a story, he was galloping across a misty bog with a lance couched at his side. The image was surprisingly clear, as clear as the worry it inspired in the slumbering lad. She had never read anyone this distinctly. Obviously, mortals did not have the same defenses as *upyr*.

Sleep, she thought at him in experiment. *Dream sweet and deep.*

To her delight, the boy relaxed more profoundly, his mouth curving in a smile. Since her change, she had attempted such things on her own kind but to no effect. Unbeknownst to her, the efforts must have strengthened her gift.

This, she thought, was a very convenient talent.

Confident she would not be interrupted, she moved to the bed and slipped inside its curtains. The man slept on his back with a thin gray cover pulled to his waist. His arms were bent, one hand covering his right breast, and the other curled loosely across his belly. His head was half turned away. At the sight of him, her breath caught in her throat.

He was huge.

He had seemed big to her before, but she had imagined this the effect of the relative smallness of the bird. That simply was not the case. Even in human shape, he was the largest man she had ever seen.

Fear and fascination raced through her nerves. She knew it could not be true but, in looks, he seemed more powerful than her wolves. If Ulric had been as large as he, she would never have won free. The pack leader would have crushed her into submission within a week. She gave thanks that this man—apart from sewing her familiar's eyes shut—showed no signs of a violent nature.

Then again, when they entered the inn, one man had called him the Butcher of Bridesmere. Was that why he slept alone? Because he was a killer?

Something inside her resisted the idea, more than her familiar's irrational liking for the man. Surely his size was enough to account for his isolation. He filled the bed, overflowing it where his feet hung over the lumpy end. His hands were half again the size of hers, his arm muscles thick and roped. No doubt such arms could kill, but the picture that flashed through her mind was of being tossed in the air, of being caught so that her palms landed on those endless shoulders, of laughing the way she had heard other children laugh.

When he petted her in her bird form, his hands had been very kind.

Stop, she told herself. You did not come all this way to be babied.

As if he could hear, the man frowned in his sleep. His head turned on the bolster in her direction.

For the second time that night she caught her breath. His face was scarred, its left side pulled from its course by a jagged line of paler skin. Stubble shadowed all of his cheek but this. Broad as her thumb,

the cut extended from his temple to beneath his ear. A good portion of
the lobe was missing, though she assumed that he could hear.

Whether he could see out of the affected eye, she could not
guess. Scar tissue rayed its outer corner, distorting the lid and—at
the least—obscuring his peripheral sight.

It could not have been a pleasant wound to receive.

Pity aside, apart from the awful slash he was quite handsome.

Moving without thought, she perched herself on the straw-filled
mattress near his hip. His cheekbones were dramatic, his mouth
both sensitive and full. His squared-off chin had a cleft. His brow
was high. Intelligent, she thought, though naturally she could not
know. His hair spilled thickly from his crown, shining with health,
its shoulder-length waves a silvery brown.

Unable to resist, she touched it with the back of one curled finger. Its texture was a bit coarser than satin.

He made a low, small sound, perhaps of longing, perhaps complaint. Gillian's heart jolted in alarm. She had forgotten herself
completely.

Sleep, she thought as his forehead creased. *Sleep.*

He was harder to compel than his nephew—perhaps because he
was older. Thankfully, after a few repetitions, the tension in his
body drained away.

As it did, knowledge filled her in a dark, delicious rush. For all
his apparent power, this man was at her mercy, hers to do with as
she pleased. Caught up in the guilty thrill, her gaze fell to his chest.
Despite his size, it was graceful. Each group of well-developed muscles flowed smoothly into the next. Dark hair veiled their contours,
slightly matted, as if he had been sweating in his sleep. Within this
covering, his nipples were brown as toast. Her own felt tight as her
hand fisted on her thigh.

She could touch him if she wished, touch a human for the first
time in . . . over twenty years. Did humans feel different from
upyr? Did their mortality beat through their sun-kissed skin?

Trembling slightly, she uncurled her fingers and moved her

hand until it hovered above his shoulder. Even from a distance, his warmth could stun.

She wondered if she would feel cold to him.

I was this, she thought. I was human.

Sadness squeezed her heart, though it was pointless. If she had refused the elders' offer to change her, she would not be human, she would be dead. Not even a memory would remain. There would have been no one left to mourn her.

The awareness of what she had lost overcame her hesitation. Here and now, she could reconnect to the mortal world. She let her hand fall to his warm brown skin. The contact was a shock. Her palm tingled where they touched, a subtle, sensual effect. This was a human body then, and these were human veins. Fascinated, she traced one strong, blue cord from the base of his throat to his savaged ear. His pulse was stronger than hers, quicker. And his scent was truly heady.

Suddenly she understood why Auriclus had marked humans as forbidden. Their kind was far more tempting than she had guessed. She was lucky she had fed well before he caught her.

But if she need not fear that hunger, another soon proved too compelling. Curiosity, always her downfall, took hold of her eyes. The arrow of his hair, wide on his chest, narrow on his belly, was preying on her imagination. Palms damp, she peeled the musty blanket from his hips. Like *upyr,* he slept unclothed. A pair of prominent hipbones appeared, followed by a thatch of dark brown curls. They gleamed in the moonlight. Then she saw the rest.

Oh, she thought, her mind at a loss for words. Asleep or not, his phallus was extraordinary.

Heavy, she thought, the smooth, flaring head seeming to weigh the thick shaft down. Liquid pooled between her thighs as she followed the lolling curve back to his curls. He was immense. Outrageous. And not even aroused. She bit her lip to picture that.

This engine of love was fashioned to appease the greedy.

The word reminded her of her flaws. Humans were more modest than her kind and curiosity was no excuse. To bare this man without permission was simply wrong. Reluctantly she returned the covers to his waist. As soon as she did, she longed to pull them back down.

Surely she had imagined his wondrous size.

With an effort, she shook off the urge to check. She had work to do if she was going to convince this thief of hawks to let her see.

AS he had countless times before, Aimery dreamt of the Battle of Poitiers. The dream was not a nightmare, though he often wished it were. It was memory, rather, as if time were a ribbon looped on itself. Again, with the other archers, he lay on his belly in the grass to the west of the Nouaillé wood, knowing they were outnumbered, knowing his father would beat him if he ran. Again his skin turned clammy as he heard—but could not see—the French king's cavalry massing to charge below.

His heart was beating so quickly he nearly fainted when the signal came to prepare. He tugged his shooting glove tighter with his teeth. He rose to his feet and notched an arrow. He drew and sighted, arms straining as they never had strained before. Even at fifteen he was strong enough for a longbow. His muscles shook because fear had made them weak.

And then the magic happened, the mystery he could not explain to this day. His fear drained from him like ale from a broken cask. I can do this, he thought. This is what I was born for.

With the words, his mind narrowed down to one shining point. The battle grew still and pure. He knew he would hit his mark, a mounted knight with a bright yellow tunic over his plate. The bowstring rolled off his fingers. The arrow flew. A heartbeat later it struck with a solid thunk. The sight of the shaft transfixing the Frenchman's neck was no surprise. Aimery's shot had pierced the aventail of his coif. His target might as well have been made of hay.

It was him or me, he thought, but in truth there was no horror to overcome; no elation, either—only a sense that this was what had to be.

Ahead of him, one of Bridesmere's archers fell with a crossbolt through his side. *Mine,* Aimery thought with no more emotion than he had killed. I will help him. He ran to drag the injured man to safety, shooting steadily as he went. Enemy fire rained around him before he remembered to crouch.

Then, without warning or transition, Poitiers was gone. Aimery stood in an English wood, the one that cloaked the hills behind their home.

The change startled him. He had never dreamt about this before. Wondering what it meant, he looked around. The copse was greener than it should have been this time of year. Through the unfurled leaves an uncertain light fell in veils of gold and rose. Primroses bloomed—yellow, purple—and birds twittered in the branches. Squirrels made the underbrush crash and snap. Giving in to the moment, Aimery filled his lungs. The sap rising up the trunks was sharp and sweet.

Shoeless, he trod the old path toward the druid clearing. Between boulder and oak it wound, packed by centuries of feet. His legs were tireless, as if he had the strength of twenty men.

I trespass, Aimery thought. This is my brother's wood.

But it did not seem so. The trees seemed to belong more to themselves than to any man.

Then he saw the woman, standing slim and straight before the ancient stone. She wore nothing, not a stitch. Against the lichen-stained granite her skin glowed like ivory before a flame. Her hair was a tumble of raven curls, clean and shining, covering her breasts and falling to her hips. The shadow of her navel made his ribs tighten on his breath. It was a tiny, secret mouth that led his eyes even farther down. He stared at the triangle of her womanhood, at the soft curves of her limbs.

Beauty like this stole the senses from their seat.

His body stirred. The reaction seemed disrespectful, but he could not stop it. Want beat through him in drowning waves until he stood as hard as horn. He swallowed, his palms ablaze. He knew he must not touch her.

She was the goddess of the forest.

He was just a man.

Her arms lifted as if for aid.

"Why," she beseeched, "have you blinded me?"

His gaze flew to her face. The goddess's eyes bore the stitches with which he had seeled the falcon. A single bloodred tear rolled down her cheek.

No, he thought, and all the pain the helpless bird must have felt tore at the sinews of his breast. He should not have done this. He should have found another way.

At Poitiers he had been remorseless, but now the horror of his actions wrenched him awake. He bolted up gasping for air. The sheet beneath him was damp with sweat. Saints above. He was used to disturbing dreams, but this was stranger than all the rest. Vivid, too. He could smell the forest still, could feel the earth beneath his naked feet.

Shaken, he peered through a gap in the curtains. Curled up on his pallet, Robin grumbled but did not wake. At least he had not made too much noise.

Rubbing his face, Aimery eased from the bed. He wanted to be certain all was well.

To his relief, Princess was a shadow on the chair where he had left her. Her claws shifted on the wood as he approached, but the bells on her jesses did not jingle. Dark as it was, she should have been asleep. His thrashing must have disturbed her.

Since she was up, he found his tinder and lit the pierced tin lantern that hung from a hook on the wall. The light from the stump of candle showed she was calm. Unnervingly, her head was turned directly toward him. He could see her sutures were clean.

Despite this, he could not shake his unease.

"Did I hurt you then?" he murmured, stroking the sleek brown feathers of her breast. Strange. He could have sworn she had more down this morning.

Roused by his voice, Princess ruffled her wings.

Aimery reached for his satchel of tools, then shook his head. Generations of falconers had trained their charges by the method he had used. Was he going to go against their experience for a dream?

Sighing, he drew his smallest blade from its leather loop. Ridiculous or not, perhaps it was time someone tried a different way.

As if she knew what he intended, Princess quieted as the knife approached.

"There," he said softly. "Soon you shall see again."

When the threads pulled gently free, her relief was indistinguishable from his own.

Four

AFTER the excitement of the day and night before, Gillian napped most of the morning on Aimery's wrist. Her head was covered by a leather hood so poorly fitted she could see quite well around the edges. The way it chafed her feathers was annoying but not enough to keep her from sleep.

Then again, the meal she had eaten might account for her need to rest. Her captor had fed her morsels of chicken so fresh they were still warm, then sang her into a doze. By this time she knew his melody by heart. Rather than weary her, each repetition increased her sense of comfort. As the horses jingled and creaked across the landscape, she leaned into his chest, too soothed to worry if he bewitched her.

She had her own power, after all. She had proven that when she slipped into his dream.

When at last she woke completely, they were much farther inland than before, in an area of rolling moorland and scrub. A river wound to their left, its water turned to milk where the snow-swelled current coursed over mossy rocks.

Awareness hummed inside her. Since taking her familiar, she had learned her senses were even more acute in this new shape. She could smell the places the river had been, the earth it had dug from the banks. The way its currents pushed and fluttered the mild spring air sent a thrill of happiness through her being. She was glad to be on the move, even if that meant taking unfamiliar risks. When a small brown vole darted out from a tussock of heather, she could barely stop herself from giving chase.

But she knew she must restrain the impulse. If she proved un-ruly she had no doubt her captor would sew her eyes shut again.

She consoled herself by lifting folded wings to feel the air flow smooth as silk beneath. Her bird form felt capable and sound, as if it had finally attained adulthood. She had grown faster than her fel-low nestlings, though not as fast as she had on first becoming *upyr*.

"Soon," Aimery crooned, running his large gloved hand along her back. "Soon we'll be home and you'll learn to hunt far tastier creatures than that rodent."

As if to verify his words, the land rose up ahead, slowly at first and then more steeply, until it formed an impressive scarp above the river. Surmounting this stony lookout, almost seeming to grow out of it, was a castle.

This was no stained-glass confection, but a fortress. Gillian counted four stout towers joined by a thick crenellated wall on whose ramparts a handful of soldiers paced to and fro. In fact, two sets of walls protected the tall, square keep that rose from the mound within. Narrow windows pierced its upper level and what looked like a movable wooden bridge connected it to the walls.

Beyond the battlements and the deep dry moat, she spied a town. Plowed fields, barely hinting at green, surrounded that. Aside from these signs of cultivation, most of the land appeared to be pas-ture for flocks of sheep. Shepherds walked among the ambling white huddles, while wooden carts dragged trails of dust down a rutted road. A group of children raced around a millpond with a kite, as different as night and day from the last children she had seen. Her surprise made her realize she had not expected to find this well-peopled world.

Humanity had healed while she hid away in the forest.

Uninterested in her musing, the bird turned to admire the sturdy, high-perched keep. This, Gillian gathered, was an eyrie she could approve.

Aimery used the arm that held his reins to point. "There," he said. "That is Bridesmere, your new home."

Gillian had traveled far indeed if this imposing stronghold could welcome her.

━━━◆━━━

AS always, Aimery experienced a mix of feelings on coming home. To see the outward evidence of Fitz Clare strength, theirs since the time of their great-grandfather, made his heart swell in his breast. The Fitz Clares were a family of warriors—in Jerusalem, in Wales, in France—but also a family of survivors. Monarchic rivalries had not destroyed them, nor the Great Dying, nor would the wily Scots. "Never bow," was the motto carved into the stones above the gate.

Fitz Clares had bowed, of course, when necessity demanded, but for the most part they stood tall.

It was a sacred responsibility: to show the world one's integrity was sound. A lord could not demand better from his people than he was willing to give himself.

Aimery was not, however, the baron of Bridesmere. His half brother, Edmund, was. Much as Aimery sometimes wished he could deny it, he knew Edmund ruled well; better, mayhap, than Aimery would. Edmund was a lord for times that lay ahead—part merchant, part diplomat. He and his sons would lead the Fitz Clares into the next century as skillfully as their forebears had led them into the last.

Aimery was grateful to be a part of that heritage, grateful his brother had not cast him out as so many brothers would. Rather than being obliged to hire out his sword, Aimery served Bridesmere as master of arms, responsible for training and outfitting its men. The position was one of respect, but he was also godfather to Edmund's sons. If he wished occasionally for a place of his own to rule, that was his private cross to bear. Many had worse, as Aimery had always known.

This reminder ran through his head as they entered the barbican before the gate. The high walls narrowed around them, funneling them past firing embrasures along the way. Most were empty, the area having been free of large-scale conflict for some time. Some were manned, though; Edmund had enough military sense for that. The veterans spoke quiet greetings as he passed, one soldier to another. Aimery felt the tension in his neck relax. To them, he was neither hero nor horror. They had scars of their own.

Still perched on his arm, the peregrine's head turned from side to side, clearly interested in the voices. The echo of the horses' hooves crossing the drawbridge made her flutter, but they reached the gatehouse without him having to fight her will. Once inside the stony enclosure, Aimery's gaze went to the ironbound inner door. To his satisfaction, more men were posted there. Over their armor, they wore Edmund's livery of scarlet and green.

"Fifteen," Aimery heard a young guard murmur. "He lost that eye in battle at just fifteen."

Merciful Mother, Aimery thought. Now they could not even bother to see the eye was still there.

The new recruit, whoever he was, stumbled forward as someone clouted the back of his skull.

"Lads," said Old Wat in disgust. Squat as a boar and twice as tough, Old Wat was the captain of Bridesmere's guards, survivor of many long French campaigns. Though his position outranked Aimery's, he often deferred to the younger man. This was in part because Aimery had gentle blood but mostly, Aimery suspected, because he had saved the soldier's life at Poitiers. Aimery could not remember the particulars of the incident himself; once fighting began, he had no awareness of individuals, only of who was friend or foe. Old Wat occasionally mentioned his purported rescue while in his cups but now, as was more usual, he merely nodded before turning to welcome his liege lord's son.

"So, boy," he said, "you catch any reivers while you were gone?"

"Just a princess," Robin answered, old enough to return a jest. "And Uncle Aimery helped."

To the sound of appreciative chuckles, they clopped into the outer bailey, the horses forgetting their fatigue in their eagerness to reach their stalls. Two grooms ran out from the stables to get them while Robin slid off his fat-bellied cob.

"No sneaking off," Aimery ordered, grabbing the back of his shirt. "Your lady mother will want to see you are safe. In addition to which, you are in dire need of a bath."

Robin sighed dramatically but obeyed, probably hoping by this good behavior to earn more privileges in the mews.

As they neared the keep, Brother Kenelm appeared on the outside stair. The boys' tutor was a serious young man who had the amusing habit of clasping his hands behind him when he walked. He was meticulous in manner, intelligent, judicious, and a little too aware of all three traits. A protégé of Edmund's uncle, the powerful abbot of St. Crispin's, the tutor had—Aimery gathered—been sent into Bridesmere's service for some disgrace.

What his crime had been no one could say. A sin of pride was Aimery's guess. If Brother Kenelm had been provoked into speaking his mind to one of the abbot's more important patrons, he would, at the least, have had to be put out of sight.

But St. Crispin's loss was Bridesmere's gain. Brother Kenelm was a conscientious teacher to the boys, imposing order when needed but also kind enough that they did not fear him.

To Aimery's surprise, he was crossing the scythed grass of the bailey with more than his usual measured strides. Hood thrown back, the hair around his tonsure was downright mussed.

"Sir Aimery," he said, breathless from his haste. He glanced over his shoulder at the keep as if expecting some hellhound to issue out. "How fortunate you have arrived. Your brother wishes to consult you on a matter of some importance."

"Does he?" said Aimery, almost certain the monk was lying.

A moment later, his suspicion was confirmed. Claris swept out from her private garden with a gaggle of her ladies. All were colorfully dressed and carried small woven baskets of herbs and flowers. They made a charming picture, no doubt Claris's intent, especially since she was the prettiest member of their bouquet. Her sweet high laugh could be heard quite clearly from where he stood.

Brother Kenelm muttered an imprecation no monk should know.

With a sigh of resignation, Aimery waited for his brother's wife to reach them. His scar ached, tight from days in the cold and wet. He fought the urge to rub it. Claris would only fuss. Whatever his dread of her ministrations, he had to admit she was a lovely woman. Fair of hair and blue of eye, with the womanly shape of a Bible temptress, she made the most of her herbal skills. Though nearing thirty, her rose-petal skin was as smooth as it had been ten years before.

If her spirit had matched her form, her pursuit of Aimery would have been a far different trial.

"My lady," he said, and politely inclined his neck.

Beneath her pink velvet kirtle and pale green surcoat, her belly was slightly rounded with Edmund's child. Lady Blythe, Claris's cousin and sycophant, stopped a few paces behind, gaping as worshipfully as if Aimery and Claris were characters from a tale. When Claris curtsied playfully at his nod, Lady Blythe could not repress a romantic sigh.

"Why, Aimery," Claris burbled in her youthful way, "we did not expect you back so soon. And, Brother Kenelm, how kind of you to come to collect your charge."

Brother Kenelm's long face grew even more disapproving.

"Robin and I have no lesson today. It is your husband's brother I come to collect. Sir Edmund has need of his expertise."

"Nonsense." Claris smoothed her golden hair. A chaplet of rosemary adorned the shining waves above her brow. Married as she was, she should not have been wearing her hair unbound. Unfortunately, unless they had important visitors no one could rule her in such things. "Sir Aimery has only just returned," she said. "He should not be troubled with my husband's tiresome demands." She turned back to Aimery, her eyes aglow. "I shall have one of the chamberers heat you a bath and you can refresh yourself from your journey. I know how you delight in being clean."

Her voice sank to a throaty purr. A flush, part anger, part embarrassment, crawled up Aimery's cheek. She seemed not to care what her words implied. Her son, whom she had not greeted nor even glanced at, stood at his hip, along with a man sworn to honor both her husband and her God. Aimery tried to think of some way to discourage her that would not sound churlish. Before he could, Claris pressed one pale pink finger to the cleft that marked his chin.

Whatever tease she meant to utter was lost in a sudden cacking, flapping fury from the falcon he held on his arm. Apparently, the fit of Princess's hood was worse than he thought. Had he not been gripping her jesses tightly, Aimery was sure she would have attacked his brother's wife. The bird was so enraged, the power of her wing beats nearly pulled him off his feet.

"Goodness," Claris exclaimed, falling back with her hand pressed to her throat. "I can see that creature needs training!"

"I must take her inside and calm her," Aimery said, jerking his head to avoid a flailing pinion. "Then I shall see what my brother needs."

"Your half brother," Claris corrected crisply.

Ignoring her, Aimery turned to kneel before his nephew. As soon as she was not facing Claris, the bird subsided.

"Good Princess," Robin whispered and Aimery pressed his lips together to hide a smile. The boy should be discouraged from wishing his mother ill. Now, however, was not the time for a scold.

"You have served well," he said, "and fulfilled your obligations. I shall speak to Brother Kenelm about you helping me train our newest huntress between your lessons."

"Truly?" said Robin in the tone of one who has learned to be wary of promises.

"Truly," Aimery confirmed. With a creak of his old, scarred knee, he rose and walked toward the tower he had been given as his quarters in the outer curtain. He did not take formal leave of Claris, though he should have. She, alas, could not see his rudeness for what it was.

"I shall not forget my promise to refresh your spirits," she called gaily after.

Her ladies tittered as she rejoined them. "Did you see that great brute flush!" he heard one exclaim.

"His heart *must* yearn for you," gushed Lady Blythe.

If Aimery had possessed his brother's quickness, he might have found a dampening retort. As it was, the best he could manage was pretending he did not hear.

THE lord's chamber was situated in the keep, above the upper end of the hall. Here Edmund received important visitors and conducted the business of his estates. Sometimes he felt as if that business were never ending. Bridesmere and its various manors resembled a tiny country, with their own courts and traditions, with their own workers and soldiers and trade.

Despite the scope of what was overseen here, Edmund's chamber was not grand. Grace alone it could claim, with one arched window whose peak held a rendering of the Fitz Clare crest in colored glass. Aglow in the sun, their dragon reared fierce and green, forever spitting its scarlet flame.

Never bow, Edmund thought, his mouth curling privately in

amusement. These days, with peasants less numerous than they had been, a lord who failed to make concessions found himself with no one to bake his bread or plow his fields. Even the king was no longer a law unto himself, not if he wanted Parliament to raise taxes for his wars.

Sighing, he let his gaze rove from the window. The great carved bed stood on its stepped platform against the wall, swathed in blue velvet picked out with embroidered stars. His resting place seemed sad and abandoned this time of day, so he did not long regard it. The familiar tapestries on the walls, which showed the conquest of Wales, were a considerably more calming sight. Faded but sound, they had hung in this room for generations.

Unlike his lady, the baron of Bridesmere valued history more than show.

But thinking of Claris would not get his business done.

This afternoon he and his seneschal, Sir John Peters, stood side by side at a broad worktable, discussing cartage and supplies for the next few months. Edmund was about to question one of Sir John's figures when something inside him tensed. Light, steady footsteps climbed the stairs. His half brother had come home.

As ever, Aimery's arrival spurred a tangle of emotion: affection, resentment, fear that he relied on his younger sibling too much. Aimery did not have to stay at Bridesmere. More than one powerful lord would have bid for his sword arm. The fact that a brain, and a gift for inspiring men, lay behind his twisted visage made the arm worth all the more. For that matter, his talent as a falconer was worth competing for. Aimery was a man of numerous gifts.

Always courteous, he nodded a greeting at Sir John.

"You look tired," Edmund said because his mind was not guarding his tongue. "Was Robin too great a trial?"

Aimery shook his head. "He was no trouble. A dream kept me awake."

No more needed to be said. Most of the castle knew about Aimery's dreams. They made him cry out sometimes, even attack those who tried to rouse him. They were the reason he had a tower to himself . . . along with the likelihood that, had he not, Claris would have been creeping to his room to "comfort" him if she so much as heard him sigh.

"Robin was a help," Aimery repeated and met his brother's gaze. His expression was calm and uninformative, a kind of mask, Edmund knew, though it did not seem so. Edmund could not maintain the stare. His brother's scar was too hard to face.

He squared a stack of Sir John's accounts. "I trust your journey was successful."

"Yes," said Aimery, then: "Brother Kenelm came out to greet us. He said you had need of me."

Edmund laughed drily through his nose. "Brother Kenelm knows my lady wife has been fluttering about all morning in anticipation of your return. I suspect he was trying to head off a mortal sin."

The color that suffused his half brother's face was shamefully gratifying. His own, he knew, was cool as springwater. In the space of heartbeats, only Aimery's scar and the skin around his grimly narrowed lips remained unflushed.

"I hope you know I would never—"

"I know." Edmund cut him off. "But Claris does not. Nor would it do any good to tell her. You are the love of her poisonous little heart."

Beside him, Sir John cleared his throat. He knew the family business—had to in his position—but that did not mean he liked to have it aired before him. Because he was friend as well as retainer, Edmund forced the bitterness from his tone.

"Forgive me," he said to the steward. "Why do you not find a meal and a cup of claret? Aimery and I will discuss the disposition of the new recruits."

Sir John left with a sharp, clean bow for them both, his gaze lingering briefly on Aimery's scar. Aimery took no notice. Everyone stared at the ruin of his beauty, the proof of his youthful valor. Edmund well remembered the first time Claris saw the mark. Aimery had come late to their betrothal banquet, hair damp from a hasty wash, good doublet crumpled from sitting too long in a chest. Claris's hand had flown to her mouth in horror, her blue eyes wide, her breath coming strangely quick.

Aimery had spoken to her in his quiet, careful way, apologizing for his lateness, saying what was kind and proper but not flattering her the way all who knew her were wont to do. He sang no odes to her beauty, merely expressed a hope that she would be happy in her new home.

It had happened then. Because he was reserved, because he seemed romantic, Claris had fallen in love—or what passed for love in her foolish eighteen-year-old mind. From then on Aimery was her noble wounded hero, the object of all her dreams. She plied Edmund with questions even as they shared their promise cup. How had his brother gotten that scar? Was it true he had killed a hundred men? Was he really descended from berserkers on his mother's side? Edmund hardly had to answer. Fever had flown into her cheeks and brightened her starry eyes. Dowry notwithstanding, Edmund already had doubts about the alliance. As she prattled, he felt those doubts grow brittle as winter frost.

Idiot, he had thought. Heedless little idiot.

Despite the trouble it would cause, he asked her later that evening if she wanted to call off their marriage. She laughed the suggestion away, pretending he was silly to think she cared for a soul but him.

Edmund knew better even then. Claris did not love him. Claris wanted to be the lady of Bridesmere, not the wife of a second son, a mere knight bachelor. The last of her father's six daughters, none of whom she seemed to like, she hungered to rise above them all. What is more, she relished the thought of Aimery pining for her from afar—never dreaming he would refuse to enslave himself to her charms.

Poor Claris, he thought without much pity. Neither love object nor husband danced to her tune. His mood gone abruptly black, he made Sir John's papers flutter with the vigor of his exhalation.

"I hope you know I would never touch her," Aimery said even more soberly than before.

"I know," Edmund repeated, his voice a trifle sharp.

In truth, knowing Aimery scorned his wife heightened his irritation. He would have enjoyed seeing his brother suffer like an ordinary human being.

Not that Claris would have let him suffer long.

Shaking off the knowledge, he beckoned Aimery to his side. "Come," he said. "Tell me what supplies you need from the armorer."

Through all the business they discussed, peaceable though it was, the tension that lay between them did not abate.

Five

GILLIAN opened her eyes to a large, round room. Night had fallen and the single window was shuttered against the chill. She needed her *upyr* sight to discern the scenes of hawking painted on the walls. They were not immediately familiar. In truth, nothing seemed familiar until the scent of the room's inhabitant reminded her where she was: Aimery's chamber, on the topmost floor of his tower.

Her perch was midway between the window and a well-banked fire.

Sleep! Princess grumbled, but Gillian had been sleeping all afternoon, lulled by the sun and the leather hood. Not lulled by everything, though. She thought back to the woman who had disturbed her, the one Aimery called Lady Claris. Princess's reaction suggested more than possessiveness toward her keeper. Some creature instinct had decided she was a danger.

But to whom? Gillian had tried without success to read the woman's thoughts. Lady Claris's mind was a snarl of contradictions, her beliefs seemingly created by twisting the truth in knots. A litany of people and things she hated repeated endlessly behind it all. This one had slighted her. That one possessed something she desired. Another she had put soundly in her place. Some of these thoughts sounded like delusions, but Gillian could not be sure. Lady Claris wanted Aimery; that much was clear. Beyond that, Gillian could not guess.

Bad, the bird insisted and repeated her call to sleep.

I am going to explore, Gillian informed her. *As soon as I take my own form, you can rest.*

Through trial and error, Gillian and Princess were discovering the limits of their partnership. Gillian ruled, of course, and could dictate the actions of both forms, but their awareness could also separate. Certainly while in human form Princess was welcome to nap. Gillian would hardly need to consult her on how to operate a body that had been hers from birth.

Itching to be off, Gillian craned to free the knot in her jesses with her beak, then carefully clawed off her too-big hood. Lord willing, Aimery would never think to adjust it.

Ruffling with pleasure, she hopped to the rush-and-herb-strewn floor. A muffled jingle reminded her to remove her belled ankle strap. That done, she changed in a blink of her human eye, the whirlwind barely blowing through her before it passed. Herself once more, she wriggled her toes and stretched, resisting her urge to investigate Aimery's bed.

She knew he slept, could feel it in the quiet of the air. She had no need to touch him, no need to enspell. Interesting or not, he was a distraction. The time had come to focus on her goal.

I must discover everything I can about these humans, she thought—all of them, not just one. Otherwise, I shall never learn to walk amongst them unremarked.

With a last backward glance, she crept from the room and

down the spiral stair to begin her reacquaintance with the world of men.

World of men it was. Apart from a smattering of female servants, Bridesmere was a male preserve. Mercifully, human ears were far less sensitive than *upyr*. Like a silent shadow, Gillian flitted through the sleeping barracks and the hall, through the smoky kitchen and the stables, through the bakehouse beneath the wall. Though she was careful to remain unseen, she realized her nudity might draw attention. As soon as she was able, she filched a simple undergown from the laundry. It was stiff at first, but a minute next to her skin softened its weave.

She nearly tripped over the laundress before she left.

People slept where they worked, it appeared, on pallets and canvas cots. Where sounds told her servants stirred, Gillian shrank into the darkness and held her breath. The guard rooms were most difficult to pass for there all were alert: cleaning equipment, sharpening weapons, sharing rounds of ale and dice. Theirs was not the alertness of war but of discipline. Given their air of good-humored responsibility, it seemed wrong to spell them to sleep.

She did, however, weave a net of thought around herself to make her look ordinary—a glamour in reverse. In the illusion she projected, her skin did not shine, nor her beauty blind. She had no more grace than a sheep. Keeping the pretense in her mind required an effort, but her memory of her first glimpse of Nim Wei told her she must try.

She had to admit she enjoyed the challenge. Sneaking around the torchlit castle was as exciting as sneaking around the pack. If she liked it a bit too much, well, Lucius had told her to use her advantages. Surely this knack for trespass counted among them.

Emboldened by her success, she dipped into the soldiers' minds. Some of the guards were easy to read, others difficult, but she began to see common threads.

Human males, she concluded, were given to crudeness when in groups. While exaggerating their own accomplishments, they feared others spoke only true. Many of the men-at-arms had done amazingly brave things and yet still worried that they were cowards. Some were brutal, some kind, some unschooled but wise. Many wanted more than they had without wishing to work. Theirs were the easiest thoughts to steal, as if their sloth extended to shielding their minds. They were owed, they thought, *owed,* and they did not care who knew it.

Once or twice, she caught a wisp of thought so personal she was compelled to turn away.

But she could not turn away completely. This gift of hers, this inner sight, was a terrible fascination. She hardly noticed how crowded her head had gotten until she reached the chapel next to the keep. *Stop,* she thought, abruptly dizzy. She felt as sick as if she had stood in the sun too long. Desires assailed her, and fears, and grudges too petty to believe. Bad enough to deal with her own small thoughts without taking on the world's. Deciding she would not do this again unless she must, she put her hand to the door and pushed inside.

The smell of incense immediately calmed her.

Bridesmere's chapel was high and narrow, its peaking roof supported by a lattice of exquisitely carved wooden beams. Equally elaborate, a balcony hung opposite the altar, furnished with handsome, high-backed chairs. No doubt the family sat there for mass while the household stood below. Most likely, the door behind the chairs led to the keep.

Gillian considered slipping through it but quickly dismissed the thought. Enough spying for one night. She wanted to stand and enjoy the peaceful way the stars shone through the colored glass. The tranquillity she felt surprised her. She had assumed the god of her childhood would not want her now that she had become a sort of demon. Either this place was not very holy, or her god was more forgiving than she had been told.

Fighting a lingering doubt, she ventured carefully onto the aisle. Even then no lightning fell from the sky. Some inexplicable awareness made her look down. The stone of the floor was worn, older than the walls. The blocks were so closely fitted, she could not discern the mortar. Symbols marked them faintly here and there. She knelt to get a closer look. Not writing, she thought, at least not the writing of modern times. Her eyes traced triangles and circles and pictures of funny beasts: human-headed lions and serpents with hands and feet.

The carvings reminded her of the fountain chamber in the cave, buzzing with distant magic.

Before she knew it, she had followed the trail of pictures behind the altar to an oaken door fitted in the floor. An iron ring lay near one end, obviously the means by which it was lifted. Gillian gnawed her lip. After sunlight and fire, pure iron—especially when fashioned into a weapon—was the greatest weakness of the *upyr*. The metal drained their strength, making them vulnerable to killing blows.

This, however, was not a weapon. Making up her mind, she wrapped her hand in her gown and bent to grip it. The ring burned her palm but she heaved at it all the same.

Bad, complained the bird, disturbed by her blistered skin.

Gillian paid her no mind. This small hurt would heal. She had to see what lay beneath this door, then had to descend those shadowed stairs.

Her scalp tingled strongly as she went, but what she found was hardly dramatic. The steps led to a storeroom. The floor was icy, the walls damp and stained with lime. The only object of interest was the well that stood in the center. Disappointingly, it was covered with dark, unembellished wood.

More to leave no stone unturned than because she expected to find anything important, Gillian shoved the lid up on its rusty hinges. Still holding it, she stuck her head underneath. Light glittered on the water below, perhaps a bit of starshine from the church. Gillian inhaled. Spring fed, she thought, taking in the sweetness. Most likely, this hidden well was intended to help the castle withstand a siege.

Without warning, the bird's soul stirred within her. Princess wanted her to leave, to return to their protector. *Go back to sleep,* Gillian thought at her. *There is nothing treacherous here.*

But there was something. She stared at the water, enthralled by the shifting patterns of glinting light. Could this illumination possibly come from the church, or was its source somewhere closer by? A sound brushed her inner ear, a rough, half-broken sigh. Was it real? Imagined? It came again, deeper this time, more like a lover's groan. The sound seemed to open a hidden window in Gillian's head. She could almost see pictures: a city's moonlit spires, a rearing horse, a woman's profile. She shivered even as she squinted to make it out. Yes, there, on the surface of the water, was a woman's head.

Without warning the final picture coalesced, abruptly vivid, as real as a stinging slap. The woman turned with a swish of midnight silk hair. Dark, slanting eyes locked onto Gillian's. Petal-pink lips parted for an indrawn breath.

"Who is there?" said the woman, squinting back. "Who calls me from my mirror?"

Gillian jolted back so quickly the well's heavy cover fell with a crash.

Nim Wei. The image in the water had been Nim Wei.

She felt as if she had two hearts, hers and the bird's, both drumming out of control. Nim Wei. What if the elder had seen Gillian? What if she remembered who she was?

It seemed impossible after all these years and yet Gillian had recognized Auriclus's nemesis straightaway. She was as beautiful as ever, as seductively sweet and cool. Evil or not, Gillian did not want this powerful *upyr* knowing where she was. What if she was still angry with Gillian for choosing her rival? What if she told the pack where to find her? What if Gillian never got the chance to live out her dream? Lucius had warned her elders were unpredictable.

Lord in heaven, she thought, what was Nim Wei's magic doing here?

Gone was her giddy arrogance: Gillian felt as small and helpless as she had before she was changed. Stealing her bird soul seemed like nothing, reading minds a trick for a child.

But perhaps Nim Wei had not had a chance to see her clearly. Perhaps Gillian had pulled back soon enough.

Please, God, she prayed with a sincerity she had not known she could feel. *Do not let Your enemy track me down.*

NIM Wei adored her palace in Avignon, the decadent home of the captive pope. Rome, the papal capital until His Holiness crawled into bed with the French, had been too crowded and poor for her— a travesty of the marvel it had been. When Clement V bowed to pressure to move his court, she had been elated. Avignon's only drawback was that she could not maintain a brood. Sadly, her children—subversive little rebels that they were—could not be trusted to mind their manners in the presence of so many priests. For herself, however, this Rome away from Rome was a marvelous retreat, if for no other reason than the indulgences it afforded. She, of all *upyr*, knew who was safe to corrupt.

Her partner for the evening was a sophisticated mortal cleric, a lover of subjugation. To enhance his experience, she had tied him naked to her grandest chair, a throne really, binding him to its joints at elbow and knee. Now each rasp of her sharpened nails inspired an ecstatic sigh. Transported by the pain, he trembled on the edge of coming like a bow pulled to its verge.

Not that she would let his arrow fly. If Auriclus's gift was the ability to change himself—to become fog, or wolf, or whistling wind—Nim Wei's gift was the ability to change others. Her will reached inside her victim, into the tiny cells and channels that made him up. Those vessels that allowed him climax she had stopped. His arousal would rise until it created the agony he craved.

Given the cleric's nature, this would arouse him more.

He was most appealing, this fellow: a long, slim quiver against the wood. Old enough to know what his body liked, he was also young enough to respond as keenly as possible to her skill. The tapers she had set about the chamber threw his perspiring form into high relief. His phallus stood hard and red between his thighs, but not as red as his handsome face. The cuts her nails had scored along his torso were like a poem in scarlet ink.

Auriclus would have been shocked to see it. This was a pleasure her stuffy old sire would never allow himself to explore. *Humans are not playthings,* he liked to intone. *You must treat them with respect.*

She frowned as a trickle of sweat spoiled her sanguinary art.

"Please," begged the cleric, "I can take more."

Shaking off her distraction, she braced her hands on his straining forearms where the ties strapped them to the chair. His nostrils flared, excited at being caged, and his gaze slid down her front. Her tunic was dark blue satin with sapphire buttons and tailored seams. Her shoes were pointed, her leggings full. She had dressed like a man for him, like a Turkish sultan. Only her hair fell free like a woman's, over her small, round breasts. The tunic hugged them as if with love.

"I know you can take more," she said. "My will holds your pleasure in check until I say."

They had played this game before, but his eyes half closed with bliss. "My queen," he moaned, utterly overpowered. "I give my soul into your care."

Nim Wei had no use for his soul, but the sentiment was one she approved. She leaned close enough to drag her teeth along his neck, his shiver of lust a meal in itself.

"I am yours," he declared. "Body and blood and seed."

How nice, Nim Wei thought, amused by his sense of drama.

Then something shattered his focus. He stiffened beneath her mouth. "Your mirror," he said, nodding at it with his head. "Someone is inside it."

Nim Wei turned, her heart thumping once in shock. Her oval scrying mirror hung from the wall in a gilded frame. She knew she had left it covered but something—someone?—had blown the gauze away. Blurred but unmistakable, a woman's face looked out from the polished bronze.

"Who is there?" Nim Wei demanded. "Who calls me from my mirror?"

The face disappeared as if she had scared it.

"Is it a devil?" the cleric asked, his fear betrayed by his shaking voice.

In other circumstances, Nim Wei would have laughed at his superstition. Tonight she was merely angry. These scrying mirrors, a network she had arranged in all her cities, were her surest means of communicating with her broods. If someone dared to use one who should not . . .

Quickly crossing the room, she pressed her hands to the metal and whispered an ancient word, a key made out of sound. Her answer came in pictures. A rearing lion appeared and a tall gray castle on a cliff. England then, but not London. The scrying device on the other end must be an old one, one she had not built herself. She had found a few on her travels, their origins lost to the mists before her birth—perhaps before Auriclus's birth as well. Whatever the method by which they worked, it was these apparatuses she had copied to make her own.

"What does it mean?" she whispered, her head bowed, her hair a shimmering curtain. "Is it a sign?"

She waited, but the nameless powers who ruled this magic refused to say.

"What troubles thee?" asked her plaything.

Nim Wei's hands curled into fists, but then she sighed. Whoever the intruder was, her cleric had not frightened her away. In any case, Nim Wei had better uses for this priest than to purge her anger.

Turning back, she let him see her lengthened teeth. They were as sharp and delicate as a cat's, a gleaming ivory white. Her partner sucked in a breath, and another when her hands moved to her buttons. One by one she freed the jewels, then shrugged the cloth to her waist. She wore nothing underneath. Spurred by the sight of her snowy breasts, his sex surged up again.

Humans, especially young ones, were delightfully easy to rouse.

"Now," she said, "you shall show me what you can take."

"My pleasure," he choked out, and naturally it was.

⚬⚬⚬

GILLIAN shook with reaction as she climbed the stairs to the corner tower. Reassurance was what she wanted, what she needed more than breath. Her instincts, like the bird's, homed in on Aimery.

He is not safe, she tried to tell herself even as her fingers trailed down the parting of his bed curtains. He is a stranger and a human. He would drive a stake through my beating heart if he knew what I was.

I will just look at him for a moment, she promised. Just a moment until I calm. She would not even cast her sleep spell. The risk would force her to leave before he could wake.

Her hand shook as she pushed the dark green cloth aside, causing it to rustle like feathers sliding through dust. Aimery did not stir. He slept. She knew he slept, but suddenly his hands shot out and grabbed her. Everything went from her mind but shock. She was pulled forward onto the mattress, spun, tangled in bedclothes, weighted down by an arm across her throat and a heavy body across her thighs.

"Devil take you, Claris," he ground out, then stopped when he saw that a stranger lay beneath him. His jaw fell like a child's. "Saints above, your skin glows like a candle!"

Gillian cursed herself. In her distraction, she had forgotten to keep up her glamour.

Luckily, surprise had slackened his hold enough for her to push his forearm from her neck. As she did, he shifted his weight from her legs as well. He did not look as if he wanted to attack her. Wary now, he had drawn back to the very bottom of the bed. Still caught in blankets, Gillian struggled to sit up.

They stared at each other, both struck speechless. It may have been the strangest moment of her strange life, to be caught by this human, to be held in suspension without the faintest idea what would happen next. His eyes were gray with flecks of gold: bright eyes, piercing her like the sun. His scar twisted the left lid out of true, making his look seem baleful.

Neither eye gave much away, but—however monstrous the left's appearance—Gillian found she could not fear him. Desire him, yes, but not fear. His lashes trembled with the force of his racing pulse and his blood rose beneath his skin. The heat of it warmed her like a fire. When his gaze flickered to the place where her stolen gown had rucked up her thighs, his color darkened.

She did not think embarrassment was the cause.

Other things seemed to be darkening, too, and rising, until the scoldings of her nearly forgotten childhood were all that kept her eyes on his.

Or almost on his. His erection was too spectacular to ignore. Thick as her wrist and longer than her hand, it practically begged her to reach out. She needed all her determination to drag her gaze away.

How different he seemed awake! More human, but also more vital and filled with power. This was not the connection the bird had felt. This was a drawing of male to female and like to like. Shivering with interest, she tried to remember when she had desired a partner just to touch. His arousal was but one source of intrigue. Brawny arms and sinewed thighs called equally for her attention. His skin was brown to his waist and then milk white. His hair looked silky, his joints perfectly balanced. A second scar on his knee invited a kiss. No cat could have wanted to circle a body more.

Of course, she could hardly do that without providing some reason why she was here. As she scrambled desperately to devise one, he broke the hanging pause.

"I know you," he said, his voice coming slow and thick. "You are the goddess from my dream."

Six

AIMERY felt idiotic the moment he said the words. Oh, everyone heard tales of the miraculous: vengeful fairies, crying statues, rocks that sang aves in the wind. Aimery himself had seen marvels on the battlefield, acts of valor and strength he could not explain. But this? How could she be a goddess, much less one he had dreamt?

Things like that did not happen to men like him.

On the other hand, how could she be an ordinary woman? Beauty aside, her skin was as white as marble. And it glowed. Like marsh fire. Or a firefly turned to snow. The luminescence filled the space between his bed hangings until he could see her better by her own light than by the moon. Try as he might, he knew no sensible means to account for that.

Caught in a sudden panic, he clutched his thumping heart. "Am I dying then? Are you an angel?"

She laughed, sharp and startled. Thinking she mocked him, Aimery flushed. A moment later she grew quiet. "No," she said so forlornly he longed to cup her downcast cheek, "the last thing I am is an angel. And the last thing you are is dying."

With a glint of mischief, she smiled at him through lowered lashes. She did not quite stare at his risen loins, but he knew she had noted their condition. Abruptly conscious of his undress, he grabbed a length of blanket to hide his lap. With the shield, his normal self-possession began to return.

"You cannot be a natural creature," he said, "and you are far too solid to be a ghost. If you are not the goddess of the forest, pray tell me what you are."

She sighed and chewed her lips while thoughts flew mothlike across her face. He waited, feigning patience. Until she drew breath, he was not sure she would answer.

"I am not the goddess," she admitted with obvious reluctance. "I am merely her servant. And she is not the goddess of the forest but of the air. She was concerned about your treatment of her child."

"Her child? You mean Princess?"

"Yes. She was not happy to see her blinded."

"That is why you sent me that vision."

"Yes." Still refusing to look directly at him, the goddess's servant bit her knuckle like a girl who has told a lie. But perhaps her discomfort had another source . . .

"Are you here to punish me?" He was strangely unmoved by the possibility. He felt as he sometimes did in battle, the one cool point in a blaze of madness. This was madness, her being here. With him. Claiming to be more than human. But what was meant to happen would. What he did or did not believe would not change his fate.

"No," she said, shaking her head in denial. He tried not to watch the way her jet-black curls alternately hid and revealed her breasts. Though her undergown was simple, its cloth was as sheer as the finest silk. To his dismay he found this more arousing than if she had been naked. His body hurt from wanting her and the ache of desire made it hard to listen. When she touched his knee to get his attention, he almost went up in flames. He was not surprised to see the contact raise a blue-white spark.

The goddess's servant sucked her finger into her mouth.

"I am not here to punish you," she said once the hurt was soothed, "merely to show you that to tame without harm is the higher path. The goddess is pleased with you. Very pleased. She does you great honor by communicating in this way. Humans are not always to be trusted. By your kindness to our . . . our feathered sisters, she judged you worthy."

Even she seemed to feel this speech was somewhat ridiculous.

"You are lying," Aimery said, amusement dispersing his awe. "I do not know about what, but you surely are."

"I am not!" she said, which made him laugh outright. Obviously miffed, she squirmed on her tempting, half-bared legs. "It is simply, you were not supposed to catch me!"

"I suppose you will be scolded when you return."

"Oh," she said, obviously taken aback. The faintest of flushes crept up her alabaster cheek. "Yes, well, as to that, I must confess I have run away. Temporarily. To . . . to see the world. I am very curious about the world, but we are forbidden to interact with mortals." She put out her hand but stopped short of once more touching his knee. "You must not tell anyone I am here. If word of my disobedience reached the goddess, her anger would be fierce!"

Her fear of discovery seemed genuine, even if her words did not ring true.

"Hm," he said, squinting at her unnaturally perfect profile. Her gaze was not merely lowered but turned away, as if she knew he would try to read her honesty in her eyes. Her lips were as red as blood. By force of will, he controlled the urge to kiss them. "There is more to this tale than you are telling. You remind me of my nephew when he misbehaves. I think you must be a very young servant of the goddess."

"I am every bit as old as you, though—I suppose—to my own people, I am a novice. As it is, I hardly know anything that I wish."

Her glumness he believed. No one could fake that particular mournful tone.

"You will learn," he said kindly. "Everyone must walk before they can run."

She nodded and sniffed, and then—for the first time—looked directly at him with eyes that swam with tears. His breath caught in his chest. His dream of her had not prepared him for the power of her gaze. Against the darkness of her hair and brows, her eyes were a startling, sea-clear blue. Like gems they shone from her white, white skin. Impossible as it seemed, he felt as if he knew them.

They touched him like cat's paws, a sublimely gentle buffet to his soul.

Somewhere, somehow, he had met this woman before.

"May I visit you?" she asked, and this, too, was a blow. She seemed terribly humble and young, as if she were just a girl.

He struggled for speech. "You want to visit me?"

"I will not get in your way, but I would be very grateful if you said yes. I know you are the kind of human I could esteem."

His throat was too tight to swallow. "I am no one special."

She smiled at that, suddenly more woman than girl. Her voice turned husky and wine-rich. "You are the chosen of the goddess. That is special enough for me."

His hands clenched on the blanket, every inch of his skin abruptly beating with lust. His very nerves seemed to catch fire. Aimery was a man fond of his bed sport, though partners he could abide for long were sometimes hard to find. None, however, had ever moved him to this pitch with just a word. Whatever else she might be, this creature was a female his body liked. When he answered, his tone was strained. "What would we do on these 'visits?' "

At once she sat up straighter. "We would talk," she said, both hands flat on her glowing thighs. He got the impression she was try-ing hard not to bounce. "You could teach me how to be human."

As endearing as he found her enthusiasm, her request left him perplexed. "Why would you want to be human?"

"Not *be* human, precisely, but be able to walk between your world and mine. Humans interest me immensely. They know things I wish to learn. None of my own kind have had the will to teach me."

"Perhaps they are trying to protect you. Not all knowledge is good to have."

"I do not believe that. It is always better to know!"

"So said Eve when she bit the apple."

She frowned at him, her ripe lower lip thrust stubbornly out. Goddess's servant or not, Aimery could not resist reaching out to tweak it.

"Hush," he said when she swatted his hand away. "I have not refused you. But I do not see how you shall walk amongst us without a sack. Your looks are not the sort to blend in."

"I can bespell people," she said, "so they think I look like them. Watch."

Given his lingering doubts about her story, he expected her to fail. After a moment, however, he felt a peculiar prickling between his eyes. Like a lamp winking out, her glow was gone. Aimery crossed himself in surprise.

"There," she said with a prideful grin. "Now I am perfectly normal."

Perfect, Aimery would give her, but "normal"? She remained too pale and exquisite for that. Still, in a pinch, he supposed she could pass as human.

"Lord save us," he breathed. "You really are a magical being."

This did not please her. "You must not speak to me that way," she said. "I may be different but, believe me, I am no better than you."

"How shall I speak to you then?"

She considered this. "As a friend."

"Is that what we shall be?"

His purr of insinuation, which he had not planned but could not repress, seemed to discomfit her as much as his awe.

"Yes." She nodded firmly. "Friends is what we shall be."

Happiness spilled through him in an unexpected rush. She lied. From the tips of her blushing breasts to the curl of her tiny toes, she lied to herself and him. Difficult as it was to credit, given who she was—who *he* was, come to that—this otherworldly creature found him as desirable as he found her.

This time, his insinuating tone was quite deliberate.

"If we are to be *friends*," he said, his eyes heavy with enjoyment, "I think I should know your name."

"Gillian," she gasped.

The breathless hitch in her voice was all the confirmation he could have craved.

EDMUND would never understand how an eminently brutish thing like holding a castle came to involve so much ciphering. Dinner came and went without him or his seneschal showing their faces in the hall. Finally, when the church in town rang matins, he and Sir John closed the accounts.

Bridesmere was turning a profit, not a great one but large enough to repair the mill and dredge the fishpond. Considering the expense they had gone to training troops for the prince's recent expedition in Castile, this was no small achievement.

The Fitz Clare demesne was sound.

If they found a good buyer for their next shearing, their coffers would again be flush. Even better, Edmund might have enough of a margin to pursue his dream of establishing a community of weavers here. Why should the Flemish corner the market in fine cloth? The world's best wool grew on English soil.

Too tired to move from his leaning post by the window, Edmund rested his head against the plastered stone. In the bailey down below, a woman was slipping into the family chapel. Edmund did not recognize her, but through the wavy glass he could just make out the glow of her long, white gown.

Pray for us, he thought, who live in this fractious world.

His secretary, Geoffrey de Malleville, the still-gangly son of one of his allies, tapped hesitantly on the door.

"My lord?" he said, clearly unsure of his master's mood. "Your son gave me this to pass to you when you were free."

Edmund took the scroll from him and told the young man to go find his bed. It was late; past time for anyone to be working. His eyes gritted like sand as he opened the small rolled sheet. He angled its surface to catch the light from the fire.

"Dearest Father," said the awkwardly careful script. "Brother Kenelm says I may help Uncle Aimery with his new bird, but only if

I obtain your permission first. I beg of you, if you love your most dutiful and respectful son, please give your blessing."

The flowery language made him want to laugh. He knew it was Robin's conceit, not the more practical tutor's. His youngest was always trying to reach beyond his years.

Too bad he was reduced to sending his father notes. Edmund could not recall when he had last spent an hour with his son, or taken him for a walk, or had a conversation about anything besides the progress of his lessons. Aimery saw Robin every day, as he had Thomas when he was home. He had formed those boys' hearts and minds far more than their father.

Which, all things considered, might not be an awful thing.

With a twisted smile, Edmund pushed himself from the wall. He would grant his son's request. The boy needed someone to look up to.

Thoughts of family led him down the stair to his lady's chamber, where the flicker of candles told him she did not sleep. He knocked on the partially open door and stepped inside. Here all was velvet and silk and fancy Italian tapestries to warm the walls. Even the ceiling beams had been painted with foliage and flowers. Two of Claris's ladies worked at embroidery in the alcove by the fire. Both were yawning, but Claris would not dismiss them until she was ready for bed herself. Edmund nodded at them, grateful they were too weary to converse.

Lady Blythe, his least favorite of the coterie, acknowledged his nod with an expression between a simper and a glower. God knew how—and, frankly, Edmund did not care—but Claris had convinced the silly goose he was an ogre and she a saint. Despite her visible disapproval, Lady Blythe could not forget he was a lord, and a comely one at that. Had he paid her the smallest kindness, he had no doubt he could have had her in his bed. Reason enough, he decided, to treat her as coolly as she treated him.

Keeping these cogitations to himself, he greeted his wife.

"What do you wish?" she asked politely. Open hostility was not his lady's way. She sat at a mirrored table, smoothing some concoction of her own devising over her face and neck. The shiny cream smelled of rosewater and almonds.

Claris was nothing if not clever with her herbs.

Ignoring the ladies, who were likewise pretending to ignore him, Edmund moved behind his wife. He laid his hands gently on her shoulders. He had no delusions about her nature, but perhaps tonight they could make peace.

Surely even she grew weary of their endless feud.

"I came to see how you do," he said gravely, "you and our future child."

Her lips curved in a secret smile. "We do well," she said, sneaking a look at his reflection from beneath her lowered lids. "You might even say we bloom."

"I am glad to hear it." When he propped his hip on the corner of her table, she moved her arm before it could touch his thigh. Inwardly Edmund sighed. Claris would win her game if he showed offense. "I did not get you a gift for this child. Would you like one?"

"I need no gift for doing what is natural to any woman."

"Need has nothing to do with it. The gift is to mark a new life, to give thanks that God has entrusted it to our care."

The deepening of her smile made dimples appear in her cheeks. "God you can thank with alms, my lord. I require nothing from you."

"Claris," he said, his patience fraying, "it would not kill you to accept a gift."

Claris's expression grew, if anything, even sweeter than before. "Perhaps I would like a little merlin," she admitted, "a swift, sure huntress of the air."

Despite the innocence of her tone, Edmund knew precisely what she implied. Only Aimery could give her what she wanted. Only he was heroic enough to win her heart. But she had misstepped in her choice of wishes. She must not have known he had heard how Aimery's new falcon tried to attack her.

"Yes," he said softly, "perhaps my brother can find you a huntress with nice, sharp claws."

Then, before she could respond, he strode determinedly to the door.

I should not even try, he thought, and did his best to put her from his mind.

BECAUSE he showed no signs of tiring, Gillian spelled her captor to sleep, then hid her stolen gown in a dusty chest before she changed.

Perdition take her tongue, she cursed as she settled back on her perch. Of all the stories to come up with! Yes, Aimery had caught her unprepared with his assumption, but Gillian had never met a goddess in her life. She had sent the image of a blinded maiden into his dream as a convenient way to coax him to unseel Princess's eyes. She had not expected him to remember it, much less take it for a visitation. Goddesses were complete nonsense, so far as she knew.

She consoled herself with the knowledge that he had half believed her. And, after all, pretending to be the servant of a goddess was preferable to the truth. Goddesses' servants were not candidates for staking. A man like Aimery would feel honor-bound to protect her.

Predictable as the tide, Princess cheeped in contentment at the mention of her keeper's name.

Stupid bird. Stupid Gillian, for that matter. How could she have let herself be drawn to him? His being as sympathetic as he was attractive was no excuse. The last thing she needed was to be more vulnerable than she was. She wanted to explore the human world, not get attached to one little corner of it.

Or one not-so-little corner.

Had she been in her human form, she would have blushed. What did the size of his manhood matter? She was no maid. She was an *upyr* grown. The games she had played with Ulric would have curled his hair.

Princess crooned at her agitation, the same soothing burble Gillian remembered from the mother bird in the nest. Now, though, the burble held a hint of Aimery's song.

Stupid, Gillian thought, but succumbed to its calming lure.

———◦———

NIM Wei sat before her roaring hearth in the simple robes of a Yangtze peasant. She had been born in the valley of that river during the reign of the great Wen Ti, the year 590 by the Christians' reckoning. Dirt poor but determined, she had set herself up as a local sorceress before she realized her gifts were real. This humble garb reminded her how far she had come, and how far she still meant to go: so far she could never slide back again.

"Never," she whispered to the flames, then willed the memory away.

She had sent the priest home to his quarters in the papal palace, his wounds already healing, his mind filled with pleasant dreams. To him, she was everything; to her, he was a passing fancy, a type rather than a person in his own right. Others could have filled his place and she would not have cared.

Why did humans care? Their lives were a snap of her *upyr* fingers. Why did they struggle to do good or bad? Why did pleasure or punishment matter? Why did they want to believe?

That most of all was a mystery.

She did not believe in heaven or hell. She had killed for her own convenience, had stolen and lusted and lied and no divinity had reached down to smite her. Fate was her god, and the secret forces of nature. Patterns could be found by those who knew how to look. The signs were difficult to interpret, but as real as the symmetry of a leaf.

Form fought chaos. Creation balanced destruction.

Intent lay behind this, of that she had no doubt, but it was an intent so alien no human mind could see more than its dimmest shadow. Even the mind of an *upyr* had to strain to grasp its scope.

The gods did not care, she thought. They merely set events into motion.

Sometimes their current could be thwarted. Other times, the only course was to let their tide sweep one out to sea. To fight was to drown. To give in was to reach an exotic shore.

Nim Wei felt a current tugging her now.

Though she did not want to go to England, she felt pulled. Something moved there. Something that affected the *upyr*. Ever since her mirror had awoken, she sensed a change, a chess piece out of place.

Auriclus had always liked the game, despite his pretensions to rusticity. They had played many times as master and student before she recognized the truth. He did not want her to be his equal. He would hoard the best of his secrets to the end. What she knew she had taken by stealth. Check, she thought. Always check and never mate.

Once upon a time she had longed to kill him.

Remembering the desire—the heat of it, the energizing power— she shifted restlessly before the fire. Tonight she would settle for being able to forget.

This imbalance she sensed was his doing. She could smell his mark on it as undeniably as blood. He thought of himself as an ideal sire, letting his children find their own path within the bounds he set. But he never finished what he started. He was as irresponsible as a storm.

The wood burned and crackled before her unblinking gaze, the flames created from the tree's destruction. The tug on her grew stronger as she cleared her mind. Again she saw the lion, and the castle, and a hawk swooping over both.

England it was then. And no time to delay.

Seven

AIMERY went about his morning tasks with a feeling of well-being. Princess sat on his shoulder, as bright and alert as he. He should have been shaken by his experience of the previous night, should have been itching to consult someone about whether it could be true. But Aimery did not want to know what others would say. He was too busy being happy.

There had been little enough of that in his adult life. Contentment, yes. Satisfaction, surely. But this giddy sense of joy was rare.

He wondered when he would see Gillian again, if perhaps the next time he could coax her into letting him kiss her. Branded in his mind was the memory of her lips, soft and red, like berries in the snow. He wished he had more experience with wooing. All his life, women had pursued him, for reasons that had little to do with who he was. Women looked at him, saw a dangerous brute, and decided they would enjoy him in their beds—either with fantasies of taming him, or because they wanted to play with fire. He had benefited from this penchant, but now and then it wore on his spirits.

"What do you think?" he murmured to Princess as they entered the shuttered mews. "Do goddess's servants like dangerous brutes?"

If she had an opinion, she did not share it. She was too occupied with turning her head this way and that. He had left off her hood today—an experiment, he told himself, to see how calm she would remain outside his rooms. Thus far she had behaved, only fluffing in anxiety when one of the hunting dogs trotted across their path. Her claws had poked straight through his doublet, but he forgave her. He must not have coped her talons as carefully as he thought.

Now she seemed fascinated by her fellow hunters. This soon after sunrise, most of the birds still dozed on their scattered perches. Aimery flew a variety of breeds: big red-tailed hawks, tiny merlins, and quite a few peregrine falcons like Princess. Peregrines were the noblest of the hunting birds: fast and strong and, when raised well, full of heart.

Those who ruffled and blinked at his entry were, without exception, looking at Princess askance. "Who is that?" their attitude seemed to say. "Why is she so big and sleek?"

Far from being intimidated, Princess accepted their nervousness as her due. She did not threaten them, but neither did she cower. If she was a princess, she was one secure in the knowledge that she would be queen.

Amused, Aimery stroked her glossy back. Attention caught, Princess gaped her beak at him and cheeped. Part of him felt as if he ought to understand her. Irrational as the reaction was, he realized it was not new. Even before he had met the goddess's servant, his bond with this particular bird had been strong.

But maybe Gillian and Princess knew each others' language.

"Put in a good word for me," he said, smiling fondly at her tilted head. "Since you obviously have the ear of the spirit realm."

Princess stamped her feet on his shoulder and half-lifted her wings.

Aimery laughed. "Is that a 'yes,' little sister? Or do you think silly humans like me should do their own wooing?"

The bird did not answer, though she did caw softly at his laugh. Aimery decided he must have lost his wits. Why would a beautiful creature like Gillian bother with a big, scarred wreck like him? Still, remembering the way she had squirmed beneath his gaze, he could not relinquish hope.

Maybe she would see him, not as hero or monster, but as the man he truly was.

If not, well, he would settle for what he could get.

GILLIAN thought her heart would burst with excitement. Today, she was going to fly.

At first, when Aimery fed every bird in the mews but her, she had been annoyed. Happily, he had the habit of speaking to his charges, whether or not he thought they could understand. He wanted her appetite keen, he said, because today she would start learning to hunt.

"You are young," he explained, "but I know you are ready to try."

The prospect thrilled her so completely, she could not help flapping her wings against his back. Her blood seemed to fizz within her veins and her muscles tingled in their eagerness to be tried.

She had been dreaming of this ever since she watched Princess's mother catch that gull.

Fly! cried Princess, picking up the images in her mind. Gillian did not try to hush her. *Yes,* she exulted back. *Today we are going to fly.*

Mounted on his big gray charger, Aimery carried her on his glove to an open pasture outside the walls, with Robin and a second man to assist.

"She is a big one," the assistant said when he first saw her. "She should take down a hare or two."

His name was Ian. He had a cast in one eye and a missing thumb, but neither seemed to hamper him in his duties. From listening to him talk, Gillian learned he was originally from the town and that Aimery had hired him when he lost his job at the mill.

It was a kind act, she thought, and a savvy one since the man was skilled. Despite her wish to remain aloof, it made her like Aimery even more.

Aimery best, Princess insisted, loyal to the last.

Gillian chuckled to herself and took in the day. The weather was lovely: not too hot, not too cold, with a soft spring breeze she knew she would love to ride. She smelled sheep in the distance, and wet young grass, and the comforting scent that was Aimery's own.

Another, gamier smell proved of more interest to Princess. It came from the peculiar kitelike contraption Robin held, a pair of real crane's wings secured to a wooden frame. Gillian did not think much of Princess for being fooled by it but she, apparently, was convinced that it was prey.

"How far shall I walk off?" Robin asked, his voice piping with an excitement as great as hers.

"Out to that rock," Aimery answered. "Just drag the wings behind you and waggle them as you go."

Gillian wanted to snort but of course Princess could not.

"Whistle when she has flown most of the way," Aimery reminded Robin. "She should come down on her own, but she needs to learn the signal to land."

Eager as a puppy, Robin took off at a run with the pitiful corpse wings bumping along the grass. Anything less like a living bird she could not imagine.

"All right then," Aimery whispered. "Let us see what my girl can do."

His arm tensed and, before she realized what he intended, he tossed her gently up and away. Her wings flapped awkwardly in surprise, then steadied as she caught the invisible substance of the air. Her weight fought her, but this battle she won as well. Even the trailing cord of her creance she could not mind. Up she drove her light and speedy body, up and up, her muscles beginning to warm as her wings beat strongly down. Her heart pounded in the rhythm its instinct set.

Then she found the breeze.

Oh, how lovely it was to let it hold her, to circle effortlessly upward and soar free. In that moment, she thought she could fly forever, far, far away, with nothing to pull her down. This was why she had left the pack: to taste freedoms like these.

Voices cried out beneath her in encouragement and awe. Dimly she heard Robin whistle, not Aimery's old song but a new one.

She knew he would worry, but she could not go back just yet.

She looped around a stunted elm and cried a challenge at a passing crow. She did not dare dive, but she rose as high as she could and then sloped down until she skimmed like an arrow close to the ground. The speed she attained was heady, pressing her feathers against her skin. When she lost her nerve for the game, her momentum carried her upward almost as high as before.

Fly! cried the bird, and then, almost as an afterthought: *eat?*

Very well, thought Gillian with a mental laugh. *We had our bit of fun.*

She followed Robin's whistle to the crane wings where, to her relief, a fresh morsel of fowl's breast awaited her as reward. She did not care what Princess thought. She had no interest in rotting meat. Even standing on the wings was a bit disgusting.

"Did you see her?" Robin bubbled. "Did you see how high she flew?"

"I saw," said Aimery, having rode up on his horse. "I thought for a minute there we would lose her."

"Not Princess," Robin insisted. "Princess will always come back to you."

"Perhaps," said Aimery. "But we must remember she is a wild thing. We must ensure she wants to return."

"By feeding her," said Robin, "and by being kind."

"And by letting her follow her nature. What she would do in the wild, we can train her to do at our request. What is unnatural to her, we should not demand. A falcon is not a dog. She will please herself before she pleases us."

A hail reached them from the pasture's edge.

"Blast," said Robin, his tone so dejected Gillian looked up from her meal. "There is my stupid tutor."

"Hardly stupid," said Aimery, "and I thought you liked Brother Kenelm."

"I do. But I did not think he would come so soon. I want to learn more about the falcons. I want to know how Princess would act in the wild."

Aimery chucked his chin. "You gave your word you would not shirk your other lessons. What Brother Kenelm can teach you matters, too."

Lessons, Gillian thought, immediately perking up. Robin was getting lessons? Without a moment's hesitation she fluttered onto the boy's shoulder. He squawked in surprise and laughed, but was sturdy enough to perch on. *I want to come,* she thought at him, though she was not convinced she could do this magic in her bird form. *Please, please take me with you.*

In case this was not enough, she pecked delicately at his ear.

"I think she wants to come," said Robin. "Can I take her, Uncle Aimery?"

"What, to your lessons?"

"Yes, please, since you are done with her for today. I need to practice taking care of her by myself."

"I think you are hoping to distract Brother Kenelm from teaching maths."

Oh, no, Gillian thought at him. *You love maths. You would never let yourself get distracted.*

To her delight, Robin staunchly shook his head. "I like numbers. Thomas is the one who hates them."

The tutor stalked to a halt before them. Something about his stern expression told her not to even try sneaking into his mind. He crossed his arms over his habit.

"So," he said to his student, "you claim to like mathematics. I shall remember that from now on."

—————

ROBIN carried her to a tiny chamber off the hall. When not used for lessons, it obviously served as the tutor's room. A chest for books guarded the foot of a narrow bed whose single blanket was neatly rolled. Above the headboard hung a crucifix. Pegs held a cloak and a change of robes.

They were the simplest of furnishings, but something about

them conveyed their owner's taste. The chest, though plain, was beautifully constructed, the robes of finely woven cloth. The brother himself was neatly groomed, his tonsure combed, his nails free of ink or dirt.

This monk had known better chambers than these, Gillian deduced, but had too much pride not to take care of what he had.

He waited until Robin was settled, with her on his shoulder, behind the standing desk.

"As you know," he began, "our modern science of numbers owes a debt to the Arabs, who gave us our concept of zero. The zero, or naught, allows a single numeral to take on value as a multiple of ten or a hundred or however high you wish to go, according to its position."

To Gillian's disgust, this was the last of the lecture she came close to understanding. The cleric's fondness for Latin did not help, since she barely knew enough of that to say a paternoster. Young as he was, Robin understood. He took copious notes on a wooden tablet coated in wax. Sadly, for all Gillian could read of the whitish marks, Princess might have scratched them.

Tail drooping down Robin's back, she sighed silently in defeat. She should have known this solution was too good to be true. She would have to swallow her pride and ask Aimery for help—which was not how she had hoped to spend their time. These were lessons for children. She did not want to get them from him.

At least the glowing brazier kept the chamber warm. She was about to give in to Princess's urging to nap, when she noticed a change in Robin's notes. A simple symbol had appeared near the bottom of his slate, a squared-off circle with a curly tail. Next to it he had scratched a picture of an apple. As she craned her head in fascination, his stylus peeled the wax from a second symbol, another circle with a loop attached to its upper left. This he paired with a picture of a bird.

"B," he muttered beneath his breath. "B is the first letter of the word for bird."

Intrigued, Gillian gripped his skinny shoulder and leaned farther forward to see.

"Buh," he said. "This letter makes a sound like 'buh.'"

She could almost hear the gears turning in her mind, great wooden ones, with rusty axles, grinding closer and closer to culmination until the creaky approach dissolved in a burst of light. Yes, she thought, *yes!* Whether she would have grasped the concept as quickly when she was human she did not know. She only knew that, with a few simple words, the pieces to the mystery fell into place. When Robin scratched three more symbols after the B, she knew each represented one of the sounds that added up to "bird."

She was so elated she fell off Robin's shoulder and had to scrabble for purchase on the slanting desk.

The flutter, and her involuntary squawk, drew the attention of Robin's tutor.

"Hm," said Brother Kenelm, turning Robin's slate around to examine. "I do not believe these notes are in any manner related to ciphering."

"They are for Princess," Robin said with a lack of guile that made Gillian wince—never mind she was wondering how he had managed to understand her wishes. Maybe children, since their minds were more susceptible to influence, were also better able to hear the influence itself. If that were the case, Gillian hoped he did not tell the tutor he heard her speak. The strict-minded cleric was liable to call an exorcist—for Robin as well as her.

She was far from reassured by the boy's next words. "The lecture was boring her," he explained. "I thought she might like to read."

"Oh, I see. You thought she might like to read." The tutor's tone was as dry as parchment.

"Do you not think a bird can learn?"

"No, I do not."

No answer could have been more definite, but Robin was not quashed. "I think animals are smarter than people realize. Old Wat told me once, when he was little, he had a dog who could count to five."

The tutor covered his eyes, probably so Robin would not see him roll them. "Master Robin . . ."

"I am not trying to shirk. I swear it! I just"—the boy leaned forward to whisper—"I think she wants to learn things. She hopped right on my shoulder as soon as she heard I was coming here."

"She is a bird. Birds prefer to sit up high."

"Then why not hop on Uncle Aimery's shoulder? He is higher than me."

The tutor sighed and looked sternly down his impressively bony nose. "How old are you, Master Robin?"

"Eight and two months."

"Do you not think that is old enough to stop believing in childish tales?"

"But what if she does want to read?" Robin drew a bracing breath. "Do we have the right to deny her an education?"

This time Brother Kenelm covered his whole face. Gillian thought he might be laughing, but when his hands fell away he appeared as sober as ever. "God grant me strength," he murmured, and it did not sound like a prayer. "Very well, young man, if you wish to conduct an experiment on this bird's capacity to learn, I shall not stop you. I will thank you, however, to conduct your lessons on your own time. Perhaps you will discover how challenging teaching is."

Robin was delighted by this concession. For her part, Gillian wondered what sort of trouble they both might be inviting. Heaven forbid Aimery's nephew should puzzle out what she was. She would have no choice then but to flee.

The dread that prospect elicited was a warning in itself.

"YOU look sleepy," Aimery commented as she settled with her legs curled beneath her at the foot of his rumpled bed.

She was flattered to see her arrival had not roused him. He had been waiting for her to come. His eyes glowed with anticipation, the flecks of gold like polished amber in her *upyr* light. He seemed different tonight: more confident, more male if that were possible. They sat within his emerald brocade curtains as if within a tent— she in her stolen gown, he in nothing more than his sun-browned skin. He was propped against the bolster with the covers pulled to his waist. He put her in mind of a warrior prince, with his great muscled chest and his commanding sensuality. If she had not known how kind he was, she might have been afraid. As it was, flickers of trepidation skittered along her nerves. The atmosphere in their curtained bower was warm and hushed, the air made rich by the scent and pulse of his human life.

This, she thought, was a place for sharing secrets.

"I am a bit tired," she admitted, surprised that it was true. She had never before had the option of being active both night and day. Between flying lessons and nocturnal explorations and now learning to read, she was getting little rest.

Given her fatigue, her session with Aimery's nephew this afternoon had required all her concentration. Gillian had tried to tread a line between responding enough to encourage him, but not so much he knew for certain she understood. He might suspect she did, but even an imaginative eight-year-old would not be sure. If she recalled her own childhood aright, eight was an age when one's faith in talking birds and fluttering fairies was about to fray, an age when harsh reality began to rule. Whatever he wished to believe, Robin would doubt. Hopefully, that doubt would keep him from carrying tales.

She had promised Lucius she would be careful. She did not want to betray his trust.

"Such thoughts," Aimery said, watching them cross her face. "You make me wonder what goes on in a goddess's servant's mind."

"Nothing much," Gillian mumbled and Aimery laughed.

"That I sincerely doubt. I wager a mind like yours is never completely still."

It was when I was flying, she thought. For a while, I was serene.

"Now you have thought of something happy, for your eyes are dreamy and your face is soft."

"Stop," Gillian scolded, smiling in spite of her dismay. "I am supposed to be observing you."

"Well then, you may observe my observations. Come." He patted the space beside him. "Would you not like to observe me from closer quarters?"

She hesitated and he laughed again, a low, sweet rumble in his chest. "I promise I shall not bite, though I cannot promise not to be tempted."

"Neither can I," she retorted, perhaps a trifle too near the truth.

Without meaning to, she imagined how he would taste, how he would flinch and sigh as she pierced his skin. The exchange of blood was the profoundest act an *upyr* could share, more intimate than making love—though the urges were intertwined. What would it be like to experience this with someone besides the pack leader, with someone as exotic and forbidden as this mortal man?

Her cheeks stung with heat at the dangerous thought. When his knowing gaze met hers, she felt as if his large, warm hand had cupped her sex. She was grateful he could not know exactly what she desired.

"Sit with me," he said, his voice rumbling with more than humor. "I would consider it an honor."

She felt obliged to accept then. To refuse would have been rude. Warily, she crawled up the bed and turned to sit beside him. Though the mattress was large, he had positioned himself so she could not sit without brushing his side and shoulder. Through her undergown's sleeve, her skin tingled as strongly as if her arm had been bare.

"Magic," he whispered and turned on his hip to face her. His hand lifted to her cheek. Slow as smoke he petted her skin, first with the front of his fingers, then the back. His touch was like nothing she had ever felt, like comfort and danger and sex rolled into one. When he traced the shell of her ear, her spine threatened to collapse.

"Does this stir you to the soul?" he murmured. "Or is it only me? I feel as if you have enspelled me and yet my mind has never been so clear."

She had no breath to answer. The tip of his finger was drawing a trail of velvety warmth along her jaw. Her mouth fell open without her will. The pad of his thumb pressed her lower lip.

"Gillian," he said, "I would brave any sorcery to know your kiss."

Despite the humility of his words, his gaze was bold. Gillian fought the urge to swallow and ended up shivering instead.

"Are you cold?" he asked. His hand slid down her neck and across her shoulder. She did not dare look down. The tips of her breasts felt tight and hot.

"My kind," she gasped, "do not mind the cold." As if to brand herself a liar, she shivered again.

He smiled, his eyes crinkling with enjoyment. "Lift your legs," he ordered, doing it for her before she could ask why. With an agility that spoke of much experience, he tucked her under the covers and pulled her close.

She felt his bareness along her side—from ribs to hip to thigh. The contact seeped like brandy beneath her skin. He had his arm wrapped behind her now. Off balance, she had no choice but to brace her own palm against his chest. His hair was a teasing rasp, a reminder of how thoroughly male he was.

"This," she said, her voice gone distinctly breathy, "will not help me learn to be human."

His grin had the quality of an expression not often seen. "Are you certain? You feel more human to me than ever."

"Ha." She removed the large, warm hand that had somehow crept onto her hip. "You are a rake, Sir Aimery. Fathers must lock up their daughters when you come round."

"I assure you, they do not. No one ever gives me a chance to flirt."

"If this is your idea of flirting—" She broke off with a gasp because his hand had found her hip again and was rubbing liquid heat up and down the bone. "You have no respect! Please remember whose servant I am."

Still grinning, he relinquished her hip, though not before his thumb swept dangerously close to its inner curve. His lack of re- morse might have had something to do with the audible hastening of her breath. Certainly she was not acting like a powerful being, much less like one who scorned his caress.

"If you please," she said briskly, pretending he had not turned her to melted ore. "I would like to hear of your life."

"I am not sure the story of one man's life can tell you all you wish to know."

"It shall be a start. And I would like to listen. You intrigue me."

His brows quirked up and down. "Intrigue is to be desired."

"Aimery," she scolded, but it did no good.

"You make a poem of my name," he purred. "Sweet and just a little husky."

She pushed away and crossed her arms. "That is exasperation you are hearing."

"In that case, you make a poem of exasperation." Giving in, he settled back against the bolster so that his shoulder once more warmed hers. "Very well. My life. I was born here at Bridesmere. My mother was my father's second wife. She was kind, I remem- ber, and sweet of face and manner. Truth be told, Edmund was closer to her than I. He was a wild thing after his own mother died, a three-year-old savage with a broken heart. I think he called to my mother more than an easy child could have done. She was a stranger to Bridesmere. It made her feel needed to soothe his wounds."

"What happened to her?"

"She died of the pestilence when I was ten." Aimery sighed and wound one of Gillian's curls around his finger. "We were luckier at Bridesmere than those who lived in the cities. Most of us survived. Of course, every soul who passes is missed. We had a sister, Kate,

who was only two when she was taken. I think I cried for her more
than I did for my lady mother."

Gillian covered his hand where it lay now beside her neck.
"Your sister was the one you liked to baby, the way your mother
babied Edmund."

He smiled at her, his eyes glinting with emotion even after so
many years. "I suppose she was." He tugged at her hand to change
the mood. "What of you? Have you brothers and sisters?"

He could not have known how less than happy that question
was.

"I had a brother," she said, the admission a thread of a whisper. The shame came back to her with the words, sharp and burning. But she had lied about so much. The least she could do was be
honest about this. "His name was Colin. I was jealous of him because he was Mother's favorite."

"Was? He is not alive?"

"He died of . . . he died as well."

Aimery drew back to peer at her. "I thought the goddess's servants were immortal."

"Immortal. But not indestructible."

She had said too much and not enough. She hung her head as
she waited for him to ask how her kind could be destroyed.

But this did not seem to concern him. He lifted her curls behind
her shoulder and cupped her face. "I am sorry I asked you this
question that makes you sad."

Gillian bit her lip. "I am not as sad as I am ashamed. Many
times I wished that Col were dead."

"Ah." Aimery stroked the locks he had rearranged. "Envy is a
passion children have. It is not right, but it is natural. You probably
would have outgrown it, given the chance."

"I do not know."

"And maybe your feelings were a little your mother's doing?
Parents are not always fair."

Gillian thought back to their last exchange: her mother cradling Colin, ordering her to live. The fierceness of her words had haunted her all these years. Was the emotion behind them love or anger or something more complex? She would never know. Not for sure. Not even with her gift.

Tonight, for once, the uncertainty did not seem too great to bear.

"She cared for me in her way," she said, "as much as she could care for a female child. I believe she thought, since I was a girl, I was born to suffer."

"Have you suffered?" His voice was quiet, conveying a soft, calm sympathy that gave her the strength to answer with composure.

"Now and then. But I have also been blessed beyond my power to imagine when I was small."

"That is a good thing to know. Some people never learn to be thankful."

She lifted her gaze to find his already on her, as steady and gentle as his voice. The look went through her, touching her, connecting them, until her wonder moved her to speak.

"Is this what being human means, to be so kind and wise?"

He laughed at her question as if it took him by surprise. "I am flattered you think me wise. I promise you, though, on my behalf and that of others, kindness and wisdom are not intrinsic to humanity."

"They are intrinsic to you. I knew that the day we met."

His face darkened and his beautiful eyes narrowed in their frame of ash-brown lashes. She could hear him breathing then, rhythmically and deep. The sound excited her. The flesh of her sex felt swollen, each tiny part conveying a persuasive message. She wanted him there, the full, hot bulk of him driving hard. In that instant, she would have surrendered without a qualm.

"Do not put me on a pedestal," he said.

"I would not do that," she assured him, her voice as constricted as his. "I know every being is a mix of good and bad."

She touched his chest and a small, pained groan broke in his throat. The thought that he might not have meant to make the noise aroused her more. Heat rippled through her as his hand cradled her head.

"Gillian," he said.

It was her only warning before his mouth came down.

Eight

FOR some reason, he expected familiarity, a sense of coming home. What he got was a sensual bombardment that obliterated rational thought. Her mouth tasted of berries: tart and cool and wet. The coolness surprised him, though she quickly warmed.

She had been kissed before. That he realized as her arms came sweetly around him. The stroke of her tongue, the tug of her lips betokened skill. She was teasing him, giving him a taste and then drawing back, opening a little, then more, before surrendering so deeply, he could not contain a moan.

However her kind lived, it seemed they did not keep their daughters under lock and key.

The desire to touch more fully hit both at once. Together they squirmed onto their sides, each pressed full length against the other. Gillian was as lithe as a little mink, strong and fearless in her response. When her hands slid down his back to cup his haunches, he felt as if he had drunk too much unwatered wine.

"Your skin is hot," she gasped, breaking free of the dizzying kiss. "I want to rub myself all over you. I want to lick you like a cat."

No woman had ever said such things to him. Though he meant to speak, all he could do was groan. The images her words called up made him hard enough to explode. In truth, he feared the state he had reached would frighten her. But she was licking his shoulder, then his chest, taking the salt from his skin with a tongue that was satin smooth. She found the bead of his nipple and flicked it.

Sensation darted straight to his loins. Before he could stop himself, he had grabbed her hips and was grinding his huge erection against her belly. The silk she wore was fine and soft but not what he wanted to feel on that most sensitive skin.

"You, too," he choked out, the closest he could manage to saying he wanted to touch her all over, too. Rather than try again, he wrenched her gown up in the back. No protestations met the maneuver. His hands found thighs like sun-warmed marble and buttocks that filled his palms as if they had been carved to fit. When he squeezed them, he discovered the well-formed muscles that lay beneath.

"Sorry," he mumbled, fearing he had been too rough.

"Oh, are you?" she said and laughingly nipped his chest.

His body jerked, though he barely felt the press of her teeth. His hands had a mission of their own, exploring the curve of her bottom, and the crease, and the two tantalizing dimples that framed its top. The feel of her was addictive.

"I cannot stop touching you," he confessed. Up slid his palms, measuring the swoop of her spine, the delicacy of her shoulder blades, the fine, long arch of her neck. Her eyes were dark as he framed her throat.

"I like that," she whispered, drawing a shiver from them both.

"I am glad," he said. "I want to please you."

The words hung in the air, thick with promise. He wanted to please her more than he wanted to please himself. He was not a selfish lover, but he did not think that had happened before. She was different. She was . . . more. The feeling frightened him a little, but he ignored it. She was a miracle, not a danger. Beneath her ear, her pulse beat in time with his. The paleness of her skin made her veins seem bluer. He caressed one, marveling. By contrast, his fingers looked as brown as a Turk's.

She stretched her throat under his palm. "Is this all you want to touch?"

She must have known it was not. "No," he said roughly. "I want to feel every inch."

Even as he pushed her gown up beneath her arms, the sharp-tipped press of her nipples lured his hand to slide around. Like the halves of her bottom, her breast fit perfectly in his hold. She purred as he ran his thumb around one pouting tip. Unable to resist, he bent to take it in his mouth. Be gentle, he told himself. Do not frighten her.

The advice was difficult to obey. Again, as he suckled, he felt her flesh go through that fascinating transformation from cool to warm. What was her nature, that she could alter so at a touch? She ripened against his tongue, a pebble wrapped in silk. When he deepened the pull, her thigh slid restlessly against his own.

He made a space for it, welcome and tight against his groin. Her strength, her softness, nearly made him cry.

"Kiss me," she urged, but already he clung to reason by a thread. He knew the briefest taste would devastate his control.

He waited until her gaze refocused to shake his head. "I dare not, sweeting. Your kisses rob me of sense."

She laughed at that, but he meant the words. Willing or not, he would not risk getting her with child. "Turn," he said instead, coaxing her to it with his hands. "I want you on your belly."

She lifted her brows as if doubting his sanity, but she complied. When she was settled as he wished, she grinned at him over her shoulder. "There," she said, with a cheeky waggle of her hind parts. "How do you like this view?"

"Immensely," he assured her, hardly knowing what he was saying. He straddled her, moving slowly, aware that her gaze was on his erection. Between his legs, his organ pulsed like a leaden weight. He could not hide it, so he did not try. He was what he was. Either she would accept it or she would not.

But her eyes narrowed with interest as she measured him up and down. "Should have grabbed that when I had the chance," she said, and he surged higher as if she had.

The sharpness of his relief, not to mention his excitement, robbed him of words. Rather than retort, he smacked her buttocks with both hands. Her brows went up again, but she did not speak. In truth, her squirm of reaction told him she was aroused.

"You need a firm hand," he said, embarrassingly hoarse.

Her grin broadened as she nodded meaningfully toward his cock. "I imagine you do, too, *sweeting.*"

Another man might have taken umbrage at her impertinence, but Aimery welcomed her spirit. "I do need a firm hand," he said, "and have needed one most sorely since we met."

"That long, eh?" Her eyes sparkled with amusement.

"Quite long," he agreed, "and quite hard."

She laughed. "I wish I could say you flatter yourself."

"No," he countered roughly, too stirred to sound glib. "I think you wish anything but."

Needing an outlet for the energy of his lust, he massaged her with all his strength, squeezing her cheeks together, watching the rich, pale flesh rise up and then subside. Her ability to take the treatment, and enjoy it, made him sweat. How much more could she take? How much more would she let him give her?

A great deal, it seemed, for soon she was wriggling underneath him, making tiny sounds as if her longing were too intense to keep inside. Watching her, hearing her, brought his arousal to the brink of pain.

With a groan of helpless lust, he stretched his body over her back until his chest brushed her head and his shaft pulsed tight and thick between the flesh he had just warmed. Far from flinching in shock, she pressed eagerly back at him with her hips.

He swore with pleasure, then slid his hand beneath her mound. Her curls were crisp, her labia melting soft. Between she was wet and quivering. Two of his fingers slid inside her sheath with barely an effort. The fit was close enough to make him sigh.

He breathed hard, wondering if he dared try a third. " 'S blood, you are a hot one."

She did not answer, merely uttered a low cry of relief. Her weight shifted, turning one thigh to the side to give his hand more room. Her hand eased beneath, her fingers pushing his deeper, her thumb guiding the motion of his own. His head spun at her boldness, a tempting call to match it with his own. Her pearl was ripe under his touch, a sleek and swollen fruit. Before he had time to ask if what he was doing pleased her, she spent with a strength and swiftness he had not foreseen.

"Ah," she said as her shudders faded. "Ah, do it again."

His inhibitions had no chance against her demands.

"Lift up," he said, hoarse with excitement. "I want to try another finger."

At once, he worried he had gone too far. She stilled beneath him and turned her head. He pushed up on one elbow to let her study his face.

"You want to see if I could take you," she said. A tremor shook her voice, but he did not think fear was the cause. Her tone grew soft and caressing. "You will fit, Aimery, no matter how big you are. And you need not worry about hurting me when you do. I am too strong for you to hurt. All your size will inspire is pleasure."

She might have reached into his mind to read his deepest frustrations: always holding himself in check, always fearing his hunger would rise beyond his command. The women who pursued him loved the look of his arousal—as if his size were proof of their allure. They never considered how much he restrained himself to protect them.

The thought of letting go completely was so enticing, he nearly spread her then and there.

"Lift," he said gruffly, drawing on the last of his determination.

To his relief, she did not argue. Her bottom rose to press the throbbing fullness of his shaft. Again he thought of taking her, of tilting her hips a little further and driving in—if only to test the truth of her claim.

But it did not matter if it was true. He would not risk her health in childbed.

Gritting his teeth, he paired his first two fingers with a third. Pressing them tightly together, he eased them in. Her body gave way as sleekly as it had before.

"Mm," she hummed as if to prove there was no pain. Her sheath was satiny and plump, flickering gently at the insertion, clinging hungrily when he withdrew for a second stroke.

He would fit, he thought, shivering with awareness. She would cling to his shaft as greedily as to his hand. The realization made him ache. He could not wait much longer for release, not if he hoped to keep his passions reined.

"Take me over," she whispered, and he knew she shared his need.

This time they rocked together, he against her bottom, she against his hand. Her heat sent him quickly to the edge. He had known lusty women, but she redefined the word. Utterly unashamed, her desire was a gift she freely shared, sighing out her pleasure, urging him to take his own.

"Yes," she said when he could no longer hold back his final drive. "Let me feel you spill."

He did not know how she did it, but she lifted him off her and turned to face him. Her hand slid down his chest to find his shaft. She growled in her throat as she squeezed it, clearly pleased by his length and heft.

"I love the way you feel," she said low and confiding, "you cannot know what it does to me."

Oh, Gillian, he thought. You cannot know what you do. His every muscle tightened at her touch. When she moved the skin of his erection over its hardness, the fraction of his mind not ruled by lust was all that kept him from begging to come inside.

"Here," she said, "against my belly."

Their legs tangled together as she pressed his shaft against her matchless skin, her cupped hand rubbing the upper side with a stroke so quick and brisk the sudden increase in sensation almost hurt. His body sang; his mind whirled. Seeming to divine what he wanted most, she kissed him an instant before he could demand it. They drew on each others' mouths as if they were starving, begrudging the need to breathe. Something cut his lip but he did not care.

Impossible, he thought, to feel such longing and not break.

Then his longing did break in a tight, hot spume of delight, and another, followed by a spreading wave of relief.

He did not have nearly long enough to enjoy it.

Gillian was panting against his mouth, but with tension rather than desire. When he stroked her hair to soothe her, she rolled away and sat up.

"I must go," she said from the edge of the ticking. She had turned her back to him, her arms propped straight and taut beside her hips—as if to bar his approach.

Aimery fought a pinch of hurt. Women were different, he told himself. Some did not like cuddling after love.

Some, of course, merely needed to be encouraged.

"Gillian," he coaxed, tugging at a trailing lock.

To his dismay, she shook him off. "I must go!" Shoving back her mass of curls, she pushed through the parted curtains. He began to follow, but she pointed him sharply back. "Stay," she ordered without turning her head.

The word was more than speech. His muscles locked in place as if he had to obey her. The unexpected loss of volition made his heart race in his chest, partly angry, partly alarmed. He had forgotten she was not an ordinary woman, but who would have guessed she could do this? When he recovered sufficiently to climb past the bed hangings, he found her gone. Only Princess remained in the darkened room, her feathers as puffed and awry as they had been for the hunting dogs.

Aimery raked his hair from his face and sighed. "I do not suppose you know where she went."

The falcon sidled uneasily on her perch. Her jesses were loose. Again. Damned if he knew how she disarranged them. He was as careful with the fastenings as he could be.

Hoping the chore would soothe him, he helped her get straightened out. When he took off her crooked hood, she pressed her head in gratitude to his chest.

At least the falcon loved him.

"Very well," he said, stroking her settling feathers. "I suppose it is dark enough to leave this off."

He stayed with her longer than he had to, crooning nonsense until she slept. When he finally stepped away, a flash of paleness caught his eye.

A piece of cloth was sticking out of his second chest, the one he shoved against the wall and rarely used. Curious, he opened the dusty lid. It was a woman's gown, Gillian's gown. Even if the silk had not been glowing faintly, its quality was unmistakable. Gillian must have shoved the garment in the chest before employing whatever sorcery she used to disappear.

Helpless to stop himself, he drew the cloth to his nose and inhaled her rainy lilac scent. The reminder of her sweetness made him feel better and worse. He let the garment drop to his side. What had he done to make her run? He knew his roughness had not frightened her, nor his size. That she had found her pleasure he could not doubt.

He squeezed his temples in confusion. Women were a puzzle he had no talent for sorting out, much less women who were not human. Any of a thousand gestures could have alarmed her.

He looked again at the gown, saddened to see its glow had begun to fade. He wanted everything about her to be indestructible. He had seen more than enough things die. But the cloth felt coarser already, as if her magic were the reason for its fineness.

It was only linen, he realized, rubbing a fold between his fingers. Linen and not silk.

She deserved silk. Silk and velvet and rubies as red as her tempting lips. He could not buy her rubies, but perhaps he could afford a gown, an apology for whatever he had gotten wrong.

Hopefully, a goddess's servant was enough like a human woman to enjoy a gift.

⸺⋆⸺

THE approach of sunrise roused her, a sure sign that Gillian's world had turned upside down.

She had almost ruined everything.

Playing with Aimery had made her feel free. Even when he pressed her into the mattress with his weight, she had no sense of being threatened, only of pleasure shared. Though she suspected he liked his bed sport rough, he seemed to have no compulsion to control her. Because of this, she longed to see his strength unleashed. That would be a gift to match those he had given her.

Unfortunately, in the heat of all these discoveries, in the delight of holding and being held, she had forgotten what she was.

She had reached unthinkingly for the closeness her kind most prized. As he kissed her that final time, her teeth had sharpened uncontrollably. She had cut his mouth. She had tasted the human sweetness of his blood. A sip was enough to burn her veins. His life was in it, his hot, bright mortal life.

The potency of that one taste should have warned her to pull back, and would have warned her if she had not held him hot and shuddering in her hand. He was a breath away from climax. She could sense it in his tightened limbs. His mind had pressed at hers as his pleasure rose. He wanted to get closer. He wanted to be inside. And all she had been able to think of was plunging her teeth into his neck when he crashed through.

The saints only knew how she had refrained. Her heart had certainly not been in it.

She feared she could have killed him, could have drunk him down too greedily to stop. At the very least, she would have showed herself a monster.

She closed her eyes, wishing for once that she had the hood to hide in—not that it would have helped her hide from herself.

I have been careless, she thought. I cannot afford to get that close again. Even a kiss might be more of a risk than she could afford. No matter how terribly it would hurt, she had to keep her distance.

Too bad she was not the least bit confident she would succeed.

THE tilting yard was a stretch of beaten ground beyond the stable. Years had passed since Bridesmere had hosted a tournament; their men were too valuable to risk on jousts. The wooden viewing stands were useful, however, and so remained, allowing trainees to observe while their fellows fought. Across from the stands, where two walls met, a battered quintain dummy awaited unwary pages to come do battle with its swiveling arm.

They would not come this afternoon. Edmund and his brother had claimed the space for their weekly practice at arms.

Or, rather, for Edmund's weekly practice. Aimery did not spend his days poring over papers and getting soft.

The knowledge that his brother did him a favor was a dash of gall to Edmund's mood. Gritting his teeth in determination, he shoved his sweaty hair from his stinging eyes and braced for the next attack. They fought with halberds today, a foot soldiers' weapon with a six-foot shaft. The business end of the thing comprised an ax for hacking, a hook for sweeping knights off their mounts, and an upward pointing spear for piercing armor. Though the blades they used were blunted, the halberd's weight, and the swing a man could put behind it, meant the prospect of injury was very real.

No doubt this, and the fact that he and his brother had stripped to their waists, had drawn their audience of stable boys and laundresses. From the safety of the stands, they watched the conflict, gasping in exaggerated dismay whenever one of them took a knock.

Shamefully, the one was usually Edmund.

Despite his less than legendary skill, both men received a share of admiring looks. True, those turned on Aimery were markedly more lingering. One of the laundresses was actually clutching her hands to her breast. But who could blame her? Seen this way, with his hair tied back and his torso bare, Aimery was an animal in his prime, a creature who had earned his supremacy with tooth and claw. He needed no title to prove his power. He had only to snap his fingers and they would kneel.

Not that the noble and modest Aimery would notice their adulation. As ever, Edmund's younger brother was focused on the task at hand—though not, perhaps, as focused as was his wont. He was dripping sweat for one thing and, for another, had twice missed good opportunities to take him down.

Generally speaking, holding Edmund off did not require much effort on Aimery's part.

"You seem distracted," Edmund panted, both hands gripping his weapon as Aimery's crashed against it with bone-jarring force. The shafts formed an X between them, against which both strove for control.

Aimery's only response to his sally was a grunt. Edmund braced his feet.

"One of the milkmaids spurn you?" he suggested, struggling to disengage without giving his brother a chance to strike.

"Hardly," said Aimery, and swept his foot behind Edmund's heel.

He managed to trip him, but Edmund was up again in a trice. Though Aimery had strength on his side, Edmund flattered himself he had speed. Taking heart at his recovery, he employed a flurry of blows to drive his brother back across the dusty yard.

"You admit it then," he needled. "This humble bit is an act. You know no woman can resist you."

The ax end of Aimery's halberd swung toward his head. Edmund blocked the blow, but the strength of it numbed his arms. He danced away to shake them, covering the weakness with a laugh. "Maybe you are weary of being chased. Maybe that is why you are off your game. Too much bed sport has drained your mighty strength."

"Fight," said Aimery, swinging around the other way. "No one ever talked an enemy to death."

But Edmund knew he had found a weak spot. With a grin of relish, he jumped over a whistling blade. "I understand. You are afraid to admit to a smidgen of imperfection."

Suddenly he saw an opening. Aimery's side was undefended. Edmund ducked a blow and struck, but he had barely touched Aimery's ribs when pain exploded behind his skull and threw him forward. He heard the laundresses shriek an instant before the ground smacked his face like a wall.

He did not quite go out but nearly. His head was definitely groggy when he rolled onto his back and blinked up at Aimery's anxious face. His brother was crouched beside him with one knee in the dirt. Well, Edmund thought as he fought a groan, at least that got a rise.

"See," he said, his voice a trifle slurred. "You were distracted. You never would have hit me that hard if you had been your best."

"As you will," Aimery conceded. "I was distracted, but so were you, or you never would have fallen so badly for that feint."

"Ha." Edmund spat a mouthful of dust. "I think I fell damned well."

Aimery laughed, a snort of sound that warmed something deep inside Edmund's soul. Memories hovered on the edge of his awareness, times when their family had been whole, when he and his brother—despite their rivalry—had been close. God, he missed Aimery's mother. Lady Elizabeth had always known how to calm the waves.

"Here," Aimery said, offering his hand. "Let me help you to your feet."

Edmund accepted the aid, but pride made him spring up too quickly. The yard tilted like a ship until Aimery steadied his arm.

"One more round?" Edmund suggested, trying to look spry.

Aimery gave him a dubious stare. "Have you not collected enough bruises for one day?"

The comment stung, though that was probably not his brother's intent. A biting wit, after all, was Edmund's weapon of choice.

"Yes," he said coolly. "Perhaps I have. Please forgive me for imposing. I know you are too honorable to enjoy trouncing your brother."

"Edmund."

"No, no. You must not apologize. That would be an insult to us both. You are, as usual, in the right." He bent to collect the fallen halberd, ignoring the painful pounding in his head as he changed position.

A page rushed over with the fine white toweling Edmund favored to blot his face. He hid behind it for a heartbeat, then let it drop. He told himself he did not care that he had been bested yet again. He was lord here. His word was law. Their audience was not thinking of his shame at Poitiers. That was ancient history. No one dwelled on it now but him.

Aimery caught his arm before he could go. "I was careless," he said. "You were correct. My mind was not on the session."

Edmund's anger drained away. Emotion shone from his brother's eyes, a vulnerability he could not remember seeing since they were young. The tension in Aimery's face drew more notice to his scar. For once Edmund attached no rancor to the sight.

"Whatever is troubling you," he said, "you can tell me."

For a moment, he thought his brother would trust him. Then the paragon shook his head. "It is nothing. I shall solve it in my own way."

"No doubt," Edmund answered dryly. "God only knows why I thought you might need my help."

⸺⊱✦⊰⸺

AIMERY shook his head as he watched his brother stalk toward the keep. Aimery had stung his pride. Again. If only Edmund knew how recently he had been refused, and by the very woman he wanted most . . . Two nights had passed since he held Gillian, two endless, lonely nights.

He had not known he was lonely until she came. He had merely thought his life was quiet.

I miss you, he thought. Why have you not come back?

One of the laundresses sauntered casually to his side, her rolled-up sleeve brushing his arm. She was new; not young but comely. A widow most likely, saucy and confident with her experience. She nodded at Edmund's retreating form as if she and Aimery were well acquainted. "Luck was with you today. You might have broken the baron's nose."

Aimery gave her credit. Her gaze slid only briefly to his scar. Despite her restraint, the nature of her interest in him was plain.

"He would not have punished me if I had," he said. "His pride does not overrule his fairness."

The laundress laughed. "Only a fool would lay odds on that."

Aimery stared at her, at her merry eyes and her buxom form. He knew she meant no harm, just as he knew she would probably be a generous partner. Not, however, the partner for him.

"I am that fool then," he said mildly, "for I would lay any odds you like. Bridesmere is fortunate in its lord—as you are fortunate in your employer."

She must have heard the censure beneath his tone. She stepped back as if he had struck her. "Forgive me, sir. I thought—" She had the sense to stop before she made her error worse. Head hanging, she sketched a curtsy. "Forgive me, I was too bold."

He was about to reassure her when he noticed her peering coyly through her lashes. Her meekness was a sham. Even now, she thought he would take her, like a stallion who would cover any mare who walked past his stall.

Without another word, he strode away. Chivalry be damned. He had just sworn off putting up with women's ploys.

THE bathhouse next to the kitchen had been a gift from Edmund's father to his second wife. Lady Elizabeth and her friends had loved to gather for a gossip in the steamy room, but it was also a boon to Edmund. Once a week he closed it off for use by the garrison, thus preventing his men from getting into trouble at the more licentious bathhouse in town.

When he chose, as he had this afternoon, he could also close it for himself.

The bath refreshed him, a quick one today since visitors were expected and Edmund wished to show himself at supper in the hall. Edmund was not as particular as Aimery or his birds, but he enjoyed a good, hot soak with a cup of claret. This one, though brief, had at least eased some of the creaks from his latest drubbing.

Supper—and the delegation of Flemish merchants—could now be faced. With luck, before they left, he would have a contract for his next few shearings.

His thoughts so engrossed him that what he found when he pushed through his chamber door took him by surprise.

"Well." He propped his hands on his hips. "I can think of but one reason why you would be woolgathering at my window. Enjoy the view of the tilting yard?"

Though Claris had jumped at his voice, the expression she faced him with was prim. "I wished to speak to you."

"Of course you did." He stripped off his dampened shirt and reached for the dry one his chamberlain had laid neatly across the bed. He both enjoyed and was irked by the way Claris flinched at the sight of his naked skin.

"I thought you might want to know I have overseen everything for supper, as well as airing the north tower chambers for our guests."

"Thank you," Edmund said and pulled the new shirt over his head. He debated pointing out that she need not have waited here to tell him that. He had never demanded that she report to him. For the most part, Claris was responsible in her duties.

"I shall wear my blue gown with the pearl embroidery," she went on, "and veil my hair the way you prefer."

Edmund undid the points of his hose in preparation for removing them, knowing without even looking that Claris would turn away. "It is not a matter of my preference. Your hair is lovely however you wear it. I ask you to don a wimple because that is proper. Merchants tend to be a conservative lot."

His legs reclad, Edmund studied his wife's averted face. Her demeanor was subdued, but under that he sensed excitement. His stomach clenched. Life rarely improved when Claris was making plans.

"Mooning after him will not help," he said, the words quiet if not kind.

She put her hand to her throat. "I cannot imagine what you mean."

"And I cannot imagine why you think everyone in this household has not seen through you. Aimery does not desire you. Spinning tales of him in your head will not change his mind."

"Your brother is too noble . . ."

"He is too smart, Claris." With an effort, Edmund uncurled his fist. Lord, but he loathed that look of mulish sanctimony she got when she tried to tell him what his brother was. He put his hand on her sleeve but resisted the urge to shake her. "You are not the kind of woman he wants or needs. How could you be when half the countryside would lay down for him if he asked?"

"He rejects them," she said, her cheeks a blushing pink. "*They* are the women he does not desire."

"Claris—"

"He rebuffed that slut of a laundress after the fight. Why would he do that if he were not yearning for something finer?"

"And an adulteress is finer than a slut?"

"True love cannot be found within the marriage bond. Everyone says so. Everyone!"

She was trembling with passion, her eyes flashing like sky-blue jewels. If she had not been such a half-wit, she could have been taken for a heroine in a tale: Guinevere, perhaps, or—better yet— the maiden who died for love of Lancelot.

"Claris," he said, his eyes stinging with an unexpected prick of pity. "If you are as miserable as you claim, by all means, take a lover. You have given me two fine heirs—possibly three, if this child turns out to be male. All I ask is that you exercise discretion, and that you leave my brother alone. He does not want you. Your ladies' twitterings to the contrary, you make yourself a fool by this pursuit.

"Besides which," he added as he warmed to his topic, "you would not know what to do with him if you had him. He is a man, Claris, with all a man's nature implies. He is not about to sprinkle rose petals on your pudendum, or whatever romantic nonsense you expect."

With a dignity he was forced reluctantly to admire, Claris pulled free of his hold. "You are the fool, Edmund. For you, every-thing must sink to the lowest level. But I shall not sink. I shall keep faith with my heart."

She resembled a saint swearing on a relic. Edmund knew it was pointless to speak to her in this mood. Sighing to himself, he turned away. "I shall see you at supper then."

Somehow she made her slippers scuff righteously toward the stair, the smell of roses trailing behind. Aimery had once given her roses, to lift her spirits after Thomas's birth. The gesture had been no more than kindness, but ever since Edmund's wife had crushed the blossoms for her perfume.

Edmund waved the scent from his nose. Someday, he thought, she would have to admit the truth.

Even a fool could not fool herself forever.

Nine

DUSK had fallen when a sound drew Edmund from his reverie by the window, some altercation outside his chamber. In the seconds it took him to cross the room, he heard his secretary loudly refusing someone entry, then a thump as if a body had been slammed against the wall. This was followed by a heavy silence.

Cautious, but not alarmed, Edmund reached for the door. Geoffrey was a sturdy lad. He had probably subdued whoever was trying to interrupt him.

When he stepped onto the rushlit landing, however, Geoffrey appeared to be the party who had been subdued. His eyes were glassy and a large, brown bruise bloomed on one cheek. Most shocking of all, a trickle of blood was running down his neck. He looked as if he had been bitten.

"S-sorry," he said, swaying slightly on his feet. "Says he needs to see you."

Shadows stretched and shrank in the well of the descending stairs, but Edmund saw only a doll-like woman who seemed to be holding Geoffrey up. At his questioning glance, her delicate pink lips curled in a smile. To his confusion, she was dressed as a man. Her straight sable hair was tucked beneath a cap and a man's black velvet houpelande fell to her thighs. Her hose were so snug, they clung to every curve of her calves. Edmund dressed with a modicum of vanity, but this far outdid him. Small diamond buttons framed the slits in her baggy sleeves, the lining of which was scarlet satin. The shirt beneath was blinding white and the links of yellow gold that hung from her neck were as thick as his thumb.

It was the richest outfit he had seen outside a royal court, but only a blind man would mistake its dainty inhabitant for a male.

If her mode of dress were not mystery enough, a moonlike glow shone from her skin. Edmund's mind struggled to conceive what might account for this effect even as his anger rose. Geoffrey looked drugged as well as battered. Implausible though it was, this tiny woman—or perhaps some hidden accomplice—must have attacked him.

"What have you done to my secretary?" he demanded.

The woman's night-dark eyes crinkled to join her smile. Her tongue swept her lower lip in a manner he found both erotic and disturbing. There was something strange about her features. Not only were they very pale, but they were too smooth, too perfect, as if a painter had contrived them as the ideal of what a face should be.

"Well?" he prompted.

But Geoffrey answered instead. "You need him here," he slurred. "He is a famous minstrel. The merchants will love his songs."

Edmund's hand went to the pommel of the blade that hung from his belt. He was surer than ever someone was hiding. "What are you talking about?" he said. "I see no one here but this woman."

The woman cleared her throat, a soft, husky sound that brushed his ears like a lover's sigh. "Forgive me. In all the excitement, I dropped my glamour." Her shoulders lifted in a jaunty shrug. "I suppose I shall have to bite you, as well."

Edmund gaped at her, frozen a second too long in shock. Her smile had changed. Her incisors were growing longer as he stared, sharper, like an cat's. His heart pounded in instinctive terror, though it was different from the terror he had felt all those years ago in France. His body knew it was threatened, but his mind could not take it in. Her eyes were like an animal's, too, glinting oddly in the flickering light.

"Sweet Jesu," he had time to say before she leapt.

The heels of her palms struck his chest with inhuman strength. He flew backward into his chamber, lifted completely off his feet. When he hit the ground again, his tailbone caught his fall. He sprung up despite the pain and attempted to push her back, but he might as well have been opposing a force of nature. She shrugged off his efforts as if they were nothing. When he tried to reach for his dagger, she cuffed his head so hard he saw stars.

Even then, he could not tear his gaze away from her teeth.

"Deus salva me," he murmured, on the floor again, weight supported by his hands as he scrambled back. "Please, God, help me now."

His plea seemed to amuse her, as if she knew how little God valued men like him, as if she knew every petty impulse he had ever felt. He shuddered as his back struck the tapestry-covered wall. He had retreated as far as he could.

"Yes," she said, looming over him, "I can see into your mind, human. Why do you ask a god you do not believe in to give you aid?"

I do believe, he thought, unable to catch his breath. I simply do not believe He cares for me.

"Ah," she said, the sound a travesty of understanding. The violation was unbearable—to have this stranger inside his head, stripping all his weaknesses bare. Smile still in place, she crouched before him. She had lost her cap. Her hair hung around her shoulders like a silken cape. He should have moved then, should have tried to get away, but all he could do was gulp for air. The fact that she had not bothered to take his dagger troubled him most of all. When she stroked his cheek with her silken palm, a flush heated his skin.

His body's response astonished him. A perceptible stirring moved at his groin. This creature was about to kill him and he was growing aroused.

"Your hurt is misplaced," she said, those eyes of hers glittering like polished jet. "The gods care little for any man. You are no more slighted than the rest."

Her gaze seemed to steal his will. She bent closer, her hand curling almost tenderly behind his neck. She smelled pleasant but peculiar, like old vellum and ink. Shivers wracked him as she licked his throat, one long wet drag from base to ear. Her touch was unnaturally cool, but her gathered velvet bodice brushed him with her quickened breaths. She was excited—for different reasons than he was, he suspected, but she was.

He tried to remember when a woman had last touched him with desire.

"Wh-what are you doing?" he stammered as longing ached through his ribs. What was the matter with him? He fought an urge to cup the back of her head. He would not give her permission to hurt him by what he did.

"Mm," she hummed, oblivious to his struggle. "You smell even tastier than your aide."

Though he was expecting it, her bite stunned his mind to blankness. The pain was sharp and cold until she began to draw on his blood. Then the sensation was blazing hot. His body hardened and throbbed, every inch of his skin tingling with excitement. The sound of her moans was a caress. When her hand gripped his shoulder from the back, a delicious weakness slid through his veins. Her heart beat all around him as if he sat inside a drum. Enthralled by the mysteriously comforting noise, he forgot everything but pleasure: pleasure in waves, pleasure in pulsing, piquant spikes, pleasure like bursts of juice from foreign fruits. No fear could withstand it, no envy, no guilt. Surrendering, he closed his eyes. Only his fingers twitched with his yearning to drag her close.

They lifted feebly to her slitted sleeves when she pulled away.

Reluctantly, his lids blinked open. Her face was an inch from his. Such beauty, he thought, was too lavish to be real.

She was flushed from her meal, her lips darkened from rose to rouge, her pupils nearly blotting out her slanting exotic eyes. For an odd, hanging pause she simply stared at him. My blood is inside her, he thought. It warms her beating heart. He could not read her expression, but he sensed their interaction had thrown her off her stride. When she spoke, her voice was thick.

"Now," she said, "let us discuss my fee for singing to your guests."

At once Edmund's head grew clear. "Your fee! Why on earth would I pay a woman who bites everyone she meets?"

"A woman!" His attacker sat back on her heels. He could tell he had shocked her, though he could not imagine why. Without warning, she leaned forward to clasp his face in her hands. Since he suspected her hold would be unbreakable, he did not try to prevent her from peering into his eyes.

As she probed, the spot between his brows felt as if she were tapping it with her nail.

After a moment, she released him in disgust. "You have seen through my disguise. You are not under my thrall."

"I should think not," he huffed and rubbed his itching forehead.

Suddenly, she smiled. Her teeth were normal again and his body immediately reminded him just how potent her charms could be. Tipping her head, she pressed one finger to her flawless cheek. "You know," she said musingly, "those who offer blood of their own free will cannot be compelled. Even if your work has strengthened your mind, my kiss should have restored my glamour. I am forced to conclude you wanted me to bite you."

"I wanted no such thing!"

"Did you not?" Her finger trailed down his chest to the hardness between his thighs. "That wife of yours must keep you happier than I thought. Oh, wait, it was *you* who thought you were unhappy." Her throaty laugh made his organ thump in her hand. She squeezed its thickness and laughed again. "Really, Edmund, you are a lovely man, and lord of this little heap. You should avail yourself more often of the bounty that surrounds you. To be so hard-pressed that you welcome the likes of me is hardly wise."

His emotions were too confused to respond to her teasing

words. "What are you?" he asked, the only question that seemed to matter.

One of her eyebrows rose. "What do you think I am?"

He crossed his arms. Now that his fear had begun to fade, his wits returned. She could talk all she liked about the strength of his mind; he knew this guessing game was meant to play him the fool.

"Maybe I am a demon," she suggested. "That would explain my infernal power."

"What would a demon want with me?"

"Perhaps I wish to steal your soul."

Edmund snorted through his nose. "No man ever needed a demon's help to give up that."

"A cynic!" She clapped her hands delightedly before her mouth. "My favorite sort of human. It is so terribly entertaining to make them believe."

"What do you want me to believe?"

She rose from her crouch to stroll his room, making an impromptu dance of touching his possessions. Light as swan's down, she scooped her cap from the center of his floor. He knew he was being toyed with, being made to wait for the answer he desired. Despite the knowledge, the sight of her shapely legs and twinkling feet made his body burn with lust. When she performed a farandole with the corner of his bed arras, he wished she were partnering him.

"I am *upyr*," she said, turning the words into a spoken song. "A creature of the darkness who feeds on human blood. For centuries, I have preyed upon mortal kind: growing in power and knowledge until the forces that guide me led me here."

The flourishing bow with which she concluded would have dazzled a queen. Edmund was a bit harder to blind. "Why would the forces that guide you lead you to Bridesmere?"

"Because"—she pointed accusingly with her diminutive gleaming hand—"something in your little castle is out of balance, something that affects the future of the *upyr*."

The word was vaguely familiar. He thought he might have

heard it from Old Wat, some tale of specters that preyed on wounded soldiers abandoned on the battlefield after dark. Like the majority of Old Wat's tales, Edmund had assumed it was nine parts nonsense. But maybe not. Maybe this creature was what she claimed. His heart began to thump again, though he did his best to hide it.

"I know nothing of your future," he said.

His tormentor dropped her dramatically outflung arm. "Yes, I can see you are most admirably ignorant. No matter. I will simply stay here until I sort the conundrum out."

"Stay?" said Edmund. "Here?"

She laughed. "No need to look so horrified. For one thing, you insult me. For another, I really am an accomplished entertainer. That passel of fat merchants I passed on my way in will soon be eating out of my hand. And they will see whatever guise I choose to assume—whether male or female or two-headed goat."

Edmund finally felt able to stand, though the wall behind him was a useful prop. To his surprise, his bruises hardly ached. "You mean they shall be fooled because you are so powerful."

His skepticism appeared to amuse her. "My mind may not have conquered yours, human, but I assure you that is out of the common run. Those who train their intellect have some resistance to *upyr* glamour. However, even scholars can be thralled so long as the bite is forced. You were simply lucky you welcomed mine."

Edmund felt far from lucky as he remembered how easily she had tossed him across the room. Nonetheless, he judged it best to stand his ground. "I will not endanger my guests."

"What danger?" She threw up her hands. "Do you have any idea how hungry an *upyr* needs to be before she can drink a human dry?"

"I am sure I do not want to know. In fact, I would rather you simply leave."

Though he harbored little hope of getting off this easy, the nature of her response took him aback. "I will play you for it," she said, nodding slyly toward the inlaid ebony chess table that sat in the alcove beside his hearth.

In spite of himself, his interest quickened. For years, only Sir John, his steward, had given him anything approaching a decent game.

"You play?" he said, trying to conceal how his pulse had hastened. He might have saved himself the trouble. Her gloating smile told him she knew the precise extent of his interest, above the neck and below.

"Try me and see," she said, the challenge going through him like a flame.

He could not doubt she was offering him more than a game of chess, just as he could not doubt his own enthusiasm for the prospect, at least in a physical sense. Even his lingering fear was not dampening that.

With regret, he glanced at the now-dark sky outside the keep. "We do not have time to play. I must greet my guests in the hall."

"All the better." Lips curling suggestively upward, she stroked her neck. "The delay will give me a chance to prove the rest of my talents."

He knew he should refuse her, but his better judgment was overcome.

GILLIAN wandered the moonlit castle, unable to sleep despite her need for rest. Aimery had left her a gift, a soft blue kirtle that matched her eyes. When she found it, spread across the chest where she stored her stolen undergown, she almost cried. Apart from Lucius's map, no one had ever given her a present—not her mother, not Ulric, though she often brought small offerings to them. She could tell the gown was new. No scent clung to it except the wool. The buttons that fastened it up the front were mother of pearl. When she brushed them with her fingers, warmth budded in her breast.

She knew she should have ignored the gift, given her resolve to keep her distance in human form. Bad enough she was with Aimery constantly as a bird, smelling him, hearing him, wishing she could soothe the lines of strain bracketing his mouth. She knew she had put them there; his various mutterings to Princess about the perversity of female kind left no doubt of that.

He had not deserved to be rejected without a word. That being so, how could she reject his present?

She told herself the kirtle was more modest than her gown, and would thus be less apt to attract attention. She was being careful, as Lucius had advised.

Even as she made the excuse, she knew it was hollow. With each excursion, her ability to hide her inhuman nature seemed to increase. She should have been happy. The more she honed this skill, the safer she would be in her new life. Away from here. Away from Aimery.

Her throat clenched at the reminder. In this short a time, he should not have become essential to her contentment. To Princess's, perhaps, but not to hers. Bridesmere, and Aimery, were merely stops on the road to a future of adventure, a future of travel and learning and maybe a bit of indulgence, too. She could know pleasure without being a fiend; give it as well, if it came to that.

So why did the prospect of sharing pleasure with other men make her want to weep?

Tomorrow, she thought determinedly, I shall sneak into the town. That would distract her from these troubling thoughts.

Tonight, however, she was on the hunt for books. It was time to discover just how effective Robin's lessons had been.

Unsuccessful in her search thus far, desperation had brought her to the tutor's chamber. The door hung temptingly ajar. From the first, Brother Kenelm had intimidated her, but surely if anyone had a text she could test herself against, it was him.

Biting her lip, she cocked her ear to the darkened opening. The sound of slow and steady breathing drifted out. The tutor must be asleep.

I am silent, she thought to herself, not daring to touch his mind outright. *I have no more substance than a shadow.*

She crept inside to the finely fashioned coffer where he kept his books. The chest sat at the foot of his bed, where his body lay still and dark. She drew a breath and held it. The lid lifted without a squeak to reveal a bewildering pile of tomes.

"Try the Capellanus," said the monk. "I think his concept of 'honest' love will entertain you."

Gillian could only gasp as he struck a flint and lit the candle beside his bed. When he raised it to look at her, he seemed as surprised as she.

"Well," he said, dark brows climbing his narrow forehead. "You are not the intruder I expected."

Gillian inclined her head. "Forgive me, Brother Kenelm," she said, praying her illusion was still in place. "I merely wanted something to read."

He considered her in silence. Then, without a shred of concern that she might stare, he threw off the covers and reached for his habit. He wore a shirt to sleep in but it was thin. Gillian caught a glimpse of angular limbs and lean, long muscle before averting her eyes. She did not glance up until she heard him tie the hempen rope around his waist.

"I know what you are," he said, sending another shock streaking through her nerves.

"You know?"

"Oh, your glamour is better than most, but I have encountered your kind before. You call yourselves *upyr.* You are immortals. You live by drinking human blood."

Human blood, she thought, her mind racing beyond his words. He knew *upyr* who lived on human blood?

He must have met a member of Nim Wei's broods. She struggled to find her voice. "We do not all live on human blood."

"Do you not?" He stood over her where she knelt before his open chest. She could have overpowered him, but unless she was prepared to kill him, she was not certain what she would gain. He did not appear the type she could terrify into silence.

"No," she said, measuring his reaction. "Some of us can share the spirit of beasts. We live on what our animal forms can eat."

"Ah," he said, "a child of Auriclus. I have never met one of his shapechangers. I suppose this explains my pupil's obsession with teaching his bird to read."

His matter-of-fact tone unnerved her. Determined to reclaim the advantage, she rose to her feet. "Why are you not afraid of me?"

Brother Kenelm smiled. The candle he held, coupled with the natural seriousness of his face, made the expression look quite peculiar. Sadness tinged it, but so did a threat. "I killed the last of your kind who tried to suborn my will. That is why I was banished here. My superior was most annoyed."

"Annoyed!" Gillian could scarcely catch her breath. "I should have thought he would be delighted."

The monk pursed his lips in denial. "Damiano was the head of the London broods. My abbot hoped to make him an ally of the church. I counseled against it, naturally. I thought he was too dangerous to trust, too duplicitous and rash. When the *upyr* tried to"— Brother Kenelm coughed—"overcome my objections by other means, I was obliged to defend myself. As I would defend myself from you."

For the moment, Gillian ignored the warning. He had no weapon that she could see. Most likely he was bluffing. Head spinning with this overturning of expectations, she gripped his bedframe for support. "Why would the church want to be allies with unnatural beings?"

Brother Kenelm shrugged. Despite the situation, he seemed to be enjoying himself. Gone was the prim disapproval he usually wore, a disapproval she now recognized as a mask. Banished he might be, but this man was more than a simple monk. Alight with interest, the gaze that met hers was sharp.

"Your kind are adept at moving behind the scenes," he said.

"The church sometimes has . . . commissions that cannot be fulfilled in the public eye."

"You mean murder." Gillian's voice was flat and hard.

"Ah, yes, the sport of kings." Brother Kenelm laughed, then lifted his hand to forestall her anger. "A thousand pardons. I have been too long in this backwater with nothing better to worry about than whether the wife of the abbot's nephew betrays her vows. You are a child of the church, I take it, and do not appreciate my humor. Murder is hardly our *raison d'être,* though the crusaders' victims might disagree."

Her insides chilled to hear a churchman speak so cavalierly. Was this the authority she had trembled before all her life, judging herself by its standards, fearing she would fall short?

"What is your aim then?" she asked with cool politeness.

She was pleased to see the brother wince.

"Spying," he said once he recovered his aplomb. "Diplomacy. Even protection can be controversial. You have no idea how awkward the abbot's defense of the Jews was during the last outbreak of plague. People were convinced they had poisoned the wells."

Gillian shook her muddled head. It was all too much to take in. Knees uncertain, she turned to sit on the edge of his open chest. Baffling her yet again, the monk lowered himself beside her as if they were old friends.

"You," he said, "would make a better ally than Damiano."

She was too surprised to guard her words. "Why me? I am not anyone's leader. Compared to the one you met, I must be a child."

Brother Kenelm's hand lifted to stroke her cheek. Gillian did not stop him. For a moment, his expression held nothing but human wonder for her beauty.

"You have power," he said. "More than I think you know. I have read most of the church's records on these matters, and have trained myself to see behind the *upyr* veil. Magic has its own scent, its own vibration against the skin. Yours is like a pool hidden in the forest. Even I cannot guess how deep it goes."

She turned away, staring at but not seeing his painted walls. His mention of records suggested humans had been studying the *upyr* for a good, long time. She wondered if Auriclus and Ulric knew. Even more importantly, was what he said about her power true? Was she out of the ordinary? Was that why she had been able to capture Princess's soul without instruction? Was that why she could read the minds of those within the castle?

She could not accept the claim on faith. Not when her life might depend on it.

"Stand," she whispered, and Brother Kenelm stood. She was not sure she had put her mind behind the order, but she followed him to his feet. Sensing something, and nervous with it, the monk dropped his gaze to the floor. His tonsured scalp gleamed in the candlelight. Gillian gathered her intent. As she had with Princess, she let instinct be her guide. "Look at me, Kenelm. Look into my eyes. Tell me all you are not saying. About Damiano and these records. About anything a young *upyr* might need to know."

He uttered a sound of protest, but he obeyed. Their eyes met and a quiver, like the augury for an earthquake, shot up her spine. *Wait,* she thought, but it was too late.

As his mind roared over hers, she had a moment to realize she should not have asked for so much. Whatever training had allowed him to see through her glamour crumbled at her demand, a wall of earth rather than stone. She felt surprise from him, then terror, before pictures and sounds and tactile impressions flashed through her awareness in a bewildering flood.

Books. Scrolls. A secret reading room with iron-gated shelves stretching to its ceiling. The key in Kenelm's hand. The scratches in the wood of the lectern. An ocean of words flipped by on yellowing pages. Dust stung her nose as a tall *upyr* stepped from the shadows of a turn in a corridor. *I am a friend of your abbot,* he said. *There is no need to fear.* Kenelm's blood leapt with more than alarm. Rings gleamed on the stranger's graceful fingers, fingers that smoothed the folds of his perfect clothes. He smiled at Kenelm's fascination, aware of his own allure. *Shall I be a friend to you, little scholar? Is that the hunger hiding in your heart?* The images tumbled, dizzying. Her own voice: *Tell me all you are not saying.* A glass of wine. A tattered blanket before a fire. A kiss laid on a naked thigh.

Stop, she thought at him. *Concentrate. I want to see the part that matters.*

Quiet fell in her mind—their minds—then seemed to gather. Gillian felt her soul plummet like a stone before she was lost.

Ten

As he frequently liked to do, Damiano was holding court in the abbot's quarters at St. Crispin's. The three of them, the abbot, the *upyr,* and Brother Kenelm, had drawn apart from the other monks after supper—which perforce Damiano had only pretended to eat. At present, they were comfortably ensconced before a gently crackling fire. A pair of matching choir stalls, three seats apiece, faced each other across the hearth. The finest artisans from Paris had carved the story of Abraham and Isaac into the wood. The *upyr* had a stall to himself, while Kenelm and the abbot shared the other. The seat Kenelm occupied showed the obedient Abraham binding his son to the altar of sacrifice.

God bless the Old Testament, Kenelm thought. How much more it rules us than the New.

More proof of their far-flung commerce stood between himself and the abbot, a hexagonal table with lacelike carvings even finer than those on their seats. This fanciful creation came from the workshops of the Moors. A jug of sweet Gascon wine was sweating on its top. Whenever Damiano emptied his golden cup, the abbot would stretch out the jug to refill it.

Though the *upyr's* eyes were shining, he never seemed to grow drunk.

"The church is a power in this world," he was saying in his rich, young voice. "A force for civilization. A preserver of treasures present and past. With that responsibility—a grave one, you must admit—come certain privileges. Rightfully so. Can the peasant laboring behind his plow comprehend the importance of a rare Greek text? He would toss it into his fire if he were cold. Only men of learning, such as yourself and your clever aide, understand how precious knowledge is."

When Damiano's bright brown gaze smiled for a moment into Kenelm's, a heat that had nothing to do with the fire rippled through his limbs. *Later,* said Damiano's eyes. *Later you will welcome my demands.*

As if his hand belonged to someone else, Kenelm watched it smooth his fine black cassock across his knee.

He had long since discovered the *upyr's* eyes could lie.

Oblivious to the exchange between his assistant and his guest, the abbot leaned forward in his high-backed seat. He was a worldly man—a skeptic, truth be told—lifted to his position by family connections rather than faith. He should have been immune to Damiano's charm, but he was not.

"He makes me feel alive," he had confessed to Kenelm once. "As if my mind were about to burst the confines of my skull."

He flatters you, Kenelm thought, but did not say aloud. He makes you entertain treacherous ideas.

"Some knowledge is dangerous," the abbot was saying now, though without the heat of genuine disapproval. "It contradicts the teachings of the church."

Damiano shrugged, his curly hair gleaming blue and black in the flames. He wore satin tonight, a red so dark it resembled blood. A large gold ring gleamed on one finger and his snugly hosed legs were crossed at the knee. The bulging of his yard was the only less than elegant touch. Kenelm could just about count the *upyr*'s veins. Apart from this crude display, which probably was deliberate, the *upyr* never suffered a wrinkle or a stain—or not for more than a moment. His stylishly pointed poulaine wagged up and down with the gentle motion of his foot, making it difficult for Kenelm to swallow. He suppressed a shiver as the *upyr* steepled his long, pale hands. The two index fingers met beneath his chin.

"Simple men need simple teachings," he said. "A faith without gradations of black and white. Wrong must be wrong for them and right must be right. Otherwise their lives fall into chaos.

"The minds of more sophisticated men can encompass contradictions. The teachings of Aristotle or the Arabs need not be kept from them. Indeed, there is no one more qualified to decide what knowledge can safely be shared with the common man."

The abbot laughed, a sound of deep enjoyment. "The way you argue, you sound like a prince of the church yourself."

Damiano inclined his head as if he found the comparison gratifying. Only Kenelm observed the condescension in his smile. Brother Kenelm did not often speak at these gatherings. He understood his position as appreciative audience. This time, however, he could not hold his tongue.

"If I understand you correctly," he said, his voice rusty from the wine and his tightened nerves, "there are two classes of men. The first must be protected from knowing things that may be true and should be discouraged at any cost from thinking for themselves. The second, by simple virtue of possessing imagination and good birth, are justified in promulgating any lie that furthers their power. Convenient, I would say, had I not been so graciously assigned to this privileged few."

Hearing his acerbity, the abbot turned to him in surprise. "You take me aback, Brother Kenelm. You hardly sound the pragmatic young monk I have grown to trust."

"I have not forsaken my pragmatism," Kenelm said, forcing his fingers to release the arms of his chair. "But I am not such a fool that I think this creature cares one whit for the future welfare of the church."

Kenelm had gone too far. The abbot's eyes hardened and the muscle that signaled the rise of his temper bunched in his jaw. "I am sorry you think me a fool, Kenelm. And even sorrier you see fit to insult our guest. You know better than anyone what services Damiano has performed on St. Crispin's behalf."

"Because it serves his purpose!" Kenelm cried, unable to be wise. "Because he knows that, if you wished, you could raise a new crusade against his kind. He has no moral limits. None. The faithful rely on us to protect them, not to look the other way while our 'friends' threaten their very lives. Do you think he will only kill when you ask it? By the love and respect I have always borne you, please, I beg you, do not commit the church to an alliance with this man."

Damiano responded with a slow, resounding clap. "Bravo. Eloquence and passion, too."

His amusement caused the abbot's anger to subside. He had half risen from his chair as Kenelm spoke, but now he sank back against his leather cushion. "Too much wine," he said with a smile Damiano was meant to share. "Next time we shall have to water this hothead's cup."

Kenelm knew there was no more argument to be made. He stood and bowed stiffly to both men. "Forgive me," he said. "No doubt you are right. In any case, I should withdraw."

Damiano smiled as Kenelm brushed past his knees, his eyes guarding his secrets with heavy lids.

"*In vino veritas,*" he murmured just loudly enough for Kenelm to hear.

Kenelm knew it would not be all the *upyr* had to say, just as he knew he could not truly escape. In the best of circumstances, St. Crispin's had few places for its residents to be alone. Kenelm hurried around the cloister's columned loggia, passing monks walking solemnly in pairs, cowls raised, hands clasped and hidden within their sleeves. None spoke, but a few turned to watch him in disapproval.

Ghouls, he thought, though he knew they were in the right to judge him. He was not one of them anymore. He had been tainted by worldly lusts. Ducking through an ivy-covered door, he entered the herb garden, blissfully empty this time of night. The object of his unseemly haste, a small work shed, rested drunkenly against one wall. Seed was stored here, and pots, and other tools of the gardener's trade. The gardener himself would be praying at chapel, too old and forgetful to notice if someone disarranged his things.

The shed smelled of herbs and stone and aging manure, plus a few small mice who had escaped the abbey's cats. In the months since the *upyr*'s arrival, Kenelm had grown familiar with these scents. More than once they had come here for assignations. The odors aroused him in direct contradiction to his mood, as if his body were ruled by different forces than his mind. These worktables, these hoes and rakes and straw-stuffed sacks, had witnessed so many heady pleasures, they could suggest them all by themselves.

Such was Damiano's unnatural fleetness that, despite having left the abbot after the monk, he was waiting in the cluttered building when Kenelm arrived. His glow lit the space better than a lamp. He held a dirty spade in his pristine hands and was rolling it idly round and round.

"You know," he said as if continuing a conversation, "your opposition is not helpful. I am this close to introducing your worthy abbot to my queen."

"Marvelous," Kenelm responded, meaning it not at all. "Then the man I have looked up to for years can become embroiled with someone even more depraved than yourself."

"Such sarcasm. I must admit it suits you . . . almost as much as sighs of ecstasy."

"Do not try to distract me with your seductions. I do not trust you, Damiano. I never have."

"I could make you trust me. Indeed, with one sweet bite, I could make you my slave."

Kenelm's heart thumped faster with his fear. "You forget," he said as coolly as he could manage. "I have access to the abbey's private library. I have studied the records concerning your kind. Those who offer—"

"Yes, yes." Damiano waved his hand as if swatting a bug. "Those who offer their lifeblood voluntarily cannot be thralled. You forget, however, that I can insure there is nothing voluntary about your participation. Even you, dear Kenelm, have boundaries you would dislike having me cross."

While he spoke, Kenelm had been edging toward the gardener's makeshift bed, shuffling backward step by step as if retreating from a threat. When the back of his legs hit the musty blankets, Damiano became a blur of speed. His fist struck Kenelm's breastbone, knocking him to the sacks and nearly stopping his heart. Then the *upyr* leapt atop him and pinned his hips with his thighs.

Stunned breathless by the blow, Kenelm could only lay there as Damiano gripped his robes at the neck and tore. The ivory crucifix he found beneath inspired a laugh.

"Now this," said Damiano, "will do you no good at all." The *upyr*'s teeth were already sharp. They extended even further once a suitable portion of Kenelm's chest was bared. With the side of his nail, Damiano cut a wound. The blood welled hot and wet. Pain was not Kenelm's pleasure, but as his attacker hardened, his body reacted in sympathy. It was a victory, of sorts. To effect his thrall, Damiano could not drink until he was unwilling.

"I shall miss your spirit," Damiano said, "if that is any consolation. Slaves are dreadful bores in bed."

"I shall miss you, too," Kenelm responded. "I wish our natures had been more in tune."

The *upyr* gave him a little smile for this, caught between perplexity and being charmed. His vanity was his undoing. He did not realize how thoroughly Kenelm had studied the secret texts, and how well he had learned to hide his mind. Kenelm fumbled between the sacking and the wall, searching for the weapon he had commissioned from the blacksmith days before. His fingers found it and curled tight. The iron stake was cold and heavy in his grip, both frightening and reassuring. Wood would have transfixed the *upyr*, but only iron could kill.

Damiano's smile did not have time to fade before Kenelm drove the sharpened implement through his heart. The *upyr* gasped in shock and stared down at his chest, human in his befuddlement and pain. *No,* thought Kenelm, wishing he could recall the blow. It was too late. There was no blood, no screams of accusation. With a flash of cool white light, the church's would-be corruptor simply ceased to be.

BROTHER Kenelm reeled as Gillian released him, stumbling back against the edge of his simple cot. The candle fell from his hand and guttered out on the floor. Gillian was none too steady herself. One of her own had been killed before her eyes. In fact, linked as she had been to Kenelm's mind, she felt as if *she* had slain the *upyr*.

For good or ill, because of one man's decision, the creature who had been Damiano was forever lost. His schemes might—and probably did—go on, but he himself was gone.

Gillian had known death was a possibility, but that possibility was more real now than it had been since she had run from it as a child. Immortal or not, she could be killed. This human, and unsuspected others like him, knew her weaknesses better than she did.

"You read my memories," said the monk, his arms hugging his body as if he were cold. "You saw me kill Damiano."

"Yes." She rubbed the lingering pressure behind her brow. None of what she had seen was fading, not even that first overwhelming flood. The contents of his mind had poured into hers like honey filling a comb. She could sort through it now, at her leisure, as if those events had happened to her. To test the theory, she reached for his memory of the abbey's secret files. Yes. Records *had* been kept by members of the upper echelon of the church, an elite within the elite who hoarded every scrap of information they could find.

Only yesterday, Gillian had struggled to understand. Tonight she could read the words as easily as the monk. She fought to contain her wonder as she absorbed what the books had held. Conversations. Drawings. Theories too wild to be believed. The church was aware of the rivalry between Auriclus and Nim Wei. Nim Wei had been his student, it seemed, before striking out on her own.

She had formed her own organization after her rebellion. One scroll contained a list of cities and the leaders of their broods. Another enumerated payments made for services to the church, though the descriptions of the services themselves were vague. "Relic recovered," said one entry, the fee for which had been a hundred ducats.

Less information was to be found about Auriclus's packs, but they were there as well. More than one reference spoke of "Lucius the White" who "drank of Lethe and woke no more." The accompanying sketches left no doubt this was the Lucius she knew. But what did it mean? What could she make of this jumble of fact and supposition?

The only mention of herself was in a list of children missing from London. "Gillian, daughter of Ilsa: fate unknown," wrote the local priest, who went on to add that humans her age made risky candidates for the change. "Madness common. All known to date have been marked for destruction by their superiors." Cold words for a colder fate. They made her think her rearing by the pack could have been a godsend.

She was pulled from her musings when Brother Kenelm began to laugh. The sound was more hysterical than amused.

"You should not have been able to breach my defenses," he said through chattering teeth. "You did not even bite me."

She looked at him. His eyes were wild, his skin pale enough to have been drained. She saw that she had hurt him, though he was trying to pretend she had not.

With a stab of guilt, she grabbed the coarse wool blanket from his bed and wrapped it around his shoulders. She felt strangely close to him and it disturbed her, as if reading his history had linked them, making them not so much friends as fellows in tragedy.

"I am sorry," she said, trying to shake the feeling off, "though you must admit I had reason to fear what was in your thoughts."

"My, yes," he said with another brittle laugh. "I am a dangerous individual compared to you."

"I thought you were lying!"

"So you raped my mind?"

She opened her mouth to object, but his words were too close to being true. Though she had not intended harm, she had forced him to her will just as Damiano had tried to do. The only difference was that she had been successful. Perhaps her strength was greater than expected because she had possessed a hint of this ability when she was mortal. Being changed must have magnified the skill.

"I am sorry," she said again. "I cannot undo it."

Brother Kenelm pulled the blanket tighter around his throat. He huffed at her, but seemed to be recovering. "You see what I meant about your power? It is deeper than you know. Maybe as deep as an elder's. I confess I am curious to see how Nim Wei reacts when you two meet."

Gillian stilled at the name that had haunted her for twenty years. "Why would you expect us to meet?"

"Why?" The monk wore an odd half-smile. "Because tonight, in this castle's hall, I heard her sing for her supper. When you sneaked into my chamber, I assumed that you were she."

"CHECKMATE," the human said. His voice was soft. Only his sharp gray eyes danced with enjoyment.

Astounded, Nim Wei stared at the board. He must be mistaken. No one had beaten her at chess in a hundred years, and never had she been beaten by a human. But there his victory was, now that she looked more closely. Her king was destined to lose his pieces before the human's. She could envision no move by which she could prevent it.

"I cannot believe it," she murmured. The Fates had brought her here for this? To gamble her chances on a game—and lose?

But she had set the terms of this contest herself. She could not renege without loss of face.

Regaining her feet, she smoothed the soft black folds of her houpelande. "Thank you for the game. I shall see my purpose through from some other vantage point than your home."

She turned to leave, but he caught her wrist where it emerged from the velvet sleeve. His warmth moved through her like molten copper, causing her gaze to lift to his.

"Stay," he said. "Next time you will take me seriously and play harder."

She had already noticed he lacked a propensity for blushing. Nonetheless, she marked a subtle darkening of his face and neck. The sound of his quickened pulse was easily audible to her ears.

She allowed herself a gentle smile. "I can play as hard as you wish, for as long as you wish."

Even a human would have heard the catch in his breath. "I meant, I would invite you to stay for the pleasure of matching wits again . . . if you would be willing to guarantee the safety of my household."

She moved swiftly enough to startle him, from her side of the heavy table around to his. She rested her hip on the inlaid edge. Like any male who must fill as much of his world as he can, the human's legs were sprawled in his chair. Her shift in position put one of her calves against his own.

"You would accept the promise of an *upyr*?"

"You kept your word when you lost your wager." His gaze was forthright. Despite what he had seen her do, he showed little fear—unusual, but not unheard of. Some humans felt too much fascination to be afraid.

The sense she used to read the Fates moved within her like a minnow flitting from shadow to light. What if this mortal were the reason she had been drawn here? She felt no threat in him to her kind, no disturbance to the future balance of their lives. He did, however, have the hunger she sought in her broods, the intelligence and imagination. Could that be all the pull to England had been: to find another child to change?

And maybe this one could be more than a child, thought the corner of her soul that still harbored dreams. Maybe he could be a companion.

She shook herself, uneasy with her turn of mind. "What promise would you require in return for allowing me to stay?"

"To do no harm to me or mine."

"My word on that I cannot give. I might need to defend myself."

"Then promise to do no irreparable harm."

She considered this as she would a chess move. "I can agree to that request."

"And you will maintain your pretense"—he waved a hand at her clothes—"that you are a minstrel?"

"It is in my interest to do so."

"Then we have an agreement," he said, his smile a flash of boyish charm.

"We almost have an agreement," she corrected. She leaned toward him until her left hand gripped the farther arm of his chair. "First we must decide how to seal it."

He swallowed, his gaze dipping briefly to her mouth. Images too vivid to conceal slid from his mind to hers: of kisses, of coupling, of naked, firelit skin. His scent changed with his thoughts, growing muskier and warm. In that instant, she knew exactly what he wanted: not pain, not domination, but pure sensuality.

At least, that was what he wanted tonight.

"Yes," she said, letting the word hiss seductively in his ear. "It is more than time you claimed some happiness of your own."

He touched the side of her waist with one careful hand.

That was enough permission for her.

She pulled his clothes from him, then let him pull hers from her. His hair was ashen blond all over, even between his legs.

"Pretty," she said, fingers sifting slowly through those hidden curls. He was well made, this human, smooth of skin and tightly muscled. Her thumb curled around the base of his hardened cock. "Pretty and hot as fire."

He laughed like someone setting down a burden. "Come over me," he said. He closed his knees to make room for hers on the wooden seat. "I want to see if your coolness can be warmed."

He shivered as she sank down on him, then threw back his head and groaned. His organ twitched pleasantly inside her, like a horse eager to run. Nim Wei stroked his shoulders with admiring hands. They were trembling just a bit.

"Shall I make you wait?" she offered. "I can hold you on the edge as long as you like."

"Pray you, no," he gasped, his hands caressing her thighs. "Unless you want to hear me cry."

She considered how long he must have been waiting to be well ridden, and decided he did not need to cry much at all.

—————

STAYING away from Aimery had never been as difficult as tonight. Gillian returned to his tower knowing he slept, knowing she had only to push the arras aside to see him. Twice now she had resisted, but after all she had seen and done in Kenelm's chamber, she felt such a hunger to be with him, as herself, that the craving became a pain.

Reality was not what she had imagined. Undreamt dangers, both within and without, hedged her on every side. Was she powerful or threatened? A good being or a bad? And who could advise her? Lucius was too far away and perhaps not what he seemed. Brother Kenelm's alliances were questionable at best. Even her own judgment was suspect. Certainly, she could not approach Nim Wei, not if Damiano had been an example of what her guidance produced. With *upyr* like him around, maybe she dared not live out-side the protection of the pack. Maybe her hope of exploring the world was doomed.

She wanted to crawl into Aimery's arms and forget, to soak up his kindness and his strength. Fighting the inclination, she stood in the middle of his floor with her eyes squeezed shut and her arms wrapped tightly around her ribs.

Change, she thought. Change and be done with this temptation.

The creak of the wooden bedstead warned her it was too late. Aimery stepped outside the bed hangings, naked and fine and tall.

"Gillian?" he said, his weak human eyes squinting through the dark.

She covered her face as if, by blinding herself, she could disap-pear.

Two thumps told her he had descended the platform steps. He said her name again, warmer this time and nearer. She shivered as he pulled her against him. Helpless not to, she sighed melodically and nestled close. She would have burrowed inside him if she could.

"Sweeting," he murmured against her temple. "Are you all right?" He gave her shoulders a squeezing shake. "I worried when you stayed away so long. Have I done something to offend you? I did not mean to, but if I can, I will right the wrong."

He should have been offended. Instead he was trying to make her feel better.

It is hopeless, she thought. No woman could resist this man.

She shook her head against the muscles of his chest. "I should not be here. We are growing too attached."

"Too attached." His hand combed through her curls until it reached the small of her back. Against her temple, she felt him smile. "For my part, I do not think that is possible."

"We come from different worlds. There are dangers . . ."

His second hand eased her head back from his chest. As she gazed up at his face, she was shocked to see his scar. When she pic-tured him in her mind, it was not there.

"Do I strike you as a coward?" he asked, his voice as soft as it was deep.

"No, but—"

"Hush." He covered her lips with the tip of a single finger. "Let me enjoy just having you in my arms." His ribs expanded as he filled his lungs with air. "There. That is the scent I missed. Like lilacs sparkling with dew."

She took her own breath, but for different reasons. "Aimery, there are things you do not know about me, secrets that would change how you feel."

"That is the way of fairy tales," he teased. "The dreadful secrets always keep the lovers apart."

She pushed back until an arm's length stretched between them. "I am no fairy tale."

"Are you certain?" Still he smiled, though his eyes had grown less sure. "You are the first woman who made me hope I might be loved for myself, that I might be known as I truly am."

She ached to confide in him, to tell him that she loved him. The impulse was absurd. She knew the truth of nothing, not even her own heart. She struggled to find a sensible retort.

"You speak of love?" she said. "You barely know me."

His hold fell from her arms. Her words had pricked him, but when he answered, his voice was firm. "I am aware you have not been entirely truthful, but if I do not know your secrets, I know you. I *feel* you—in my head, in my heart, in the very marrow of my bones. I know that the fire between us is passing rare. I feel it every time we touch."

"You feel my magic! You feel my lust for humankind."

"I know you," he insisted, his hands bracketing her face. "I cannot explain how, but I knew you before we met."

You knew Princess, she thought, tears welling in her eyes. You met Princess before you met me.

"Do not cry," he pleaded, kissing each trembling lid. "I know you are frightened. Falling in love is hard."

"I cannot love you! I do not!"

"I understand." His kisses brushed her cheeks. "You do not love me. Not even a little bit."

"I do not," she said as his mouth found hers. He was only humoring her, but it did not matter. She clasped his face as he clasped hers, pouring her longing into the sweet, wet kiss. She tasted her own tears and swallowed his muffled groan.

"Lie with me," he whispered against her lips. "Know me as I know you."

She closed her eyes and let him nuzzle her neck. He lifted her, arms locked beneath her bottom, and started carrying her to his bed.

"No," she said, and put the force of her mind behind the command.

When he set her down, the blood of injured pride flew in his cheeks. She knew he did not like being ordered against his will. "Tell me you do not want me," he said. "Tell me you do not want this."

"Want is not enough."

"I offer you love—"

"Love is not enough."

"Then what? What, pray tell, is enough for the goddess's servant?"

His pain and anger were too naked to confront. "I am a stranger to you," she said to her unshod feet. "And I do not trust myself with your heart."

"Are you going to leave again?" The question was low and guarded. The sound of it gripped her throat like a fist.

"I do not know. I should leave. For good this time."

"Do not," he said, the steel in the words a poor mask for his vulnerability. He touched her shoulder. "Give us a chance, Gillian. Do not make me beg."

The knowledge that he would was humbling.

"I must think." She turned her head away from his searching eyes. "I must discover what can be risked, for your sake as well as mine."

He released her shoulder and stepped back. "That is fair," he said. "As long as you do your utmost to return."

She could feel the cautious hope in him, as well as the restraint. She knew he wanted to demand more: answers, promises. She could not give them, not with Nim Wei here, not with her own future so undetermined.

All she could do was leave.

———

WELL, now what? Aimery thought as he watched the woman he probably loved hasten down his stairs. Her need to escape completely mystified him. He failed to see how he could have been more understanding.

When he saw her tonight, he had assumed that she had gotten over whatever, if anything, he had done wrong. And now she went off like this. *I am a stranger to you,* she had said. *I do not trust myself with your heart.*

What in Hades was that supposed to mean?

Aimery raked his hair back with his hands, suddenly feeling the cold of the floor seeping through his feet. With a sound of disgust, he stomped back to his bed. Alone. Again.

But there was nothing to gain from sulking. Clearly, Gillian was drawn to him. Whatever the shortcomings in his looks or character, he did not repulse her. He simply wished he had not begun to think her story about the goddess was a load of ballocks from start to end.

He growled to himself, then hoped he had not disturbed Princess. A muffled clatter from her perch told him he had.

"Damnation," he said, flopping back against his bolster.

For once, he was not cursing himself.

Eleven

I F Gillian had learned one precept from the pack, it was "know thy quarry." She could make no sound decisions concerning herself or Aimery until she addressed her ignorance about Nim Wei. She would have to stalk the *upyr*, to learn her weaknesses and strengths. Then maybe she would be able to plan a future.

She realized, with a resigned nod to her heart, that she wanted that future to include staying at Bridesmere. For a while at least. If it did not prove too risky.

Risky was all it could be until she knew Nim Wei's aim.

Her shoulders were knotted with tension by the time she reached the shadowed gallery above the kitchen end of the hall. Bridesmere's hall was imposing, lofty and large, with banners of brightly colored silk suspended from thick wood beams. The rushes were clean and strewn with herbs, though the predominant smell at present was roasting meat. Gillian's mouth watered, despite being unable to eat it.

Careful to remain unseen, she slipped behind a heavy column. Down below, a procession of liveried servants in green and scarlet were winding between the crowded benches. Arms held high to thwart the dogs, they carried platters of boar's heads and broth and baked capon—so much food it boggled her mind. Ale was being poured for the lower tables and spiced hippocras for the dais.

Curious, Gillian looked for Aimery's brother. The baron of Bridesmere would have been easy to pick out even if he had not been seated at the high table. He had an air of authority about him, a seriousness even Aimery did not possess. A slim, elegant figure in dagged green wool, his doublet required no padding to augment his fine physique. Both his face and hair were fairer than his brother's, though the expression in his eyes was dark. Not an easy man, she thought, either to know or be.

She had seen his wife before, greeting Aimery in the courtyard. With her coiled flaxen braids and her sumptuous curves, Claris made an even richer picture than her husband. Her rose-pink kirtle boasted fur-trimmed tippets on its trailing sleeves and many golden buttons to pull the bodice close. When she laughed at something the man beyond her husband said, more than one pair of masculine eyes turned toward her beauty.

Not Aimery's, though. He sat beside her, looking stiff and plain, his shoulders angled distinctly toward the portly man on his other side. They were deep in conversation, though they paused when the music began.

The sound caught Gillian by surprise, a leaping cascade of sunbright notes. A moment later, Nim Wei's voice joined the harp like a fish slipping through a stream. Gillian shuddered as if she were being plucked. The vibrancy and sweetness of the *upyr*'s song thrust her back twenty years. *She is mine,* the elder had said then. *I chose her.* Her powers of attraction had not faded in the least. As if caught by a golden net, the household swayed. Fingers waved in time and appreciative murmurs rose. Only gradually did the company resume what they had been doing before she commenced.

She had them in her thrall, all of them, by voice alone.

Though Gillian struggled to free herself from the charm, when Nim Wei sang of an enchanted princess and her desperate knight, her throat grew thick. Not until she noticed Claris casting meaningful glances Aimery's way did the music release its grip.

This is power, Gillian thought, seriously doubting she could match it.

All the same, she had come here with a purpose. If her adversary was stronger than she could face, better Gillian should know. She peered past the pillar that hid her, trying to make out Nim

Wei's figure in the opposite balcony. She was there, at the other end of the hall, a boyish shape too slight to be such an object of dread. Seated with her traveling harp, she was wrapped in a shimmer of force so thick she appeared to be underwater. Gillian assumed it was a sort of glamour, one that would hide her true appearance from human eyes. She was reassured that she could see it. To this magic she was immune.

And maybe she could do her own magic if she was careful. Delicately, she reached out with her mind, hoping to discern the nature of Nim Wei's spell without alerting the elder to her presence. It was a kind of personal force, she decided, similar to the one that kept their clothes pristine but far more potent. Nim Wei was sharing it with the humans, and using it to change the tenor of their thoughts. By some unknown process, she was altering how they felt, making them happier, calmer, more receptive to her beguilements.

When the change was complete, Nim Wei reeled the force-flow back. Gillian could see the current if she blurred her gaze, gossamer arcs of pink and blue. A few of Nim Wei's listeners were unaffected: some of the older soldiers, Aimery . . . and Claris, oddly enough. Perhaps that one lived too much in her own dreams to be moved by anyone else's. Affected or not, the crowd seemed unaware that anything otherworldly was going on. Lord Edmund sat in a positive pool of glowing gold. She thought he must be receiving a different treatment from the rest. He did not have the glassy look of a man bespelled, though his face was discernibly more at peace.

With the strain gone from his features, he was very handsome, almost as comely as an *upyr*. The resemblance between him and his brother made Gillian realize just how much beauty Aimery's injury must have marred.

It does not matter, she thought. *His scar is the least of what he is.*

Unfortunately, none of this answered the mysteries she had come to solve. She would have to try again, maybe find a chance to get closer. She suspected the *upyr*'s link with Bridesmere's lord would be an interesting one to watch.

As the song of the tragic lovers neared its end, Lady Claris chanced to note her husband's serene mien. The tiny frown that pulled her mouth told Gillian she disapproved.

"Come!" she said, clapping her dimpled hands. "Where are the tumblers? We must have happier entertainment for our guests."

Her husband leaned back in his chair, hands laced on his flat belly, a hint of wry amusement narrowing his eyes. Even when the guest beside him protested he was content, Lord Edmund did not gainsay his wife.

Nim Wei's music ceased to a general murmur of regret. Though she pretended all was well, Lady Claris's color rose. She stood and gestured regally to the jongleurs. Three of them, lean as alaunts in parti-colored dress, tumbled into the space before the dais, juggling noisy tambours as they went.

Gillian lifted her gaze in time to see a shadow slip out the far balcony's door. Nim Wei must have judged her talents would not be called upon again this evening.

Gillian wondered where she went. To hunt? To join an accomplice?

She seized the opportunity to find out.

———✦———

SO, thought Nim Wei as she stomped angrily down the dim and flickering stairs. The pink-faced cow would act the queen.

Happier entertainment, she mouthed disparagingly to herself. As if that pot of human vitriol had ever wanted anyone's happiness but her own. Nim Wei knew Claris's type, had killed her type with pleasure. What, after all, was one annoying human more or less? So long as one was not caught, destroying a few of them hardly mattered.

Nim Wei had meant her song to secure her position here, but also as a gift to Bridesmere's lord: to lighten his burdens and soothe his mind. She had refrained from trying to cloud Edmund's thoughts—assuming she could—because she wanted to discover how far she could trust him.

Not to mention how much affection he might come to feel for her uncompelled.

Nim Wei laughed at herself and rubbed her night-cool cheeks. In her way, she was as childish as Edmund's wife. *Will the handsome human like me as I am?* Pah. She knew such sentiments were born to fade. Love lasted no longer than a budded rose. Only power could shape worlds.

Pulling more of her glamour around her, she moved unseen through the busy kitchen. A giant of a man with a shiny bald head was berating his underlings for letting the fire die down. Too busy cowering, no one paid one drab stranger any mind as she followed the scent of earth and darkness to the undercroft. Accessed by a sunken door, this vaulted space extended beneath the hall. Nim Wei could tell it was little used. Its floor was dirt, its few stingy windows besmeared with grime. Good. This could serve as her resting place for the day, once she explored it. Nim Wei wanted no surprises from her retreat.

But there was a surprise, a prickle of power that caused tiny hairs to stand on her arms. Anger snapped inside her like a whip.

Someone was following her.

And that someone was not human.

Nim Wei decided to give the intruder a welcome she would not forget.

———————

THE undercroft reminded Gillian of the cave, so dark she had to use more than her eyes to see. With night fallen outside and the windows next to useless, the gloom was thick. For some reason, her *upyr* senses were not working as well as they should.

Determined not to lose her chance to discover what Nim Wei was doing, she extended her arms before her, feeling her way inch by inch as she strained to hear the noise of the elder's progress up ahead. The undercroft was full of supporting columns; already Gillian had jarred her elbow and her knee. She would have plenty of places to hide once she located the quarry she was supposed to be hiding from.

The sound of dust falling from the ceiling made her freeze. It came from her left, no more than a body length away. Was it Nim Wei or just a spider skittering between the stones?

She held her breath and cursed the blank, black nothing that veiled her sight.

"What is the matter?" asked a chilling whisper. "Cat got your eyes?"

Gillian's muscles tightened to flee, but the reflex stirred too late. A hand clamped the front of her neck in an iron grip, wrenching her off her feet and throwing her to the ground. She slammed down hard enough to lose her breath, but struggled nonetheless. Her efforts gained her nothing. She felt as if she battled a woman of stone. However Gillian kicked or twisted, the only part of Nim Wei that moved was the hand that squeezed her throat.

Unfortunately, it did not loosen.

"Nim Wei," Gillian choked out as her muscles and bones fought to keep their proper place. "Please. I only want to talk."

"You lie," hissed the *upyr*. "You are a spy. Worse, you are a danger to our kind."

Gillian's vision began to change in a different, more ominous way. Deep red blotches swam across her eyes. Clasping Nim Wei's wrist, she strove desperately to pull it away. "We can talk about why you think I am a threat. Maybe find a solution."

She burst into a fit of coughing as Nim Wei's hand released her neck. *Thank you,* she began to say, but the elder must have decided throttling was too good for her. Gillian felt a sickening tugging at her center. Nim Wei had laid her palm atop Gillian's heart and was draining her energy off so swiftly that, by the time Gillian understood what was happening, she did not have the strength to lift her head.

Stop, she pleaded without sound. *Please.*

Frightened by this threat to her partner, Princess began to

squawk. *Fly*, the falcon urged. *Fly!* Gillian would have been happy to change form had she been able. Her head was spinning, her thoughts confused. Her rib cage felt as if it were going to collapse in on itself.

This punishment was not fair. Whatever made Nim Wei believe that Gillian had to die, Princess had no part in it. For her familiar's sake as well as for her own, Gillian tried the only defense her blood-starved brain could come up with.

As she had with Brother Kenelm, she reached out with her thoughts. If she could get inside Nim Wei's head, perhaps she could find a way to daze her enough to let her go.

This was far easier conceived than done. Trying to penetrate the elder's barriers was like chipping ice with her nails. Only her fingers seemed to bend. *Let me in,* she thought, reduced to a mental pounding on the door. Princess was not impressed. *Fly through,* she said, conveying her instructions as best she could. *No more thinking.* Gillian's control of their partnership seemed to slip. Princess was taking charge. A roaring filled her ears, like a wind met at top speed. Though she had not truly changed, in her imagination she dove from a dizzying height. Fast. Faster. She was an arrow in the darkness. She was sharp as steel. Ice shattered.

She was in.

But where was in? No deluge of memories swamped her, only a thick gray fog through which silent glimmers of lightning forked, clearly another layer of protection. Gillian had lost her sense of her own body—Princess's, too, for that matter. *Ask,* said Princess. *Say words.*

Then Gillian understood. Bodiless or not, she still had the power of her suggestion. *Tell me your greatest weakness,* she thought at the formless fog. *Show me the moment that is key.*

The fog ripped like a veil tearing in the rain. Gillian had a body again. Her heart beat hard, but she was fine. She was on her feet and dressed in silk so light it floated around her knees. She clenched something in her fist, a knife with a hard, jeweled hilt.

She was Nim Wei. For a breath, Gillian marveled at the strangeness of inhabiting the elder's form. Then she simply lived the time that was gone.

———

OLD blood stained the altar of the formerly pagan chapel. Christian now, both animal and human sacrifice had soaked the moonlit plinth of stone. As Nim Wei lifted the iron knife, her sire stumbled back against it. Auriclus was trapped. He could not change form and escape. The spells her children had painted along the walls would insure that.

How appropriate, she mused, that I should kill him here, where his precious mortals pretend no god but theirs ever was a force.

"Wait," Auriclus gasped, blood-sweat broken across his brow. No human would have seen the subtle tinge of pink, but Nim Wei marked it. She had frightened him. At last.

She smiled. "You want me to wait? As I waited for you to share your secrets? Wasting centuries I might have spent building empires instead of trying to prove my worth? I think not, Father. My waiting ends when I spill your heartblood down my iron."

"I loved you," he said with such beautiful, throbbing pain she could scarcely believe he lied. "I taught you everything you know."

"Everything *I* know, perhaps, but not everything you do."

"Such knowledge is a grave resp—"

She cut him off by pressing the tip of the ritual knife against his throat. She had heard this tired old song before. Slowly she dragged the point toward his heart, slicing through snowy linen down to skin. The slash to both healed almost as swiftly as it opened. He was powerful, damn him, and he would not share that power with her.

As if he sensed her doubt, Auriclus straightened, pulling around him the righteous confidence she had long since learned to hate. "If you kill me, I shall send my power to my children. Already they possess more strength than yours. Are you willing to risk what they would do with more?"

"Your children are beasts grubbing in the dirt."

"My children are the earth and the sky and the sea that swallows rocks. My children will survive when yours are dust."

I am your child, part of her longed to cry. *Why do you not love me as you love them?* Instead she notched the knife against his breastbone. His heart beat steadily, even calmly underneath. That alone made her want to thrust. "My children are clever," she said, "clever enough to lure you into this trap."

"Monkeys are clever, but the lion eats them all the same."

"Enough!" She tossed her straight black hair. "I know you do not want to die, no matter whose children can best whose. I suggest you tell me what I wish to learn. My broods have as much right as yours to take familiars."

"You speak to me of rights? You who steal not only human blood but human will? You who murder without remorse? I am sorry to say it, but with every act you prove you are not worthy. I will not grant you dominion over innocent creatures' souls."

Rage blinded her. She shoved until the blade cracked through his bone. Blood welled, steaming in the cold, as the iron pricked his treacherous heart. One more inch and he would die.

"Nim," he rasped, his pain no pretense now. His hand wrapped hers. He did not tug but simply held. Even in her rage, the touch was sweet. "Daughter, be sure this is what you want. Think how lonely you would be without me. I am the only one who knows your past."

This was true. All the other elders were gone, not that she had ever been close to them. Sad, silent creatures. One by one they had walked into the sacred fire. *Tired,* was all any of them would say when she asked why. *I am tired and it is time to go.*

Would she grow as hopeless if she destroyed the one who had made her?

She released him with a scream of fury. "I will kill you," she promised, trying not to feel as if she betrayed her deepest self. "Next time I swear I will."

"Verily I believe you." Panting, Auriclus pulled the knife from his breast. Her body trembled in reaction when she saw how close she had come to ending his life. Blood flowed again, then ceased. "Perhaps you would accept a truce?"

"A truce?"

His mouth curled sardonically at her suspicion. "A division of territory."

"I will not cede London. Or Novgorod."

"You may have both," he said and returned her weapon by its gem-studded hilt. "Along with Paris and Peking. In fact, you may have all the cities you desire. I want the wild places and the villages, anywhere civilization does not hold sway."

Nim Wei turned his offer over in her mind, examining it for flaws, wishing her thoughts were not so rattled by what she had almost done. The countryside was safer, and covered more land, but cities were bases from which to shape the world. "Do you swear you will not poach on my territory?"

"No more than you would poach on mine."

She knew he was lying. Never would he let her achieve true independence, not if it threatened him or his darling mortals. A truce gave her time, though, during which a clever monkey could gain many advantages.

History was, after all, the playground of their kind.

She retreated toward the door, guarding her front again with the knife. She felt as sick to her stomach as if she had eaten human food. She had not done what she meant, had not gotten what she hoped. She dreaded facing the questions her children would ask, but this was nothing when weighed against her resolve.

In the end, she would rule them all.

———

WITH an angry scream, Nim Wei wrenched free of her invader, throwing her back against a cobwebbed column. Dislodged mortar rained down in a cloud, which the girl batted feebly as her legs collapsed. Nim Wei was too furious to renew her earlier blinding spell.

Let the girl see her. Let her witness an elder's wrath. Nim Wei recognized her, of course. She was the figure she had glimpsed in her mirror at Avignon, the urchin Auriclus had seduced away from her outside London.

The outrage of that old wrong doubled the new. How dare this puling infant, this child of her enemy breach her mind? More importantly, how was she able? It was one thing to read a human's thoughts and quite another to steal the memories of an *upyr*. Nim Wei herself had imperfect command of the gift.

Not that she was going to tell this creature that.

"Where is the mirror?" she demanded, pulling her adversary to her toes by gripping her gown. "Why did you call me here?"

"I d-didn't," stammered the girl. Her eyes were huge, the shadows beneath them a testament to Nim Wei's skill at stealing power. "I looked into the well, but contacting you was an accident. I found it when I went exploring beneath the chapel."

"Ah," said Nim Wei, "a scrying pool." She probed the girl for more, but she was vexatiously hard to read.

She shoved her away from her in disgust. Playing with force was Nim Wei's special gift. She had been honing it since before she changed. In fact, the skill was what had drawn Auriclus to her in the first place: his peasant sorceress, he liked to call her. Any other *upyr* would have been reduced to pudding after a minute of Nim Wei's treatment. Still, the girl seemed to speak the truth about not having meant to call her.

She does not know, she thought. She has no inkling how strong she is.

Which was, when Nim Wei considered it, all the more reason to kill her now. Before she became more dangerous than she was.

She moved to do it, then stopped. The message from the Fates had been vague at best. Perhaps the girl was a danger Nim Wei could use. Like called to like when it came to reading minds. She knew Auriclus and she knew a thing or two about this child. She had been a hungry little mortal: for luxury, for knowledge, for love—none of which her sire would have indulged. Sufficient time had passed for her enchantment with Auriclus to have soured. Knowing him, this girl would have felt abandoned within a week.

Yes, she thought, mentally rubbing her hands, let us see if she can be wooed. Bringing her over to Nim Wei's side would prove how wrong Auriclus and his methods were.

GILLIAN doubted her legs would ever hold her again. Unable to stand, she began to crawl away while she had the chance. Thankfully she could see, though the room was still very dark—as she realized when her head bumped a broken table. Swallowing a curse, she crawled around the splintered wood. She must do nothing to draw attention to her escape.

Something had distracted the elder from her murderous rage—some thought, Gillian suspected, though when she reached tentatively out, Nim Wei's mind was again a blank.

She had dragged herself past two columns when the *upyr* moved in a blur of swiftness to block her path.

I must learn that trick, Gillian thought, remembering Damiano had done it, too. How handy it was for scaring people half to death!

"It was wrong of you to read me," Nim Wei said. Considering her previous temper, her tone was calm—even prim.

"Quite wrong," Gillian agreed, feeling much less guilty than she had after reading Brother Kenelm. "I shall strive to remember my manners the next time someone tries to kill me."

Probably this was not the best time to be recovering her sense of humor, but Nim Wei laughed. It was a soft, friendly sound, no doubt as much an illusion as her glamour. The elder sat on her heels, lowering herself at merely human speed. Her hand brushed Gillian's curls back from her face. Time folded backward at the gesture. Just so had she touched Gillian in London's woods.

"You must be hungry," she said. "I stole a significant portion of your vital force."

"I shall live," Gillian said, hoping it was true but almost too exhausted to care.

"Here," said Nim Wei, and held out her arm. Her sleeve was pushed up and her flesh gleamed in the darkness like marble lit from within. When Gillian proved too astonished to move, Nim Wei used her nail to slit the slimmest vein at her wrist. The cut bled slowly, a delicate drip of lacquer black.

Unable to look away, Gillian dragged the back of her hand across her mouth. "I do not want your blood."

"Are you certain? I admit humans taste better, but elder blood is most fortifying."

"I do not want anything from you."

"What about your life? Do you want that?"

Gillian shivered at the insinuation. "Not if I have to drink your blood to keep it."

"Such principles. I wonder that you think you can afford them." Nim Wei pressed her bleeding wrist with the fingers of her second hand. When she removed them, the cut was healed. "My blood is not tainted, you know. If you drank it, your will would remain your own."

"I appreciate the information."

"Of course you do, having been starved of knowledge for so long."

Rather than admit this was the case, Gillian shifted from her hands and knees until she sat—more or less upright—with her back braced against the nearest column. Her head throbbed in protest, but she did not faint. The heaviness of her eyes forced her to close them. "Why did you spare me?"

"I am still deciding if I should kill you. I must confess your spirit intrigues me."

You mean my power, Gillian thought—much good as it had

done her. For all Brother Kenelm's predictions, the elder had proved more than her match.

Nim Wei must have taken her silence as understanding. "No law requires us to be enemies," she said amiably.

She refrained from mentioning Auriclus, or Gillian's long-ago choice, though the memory of both hung in the air like stale incense.

"You want a truce," said Gillian.

"I have made them before, as you now have reason to know."

Gillian opened her eyes to find the *upyr* picking a nonexistent speck from her short black garb. Someone wiser than she might have taken the hint and apologized for her invasion of Nim Wei's mind. Gillian, however, had been taught by the pack to show no weakness. She trusted that lesson now.

"Very well," she said. "We are not enemies. Neither of us will try to kill the other."

"Heavens," exclaimed Nim Wei, her voice like opium-sweetened smoke. "I can offer you more than that."

Gillian was sure she could, but she was also sure any offer would come with strings. With a groan she could not contain, she hauled herself to her feet. "Not being killed is enough for now."

The undercroft swayed as she stepped away from the column on which she had been leaning. She prayed her exit would not be spoiled by collapsing into a heap.

NO more than a quarter hour later, Gillian sat hunched and trembling at the foot of Aimery's stairs. Despite having drained two rats, half a jug of wine, and—to Princess's delight—an incautious goose on her return, Gillian had been unable to manage the climb. Three steps from the bottom she gave up.

The emotional impact of her time in Nim Wei's head was slower to leave her than the time she spent with the monk. Though she had stolen less information, the feelings clung to her like brackish water creeping up a dock. In the memory, Nim Wei's anger at

Auriclus had been fierce, a strengthening, righteous passion. Gillian had more than sympathized with her resentment; she had shared it. But she had never hated Auriclus, only been disappointed.

At least, she thought disappointment was all she felt.

She recalled the order she had issued before Nim Wei's barrier fell. She had asked the elder to reveal her greatest weakness. But what was her weakness? That she wanted to kill Auriclus, or that she had not quite had the nerve?

Gillian shook her head at her own confusion. She was weary of fighting, and wearier still of being scared. She wanted a life again. She wanted to be safe. Returning to the simplicity of her existence with the pack almost seemed attractive.

With a gusty exhalation, she let her skull clunk against the wall. She did not hear Aimery's approach until he was there. He must have come back from supper.

"You look awful," he said, scooping her up in his arms. "Whatever you have been doing, you are clearly better off with me."

Presumptuous though it was, his behavior was too welcome to mind. Against his warmth, a portion of her tremors eased.

"Truce," she said, the slur in her voice making her sound foxed. "We have a truce."

"Glad to hear it. I never wanted to fight with you in the first place."

Her hand curled cozily around his neck. "Silly man."

"Silly is when two people who are meant to be together remain apart."

Gillian rubbed her nose against the smoothness of his scar. "Only God knows who is meant to be together."

"Maybe so, but until you hear from Him, you should consider I may be right."

He laid her on his bed as if she were precious, hanging over her when she refused to unwind her arms from his neck. His eyes were even warmer than his skin. He was happy. It might not last, but because she was with him he was happy.

"You make me feel loved," she said, "as if you genuinely cared for my well-being."

His features tightened with what looked like anger, though she knew it was something else. Emotion had overcome him. When he answered, the words were gruff. "I wish all that is good for you, all that you hope for and desire."

"I wish the same for you!" she cried, then covered her mouth because she had sounded as if she loved him back. "I believe I am drunk," she announced in her own defense. Normally, *upyr* threw off the effects of wine. As weakened as Nim Wei had left her, however, the excuse might be true.

Aimery chuckled and pulled his covers to her chin. "If you are drunk, you will need to sleep. All night, Gillian. All night in my arms."

The prospect was so appealing, she put it into action almost at once.

"Feed Princess well tomorrow," she remembered to mumble.

Her last waking thought was that she could belong to him until dawn.

———

AIMERY watched Gillian sleep, far more troubled than he had let on. She was curled away from him on her side, breathing heavily, as if working hard for air. The change in her appearance worried him. Before she had been slender. Now she looked as if she had undertaken a sennight's fast. Her eyes were sunken, her cheekbones much too sharp. Even her curls did not gleam the way they had.

He had grown accustomed to the hum of her vitality. She—so he had thought—was a creature Death could not steal from him on a whim. Now she shone so dimly, he had to light a candle to see.

When he stroked her shoulder, he found the beginnings of a bruise above the back of her dress—a stain on the white perfection of her skin. It was the kind of mark a person got from being shoved against a wall. Had Gillian been fighting and, if so, with whom?

The mysterious people she came from? Had she earned their disapproval by confessing her link with him?

It struck him as wrong that a woman should have to fight on his behalf. For that matter, she should not have to fight on her own.

Next time I shall go with her, he decided. He would not let her stop him. Whoever her people were, however magical, she would only face them at his side.

AURICLUS could have floated up the tower as a mist, but it was a matter of no moment for Nim Wei to climb. Her fingers discovered crevices no man could see, nor cling to even if he found them. For her, the ascent was a mild exertion, a bit of excitement before her rest.

She enjoyed turning the tables on her little spy. Knowledge was power, as the sages said.

And who could resist following someone who left a trail this wide? Really, the girl was in desperate need of her guidance. Feeding from rats and fowl. Pah. Nim Wei grimaced with distaste as she reached for another handhold. Her year-old fledglings could do better. Human blood was the drink of rulers. Humans existed to make *upyr* strong.

Or so Nim Wei liked to think. It might have been true—assuming the powers that made the races cared who had the upper hand.

With a last contraction of her well-warmed muscles, Nim Wei sprang soundlessly onto the window ledge. The opening was narrow, but deep and high enough for her to stand within it. A simple folding shutter closed off the space. Nim Wei did not have to open it. She simply peered through the center slit.

If the sight of the curtained bed was uninformative, the two twined forms she sensed inside were not. One of the souls was mortal. The other was her prey. Emotion wafted in the air even as they slept, the hopes and fears of newfound lovers.

So, she thought, Father's pup has taken a mate. Nim Wei won-

dered if the girl knew just how staunchly her human meant to protect her, imagining he could face "her people" down. But his presence would make Nim Wei's conquest more of a challenge. Better
the girl had been friendless.

She shrugged to herself, content for now to have the situation
be what it was. A path would be revealed—to endear herself to the
girl, to put her in her debt.

Nim Wei knew how to wait, especially when she did it on her
own terms.

Twelve

E DMUND'S strapping young secretary slept on a pallet outside
his door with a small covered brazier to keep off the spring
night's chill. His master must not have realized his loyalty had been
compromised when Nim Wei bit him. Though his size made him an
effective guard, his mind no longer would.

He rose up on one elbow when Nim Wei's swift approach
caused the torches to dance uneasily on the stairs. His dark brown
hair was tousled from sleep.

"You," he said, his eyes losing their focus even as his will strove
to stay firm. "Minstrel boy."

He was about to tell her she did not belong here, but Nim Wei
pushed at him with her thoughts and he went quiet. Not for nothing was she famed for the persistence of her thralls. While most
upyr's influence faded in days, a year from now Nim Wei would be
able to direct this man.

"Call me sir," she said, "not minstrel boy. And stay where you
are. I have come to visit your master and I mean no harm. You will

hear nothing that passes between us, no matter how boisterous we may get."

The young man's eyes grew dark. Despite her male disguise, he betrayed an intriguing amount of interest. But "yes, sir" he said and inclined his head.

"Anything that passes outside this room," she added, "you will hear as well as ever. You will notify us at once if anyone seems likely to disturb us, and you will mention my visit to no one."

"Yes, sir. It is my honor to serve my master's friend."

Nim Wei laughed to herself at that. Human manners could be amusing.

Her privacy assured, she passed into Edmund's chamber. Her skin buzzed with the energy she had stolen from Auriclus's child. She was overfull with it and in need of a strenuous outlet, more strenuous than climbing a little wall. She stripped off her clothes with neat dispatch. Then, not caring to wait for Bridesmere's baron to rouse on his own, she grabbed the edge of his covers and snatched them off with a billowing snap.

He lay naked beneath them, much to her delight. One of his knees lolled invitingly to the side.

"What?" he said throatily, but she had already pounced and was raking her nails gently through his chest hair.

His groan of interest gratified her, as did the incipient swelling of his shaft. Watching it twitch, she smoothed her hands up and down his sides. The feel of him was like a fire on her chilly skin: his ribs under her palms, his hips between her thighs. He had his own glow, this human, though no one could see it but her.

"Shh," she said as he tried to speak. "No words tonight. Only acts."

He was hard-pressed to obey when she lowered her mouth over his erection. Her tongue made short work of any lingering softness, finding spots of pleasure long experience had taught her to seek out. Her lips tugged while her teeth grazed skin too sensitive to bear the touch. Only her will could help him stand it, only her *upyr* mind. Soon he was squirming beneath her and gasping in pleasured shock. Thinking his man was listening, he struggled to be quiet. Nim Wei would have none of it. Pinning his knees wide beneath her hands, she shifted and nipped his stones.

That inspired a muffled curse.

"No words," she reminded him, "but feel free to make noise. I have instructed your secretary not to hear us."

His head came off the pillows. His eyes were wide, his breathing rough. "You can do that?"

"I can do many things." She pinched the points of his nipples until he jumped.

"Ow," he said, rubbing one with his palm, though she noticed both his face and sex had darkened another shade.

How nice, she thought, a lord who likes a little pain. Smiling at his reaction, she pressed a love bite to the tender skin of his inner thigh. Though her teeth had lengthened the moment she stole his bedclothes, she was careful to refrain from drawing blood. This way, Edmund might feel a sting, and he would probably have a mark, but his strength would not falter when she craved it most.

She pressed a matching bite to his other thigh. His sharp intake of breath was all the encouragement she required.

He was ready then, his organ standing full and taut. Knowing the end would be more appreciated if delayed, she made them both wait as she kissed and nipped her way up his torso—his hipbones, his belly, the shadowed curve just beneath his arm. He was delightfully sensitive, writhing so violently when she kissed his already bruising nipples that she had to hold him down. Not that she minded. No, indeed. Nim Wei enjoyed being in command.

She grinned as she licked his throat, taking in the salt of him, the human strength and tension. He must have remembered the ecstasy of her bite from the night before. That alone could teach a man to welcome a little pain. His hands clenched the ticking of his mattress, nearly ripping through it in his desire.

She held her weight above him until her face hovered inches

from his. His eyes glittered with arousal, with fear, with thoughts she did not try to read. She told herself she knew what they were: a man's first hesitant exultation at being mastered. In some dark corner of their souls, they all wanted to give in. Let someone else take the worry of what should be done in bed. Let someone else see to them.

His lips moved, saying *now*, saying *please*. Still she made him wait. Would you be different, she wondered, if I took the time to look deep?

She would never know, would never *want* to know. When she finally kissed his mouth, his answer was ravenous agony.

The last of her patience shredded like silk. With a swiftness just short of violence, she positioned his shaft and took him with a single thrust. Then she could not help but pause. He filled her to perfection, a column of pulsing heat. Equally enchanted, Edmund grunted at being surrounded, and again when she rose on her knees to ride.

His neck arched uncontrollably as she moved.

Letting his hunger twine with hers, she told herself this was all the pleasure she needed. His hands slid up her ribs to grip her breasts. His hold was almost too strong as he squeezed her flesh between his fingers. Men did not do this to her. Men let her set the rules. Rather than stop him, she stroked his arms up and down. The unfamiliar edge of danger made her head fall back with lust.

Their rhythm changed with her reaction. His hips were pushing off the mattress to intensify every blow. Harder he went, deeper, snarling in his effort to get close. The sound sparked sweet reactions between her legs. Control abandoned, her climax rose like flame burning up a rope. Her upper body fell to his. She pressed herself to him, his chest, his neck. The demands of her flesh overcame her mind. Her senses jumbled together, tastes and smells and feelings a tumbling whirl. She felt him clutch her back, then her bottom, as if in distress. She was not certain, but she might have cried his name out when she came.

She knew he hissed out hers, his seed gushing into her in heated bursts. She accepted the offering, though no child would ever come from her womb. In pleasure, too, there was worth.

For long minutes after, she knew nothing but an unaccustomed sense of peace. Her mind was quiet and perhaps her heart as well. *Upyr* did not need to move their blood as much as humans. When required, they could erase most signs of life.

She came aware to the knowledge that dawn was approaching but not there yet. Her head rested against the human's perspiring shoulder. His arm circled behind her and his fingers were drawing patterns on her upper arm. The position was more comfortable than she could be comfortable with. She shifted restlessly on her back, the coarse linen sheets these mortals used beginning to soften with her gift. Her mouth held a taste like summer berries.

She had bitten him again, at the moment of her bliss. She had not planned to, though he did not seem to mind. His initial fatigue had passed and he was basking in the glow of contentment that came from giving blood without duress. For the next few days, until the effect wore off, he might notice he was a little stronger, a little faster, a little more resistant to harm.

Nim Wei had never met a human male who did not enjoy this. If she was not careful, she would addict him.

That result she doubted he would like. She had read quite a bit of Edmund's past when his guards were down. His perception of his right to rule was shaky as it was. If he discovered he might grow physically dependent on her, a stranger and a threat . . .

Of course, no law said she had to tell him.

She turned until his heart beat against her cheek, a soft, percussive caress. She could barely remember the last time she had lain like this with a lover.

Prague, she thought, reaching back. When Thibaut accepted her invitation to oversee the eastern broods. As she recalled, she had entrusted him with one of her precious mirrors. He had not misused it even once.

Reminded of the mystery she had yet to solve, she stroked Edmund's chest and spoke. "This castle is not very old, is it?"

His hand moved to her hair. "Not by your standards. When my great-grandfather was granted this land, he hired James St. George—the man who designed castles for Edward the First—to build it on the ruins of a fort."

"A Roman fort?"

"I do not know. If it pleased you, you could explore. Some of the previous foundations still exist."

"Beneath the chapel, for instance?"

His head lifted. "How did you know?"

"Just a guess." She remembered Gillian's tale of accidentally contacting her through a well. "I think my kind have passed this way before."

"Truly?" He sounded intrigued. "Do you think they knew the people who manned the fort?"

I think they *were* the people who manned the fort, she thought but did not say. She saw no profit in letting Edmund know how closely her kind sometimes dwelled with his. "It is possible," she said and smoothed her hand down the solid muscles of his side.

He was not distracted. "My uncle might know something about the site. He loves collecting old records."

"Your uncle?"

"The abbot at St. Crispin's."

"Ah."

"You say that as if you know him."

"I almost met him. Because of our mutual interest in ancient texts. The . . . arrangements fell through."

Damiano's death had changed her mind about doing business with the abbot—at least for the present. If, in the future, she decided she needed him, she might reconsider the association. She had refrained from taking revenge for that very reason. Of course, the fact that she had been thinking of deposing Damiano anyway had not hurt. The *upyr* had never been quite as clever as he believed.

Edmund drew her attention back to the present by shifting beneath her head. She had the feeling he was going to say something, or ask something, then changed his mind. Perhaps he remembered he should not speak openly of family matters with an *upyr*. Or perhaps—knowing his uncle and the deep sort of games he liked to play—he decided he did not wish to know.

Nim Wei preferred the latter explanation. She would have been sorry to think Edmund was as wary of her as she was of him.

"Why was your ancestor granted this land?" she asked.

"Ah, that." His tone of self-deprecation had grown familiar. "He earned it on the field at Wales. For acts of valor."

She said no more. She knew well enough why Edmund thought his predecessor had been the better man.

———

AIMERY honored Gillian's request and fed Princess well at daybreak. "But no early flight for you," he said as she tore at the welcome meal. "You shall have to wait for your lesson until afternoon."

Too grateful for the food to mind, Gillian watched from a weathering block in the yard while young Robin readied a bath. Here on this wooden stump, in this quiet section of the bailey, she and the other birds could grow accustomed to the world outside. No one entered without Aimery's leave. She was as safe here as she could be.

Even more important, she felt much better for her long night's rest. Her dreams had been unusually pleasant and she had woken in Aimery's arms. Though she had to leave him almost at once to take her other form, she could not regret that sweetness. Even in sleep, Aimery held her close.

He, too, had awakened happy, whistling so cheerfully at his chores that people had grinned and nudged each other when he passed. The memory warmed her as Robin dumped a final bucket of tepid water into the tub, his body listing sideways at the weight.

With his second hand to support his wrist, he carried her carefully to the rim.

Princess—and Gillian, for that matter—loved these morning baths. With a creel of pleasure, she jumped in and began to splash, rolling around and combing her beak between her feathers to get them clean. As always, Robin had gotten the temperature just right. It was only after a few minutes of preening play that she noticed he was not joining the fun. With a few last soggy flaps, she climbed awkwardly back to the edge. Still Robin did not smile. Curious, she craned her head at him. He had been uncommonly quiet this morning—sullen, she would say, though he was kind enough to her. When the sun fell across his face, she saw that his eyes were rimmed in red.

Concern squeezed her heart at the thought that he had been crying. On a day like this, the world should be happy. Hoping to cheer him, she pecked gently at his ear. Rather than giggle, he turned away. He looked uncannily like his father with his lips pressed into that whitened line.

"This is our last day together," he said in a quivering voice. "Brother Kenelm says I may not see you after this. He says you are a bad influence—whatever that means."

Outrage stunned her beyond response. How dare that devious, two-faced monk call *her* a bad influence? Saying she would make a better ally than Damiano, then forbidding Robin to see her. She would never harm him—never! Nor any other young person. Her own experience had instilled in her a reverence for childhood and how easily its innocence could be lost. Did the monk think she was going to make Robin her next meal? She would die before she stole one drop of his precious blood!

Too angry to control herself, she took off in an explosion of spraying flaps, snapping her tether as she went. A real falcon would have been too damp to fly but her feathers dried in seconds, leaving her to circle the rising air currents around the keep. She was not certain what she intended. To fly in Kenelm's window? To confront him with his injustice? That would hardly convince him of her self-command, especially since she had been wondering what sort of creature she was herself.

Biting Robin was not the only way she might hurt him.

Her wing beats slowed as her temper calmed. Maybe the monk was right. Maybe she should avoid Aimery's nephew. Robin understood her too well already. Young and fanciful as he was, if he worked out the truth, he might find her life too appealing. He had his own to live. She wished that for him, wished him to grow and marry and have children of his own. He should look back and laugh at his youthful attempt to teach a bird to read, not spend a lifetime pining for the magic he thought he had lost.

No matter what happened with Nim Wei, her time at Bridesmere would have an end.

Wearied by her precipitous flight, and not completely recovered from the night before, Gillian returned to the yard. Robin welcomed her landing with relief. Two shiny tear trails marked his cheeks.

"You scared me!" he scolded even as he stroked her head.

Gillian nudged his hand in contrition. She prayed she would never scare him again.

⸻ ◈ ⸻

AS if she were not wound tightly enough, two large greyhounds were included in the party for her practice hunt that afternoon. During the period when she had hid away in her bird form, Gillian had worked with them catching hares. The dogs drove the prey out of cover for her to chase. Useful as this talent was, she could hardly imagine being comfortable with them around, not when they strained at their collars and slobbered down their pointy teeth and barked loud enough to split her ears.

That her *upyr* self could easily subdue them mattered no more than the competent hold Aimery's assistants had on their leads. Princess's instincts, that these creatures were her enemies, were too powerful to ignore. As they trotted upriver to the edge of a shining marsh, Gillian clung so hard to Aimery's gauntlet, she nearly pierced the hide.

He sang to her, his usual soft and soothing song, but she could not conquer her growing dread. Her buoyancy of the morning seemed the most arrogant folly—as did her plan to learn to pass for human. Losing Robin's company was merely the latest evidence that it was doomed.

I am not clever enough to do this, she thought from the blackness that surrounded her. I am not good or strong or anything I want to be.

When Aimery removed her ill-fitted hood and she saw her quarry for the day, she knew she was destined to fail here, too.

Her intended victim was a full-grown crane, a snow-white frigate of the skies. Once it had been beautiful. Now it elicited only pity. Aimery's men had plucked half its feathers and put out its eyes. Still bleeding, still alive, they had tethered its leg to the center of a stretch of grass. There they left it, surely uncomprehending, to cringe in terror and pain.

Intellectually she understood this was the next stage in her training, providing her with experiences that, bit by bit, more closely mimicked a real hunt. A crane that size, had it been sound, could easily savage an inexperienced falcon. By crippling it, Aimery and his men were trying to protect her.

None of this knowledge calmed her horror. Worst of all, the crane's helpless cries—what cries it could make with its beak bound tight—excited Princess. The falcon could not help it. Her nature dictated her response. In spite of understanding that, Gillian feared she would be sick. I cannot do this, she thought as she recoiled up Aimery's arm. He cannot mean for me to do this.

"Shh," Aimery crooned, petting her half-lifted wings. "The crane cannot hurt you now."

Of course it could not hurt her! It was a mutilated wreck. It had not the slightest chance of escape, even against an ordinary falcon. All it could do was die.

This was not her idea of sport.

When Aimery tossed her upward and whistled the signal for pursuit, she fluttered straight to the ground. Twice she did this, despite Aimery's disgust.

"God's blood," he muttered. "One would think you had turned coward. The poor creature cannot even see you."

She tried to plead with him with her eyes, almost but not quite desperate enough to touch his mind. She supposed a falcon's eyes were not designed for pleading. Shaking his head at her, Aimery gathered her up.

Before he could toss her out again, Robin slid off his horse. "Let me try," he said. "She knows this is my last day. Maybe she will fly for me."

Aimery shot him a doubtful look but handed her off.

Perdition take him, Gillian thought as the boy whispered what was meant to be encouragement in her ear. How could she dash Robin's pride when this might be his final memory of their friendship?

Resigned and near despairing, she went at his whistle, up and up into the sky. Following her like a curse, the breeze carried the scent of horse and man and marsh and, under that, the sticky-sweet smell of the bleeding crane. Gillian was tempted to leave them all behind, to live on her own again and be free. Surely this time she would get used to being lonely. Aimery might miss her and she would miss him, but was it not better to leave before more disaster struck? Was it not better to avoid becoming the sort of killer Damiano and Nim Wei were?

She spiraled higher, ringing up toward the wispy clouds. The unpeopled land beyond the town called strongly for her to leave. Indecision, and affection, was all that held her back.

As she wavered, a voice rose in her head, a voice she was not sure she recognized as her own. It seemed foreign, both older and harder. With a shudder, she wondered if it were a remnant of her time spent as Nim Wei.

Every meal Princess ate was killed on your behalf, it said. *If*

you refuse to hunt that bird, you will not save it. It will simply suf-
fer longer before it dies.

Whatever its source, the message was irrefutable. Gillian had to
return.

The intensity of her emotions must have weakened her judgment, or maybe the cause for what came next was just fatigue. Certainly she did not rely as strongly as she should on Princess's
instincts. The falcon's eagerness to kill, natural though it was, made
Gillian reluctant to draw her awareness close.

I shall strike its neck, she decided, a single lightning blow. The
crane will not even feel it. Positioning herself, she turned in the air
and tucked her wings. Her dive was steep, the force of the wind
seeming to compress her flesh. Closer and closer the green ground
rushed as her mind filled with the thought that she was the monster
she always feared.

She could not escape her destiny. Ever since her childhood,
since the birth of her brother, Col, this had been what she was.

Her angle of descent was as ill chosen as her speed. Just when she
most needed her sight, the sun caught her eyes in a glaring flash. She
was blind. Her claw glanced something solid. The crane's bloodied
wing. Hit. Too late. Too fast. She could not check. Fear barely had
time to gather before she slammed into the ground. She felt parts of
her snapping: feathers, bone. She tumbled and came to a halt. A
scream of avian triumph split the air as something sharp tore at her
side. The pain was overwhelming. The thought that Princess might
be left alone to face her mistake was all that kept her clinging to con-
sciousness. With the last of her strength, Gillian would shield her.

The greyhounds were going mad.

"Mary in heaven," someone swore. "The crane is loose. Get it
away from her!"

"I have her," Aimery shouted back. "She is alive."

The world bobbed like a piece of bark dropped in a stream.
Gillian's body seemed formed of torment, burning with it, every
panting breath another spear.

"Hush," Aimery crooned, cradling her with infinitely gentle hands. "I have you now."

I am losing him, she thought, before we even knew how much we could share.

Robin's frightened sobs matched her own wildly pulsing heart. Her panic was making her bleed faster. Too much, she thought. I cannot lose this much blood. Though she tried to hang on, her awareness flickered and died. She heard no more until she opened her eyes to the musty dimness of the mews.

She lay on a nest of blankets on the sanded floor. Two peregrines and a kestrel, their feathers puffed with anger and fear, were staring determinedly away from her on their perches—as if they wanted to deny her existence.

Well, she mused, if those birds thought she was dangerous, she knew she was alive. She tried moving her wings. The pain seemed less, but so did her strength. Her vision blurred in and out while a cold like the grave crept up her bones.

"Save her," Robin was pleading. "You have to save her!"

Aimery held him back by the shoulders, his murmuring answer low. Gillian did not need to hear his words to guess their meaning. Her injuries were beyond his skill to mend—and maybe beyond her own. She was not healing as fast as she should. With every second, her powers ebbed. If she did not do something, and soon, she and Princess would die.

One hope remained: to take her *upyr* form and pray the transformation would help her wounds. This would mean betraying her secret, but she did not see what other choice she had.

Monster though she might be, Gillian wanted to live.

She reached for the mystery, faltering in her fear. The change had always come with a thought. Never had she analyzed what she did. Wishing now that she had, she tried to recapture her sense from the first time, that she and the heavens were one. *Please,* she thought. *For Princess if not for me.* With the prayer, her awareness shifted. *Love is the center,* said the silvery whisper she remembered. Its coldness, its distance was something new. *All flesh,* it said like a chime ringing fitfully in the wind. *All flesh is but a dream.*

The words seemed to freeze her spirit. She was a gust of snow against a field of black. *Aimery,* gasped her mind, stretching for a warm love, a love a being like her could comprehend. *I am warm,* reprimanded the whisper. *All love comes from me.*

Her eyes snapped open. Her body felt bruised in every inch but it was whole. She lay on the scuffled floor with Aimery and Robin on either side. They were gaping at her with matching open mouths. She curled her fingers and her toes. She was alive. And she wore her *upyr* form.

⊰⊱

AIMERY stared so hard his eyes were aching.

"I knew it!" Robin crowed, his triumph cutting through his tear-roughened voice. "I knew Princess was a magic bird."

Aimery felt as if he should have known as well, but even now, with the evidence in the flesh before him, he could scarce believe.

His Gillian . . . His little goddess of the air . . . Her curls fanned beneath her, black as coal beside her snowy skin. She was his falcon. And the temptress he had welcomed to his bed. She had been with him all along. Even when she seemed to leave him, she had remained. No wonder being with Princess had brought such comfort. But he had almost lost her. He knew he had. No natural creature could survive the damage he had seen. With renewed alarm, he surveyed her from head to foot.

Apart from a line of red along her ribs where the crane had slashed her, her wounds were gone.

"Bar the door," he said to Robin, the order sharp. "No one else must enter."

He used the boy's retreat to cover her with a blanket. She was dazed yet, but with his help she sat up.

"Are you well?" he asked because he could not conceive of what else to say.

She nodded, then brushed his chest with the back of her hand. The touch inspired a pang of more than physical longing. "Aimery," she said, "I am sorry. As soon as I saw how honest you were, how honorable, I should have told you the truth. If you had known what I am, what I can do, you would never have harmed that crane and I would not have almost destroyed us both."

"You could have trusted me," he conceded, matching the seriousness of her tone. "But I knew you were lying. I wanted you to stay enough not to push."

"I might not have told you even if you had. I was afraid that you would hate me."

Despite how much he needed to reassure himself that she was there, he found it difficult to hold her gaze. The emotion it contained was raw: guilt, fear, worry. Immortal or not, she could not have looked more vulnerable.

"Because of this?" he asked, trying to understand. "Because you can take this other shape?"

"There is more," she said, the words low with regret.

He was trying to formulate an answer through the turmoil in his mind when Robin returned.

"Are you all better?" he asked, shy now that the marvels he had witnessed were sinking in. To a boy like Robin, a woman who could change into a bird was better than a queen.

She smiled at him, her amusement gentle. "I am much improved. And now I can finally thank you for your aid."

Robin dug his foot into the sandy floor. "Uncle Aimery carried you back."

"I meant for helping me learn to read. That was kindly done."

"Are you a fairy?" Robin blurted out.

"No," she said just as courteously as before.

"Then what about an angel?"

"No," she said again, with a hint of firmness. Aimery leaned instinctively closer to his nephew, prepared to rise if need be. When Robin's chin quivered, she squeezed his hand.

Whatever flash of concern he felt dissolved. Even if she had not been this caring, he could not think of her as a threat. She appeared much as she had when he found her huddled in his stairwell the previous night. Her magical glow was gone, her beautiful features worn by fatigue. The eyes that met his nephew's were simply blue. Any descendant of the Saxons might have possessed them. Her pallor alone marked her as otherworldly—none of which mattered in the least. Every inch of her was dearer to him than ever, not because he desired her, but because of who she was inside.

Her soul shone in her gaze. Her kindness, her grasp of a young boy's pride, even her shame stirred his regard. In all the ways that mattered she was human. Flawed, but not blindly flawed. She acknowledged her imperfections. Regretted them, he expected, but did not wallow in that regret. She could smile, and understand others' weaknesses through her own.

She was, he thought, his own more beautiful reflection.

"What I am," she said, her hand rubbing Robin's wrist, "is not for one so young to know."

"But—" said Robin.

"Do not force me to bespell you," she cautioned. "If you press me, I shall have to make you forget."

Robin's eyes went wide. Aimery knew he was debating how far he could push the limits of this strange adult. In the end, his faith in Gillian's powers proved stronger than his rebellion. "Very well," he conceded. "I shall not press."

Aimery was almost sorry the boy gave in. If Gillian could make him forget, that might be wise. Unless her threat was merely a bluff . . .

He must find out. He must discover what she meant when she said that there was more.

"This lady and I need to speak privately," he said to Robin.

"And you need to be about your duties—without telling anyone what you have seen."

Robin nodded glumly. "I do not suppose Brother Kenelm would like Princess any better if he heard she could turn into a naked woman."

"No," Aimery agreed. "I am certain he would not."

Thirteen

FORTUNATELY for Gillian, the mews were close to Aimery's tower. Gathering her up in the rough gray blanket, he carried her across the distance between the doors. Though her exposure was brief, Gillian's head spun from the sun. She buried her stinging face against his neck, sighing in relief once they were inside.

"What is wrong?" he asked, taking the stairs two at a time.

After what he had just witnessed, she judged she might as well speak plainly. "The sun," she explained. "When I wear this form, it affects me like a poison."

He asked no more until he set her on his bed and closed the shutters. "Now," he said. His tone was quiet, his arms folded stubbornly across his chest. "Tell me all you have not said."

She pulled her legs up and hugged her knees. "All?"

"All," he insisted.

He stood beside the bed and opposite the window. The light from behind the shutters painted his face with a line of gold. She loved seeing him illuminated this strongly. Danger notwithstanding, for her the day possessed a poignant beauty no night could match. The stars were timeless. The sun reminded one life was short. By its light the colors of his hunting murals revealed how much they had faded, a mend showed in his arras, and lines fanned out from his clear, bright eyes. Perhaps to humans these would seem flaws; to her they were exotic treasures.

From his look of determination, she knew he intended to make her explain. She plucked at the blanket that covered her knees, watching her fingers rather than him. "Do you know the term *upyr*?"

The air between them tensed. "The children of midnight? The blood drinkers? We heard stories of them in France. The people of Aquitaine called them the soldiers' nightmare. Do you mean to say they are real?"

"They are real and I am one of them." She made herself lift her eyes. He blinked at her, his lips parting in disbelief.

"You? But they are demons!"

She laughed despite her fears. He could not have been more reassuring if he tried. Then again, he might feel differently once he heard what she had to say.

Her thoughts must have been obvious from her expression. "I know you are not evil," he said as if the mere suggestion provoked offense. "You would not even hunt a wounded bird. I have seen how you are with Robin. I have slept with you in my arms. If you were a demon, I would know."

"Allow me to tell you everything," she cautioned, "before you decide how virtuous I am."

Clearly expecting a lengthy tale, he sank to the topmost of the steps that ran alongside his bed. He propped his chin in his hand and his elbow on the mattress. She could see his attention was hers. Determined to do this right, she began the story at the beginning, with her brother, Col, and the pestilence, with her choice between Auriclus and Nim Wei. She told him of the cave in the forest, and Ulric, and her longing to live in the world. She told him everything she had discovered or suspected about her kind. She threw Lucius's warnings to be circumspect to the wind. If men like St. Crispin's abbot knew these secrets, why not Aimery? Surely he merited trust.

Aimery listened to it all with great concentration, perplexed at points but seemingly not shocked. Only when she described taking Princess as her familiar did he rise and begin to pace.

"I thought—" he said, then stopped and turned. "I did not realize . . . You have another soul inside you?"

"It is a choice Princess and I made together, to share the adventure of immortal life. We are friends of a sort—though, as to that, I think she likes you better than she likes me."

Aimery did not return her grin.

"I suppose this seems strange to you," she said.

"More than." He sat again on the step, rubbing his head as if he were dazed. "Who were you fighting the other night? Did one of your pack try to bring you home?"

Less eager to share this, she explained about Nim Wei and the mirror, about following the elder from the hall and getting caught in the undercroft.

Aimery pressed his fingers into his brows. "Edmund's new minstrel is an *upyr*?"

More than his minstrel, Gillian thought but kept to herself. For the moment, Lord Edmund's affairs could remain his own. "Nim Wei charmed everyone into thinking she was male—not to mention human."

"As you did when you showed me how you dim your glow."

"Yes," she said. "Both are forms of glamour, though Nim Wei is better at spinning them than I."

"Are you good enough to make Robin forget what he saw?"

She hesitated at that. "I do not know. My powers are not as practiced as hers, or as finely controlled. The effects I have achieved—by chance, for the most part—have not been subtle. I think I would be afraid of making him forget too much." She turned her eyes earnestly to his. "Do you believe Robin will speak of me? If I . . . If I bit him, I would have more of a hold but, truly, I would rather avoid that."

"As would I," said Aimery. "But perhaps I worry overmuch.

Robin is not an ordinary boy. He may keep this confidence to himself." He gazed at her, his forehead furrowing with concern. What he said next took her by surprise. "I am sorry about your father. And Auriclus. I know they hurt you when they left."

She put her hand to her suddenly constricted throat. Tears she had not known were there welled in her eyes, making it hard to speak.

"It was not your fault," he added. "I am sure they left for reasons that had nothing to do with you."

Her tears spilled over in burning streams. To think she had imagined she could read him!

"I was never very good at being good," she confessed when she was able. "Not even when I wanted to be. But most likely you are right. Auriclus and my father had their own concerns, none of which included me. I doubt they deliberately meant to hurt me."

Aimery reached past the dark green arras to draw one finger along her jaw. The set of his mouth told her he heard more than she said. "You deserved more than they gave you, Gillian. What matter that you were not perfect? Do you honestly think they were?"

She swiped her eyes before he could see another tear. She did not want him to think she needed pity—or that she held a grudge. "That is past," she said firmly. "Done. My life is now. Sometimes I cannot even remember what they were like."

Aimery tugged the curl that lay against her neck. "I know something of what you speak. When my father fell in battle at Poitiers—while I was becoming a 'hero'—I thought his dying words would haunt me forever. Today I barely recollect his voice. But whatever time heals, the scars remain."

He gestured to his own scar, something she had never seen him do. She looked at its twisted smoothness, then down at her knees. "If I left . . ."

"No." He took her face between his hands, lifting it like a chalice. "If you left, you would scar me deeper than any sword."

Gillian's lip trembled at his sincerity. Knowing she was important to him gave her the courage to say what she must. "I should
leave," she said. "Already I have drawn a dangerous being into
your home. For now Nim Wei desires my goodwill, but what if that
changes? What if she hurts your brother?"

"You said she has not thralled him. He has to know what she is.
He must not consider her a danger."

"I think he is counting on supping with a long spoon."

Aimery's eyes crinkled at her wit. "If she was a devil, Edmund
would know. My brother is no one's fool."

"Maybe not, but she is not safe, Aimery. She is not tame."

"From what you say, neither is Brother Kenelm. I guarantee
most of the garrison is not. If we bar everyone who is dangerous
from Bridesmere, we would quickly empty the keep."

Gillian covered the hand with which he cradled her cheek.
"You truly want me to stay? Even knowing what I am?"

His eyes gleamed in the shuttered sun, his soft, fond smile a
balm to wounds old and new. "We can work this out, my love. In
that I have full faith."

Though she failed to see what basis his faith could have, she
rose to her knees, twined her arms behind his neck, and lowered her
lips to his. When he groaned at the meeting of their mouths, the
sound blotted out the world. The kiss was heartfelt promise and
shameless greed. With a low, impatient sound, he climbed the final
distance onto the bed. Gillian's hands tangled in his silky hair while
his slid down her back. The blanket fell beneath the push.

Aimery laughed and nipped her lower lip. "Now that is an im-
provement."

"If it makes you stop kissing me, I cannot grant that claim."

He teased his mouth over hers. "Does my goddess crave a kiss?"

"Yes," she breathed. "Very much."

Determined to tease him back, her thumbs drew delicate circles
beneath his ears. Shivering, he pulled their bodies together hard.
Her naked hipbones met his thighs. He, too, was on his knees, his

palms warm on her bottom, his arousal a burning thickness beneath his clothes.

She rubbed her belly against it, luxuriating in his heat. "God's blood, you make me ache," he swore against her cheek. "How can I want you more than I did before?"

"Because I am lucky," she whispered and dragged her nails down the furrow of his spine. This time his shiver was violent.

"I shall kiss you all night," he swore, "until the sun comes up in the morning."

Caught up in their pleasure, neither noticed how long the shadows had grown. By the time they did, it was too late. They jolted apart as the shutters clattered opened and a figure crawled through the arrow slit, landing lightly as a cat upon stylishly shod feet. Naturally, the intruder was Nim Wei. She wore her minstrel's garb— scarlet and green like Bridesmere's livery. A velvet cap sat jauntily on her head. Her shining hair, not even a little mussed, was braided behind her back.

"Forgive my untimely interruption," she said as Gillian grabbed the blanket. "The keep is abuzz with news. A fatally injured falcon. A naked woman carried into Sir Aimery's tower. I summed the two together and thought you might need my aid."

Before Gillian could stop him, Aimery left the bed to step between her and the elder. He appeared calm, but his hand rested on the pommel of a dagger she had not noticed he wore.

"Gillian needs no aid but mine," he said.

His voice was different, a soldier's voice, as lethal and cool as iron. His stance said he was fully prepared to carry out the threat. He seemed so confident, Gillian half believed he could succeed.

Nim Wei responded to his manner with a knowing smile. "Taken your blood then, has she? She cannot heal completely without it, you know. The lower forms of life do not offer what she needs. Like me, she is what she is."

"I know what she is," Aimery said, unmoved by her derision.

Nim Wei narrowed her eyes. "Stand away from her," she said

in a low and throbbing tone, her power behind the words. Gillian braced, but Aimery stayed as he was; his muscles did not so much as twitch.

"You shall not touch her except through me," he said.

Lord save us, Gillian thought at this open challenge. Even if Aimery was resistant to Nim Wei's thrall, he did not, could not have the physical strength to overcome her. Gillian did not have that herself. She prepared to leap to his defense, but the elder merely tipped her head.

"She *has* bitten you," she said. "You withstand my mental force."

Aimery drew his dagger slowly from its leather sheath. With the index finger of his left hand, he touched its gleaming point until a bead of red welled from his skin. *I shall not shrink,* said the silent gesture, but at least he had the sense not to contradict Nim Wei's assumption that Gillian had bitten him. The elder might be angrier if she thought he acted on his own—or she might consider Gillian more of a threat. Gillian *could* compel Aimery, at least in small things, and she had never stolen his blood. Until she read Kenelm's memories of Damiano, she had not known a bite would grant her extra power. Now Nim Wei implied that the bite of one *upyr* could shield a human from the influence of another's. Gillian had not known that, though she kept her surprise inside.

Better her enemy not suspect the extent of her ignorance.

Unaware she was being misled, Nim Wei smiled pleasantly at Gillian's lover. "If my friend here has marked you as her own, I shall not interfere."

Aimery responded with more silence.

Faced with his impassivity, Nim Wei stepped around him to speak to her supposed friend. When Aimery countered the shift with his own, the elder rolled her eyes. "What a loyal pup," she mocked, "who guards his mistress at every turn."

Despite her tone, Gillian could tell the elder was rattled.

"You have business with me?" Gillian asked, striving to match Aimery's calm.

"Not business," Nim Wei said. "Concern. But I see you have matters well in hand." Her gaze slid suggestively down Aimery's body. His erection had not entirely subsided and her eyes widened at the size of what remained. When she licked her lower lip, Gillian suspected the gesture had more to do with being female than *upyr*. "We shall speak further when you are not occupied with other things."

Gillian felt Aimery's temper begin to boil. Before he could push beyond the elder's tolerance, she stepped down from the bed and laid her hand on his shoulder. Beneath her touch, his muscles were tense and hot, like a bowstring about to snap. She dared not send a thought, for fear the older *upyr* could intercept it. Luckily, Aimery understood her wordless message. To her relief, he curbed his tongue.

"When and if our interests coincide," Gillian said, "I would be happy to discuss them."

Nim Wei laughed as if she were pleased. Perhaps she was. Gillian could not pretend to understand how an elder thought.

"I shall look forward to it," Nim Wei said and moved with unnerving facility back out the arrow slit. Tiny sounds marked her rapid scuttling down the wall, like a spider in human form. Remembering how long her descent from Ulric's cave had taken, Gillian knew this, too, was a skill she wanted for her own.

Neither she nor Aimery stirred until the elder was gone. Aimery was the first to move. "So," he said, his voice steady but tight, "I meet the *upyr*'s infamous queen."

"Yes," was all Gillian could say. After this encounter with the dark side of her kind, Gillian feared he would never see her the same.

WHEN Edmund heard about the accident, his first concern was for his son. They had no fosterlings Robin's age and that bird had been his new best friend. From what Aimery's assistants said, there was no chance the falcon's injuries could be healed.

"Flew straight into the ground," said the one with the crooked eye whose name Edmund thought was Ian. He seemed more dignified than usual, his bluff Welsh face pulled into mournful lines. "Made a right mess—even before the crane got at her. Shame, that. She was training up to be a plucky hunter. Your lad was quite tore up."

"Mind you," said the second man, "your boy dinna lose his ballast. We just thought you would like to know, since he was so partial to Princess and all."

Edmund thanked them for their report. It was telling, if not surprising, that neither man thought to take this news to Robin's mother. A brief acquaintance was generally sufficient to reveal what sort of woman Claris was. Edmund was glad these men knew what sort of boy Robin was, and cared enough to recruit some parental comfort, however unsuited to supplying it Edmund might be. He could pat a back, though, and dry a tear or two if he must.

Resolved to do exactly that, he pushed aside his correspondence and took himself to the dormitory where Robin slept with the other pages. If he was not there, Edmund would try the stables. He remembered his own childhood well enough to know boys of Robin's years cried alone.

As it turned out, he did find Robin in the dormitory, along with the last person he expected. As Edmund paused in the shadow of the open door, he saw Claris sitting next to him on his cot. Though her attention was clearly, even sympathetically, focused on the boy, he was the picture of dejection. He sat hunched on the mattress, his hands clasped between his knees, his feet swinging dolefully above the floor. A slice of blanket separated him from his mother. He seemed in no hurry to close the gap.

Immediately suspicious, Edmund stayed where he was. Claris's sort of solace came with a price. His ears were just sharp enough to make out her words.

"Lady Elspeth says the woman Aimery carried only wore a blanket."

Ah, thought Edmund. Claris would be on about that.

"She was hurt," said his son with an innocence Edmund mistrusted, even if Claris did not. "And her clothes got torn. She is not Uncle Aimery's leman, Mama. He was just trying to help her."

"But how was she hurt?" Claris prodded. "And why has no one seen her before?"

Edmund's son rubbed the tip of his nose. "I think one of the birds attacked her. And maybe she came from town."

"From town," Claris repeated, obviously not satisfied with this answer. Trying another tack, she asked, "Is she pretty?"

Robin responded with a shrug, either because he was too young to care, or because he distrusted his mother's mood.

"Lady Elspeth said she was skin and bones."

"I guess," said Robin.

A flicker of impatience tightened Claris's face. "Well, do you know how long she intends to stay?"

Robin slanted a guileless glance up at his mother. "Why not ask Uncle Aimery yourself?"

If Edmund had not been lurking, he would have laughed. Even a boy knew Claris was too proud for that. Confronting him directly would be tantamount to admitting the object of her desires might be interested in someone else.

Rather than answer her son's challenge, she stroked his hair. "Tell me, love, why were those boys teasing you when I came in?"

Robin grimaced at the reminder. "They said I would have no one to play with now that Princess is gone."

"Princess?"

"The falcon who got hurt today."

"Ah," said Claris. "That Princess. I do not think she was a nice bird. From what I saw, she had a tendency to be violent."

Though the words were mildly spoken, they sent his son into a fury. "Princess is not violent! She is smart and good and—" Robin stopped midsentence while the most extraordinary expression crossed his face. He seemed to realize he had betrayed himself in a mistake, and yet forgetting Princess was dead could not account for the horror Edmund saw. "I mean, she *was* smart and good," he corrected hastily. "She is not anything anymore and Brother Kenelm says we should not speak ill of the dead. I liked her. I liked training her with Uncle Aimery."

"Of course you did," said Claris in her sweetest, most approving tone. "I know you love your uncle. I imagine you sometimes wish he were your father."

Robin's eyes widened in surprise. He seemed too befuddled to answer. Whether this was because his mother had actually seen into his soul, or because the comment was inappropriate, Edmund could not guess.

In any case, the fact that Robin failed to deny it was enough to twist Edmund's heart. In his imagination, he felt again the clout with which his brother had flattened him at their last practice. Aimery was always first, always better—with everyone and at everything.

His teeth ground together in disgust. Lord above, he told himself. You are a grown man. Do not be so damn maudlin. So what if you are no warrior? You fulfill your responsibilities better than nine lords out of ten. Aimery has spent more time with the boy. It is only natural Robin should love him.

Natural or not, Edmund turned away with his hand clutched to his breast. That he had known the truth all along did not make it hurt any less.

"WAS she telling the truth?" Aimery asked. "About you needing my blood to heal?"

Full dark had fallen while Gillian waited for him to make sense of the day's events. He stood by the needlessly shuttered window, running his fingers across the heavy wood. His expression was shuttered as well, as if he were reluctant to share his thoughts. Though she did not invade them, Gillian knew his mood had changed considerably since Nim Wei's visit.

Hoping to avoid making matters worse, she approached no

closer than the bottom post of his bed. "I am well enough," she said.

"Well enough," he repeated, fiddling the latch back and forth. "But not as strong as you were before. I can see that for myself. Your glow is gone. You look like a penitent who has overdone a fast."

"Thank you kindly."

He spun at her attempt at humor, his face bearing all the trouble he had not wished her to see. "I am not making jests. I need to know. Will my blood help you to heal?"

She stepped instinctively back, her heart beating in her throat. "I do not want your blood."

Except she did. In that moment, she wanted it more than she wanted to bed him—and she wanted that rather much. Blood was the ultimate token of *upyr* love, their greatest intimacy, their sweetest gift.

"I do not want it," she whispered.

He was there in front of her then, holding her arms before she could retreat. He shook her just hard enough to let her know he meant it. "I thought you were done lying to me."

She pressed her lips between her teeth. Her incisors had sharpened hungrily at his words and she cut the inside of her mouth. "I do not know if I need it!" she cried. "Maybe Nim Wei was lying."

"Why would she lie?"

"I do not know. No one understands the elders."

He let this feebleness go unchallenged, his fingers tightening and releasing on her arms. Whether he realized it or not, the rhythm was that of coition. When she thought she could not bear the tension an instant longer, he spoke again.

"Have you ever?" His voice was husky, dark, almost as dark as his eyes. He might as well have kissed her sex. Her body tightened and her hands clenched into fists. She knew what he was asking, just as she knew fear was merely a portion of his response.

"Have you?" he said. "Have you drunk blood from a human?"

To her shame, she had to pant out her response. "Only from Ulric."

"Whom you loved."

In these words there was anger. Hearing it steadied her enough to meet his gaze. "You said you did not want me to lie."

"You loved him."

"Yes," she said, admitting it fully to herself. "Not the way he wanted, but I did."

"And me?"

Her touch flowed up his arms and over his shoulders. "You I love so much I cannot bear for you to see the monster inside me."

His smile was crooked, his eyes immeasurably sad. "I have been to war. I have seen what humans do to one another in the pursuit of power. The French had a term, *chevaucheé*, for the destruction armies wreaked to soften up the enemy before a battle. Burn a village, burn a field, burn a peasant and rape his wife. Then, when the enemy soldiers come to fight you, they have nothing to eat and no one to tax and nowhere to run if they need to hide. Armies fight wars, Gillian, kings profit from them, and peasants always pay. Someone like you cannot be a monster to me. I have killed." He jabbed his thumb into his chest. "I have killed more men than I can count. I took no joy in it, but I also felt no remorse. It was them or me. Not right. Not wrong. Just them or me."

"You fought for your king. For your country."

"I fought because my father told me I must. Even then I was unconvinced Edward's right to France was any stronger than King John's. Who knows if Edward is convinced himself? The chance for plunder is reason enough for most rulers to hone their swords."

She touched his scar, stroking it gently until the muscles it pulled relaxed. He shook himself.

"I am sorry," he said. "I did not mean to air old angers in front of you."

"You need not be sorry. This is part of your story, as much as Nim Wei is part of mine. I want to hear it. I want to know who you are, even if it is not pretty."

His breath caught in an ironic laugh. "No," he said, "it is not pretty."

She stood on tiptoe to kiss the cleft in his chin. "There is more hero in you than killer, love. Just ask Princess if you doubt me."

He wrapped her in his arms so tightly, he lifted her off her feet. "Let me be the one to heal you," he whispered hoarsely in her ear. "I want you to be strong again. Strong enough to fight. Strong enough to love." His mouth drifted across her cheek to lick her lip. The point of his tongue touched her sharpened incisor, then slipped behind it to stroke her palate. Gillian shuddered with temptation.

"I know this means you are excited," he said, sounding, and feeling, rather excited himself. The bulge that had impressed Nim Wei was nothing to what he sported now.

Gillian struggled to find the remnants of her voice. "You do not know what you are playing at."

Smiling, he licked the tooth on the other side. "I think I do," he said. "I think tonight I want to sate all your hungers."

Fourteen

TREPIDATION and desire chased each other across her face. The emotions amazed Aimery with their strength. Gillian needed him, and feared the need. The awareness filled him with unexpected exultation.

She wanted to protect him.

As a young man—a boy, in truth—others had looked to him to lead, to be their spar to cling to in a storm. He had not minded. The warrior's gift had been his from birth, though in Aimery's case its nature was rarely what people thought. For him, danger brought a heightened awareness of the world around him, coolness of mind rather than lust for blood.

What it had never brought was someone to shield him.

He almost smiled. Gillian's strength might outstrip his, but experience made him more than her equal. He was willing to kill where she would hesitate. Had she needed to defend herself, he would happily have spared her that burden. He would have felt ennobled to serve her, on bended knee, if she required.

The recognition was humbling, but not without its pride. He felt for her what he should have felt for his king—not blind obedience, never that, but a willingness to set her needs above his own: a willingness to *choose* to serve her. The knowledge that he was capable of such fealty roughened his voice.

"Surely," he said, "you do not think I am too weak to give you what you need?"

She trembled at his tone, still rigid and resistant within his arms. The faintest of flushes stained her ashen cheek. As if she could not stop herself, she moistened her lips. This small sign of arousal made his sex stand like a marble column between his legs.

"Must I open the vein myself?" he growled.

"No," she whispered and searched his eyes. "Aimery, are you sure?"

He kissed her in answer, licking into her mouth until her tension eased. The knots in her muscles melted beneath his hands. Languorous and warm, she moved against him, her body brushing his, her palms sliding restlessly up his arms. He did not know how he would wait to take her.

"Here," he said, turning his head aside and guiding her to his neck.

She shook again, a fine vibration like the plucking of a harp.

He heard her breathe his name into his skin, felt her dragging too-sharp teeth and a too-soft tongue along his vein. His heart hammered in his ears: a primitive reaction, beyond his mind's control. It seemed disloyal to doubt for an instant that she meant him well, and yet that very doubt was exciting. Perverse, he thought, as he breathed faster through the tangle of anticipation. His lungs seemed to hold less air than they had before. Do it, he thought. Do it and be quick. Her fingers stroked his throat as if to reassure him, as if to say she understood.

He closed his eyes and willed the fear away.

"I shall not thrall you," she said. "I want you to know how being bitten really feels."

He shuddered as she kissed him, her mouth pressed tenderly to his flesh. She licked him again and made a little noise inside her throat. Her lips were warm now, satiny and plump. He could not swallow back a groan.

"Shh," she said against his drumming vein. "Shh."

The sting of her teeth was such an ordinary pain it calmed him. There, he thought. Nothing to fear in that.

Then she began to suck.

He had thought he was as hard as a man could get, but the pitch her feeding brought him to was astounding. He ached with agonized desire, as if pure pleasure were being drawn through all his veins, were being tugged from each throbbing nerve. Gasping in shock, he clutched her closer.

Their knees gave out simultaneously, but he barely felt the floor. Everything was her mouth, her ragged exhalations, her hands kneading his back and neck. His blood sang between them. The intimacy of what they were doing overwhelmed him. Emotions rose in waves. Tenderness like a father for a child. Love so deep it was adoration. My life, he thought. I share my life with you.

She moaned as though she heard him. Images swam through his mind: a loaf of bread sitting on a table, a bird wheeling gracefully through the sky. These were her memories, haloed in gold and

scented like morning grass. The barriers between them blurred. He
felt her love for him as a tangible reality—young as a tumbling pup,
needing to grow into its paws, but so strong and full of promise he
could have wept. In that moment, he knew what they shared could
grow.

I will make it happen, he vowed. I will not waste this chance.

He was sorry when her mouth released him, though he enjoyed
the way her head fell back with savored pleasure, the way her
tongue swept over her lower lip. With her hair curling wildly and
her breasts rising with her breathing, she looked as if she had spent
a long night in bed.

"You seem better," he said, his throat almost too tight to speak.
Now that he did not have her feeding to distract him, he became
aware that his skin was tingling all over, itching almost. His erection
pounded so demandingly, he feared he would fall on her like a beast.

When she hummed in answer, low and carnal, he nearly did.

She opened sleepy eyes and rose from the floor. Her body dazzled him, its nakedness slightly flushed, its curves plump and glowing once more. Her breasts were ivory tipped in pink. He was so
caught up in staring, he nearly did not see the hand she offered to
help him up.

"If you do not remove your clothes," she said, "and quickly, I
believe I am going to scream."

He froze, then grinned and began to tear at his laces. His plain
brown tunic was sturdy enough to resist his cursing efforts. In the
end, he yanked it over his head.

Gillian knew how he felt, because she felt the same—as if she
would go mad before she could touch him. Her skin yearned for the
friction only his could give, her sex for the plunge and pound of his
size.

He was even more formidable in the lamplight, his muscles
bunched and shadowed as he wrenched his shoulders free of his
sleeves. Her own hands untied the points of his hose, practically
throwing them to his ankles in her haste.

"Oh, God," he breathed as she cupped his turgid cock.

Her hands were greedy, praising his length, his girth, with caresses she was unable to keep restrained. He pulsed like a wild thing, and trembled, and bit his lip hard enough to bleed. He groaned when she ran her tongue across the tiny wound, then gripped her arms to push her back.

"I need to be inside you," he said, his face gone dark and grim. "If you value my sanity, you will not stop me."

As a warning, this did not frighten her in the least. She stepped back to his sleeping berth, climbing the two low steps without needing to look until the mattress bumped her legs from behind. He remained where he was. He seemed afraid to follow, though his hands were clenched as if in anger at his sides. Part of her was laughing at his turmoil, though she knew enough of men not to let it show. For once, her height surmounted his. With only a hint of teasing, she pointed regally at his groin.

"I want to kiss you first," she said. "There. I want the swollen tip of you in my mouth. I want to push my lips down your shaft until I cannot take any more. I want to taste how big you are."

The knuckles of his fists went white. "I need you now. I cannot wait for that."

"You can," she purred. "You want to."

With a wordless growl, he took two long strides, gripped her waist and tossed her through the arras onto the bed. Even as he crawled over her, she slid down, slipping between his straddled legs, wrapping her arms around his thighs and pulling up until she licked the sack that swung between. Immediately it drew higher, as if it were excited, too.

Aimery cursed with exasperation.

"I am a cruel, cruel being," she declared, unable to keep her amusement inside. "I must torture you with my tongue!"

He laughed in spite of himself, then groaned low and rumbling in his chest. "Do your worst then," he said, "and I shall do my best to bear up."

Taking himself in hand, he angled his shaft until the crown pressed slick and hot between her lips.

For all his eagerness, he was careful. She could not be frightened by his maneuver to take control. As he pushed slowly within, the feel of him was everything she had dreamt: humanly salty, mortally hot, too big for any sensible woman to entertain. Fortunately, Gillian did not have to be sensible. From her first forbidden glimpse, she had wanted to explore this part of him to the fullest. Replacing his hand with her own, she drew him further in, her tongue swirling over the sensitive crest and rim. He gasped as she rubbed his solid shaft with tightened fingers. His skin was silk, his moan pleasure turned to sound. Hearing it made her burn, as did the feel of his pulse racing on her tongue.

If she had not been starved for different touches, she would have kept him where he was all night.

"Enough," he said with a violent shudder.

She let him go, watching him spring hard as a pikestaff against his belly. She smiled to herself in secret enjoyment. She had wondered how big he could get and now she knew. To her delight, he was darker than before, a sweet rose-madder flush. Like ropes of midnight, his veins ran beneath his skin. That same blood beat inside her, binding them together as surely as desire. She was drunk with it . . . and strong. Though she had not taken enough to weaken him, she felt completely hale. He seemed considerably more than hale, his vigor as impressive as his lust.

She sensed his control hung by a thread.

With the backs of two admiring fingers, she stroked his shaft to the swollen rim. A spurt of excitement made him bounce.

"It is more than enough," she agreed, the curl of her smile warming her face. "In fact, it may be too much."

His answer came through clenching teeth. "After all you did to get me like this, you had better pray it is not. I intend to give you every inch."

She doubted he meant the threat but, rather than protest, she scooted back on her elbows and let her legs fall, bent and ready, to the side. The invitation was as obvious as his need.

He swore and gripped her thighs, his fingers digging in where they met her hip, stretching her even more for his assault. The position bared the quivering tissues of her sex. Warmth slid from her, a sheen of wetness he could not fail to see. She heard him catch his breath.

"Gillian," he moaned as if in pain. His hands moved, gentling now, exploring, sliding inside her and smoothing out. One finger caressed her sheath, though she could easily have taken more. His thumb roved up her folds to arouse her further. He kissed her breast as tenderly as a dream. He was being careful of her, the very last thing she required.

"Come," she said, reaching for his hips. "Let us bring this hunt to a close."

He came at her coaxing, shifting over her, his body filling the space between her thighs.

"Gillian," he murmured. "Oh, Gillian."

As he began to lower himself, her skin jumped with exhilaration. This was what it yearned for, this close and weighted press. When the probing tip of him did not find her gate, she took him in her hand. He was hot enough to sear her. She squeezed the flare of him just inside, her breath catching at the small insertion. The linked place throbbed and clung. Their gazes met. His still held a touch of fear.

"You cannot hurt me," she reminded him. "I am not fragile like a human woman."

"You are saying I can be rough."

"You could pound me like a hammer."

He laughed at that, breathless and flushed. His hands caught hers, his fingers trapping her wrists above her head, his thumbs stroking her palms. "I feel as if I have been waiting all my life for you. For this. As if I had never truly bedded a woman before." He shook his head. "My body is on fire. I doubt I can be gentle."

She smiled and showed her fangs.

The sight startled him but sent the message she intended. She was as much an animal in this as he.

"All right then," he said, his muscles gathering in preparation. "All right."

She had underestimated his power, or perhaps his need to set his pent-up urges free. His first thrust was a blow that resonated through her spine. She cried out, overwhelmed—by his size, by his strength—nearly at crisis with a stroke. He did not misread the sound.

"All of me," he said, slamming into her again. "All . . . of . . . me."

Only her unnatural strength kept his from pushing her past the bolster. She braced one arm against the headboard as he pounded the deepest part of her, waking nerves she had not known she had. Pleasure rose in giddy, dizzying waves until her body seemed to belong to a stranger. Surely she was not making those noises. Surely she was not so overcome by greed. But she did not want to hold her responses back. She matched and met his next downward thrust even as a climax spasmed inside her.

She wanted another almost at once. She gripped his driving phallus with her sheath, half by intent, half uncontrolled. She was afraid she had hurt him, but he went wild, knees and hands digging in, muscles clenching like stone. It was a ride to glory in, reckless and wholly free. He merely grunted when her nails pricked the skin of his back.

The scent of blood joined that of sweat. Gillian tried to hide her hunger, but Aimery knew what she craved.

"Do it," he ordered harshly, cradling her head in one big hand. "Drink from me."

She was beyond hesitation. She pierced the muscle of his shoulder, drew a single swallow and came again.

Her pleasure seemed to infect him. His lungs expanded in a desperate bid for air. Tearing free of her mouth, he pulled her roughly down until her hips hung off the mattress's edge. He kicked out and the chest that sat at the bottom of his bed rolled away with a crash. He was standing then, pounding into her from the floor. He pressed her legs up and back until her ankles met behind his neck. His left hand stroked the arch of her foot while his right secured her hips.

She quivered inside to see his expression. A soul in hell could not have looked that tortured, nor an angel that lost to bliss. His face was so strained she could not tell where his scar began. Whether he was striving for culmination or trying to stave it off, the sounds he made were whimpers of ecstatic pain. His hands shifted again. Both held her thighs for purchase, then reached beyond her to grip the bed.

"Aimery," she gasped, her tension mounting with every plunge. She wanted to soothe him, and she wanted to make it worse. Hardly knowing which was which, she drew her fingernails up his back. His skin shivered at the touch. When she moved the caress to his mouth, he nipped her thumb.

"Do you wish to taste me," she whispered, "to take my life into you?"

He groaned, giving over to the flood of rising sensation. His end was irretrievable. His hips slung forward and locked. She felt him swell inside her, felt him gush as his breath rushed hot and loud. When he ground himself against her at the final tremors, she had no choice but to join.

His weight collapsed atop her with only their breathing to break the silence. Sweet, she thought, and wrapped his heavy body in her arms. His face turned back and forth across her hair as if the simple feel of it brought him joy. She sensed an immense relief in him, one that went as deep as bone. His fears had been assuaged, his lust appeased, and he had set his seal on her in the most primitive manner a human could.

"Praise God," he sighed, which made her laugh.

"Stay there," she said as she wriggled out from beneath him. "Rest."

She doubted he could have moved. He lay like a felled tree with the good side of his face pressed against the ticking. She straddled his buttocks and sat. Streaks of sweat and blood mingled on the broad expanse of his back.

"What are you doing?" he mumbled indistinctly.

"I scratched you." She traced the side of one mark with her finger. His skin shivered like a horse.

" 'S fine," he said. "More than worth it."

She hesitated a moment longer, then bent to lick the leftmost wound. It stretched from his waist to the base of his shoulder. When he felt the wetness of her tongue, he gave a little gasp.

"You will heal better," she said and paused above the second scratch. "The pack does it all the time."

He rolled his shoulders, but the tightness did not leave them. "Do you like doing this?" he cautiously asked.

"Yes," she admitted. "Does it hurt?"

He shook his head. "It tickles and it is sort of . . . sexy."

"Ah." The word was a smile made out of sound. She feathered her fingertips across his buttocks. "In that case, I shall take my time."

His spine was very sensitive, and the small of his back. His breathing deepened as she licked it. She wondered if anyone had ever taken such care with him before, if he had let them. He seemed to like it very much. His toes curled as she worked and his hips lifted for room. He turned her beneath him as soon as she finished, pressing the solid length of his arousal between her thighs. He needed no help to find his mark. His entry was as sure as if it had been oiled.

"I did not think I could feel this," he said, his movement inside her gentle and slow.

Gillian crossed her calves behind his waist. She did not squeeze him, merely kept his thrusts secure. " 'This'?" she asked.

"Trust," he said.

The explanation required no answer. They both sighed with enjoyment when he came.

PLEASURE had stunned Aimery to silence, not only for the storm of lust but for the peace that had come after. This was an ease he had not thought to know. One of Gillian's breasts pillowed his cheek. The other he caressed with gentle fingers, watching the rise of its pale pink crest.

She was herself again as he had first seen her, the flawlessly beautiful *upyr*—despite which he was utterly confident she was his. Their possession of each other had marked their souls.

He marveled at that as he kissed her silken skin.

She had closed her eyes, but she hummed approvingly and stroked his hair.

"I spent inside you," he said, letting his hand slide to her hip. "Twice. I know you said your kind cannot have children in the normal way, but—"

Two slender fingers covered his mouth. "We cannot have children at all, not after we are changed. It is the price we pay for what we gain. So you need not worry"—her voice warmed with amusement—"however virile you clearly are."

"I do not feel virile at the moment. I feel as if I could lie here all year."

Smiling, she pressed her lips to his brow. "Strangely enough, I feel the same. If I did not know better, I would swear your . . . virility had bruised me."

"I never meant—"

"Believe me, I am not complaining." Her laughter jiggled his head. "And there I was, thinking size made no matter."

He was tempted to press for details but refrained. He understood what her words implied. He was larger than that Ulric whom she loved. Childish though it was, he would claim the advantage and be glad.

"You are gloating," she teased, reading him as easily as if he had spoken.

"Only a little. The memory of my roughness is too shameful. Especially the first time, I did not use much finesse."

"Did I say I wanted finesse?"

"No, though you might lie and tell me I am the best lover you ever had." He shifted until he was propped above her on his elbow. His scar stretched with his grin, the sensation oddly painless. Making love to her had done him good.

Her hand drew a line from the base of his throat to his heart. "To say you are my best lover would be no lie."

He did not need the words, but they pleased him. "I am glad," he said. "For that is what you were to me."

"Goodness." Her laughing eyes glittered like stars. "Methinks both of us may gloat."

"Later I shall gloat. After I have loved you slowly again and proved myself better than a brute."

"I believe I might enjoy that as well."

Her drollery amused him. He kissed the palm of the hand that had touched his heart. "Do you mind?" he asked on impulse. "Not being able to bear children?"

He regretted the words the moment they left his mouth. Her lashes fell, a cloud shadowing her mood. "Truthfully, I had not thought of it before. My life seemed full as it was. But I know you are fond of children. No one who has seen you with your nephew could doubt that."

When her gaze lifted again, he could not meet it. Instead, he settled onto his back and tucked her close.

"It matters not," he said, spreading her curls across her body like a cloak. In case she guessed that he was lying, he searched for something to distract her. "My mother liked to say that children should be heard but not regarded."

"Did she mean it?"

Aimery caressed her upturned face. "No. She always listened with attention to what we said, whether myself or Edmund or our sister, Kate."

As ever, the thought of bright-eyed little Katie, taken from them so young, made his heart constrict. He could still feel the weight of her if he closed his eyes, bouncing on his shoulders as he pretended to be her steed. Kate, he prayed to the darkness, may God always keep you safe.

Gillian's touch brought him back, petting through the hair that covered his chest. "Did your brother mind that she treated you all the same?"

"He had no cause to, for—though Lady Elizabeth was not his mother by blood—everyone knew Edmund was her favorite. Once, I asked her why she was so fond of him. He was a bit of a coxcomb as a boy, very conscious of his rights as the eldest son. I thought my mother would say it was because he would be lord, but she told me she loved him because he taught her to be a mother. Because of him, she knew better how to love me. But I think sometimes Edmund did wish he were her child—as I sometimes wished he had not been born."

Gillian rubbed her cheek against his skin. "It must have been difficult for her, knowing you were jealous of each other."

"My mother had a gift for smoothing troubled waters."

"A good gift to have."

"Yes." He missed her suddenly, as he had not for many years. He had lost her so early, sometimes her part in his life hardly seemed real. But even though she and Edmund had been closer, and even though he doubted she would have understood what Gillian was, he knew she would have been pleased to see him happy. Of all the people in his life, she would have cared. That was, after all, what mothers were for.

Gillian kissed his jaw, which he had tightened against his emotions. "When you have children, I know you will raise them well. You have a gift just like your mother, Aimery, and it has naught to do with war."

Overcome, he wrapped her in his arms and rocked her, her dearness a kind of pain. She spoke of experiences he could not share with her. Though he wanted them, the thought of letting someone else supplant her made his heart cry out in dismay. Once, Gillian had said love was not enough. He found himself praying that she was wrong.

—————

HE had not dreamt of Poitiers since that night at the inn with Princess and Robin. Now the memories returned, not of the kill that made him a soldier, but of his father's death.

As the dream began, heavy bandages wrapped Aimery's face until it throbbed from the tightness and the slash he still half feared would take his eye.

He dreaded ending up a cripple before he truly became a man.

"I am fine," he told the surgeon firmly as if the words would make it true. Despite the man's objections, he pushed up from the canvas cot. He needed to leave this tent with its stench of death and pain. Battle itself had not shaken him like this.

As he stood, he saw Edmund entering the tent—gray and drawn, his armor battered—accompanying a litter that was being carried by two attendants. Though Edmund and Aimery had both started the day with the archers, they had lost each other in the melee. Until that moment, Aimery had not thought to wonder if he survived. Despite his injury, his face split in a grin. Something new linked him to his half sibling: the bond of soldiers, the pure and primal pleasure of being alive.

"Come to see if I am well, brother?" he teased.

Edmund did not smile. "It is Father," he said. "He has been wounded."

The blood in Aimery's veins ran cold, leaving his face an icy mask. He looked at the figure lying on the litter. No. That bloodied, wheezing man could not be their father. Beneath his visorless bascinet, his head was a mass of bruises. A crossbow bolt protruded from his upper thigh. Slower to fire than an English longbow, a hit from a crossbow could be cruel, penetrating plate and muscle with equal ease. This hit welled a steady flow of blood where it had punctured an artery. From waist to knee, the rings of mail were painted red. Aimery blinked in disbelief. How could his father be this grievously injured when his sons were sound? The man was indestructible.

"Father?" he croaked, kneeling by his side as the litter bearers laid him gingerly on the ground.

Lord Thomas tried to swallow, obviously in pain. Fighting panic, Aimery cradled his hand.

"Warwick will knight you," his father gasped between labored breaths, "for the bravery of which all speak. Were it not . . . for you . . . rallying the archers to Sir James's aid, our side might not . . . have captured the king."

"Father." Aimery's stomach felt as if it were dropping to his feet. "You shall fasten my spurs yourself when you are well."

Lord Thomas's head made a tiny movement of negation. Beneath his chain-mail coif, his hair was plastered to his skin. He had a stern face and a strong will—like his eldest, though without the pinch of self-doubt. He was a fair man. Unimaginative, some would say, but worthy of respect. He had always let his sons know he respected them. Now lines Aimery had never noticed were scored across his brow. He looked old of a sudden, but not old enough to die.

He gripped Aimery's hand with surprising strength. "Your brother," he began, then had to stop. A whine like an abandoned dog broke in Aimery's throat. He could not hold back the sound. He sensed what his father was about to say and that it meant the end.

"Your brother will be baron now," Lord Thomas went on. "I want you to swear yourself to him as you would to me. He is a good man and will govern Bridesmere well. Between the two of you, I know you can hold our lands."

Aimery clutched the cross-shaped grip of his sword until his hand went numb. He wanted to draw the blade, to scream with resentment and lash out. Despite the enemy soldiers he had slain, he had desired no man's death until then. That the man whose death he longed for was his brother disgraced his soul.

Breathing hard, he bowed his head and willed his fury to subside. Aimery's gift for leadership, briefly tasted today, could not
have mattered less. His father had said what he must, what justice
and honor demanded. Edmund was his firstborn. Edmund was his
heir.

"I swear," he said in a low and shaking voice. "Edmund shall
have my loyalty and respect."

"Good," said his father. "Good." His hold on Aimery loosened,
his energy exhausted. His eyes were closed when he spoke again.
"Leave us a moment, son. I have things to say to your brother."

Aimery drew back and stood, his sight blurred by tears, his
limbs quaking in reaction. He heard murmurs between the two,
worry from Edmund and what sounded like reassurances from their
father. "They know," Edmund said, his voice momentarily rising.
"Everyone saw what I did."

Aimery had no idea what he referred to, only that his brother
looked stiff and scared—and far younger than his nineteen years.

He shall be my liege, he told himself. I have just given my oath.
He tried to make himself accept the change in fortune with good
grace, but his every muscle seemed tied in knots.

"I shall commend you both to Lady Elizabeth," their father
rasped and then, with no more effort than drawing breath, his soul
departed the earth.

Edmund's eyes met Aimery's across the body, his gaze gone
blank with shock. Then he blinked and Aimery read a new sort of
wariness there, as if Edmund realized for the first time that his
younger brother could, if he chose, challenge his rule. Aimery
would tear Bridesmere apart in the process, but similar attempts
had been made before—by no lesser men than kings.

"I will hold you to your promise," Edmund said.

"You will not have to," Aimery answered coolly, "for I shall
hold myself."

AN arm struck Gillian's face, startling her from her sleep. She grabbed it, about to attack, when she realized it was Aimery's. He was flailing out in his dreams.

"No," he mumbled as his body thrashed. "No, Father, do not go."

"Aimery," she said and touched his perspiring face.

He came awake with a choking gasp. "God. Sorry. Must have been having a nightmare. I hope I was not too loud."

"You were talking about your father."

He nodded and rubbed his cheeks. "I was dreaming about the day he died."

"May I . . . look?" she asked, unsure he would welcome the intrusion. His eyes widened but she saw he comprehended her request. He hesitated. "If you think it is too personal, I will not."

"No. It is no worse than what I have told you already, and easier to let you see than to explain."

She leaned forward to kiss his brow. She was not yet trying to read him, but at the first brush of contact the dream was hers. Without resistance or evasion, he allowed her to see it all: the tent of injured men, his dying father, his brother's eyes. Oh, she understood him, better perhaps than he could imagine. Even his lust to rule she had known herself. No small part of Ulric's appeal was that he would have made her his queen—queen of not very much, but queen.

"Thank you," she said when it was done.

No other words seemed right; the gift he had given her was too profound.

She snuggled back down against him, her *upyr* magic drying the sheets that had been dampened by his distress. When he realized that was all she was going to say, his muscles relaxed as she had never felt them relax before. She had seen the worst and accepted it. He need never fear her judgment again. His arms came around her warm and firm.

"God keep you, Gillian," he murmured against her hair. With those comforting words, she found sleep again.

Fifteen

IMERY'S hand jiggled her shoulder. "Wake up, sleepyhead. You and I are going out."

Gillian struggled up in his bed. The hangings had been tied back and one long slice of light filtered through the shuttered window, gold and slanting like the setting sun. It seemed she had slept the day away.

"Out?" she said, rubbing her eyes.

"To the very exciting town of Bridesmere. You said you wanted to see the world. Admittedly, Bridesmere is not Paris but, considering you have been living in a cave, I think you will find it lively enough."

Still not awake, she let him help her dress. Only when he handed her a long black cloak and matching hood did her mind completely clear.

"This should shield you from the last of the sun."

"Thank you," she said. "It was good of you to remember."

With a wink to say it was nothing, he led her down his curving stairs. As soon as they emerged into the balmy air, countless pairs of eyes tracked their course across the bailey. Gillian knew she must look an oddity in her crowlike garb, but since Aimery ignored the watchers, so did she. Head held high, she followed him out.

The sky was a deep robin's-egg blue with shreds of pink and crimson clouds. One small star glimmered on the horizon. Turning toward it, they left by the postern gate, an entrance too narrow to admit more than a single horse. Aimery's charger would have scraped the sides, but this evening they went on foot.

The guard spoke to him briefly, a consultation rather than a challenge. Gillian could tell from the measured way Aimery responded that he had his father's respect for his subordinates. Watching him reminded her that his responsibilities extended beyond the mews. As intimate as they had been, in body and in spirit, much of who he was remained unexplored.

I want to know him, she thought, and I always want to have more to know.

The sentiment was new to her, and perhaps a bit uneasy. For the moment, she put her curiosity away. Later she would think about what it meant.

Once outside the castle's defenses, the walk to town was of short duration. It led them down a sloping path, past small market gardens to Bridesmere's gate. The town possessed its own walls. Roofs rose above them, evenly divided between thatch and tile. The gate itself was sturdy. Two round watchtowers flanked it and above the arch a room had been hollowed out in the stone. As they approached, the gatekeeper leaned out the window to wave them in. His appearance was very different from Lord Edmund's soldiers. A man of middle years and generous girth, he dressed more like a burgher than a guard.

"Ho, Sir Aimery," he called in greeting. "Welcome to Bridesmere with your friend."

As they passed beneath, Aimery explained the familiarity of the hail. "I trained him," he said, "along with most of the town's guards. The council, and Edmund, prefer hiring residents to mercenaries. This close to the border we must be able to trust our men."

Gillian was too busy gazing about her to do more than nod. The gate had led them to the town's main thoroughfare. Her steps immediately slowed in fascination. Though no match for London, the street was wide and paved with stone. Houses and shops lined it side by side, their corbeled upper stories shadowing their lower. Their construction was a good deal finer than she expected. Fresh paint brightened the signboards and the footpaths were neatly swept. This was a prosperous place. The few trundling carts were loaded with goods, the pedestrians corpulent and well dressed. Whether housewife or merchant, artisan or priest, the citizens of Bridesmere seemed to glow with satisfaction—too much satisfaction perhaps, but Gillian could appreciate the rarity of their contentment.

With a shiver she strove to suppress, she wondered if this was enough a city to fall within Nim Wei's power.

"How many people live here?" she asked as Aimery steered her around a hound snoozing in a doorway.

"Two thousand, last count. I'll have you know"—he paused to nod at a haughty woman in a bright red mantle—"we have two thriving churches in Bridesmere."

"Two?" Gillian marveled, hiding a smile.

"Indeed. And the second, the church of St. Batilda, is particularly impressive. The wool merchants, who sponsored its erection, were determined to outdo the millers. There were fisticuffs in the churchyard when the millers discovered Batilda's spire was going to be taller than St. Gervase's, and never mind the wool merchants built on a rise. In the end, the millers contented themselves with buying a reliquary containing the sacred thumb bone of their saint. I am told it has already healed an ailing pig, though that may be a story the millers put out to make the wool men jealous."

"Such drama," Gillian exclaimed. "I wonder, though . . ." She slanted a smile from beneath her hood. "How many taverns does Bridesmere boast?"

"That is the shame," Aimery conceded, shaking his head in mock dismay. "Seven taverns outmatch those two godly churches, and Lord knows how many alewives brew from home."

His humor was as much a pleasure as the trip. Gillian hugged his arm to her side, reveling in its strength and warmth, in the ease with which they strolled together. Aimery grinned down at her while an old man with a rolling barrow of pans beamed at them both.

Gillian knew the stranger had taken them for sweethearts.

But we are sweethearts, she thought, whatever else we may be as well.

Unaware of her turn of mind, Aimery pointed out a timbered

building with a painting of a mermaid above the door. "Those are the public baths," he said, "and a bigger den of iniquity you could not find. Every few years, the priests try to shut them down. It seems that cleanliness and debauchery go together."

"Really?" said Gillian, peering more closely at the plastered walls.

Aimery laughed. "I thought that would catch your interest."

Suddenly overcome with happiness, she grabbed his hand and skipped backward before him. "I want to see everything!"

"Everything, eh?"

"Well, the market at least, and a workshop or two. I used to love watching the goldsmiths back at home. Then I want to drink wine at a tavern. I was never old enough to do that."

"This is your idea of studying humanity?"

"Yes," she chortled, forgetting herself enough to toss her head back and spin around. The dying sun fell like watered claret against her face, a delicate pink seduction. She wanted to get drunk with it, to leave every worry behind.

"Careful," Aimery warned, gently returning her hood to its proper place. He leaned to murmur warmly in her ear. "You are far too pretty to flaunt yourself before these town roughs."

Gillian rose on tiptoe to kiss his chin. "I have no doubt of your ability to defend me."

Aimery's eyes were wistful as he traced the curve of her cheek. "My sword is yours, sweeting."

"I did not mean to sadden you," she said. "I would not truly ask you to fight some poor fool."

"Other women would be eager to have me battle on their behalf. As proof of my devotion."

"That is not the kind of devotion I need. Or the kind of sword."

Her voice was tellingly rough. Aimery wagged his brows at her in amusement, his spirits obviously restored. "Come," he said, capturing her arm again. "Let us see who is still stirring at the market."

Not many were, with vespers rung and the supper hour arrived.

To make up for the absences, Aimery told her stories of the shuttered stalls: the fruit seller where he and a friend once stole a whole bushel of apples, the saddler who spoke to his tools more fondly than to his wife. Listening, she realized Aimery was a part of this place, more perhaps than his brother. He had trained its defenders and left his guilty footprints in its dirt. Even if some of its inhabitants viewed him with alarm, his face—scars and all—was as familiar as their own.

The knowledge made her glad for him, and a little sad for herself. He was tied to this town in ways he could never be tied to her.

They wound past the infamous St. Batilda's into a warren of narrow streets that reminded Gillian so much of London, she half expected to hear her mother calling her home. Night had fallen between these walls, but she did not throw back her hood. She had a presentiment something was coming, a change whispered on the wind. *Take care,* it said. *Happiness can be stolen with a breath.*

If that was the case, no one at Aimery's favorite tavern seemed to care. At the Dancing Cat they found heat and noise and the yeasty smell of new-brewed ale. Aimery nabbed them a bench to share in the corner, along with a cup of wine. The drink was strong but palatable and Gillian settled in to enjoy. A group of men were throwing dice against the nearest wall. The table next to them was full of women. As loud as the gamblers, their cheer seemed much less strained. Aimery told her they probably worked at the local tannery, which was owned by a widow who refused to apprentice males.

"Her husband, the former tanner, beat her," he explained, "and by this exclusivity she takes revenge."

Watching the women, Gillian wondered about their lives. She had no wish to read them with her *upyr* power, only to study them with her eyes. Soon enough, though, she realized her eyes saw more than a human's.

"Amazing," she murmured over the rim of the battered cup.

"What is, love?"

She waved her hand at the people around them. "I can almost

tell what they are thinking by the way they hold their bodies, by the sound of their voices and their scent."

"Their scent?"

"Yes. It is telling me who is dominant to whom, who is frightened or unhappy, and which of those women is pretending to be indifferent to that blacksmith when she is not. Living with the pack must have taught me more than I knew—not that I know everything," she hastened to reassure him.

"How relieved I am to hear that," Aimery said dryly.

Gillian touched his knee. "I stay with you for more than what you can teach me."

"I know you do." He flashed a wolfish grin. "You stay for the feel of my rock-hard yardarm up your quim."

"Beast," she scolded.

"Only when it pleases my lady."

Leaning back with his arms crossed over his powerful chest, he seemed the smuggest creature who ever lived. Ulric could not have gloated more. Strange then, that in that moment she felt such deep affection for Aimery's flaws.

———

A fat, bright moon silvered the castle when they returned. To Gillian's surprise, the gate was open and unmanned. The sounds of some disturbance—raised voices, creaking harness and clinking mail—issued out from within.

Expression stern, Aimery told her to wait outside. Gillian fell into step behind him. Aimery narrowed his eyes but did not repeat the order. Perhaps he remembered she could defend herself or, more likely, decided she would be better off inside the walls, where Bridesmere's garrison apparently was.

Whatever was happening, it was not a fight. More people hurried from the buildings as they watched, and every torch in the castle looked to have been lit. Without pausing to ask questions, Aimery grabbed the scruffs of the first two guards he saw.

"You," he said in a tone that made them flinch. "And you. Back to the gate. Both of you are old enough to know better."

"But the messenger—" said the younger of the two.

"I do not care if Gabriel himself has come with news. Resume your posts!"

Faces pale, they did not grumble as they complied. Aimery watched them for a moment, then pushed through the murmuring crowd. They found Edmund, Old Wat, and an exhausted shepherd at the center. A number of the men, Edmund included, wore light riding armor: hauberk, chest plate, and helm. As a goggling stable boy led out his horse, Edmund pulled a sleeveless jupon over his mail. When he looked up from fastening its front, he caught sight of Aimery's approach.

"Good," he said in a falsely hearty tone. "My brother has returned."

"God be thanked," said Old Wat with less than politic relief. His grizzled face was a picture of exasperation. "Please tell this young idiot, I mean our gracious lord, that he cannot be rambling about the country waving his sword."

"Perhaps someone would be good enough to tell me why he wants to." This Aimery addressed to Edmund, who opened his mouth, shut it dourly, then jerked his head at the shepherd. A young man in baggy blue fustian garb that was faded from many washings, the shepherd's skin was so drained of color, his freckles stood out like mud spatters on his cheeks. Gillian's first thought was that one of her own had attacked him. To her relief, his neck was unmarked. And his eyes were clear, just very tired. Some kind soul had found him a barrel to lean against and some ale. He braced the tankard on his thigh before he spoke.

"William Walker's farm," he said to Aimery with the air of one who has told a tale many times. "Out past the copse. It was raided. They hamstrung his horses, stole his sheep, then burned the place to the ground."

"Is he alive?"

The shepherd pulled a face. "Old William is too ornery to die, but his sons were killed in the fight. The bastards hacked them up."

"Scots?"

"Who in Hades else?" Ale sloshed as the shepherd gestured in anger. "The family has had trouble with them before, but not for years and years."

"Maybe someone has a long memory," Aimery suggested.

"They had no call to burn the place! Nor to butcher his sons!" The shepherd leapt to his feet, his eyes still holding the horror. "I knew them," he said. "I knew them both."

Aimery sighed and clasped the shepherd's arm. Their gazes held, two men whom Death had brushed. The look seemed to calm the shepherd. He dragged his sleeve across his reddened eyes.

"Sorry," he mumbled, subsiding back against the barrel. "I know you will not let them escape."

"*We* will not let them escape," insisted the baron.

"Edmund," Aimery cautioned, but warily, as if he was not certain how his brother would react to being checked. He pitched his voice not to carry beyond the circle of those nearby. "You have an obligation to Bridesmere. We cannot risk you on so small a matter. If nothing else, consider your family."

Edmund's laugh held little humor. "Who do you think I am considering? Or perhaps you believe my son would rather I cower while you risk your life."

"I doubt it shall come to that. In any case, your son is a boy yet. He knows next to nothing of what it takes to lead."

"Unlike you," said Edmund softly. "You have known what it takes since you were fifteen."

"You are speaking nonsense."

"Am I? Tell me you do not gaze about this place and imagine what you could build with these materials."

"What has happened to make you ask this now?" Aimery said. "You have your responsibilities and I have mine."

"Ah, but yours are much more glamorous. More to the point,

you do not have to look at every face and wonder if they know what you really did at Poitiers."

"You did what you thought you had to, Edmund, same as I."

No one but the brothers and Gillian could hear their words, though all surely sensed the tension. Aimery's face was flushed, Edmund's pale and tight. Lord Edmund seemed utterly controlled. Only his eyes, glittering in the torchlight, betrayed emotion. He was speaking things that had been locked inside him for quite some time. Gillian did not know what had triggered their release, but she hardly dared breathe for fear of tipping the balance in the wrong direction.

"Tell me," said Edmund, barely a whisper. "Tell me you do not dream of being lord."

"And if I did," Aimery responded just as intensely, "what would it gain me to admit? You rule here, brother. I have never done anything to undermine that."

"Of course you haven't. The great Sir Aimery would never stoop."

With an effort Gillian could almost taste, Aimery relaxed his fisted hands. "I see I cannot win with you."

"Would that were true!"

"For God's sake, Edmund, Bridesmere is yours. Robin is yours. None of this is in dispute."

"But you wish it were. And maybe others at Bridesmere wish it, too. I am not blind. I saw their relief when you walked in. Me they trust to balance the accounts. You they trust with their lives."

"You ceded me the training of the garrison. If you regret the appointment, you have the power to take it back."

"Stop," said Gillian, frightened by Aimery's expression. "Please do not do this to one another."

Edmund seemed to see her for the first time. His gaze sharpened on her face, then on the hand that held Aimery's arm. "So," he said, "I finally meet my brother's whore."

"No," Gillian pleaded as Aimery began to move. "They are only words, and he only says them because he hurts."

She knew at once she had guessed true. Edmund colored but did not speak. Beside her, some of the tension left Aimery's stance. "We do not have time for this," he said. "Even now our quarry flies."

"Go then." Edmund waved his hand. "Let it not be said I kept Sir Aimery from another triumph."

Aimery hesitated, then seemed to judge it better that he leave. "As you will," he said with a bow that at least attempted to be respectful.

Gillian followed him through the press.

"You must let me come," she said in an undertone as he entered the armory. "I can help you fight."

"Oh, certainly." Aimery's acerbity rivaled his brother's. "And perhaps after that we can hire a herald to tell the rest of the countryside what you are."

"I can come as Princess."

"Princess is dead," Aimery hissed. "At least to everyone in this keep. Please, Gillian, let me do my duty without interference. As nasty as the damage was, I doubt the culprits were more than a few drunken lordlings feeling their oats."

Gillian pressed her knuckles to her lips. His refusal stung, but she could not argue its logic. Naturally Princess had to be dead. No ordinary bird could survive the injuries she had sustained. Even more naturally, Aimery did not want her to question his competence. In truth, there was no need for her to do so. He knew what he was doing. He could handle whatever came.

Nonetheless, she could not watch the sleepy squire help him into his mail with anything like peace of mind. Even the efficiency of his orders to the men he chose as companions did not ease her concern.

He clucked his tongue when he saw her face.

"All is well," he said, bussing her soundly. "Keep the bed warm for my return."

"I shall," she promised, trying to smile. He did not see it. He had turned to mount his horse before she could wave.

The mournful flutter inside her breast told her Princess was worried, too.

———❧———

EDMUND sat on the edge of the dais in the empty hall, the symbol and center of Bridesmere's power. The only light came from the moon shining through the windows. Their high-set, pointed shapes stretched down the wall and across the bare stone floor. The rushes had been swept, the tables disassembled and set aside. A draft waved the banners hanging from the crossbeams. Aside from this, the place was still. Even the castle's dogs had left for more exciting climes.

Edmund was alone with his humiliation.

He had made a fool of himself. In front of people he was sworn to lead. He thought he had made his peace with the past, or at least put it behind him. He had skills his people needed as much as they needed Aimery's, even if they did not always know it. But he had wanted to prove his courage, to prove he would go to battle if he must. Because of the endless public drubbings. Because of Robin. Because of Claris—God help him—though her opinion should not have mattered.

Elbows propped on his knees, he rubbed two circles into his temples. Nim Wei was probably part of the problem, too. He knew a woman like her could do better than a man like him.

Of course, none of these reasons excused him letting his fears run wild. His people did respect him. If they had not, Bridesmere could not have been as stable as it was. In the end, the garrison would have obeyed him, not to the letter perhaps, but close enough. And the evening could have gone worse. At least Aimery's new lover had kept them from blows.

Edmund had been curious to see her, if only for the pleasure of meeting the woman who had put Claris's nose out of joint. He had hoped she would be pretty, and expected she would be kind. What he had never imagined was that she would be *upyr*.

The signs were unmistakable: the flawless features, the faint, unearthly glow. Whatever disguise she used, it was as easy for him to see through as Nim Wei's.

His brother, it seemed, was having his own adventures in amour.

Edmund could not deny he was small enough to resent this.

The lightest of touches on his neck spun him around. Nim Wei stood behind him, grinning at having caught him unawares. She bent to press her lips to the top of his head, then swung to the step beside him. Her cheek seemed to snuggle naturally into his shoulder. "Good evening, O beauteous human male."

She smelled of wine and spices.

"You have been drinking," he said with some surprise.

"Only in your cellar—and a very fine one it is. I saved the rest of my thirst for you." She trailed her slender fingers along his jaw, sending a forceful tingle down his spine. "I hope you dined well tonight. I have an appetite."

Her dark, shining eyes told him her appetite was for more than blood. Seeming to know the moment he reacted, her hand slid down his belly to cup his groin. In heartbeats, she had him hard.

She was everything he dreamt of in a woman: uninhibited, intelligent, beautiful, with a core of mystery he knew he would never solve. And she wanted him. That most of all seemed miraculous. At least for now, this exotic creature wanted him. He turned toward her on the step until their knees sidled together.

One concern kept him from giving in to her charms.

"The other one drew you here," he said, then stopped to gasp as her nails strafed his erection's tip. "My brother's lover. She is an *upyr* like you."

Nim Wei's hand left off teasing him through his clothes. "Yes," she said, her fingers resting on his thigh. "Gillian is an *upyr* and she is probably the source of the disturbance that pulled me to Bridesmere. That said, I am not sorry to have met you."

"You must get bored with us humans, living out our paltry lives."

Nim Wei laughed and squeezed his knee. "You might be surprised how few *upyr* are any different, though our lives are generally longer. We were made of the same stuff, once upon a time. Our fears and hopes—and loves, for that matter—can be quite pedestrian."

"Can you love?" he asked. The question was undoubtedly inappropriate. He did not love her. At least, he did not think this fascination could be called love. Nor was he certain being loved by her would be a pleasant thing.

But the way the other *upyr* had looked at Aimery compelled him to ask.

Nim Wei furrowed her perfect brow as if wondering herself what the question meant. When a spot between his eyes prickled, he knew she had read his thoughts. "I do not suppose it would do any good to tell you that envying your brother is a waste of time."

He offered her half an ironic smile. "Probably not."

"You are different people, Edmund. He is neither better than you nor worse."

"I am afraid I cannot convince myself of that—and, believe me, I have tried." He let his breath out in a gust. "If I could just best him at something. Always he gets the better of me. The worst part is he deserves to."

"Now you do grow tiresome." Nim Wei gave his chin a scolding pinch.

Though her tone was teasing, it held an edge. He shook himself, willing the mood away. "Perhaps"—he stroked her arm down to its bend—"you could help me forget my tiresome self."

Her eyes slanted with her smile. "How do you propose that I do that?"

He had just leaned down to kiss her when a sound from the stairs brought both their heads around. It was Claris, in high dudgeon at seeing the picture they made.

"I knew you were rolling in the mud," she said, as venomous and triumphant as he had ever heard her. "These last few days you have been looking odiously smug."

Her outrage was absurd, given how clear she had made her own distaste for his attentions. Rather than say so, Edmund contented himself with a shrug. "Enjoying oneself in bed can do that. But I am sorry if my happiness offends you."

"Sorry!" Claris exclaimed, her pitch beginning to rise. "You are depraved, dallying with that"—her hand flapped at Nim Wei—"that minstrel boy. No one will trust you when they hear this. No one will—"

"Quiet," ordered Nim Wei. Though her voice was soft, a chill like an icy wind moved through the room. Claris not only fell silent, she fell still—as if her body had turned to stone.

"What did you do to her?" Edmund demanded once he had caught his breath.

"Froze her." Nim Wei poked Claris's shoulder without it having the least effect. "But I shall have to take the spell off soon. She cannot go too long without breathing. Unfortunately, I could not do anything more delicate to shut her up. Your wife has a mind like a nest of eels. Brute strength is the only influence from which it will not slither away."

"Well, you cannot kill her! She is the mother of my children. She carries my next in her womb."

Nim Wei muttered something along the lines of a broodmare being able to do the same. "Oh, very well," she conceded when Edmund glowered. "I warn you, though, I cannot erase her memory of what she saw."

"Fine. Just let her see you are a woman."

Nim Wei sniggered at that, but altered her glamour. Edmund witnessed the change as a heat-like shimmer around her limbs. Hopefully, what she had done would convince Claris she was not his catamite.

With a roll of her eyes and a flicker of her smallest finger, the *upyr* released his wife.

"I am no boy!" Nim Wei huffed as if no time had passed. "Or did you lose your eyes along with your spouse?"

Claris gaped at her temerity, gasping for air like a landed trout.

Despite the physical response, she seemed unaware that her mind had been in suspension. "You were in disguise," she accused.

"That I was," Nim Wei agreed, "but your clever husband saw straight through it."

"I shall dismiss you!"

"You could," said Nim Wei, complacently snuggling Edmund's arm, "if you were the one who had hired me."

"Edmund!" Claris cried, looking as if she wanted to stomp her foot.

Edmund found himself enjoying her frustration. "She has fulfilled her duties well," he responded mildly. "I see no reason to let her go."

Claris's flush of anger was deep enough to show by moonlight. "I shall not forget this, Edmund."

"I hope that is the case, for it strikes me you have forgotten who rules whom in this marriage."

Claris's jaw dropped in disbelief. Never had he spoken to her so bluntly. She shut her mouth, then turned to flounce back up the stairs. He had no doubt she would immediately wake her ladies to complain.

Let them have the joy of her, he thought, but Nim Wei was not so sanguine.

"You will have to be careful of her," she warned. "If she thinks she has lost the power to make you unhappy, she may turn to more devious tricks."

"She can do nothing by herself," he said, "and not a soul in this castle is ignorant of what she is."

He saw the advantage to that for once, that her machinations were so transparent. Dismissing all thoughts of Claris, he gathered his lover into his arms. "The sun is not yet risen. Shall we spend the time more agreeably?"

Nim Wei's small white hands slid up his chest. "Oh, yes," she said. "I should like that very much."

Pleasure suffused him at her kiss, but he could not lose himself as before. What if Claris had the right of it? What if he were depraved, though for different reasons than she thought? He had seen tonight how casually Nim Wei would kill. What did it say about him that he wanted her just as much now that he knew?

Sixteen

WITH Aimery away, Gillian felt as if her limbs were misattached. Gone was the physical ease she had taken for granted as an *upyr* and in its place were rusty joints. Poets rhapsodized about lovers being part of one another. Until today, Gillian had not known what they meant.

Too upset to sit, she paced the circumference of Aimery's chamber—or trudged it, since the sun was high. Given Princess's supposed death, flight was out of the question. Sleep, too, was elusive, despite her fatigue.

Surely it should not take this long to catch a few drunken Scots.

As the hours dragged, she pictured every injury a man might take in battle, then every means by which she might heal it. When she tried to reach Aimery's mind, she could not find him. No doubt he was too far away, or too focused on his task. She hesitated to repeat the attempt for fear she would distract him at a crucial moment. She told herself if he had been hurt, she would have known.

At least she thought she would—unless the unions poets wrote of were forbidden to *upyr*.

Stop this, she ordered, resting her head against the shuttered window. Her fingers played longingly across the wood. The cracks where the sun came through stung her skin, that small exposure enough to blur her thoughts. She sucked one reddened fingertip into her mouth. She could not even watch for Aimery's return. She could only strain her ears.

Fighting tears, she slid to the floor and hid her face against her knees.

It was far too late to wish she did not love him. Wisdom had deserted her with her heart. The adventures she had longed so desperately to have were now tied up with him. When she pictured her future, he was with her. Without him, it lost its shine.

Aimery, she thought. Do not leave me alone.

A night of grueling riding brought the men-at-arms to their goal. Twice the dogs had to double back on the trail. Finally, soon after sunrise, they ran their quarry to ground at an abandoned pele tower. Located near the border, the crumbling structure had once been used as a defense against English strikes, to shelter livestock and warn neighbors with signal fires. Believing themselves free of pursuit, the raiders had stopped here to rest.

Their stolen sheep, driven hard and far, were too exhausted to bleat when Aimery and his men rode in.

They took the raiders unawares, stumbling up from their makeshift beds with sleep in their startled eyes. Probably they had sweethearts back at home who thought them glamorous and daring. They certainly were the age for it. As Aimery suspected, not a one had seen more than twenty years. They had killed like men, though, and fought like men in their own defense. Aimery and the guards had little choice about how to treat them.

They killed two in the struggle. Three more they bound by the wrist to lead back to Bridesmere, from whence they would probably be taken to the prison fortress at Carlisle. If the criminals were lucky, they would be ransomed. If not, they would be hanged. Justice, Aimery supposed, though he took no pleasure in its execution. He knew these boys had convinced themselves that justice was on their side.

As they rode more slowly home, his men talked quietly with each other. They neither bragged about their victory, nor expressed compassion for their prey. To them, this was simply a task well done.

Aimery wondered when it had ceased being that for him.

He could not have felt more alien from his companions. Could no one but he see the tragic waste? Four young men had died—and for what? To prove their manhood? To score a point in a conflict so tangled the right of it could no longer be sorted out? Why did people do this to each other? Why could they not use a quarter of the intelligence the Almighty gave a flea?

I am tired, he thought. I will feel better after I sleep.

His limbs were leaden by the time he swung down from his horse in Bridesmere's bailey. Let the others tell the news and enjoy the claps on the back. Aimery stopped just long enough to strip off his armor and pour a bucket of well water over his head. The squires would see to cleaning his mail. Aimery had dealt with enough blood for one day.

To his surprise, his tension mounted as he climbed his tower's steps. Gillian would be waiting. He wished he could ask her not to fuss, then just as fervently hoped she would.

He craved her comfort with an unsettling intensity.

He entered to find her seated on the floor beneath his window. The shutters were folded back to reveal the final crimson streaks of the setting sun. Her eyes were red, her arms wrapped tightly around her knees. For a moment, they stared at each other like strangers.

"Are you well?" she asked, caution in the words.

He nodded, his throat too thick to speak. The tiny motion seemed to free her from her constraints. With a cry, she ran to him and caught him tightly in her arms. The embrace was more welcome, more healing than he could have guessed.

"I missed you," she said with her face squashed to his chest. "I feared you would not return."

"I did, though," he said, "as you can see." He closed his eyes and hugged her back. "All I took was a little scratch on the arm."

She insisted on seeing it, of course, tugging him to the bed with what seemed to him the perfect amount of sympathetic noise. When she removed his shirt, however, he was embarrassed. To his amazement, the wound was barely there. He swore it had been bleeding an hour before.

"That is the effect of my bite," she said. "Or I believe that is the cause. When you share your strength with me, I share mine with you. It makes you more resistant to the influence of *upyr* like Nim Wei, and also speeds your healing."

"I do not want to weaken you," he said, mildly alarmed at the thought of stealing her power.

"I do not think my strength is diminished from being shared, not when it is given in such small amounts. But you are tired." She touched his arm. "A boy from the kitchen left a platter of bread and cheese. You should eat and take your rest."

"I am fine." He smiled at the warmth her worry stirred. "Your company is better than any tonic."

She had sat beside him to see his wound. Now she braced her hands on her knees and turned to him with concern. "I was *worried,*" she said. She bit her lip in a way that made his sex stir subtly between his legs. The reaction did not prepare him for what she asked next. "Would you . . . I wish you would consider becoming *upyr.*"

Her suggestion stole his breath. Maybe he should have expected it, but his head was shaking before he spoke. "No," he said. "Gillian, no."

"Perhaps it is too soon for you to think of it," she said, her words hastening together. "Since you just found out what I am. It is only . . . human life is fragile, Aimery, even for a strong human like yourself. If you waited, you might not have a choice."

"I understand that," he responded, and he did, as well as understanding why death might be more terrifying to someone who could have an unlimited supply of life. But his answer did not calm her.

Her brows drew together with concern. "Is it because *upyr* cannot have children?"

"No." He cupped the coolness of her face. "If that were the sole impediment, I would consider saying yes, but it is not." Feeling as if he must move or scream, he rose and raked his fingers through his hair. "I dare not become what you are. Already I am a killer. I do not want to think what I would become if a hunger for blood were added to my flaws."

Gillian pulled her knees up again and hugged them. Her voice was small, her gaze troubled and dark. "I thought you did not mind what I am."

"For you I do not mind. You are strong enough to resist the urge to do harm."

"I am no stronger than you."

He had to turn from the temptation in her pleading eyes. "You do not guess how weak I am. Please, Gillian, I am flattered, but do not ask again."

Though she said no more, her hurt was a palpable turmoil in the air. He wished he could ignore it, wished she had never mentioned the possibility. All the reasons to accept assailed him, the most compelling of which being that they could stay together. Time would part them if he remained what he was. Nor could he in fairness hold her here. Bridesmere was a close and watchful community. As matters stood, he knew her nature was constrained. Princess might have lived out her life contentedly in a mews, but Gillian was not a lesser beast. Gillian needed freedom.

"I thought you did not know how to change me," he said gruffly over his shoulder.

"I would ask the pack to help me contact Auriclus. I suspect he would agree to help. He has his faults, but he wants his children to be happy. You are certainly as worthy as any other mortal he has changed."

At his ragged sigh, she rose and laid her cheek on his back. "Just consider it, Aimery. That is all I ask."

Aimery pinched the bridge of his nose. He wished he could swear to her he would not.

"TO Sir Aimery," cried Peter Timkins, raising his cup in toast, "who saved my life when that bastard nearly smashed my head with his maul."

"To Sir Aimery," seconded Old Wat, "who recovered the trail when the dogs had lost it."

Aimery's handpicked squadron occupied the head of the table nearest the dais. They had been drinking to their leader's virtues ever since the first cup was poured. No one but Edmund seemed to tire of it. Resigning himself to more of the same, he hid his irritation behind a smile and a long, cool gulp of wine.

To his surprise, when he looked down, the metal rim of his cup was bent. He must have gripped it harder than he thought, and must have had more strength in his hands. This evidence of increasing power—a gift from his lover—failed to gratify him. His wife was glowing tonight, her cheeks hectic with color, her eyes sparkling at all the praise being heaped on her One True Love.

Her joy was all the greater for knowing how much it bothered him.

"Where is our hero?" she called, her gaze darting sharp and restless about the hall.

"Too modest," said Old Wat, "to hear his own accolades."

"Or too busy," Edmund suggested, "easing his wounds in bed."

The laughter that greeted this sally made Claris frown. "No one told me he was wounded."

"Nay, my lady," said Old Wat, who was more than a little soused. "No more'n a scratch. But mayhap he had an *ache*."

Though she doubtlessly wished to, Claris could not fail to read the implication behind his words. With a satisfaction dulled by the foulness of his mood, Edmund watched her go pale as chalk.

"Excuse me," she said, pushing back from the table. "I have remembered something I must do."

"Uh-oh," said Peter Timkins in less of an undertone than he thought. "Better send a pigeon with a warning note to the tower."

Edmund let them laugh at this and similar bawdy stuff while he toyed with the crust of his meat-soaked trencher. Let Claris run to the lion's den if she chose. Let her see what Saint Aimery really got up to. Maybe she would realize what hopeless tripe her daydreams were.

Snorting to himself, Edmund stood, finished his wine, and offered some meaningless nicety to take his leave. His head was clear by the time he reached the stairs behind the dais.

"Cannot even get properly drunk," he muttered as he stomped up the cold, worn stones.

It was the *upyr*'s fault. She was changing him, making him more like her.

"No, old man," he said to his empty chamber. Nim Wei might have been making him stronger, might have been pleasuring him nearly mindless, but he could not blame her for who he was.

<hr />

HIDING her eyes against his back, Gillian strove not to feel as if Aimery had judged her and found her wanting. He was afraid to take her nature as his own—and no wonder: Gillian had been afraid once or twice herself. She had no right to expect him to give up his life for her. Why should he? Because she loved him? Because she did not want to be lonely? Those were reasons fit for a child.

Despite her attempt to control her hurt, Aimery must have sensed it. "I love you," he said, turning to clasp her face between his palms. "Please do not doubt that."

"I am trying not to," she said with barely a wobble.

His hands slid down her neck and onto her shoulders, his look growing warm with understanding and something else, something that made her feel very feminine. The pads of his fingers drew circles on her upper arms.

"Try harder," he whispered, his mouth lifting in a curve as he lowered his lips to hers.

They kissed as if time had no measure, as if their flesh would never ask more reward. Slow kisses, open kisses, with tongues that took the opportunity to explore. The leisure of it soothed her until the peace of sureness crept through her veins. He stroked her curls and caressed her back. He lifted her onto the bed's lowest step so that their hips snugged together bone to bone. Even with the evidence of his need nudging strongly against her, his touches remained soft. When her eyeteeth slid out with her arousal, he merely smiled.

I am here, said the kiss. *I could not reject you if I tried.*

She did not want him to try. She wanted him to trust her as she trusted him.

Her hands drifted over his powerful arms, up his muscular neck, and into his hair. He hummed with pleasure as she combed the ash-brown locks.

"Gillian," he murmured, his head falling back with bliss, "no one ever captured my heart like you."

"No!" came an uninvited protest from the stair.

Startled, Gillian turned to find Lord Edmund's wife on the threshold. Lady Claris trembled with agitation, her smooth pink hands clasped before her breast. In the candlelight, with her lilac gown and her golden hair, she was prettier than any human Gillian knew, like a plump and blooming princess from a tale.

The real Princess was not enchanted. *Bad,* she cawed in Gillian's mind. *Bad, bad, bad!*

The caws grew louder as Lady Claris approached. Too late to head her off, Aimery let go of Gillian and shifted between the women. It was a gesture of protection Lady Claris seemed not to read.

"I know what you are doing," she said, earnestly gripping Aimery's arms. "But you need not pretend you care for this creature because you cannot have me. Edmund has taken a lover. He has no more claim on my loyalty. You do not have to suffer any longer, my love. You can at last attain your desire."

Her voice rang with joy at this pronouncement. If Gillian had ever doubted Aimery's sincerity, his dumbfounded expression would have set her straight. He shook his head before he spoke.

"My lady," he said. "Claris. I fear I must disabuse you of this notion. I do not know why you persist in believing I have feelings for you, but never—never—have I thought of you as anything but my brother's wife."

His voice was firm, but for all the note Claris took of what he said, he might as well have declared devotion.

"Shh," she said, tenderly touching his lips. "I understand. Your honor must come first. But do not worry. I shall arrange it all."

"There is nothing to arrange! I do not love you, Claris. I never have."

She smiled as if indulging a child in some foolish humor. Then she turned to Gillian.

A basilisk could not have sent a more killing stare.

"You," she said with clear disdain, "I can only pity."

She spun away before Gillian could respond.

"Heavens," Gillian exclaimed once she recovered her powers of speech.

"Hardly," said Aimery, rolling his eyes. "I am sorry you had to see that. Claris is . . . rather fixed in her ideas, though I have tried not to encourage them. Now and then I have been kind to her. She made more of it than it was."

"She does not seem to need encouragement, nor to hear contradiction."

"No." Gusting out a breath, Aimery pulled her back to his side. "Be glad you are not one of her ladies. When she is crossed, her temper can be sharp."

Gillian shivered and hugged his waist. "From what I have seen, she is not very nice to her husband, either. Are you sure she will not try to hurt you when she finally understands you have turned her down?"

"She will not hurt me," he answered wearily. "In Claris's eyes, nothing bad can be my fault."

"But what do you suppose she meant when she said she would 'arrange it all'?"

"Write her family to complain of Edmund's adultery, I expect. She must have caught him and Nim Wei together. Not that complaining will do her good. The alliance between the families is worth as much to them as it is to us. They are not likely to help Claris fabricate any nonsense about the match—like some undiscovered consanguinity that would be grounds for annulment."

"She makes me uneasy," Gillian confessed. "And Princess, too."

Aimery smiled and kissed her forehead. "She cannot harm you," he assured her. "Either of you. No matter what, I promise you that."

His touch was as sweet as it was distracting.

"I do not know," she persisted. "Remember how I told you I could read people's scents? Lady Claris smelled odd, Aimery, like prey one has backed against a wall. Desperation lay under that rose perfume."

"She would be displeased to hear you say so," he said with a quiet laugh. "She takes great pride in her herbal skills."

"I am serious, Aimery. I think she may be dangerous."

"Hush," he said as he coaxed her toward the bed. "We are both too tired to talk of such things tonight."

"I am tired," she admitted—though from the press of his body against hers, he was no more ready for sleep than she.

<hr />

EARLY the next day, Aimery stood in the mews with his big goshawk, Delilah, on his arm. She blinked at him as he stroked her, calm and calming in a plain, animal way. He could tell from her weight that his assistants had been feeding her too richly while he was occupied with Princess. He would have to adjust her diet before she flew again.

If I am still here, came a thought like a merlin swooping from a tree.

Disturbed, he returned Delilah to her perch. Surely he was not considering Gillian's proposal. Being changed . . . Traveling the world at her side . . . Perhaps she could teach him how to take a familiar. Working as he did with falcons, he had often wondered how it would feel to fly.

As images of riding the wind slipped seductively through his mind, his brother stuck his head around the door. "Do not tell me you have forgotten."

"Forgotten?"

Edmund gestured to his own rough clothes. "Our standing appointment at the practice yard."

"Oh, that." Aimery tugged his ear, debating crying off. The last thing he was in the mood for was a fight.

"If you are too weary from your recent heroics, I would understand."

Ha, thought Aimery. Edmund wore his favorite sardonic smile, the one that said he expected his brother to let him down. Aimery could never decide if Edmund wanted to be disappointed or if he feared it. Whatever the case, Aimery supposed he ought to fulfill his obligation. "I will meet you there," he said. "Just let me finish with the birds."

The grin Edmund flashed defied interpretation. "Better gird yourself for a challenge," he warned. "I have been feeling extremely spry."

Aimery sighed to himself as his brother left. Given Gillian's effect on his strength, he would have to be more careful than ever about holding back.

⎯⎯⎯⎯⎯⎯

AS Edmund waited in the center of the tilting yard, the clouds formed a blanket of gray and black with a pallid yellow circle to mark the sun. A crowd had gathered, undaunted by the gloomy sky. Though everyone knew Aimery and Edmund's schedule for training, rarely did so many show up to watch. Half the household seemed to be leaning over the rail of the wooden stands. Even some of the garrison, normally too disciplined to leave their posts, had drifted close enough on the ramparts to look down.

Last night's tales of Aimery's triumphs must have put them in the mood for a bit of bloodsport.

Well, they can have it, Edmund grimly thought. Today, for once, he would show them what their lord could do.

Robin waved to him from a group of pages, his cropped hair glinting like a golden coin, his smile heartbreakingly hesitant.

Edmund was sure Robin's smile for Aimery would be blinding, as sure as he was that Claris was watching with bated breath from his chamber window. Edmund nodded to his son, then searched for the squire who held his fresh white toweling and sword. He strapped on the blade with dark determination, every movement imbued with the smooth, sleek vigor his nights with Nim Wei had lent. He was not the soft writer of letters who struggled to hold his own. He was as strong as a warrior himself, his mind both quick and clear, his eyes as sharp as one of Aimery's birds.

This time, in this battle, the lord of Bridesmere would not be shamed.

A rustle among the watchers pulled him from his thoughts. Aimery was striding into the yard as if unaware that the crowd had come for him. He lifted one brow at Edmund's weapon. Normally, Aimery chose how they fought.

"Swords?" he said.

"I thought you might like a change of pace. A test of skill rather than brute strength."

Aimery's faint smile said he understood the insinuation. "As you wish, Edmund. I should not like my pupil to grow bored."

"I have your sword, Uncle Aimery!" Robin piped, hastening up to give the weapon to his idol. Though the sword was not Aimery's heaviest, the boy had to drag it behind him. The plain crossbar hilt had room enough for both hands—a hand-and-a-half grip rightly called.

Aimery smiled at his nephew's efforts, his face so bright with affection, the sight made Edmund's heart twist in his breast. They loved each other, these two, as Aimery's mother had once loved him.

"Thank you," Aimery said gravely, his big, rough hand nearly covering Robin's head as he paused to ruffle his hair.

"Sorry about the dust," Robin puffed, nodding at the dirty scabbard.

"No matter," Aimery assured him. "Perhaps you could hold it for me while we train."

Robin flushed with pleasure at the charge. He began to run back to his place, then skidded to a halt. "Good luck, Father," he called as an afterthought.

Edmund knew his son expected him to be trounced.

He gritted his teeth while Aimery shrugged into the padded doublet handed to him by a squire. Edmund already wore his, along with a long mail shirt and a light kettle-style helm. Even if he was spoiling for a fight, he had not lost all sense.

Once he was appropriately garbed, Aimery tested the edge of his weapon with his thumb. "Not blunted?" he said with a hint of censure.

"If you are concerned, we can call the armorer to take off the edge."

"No." Aimery sighed softly through his nose. "I trust you have enough control not to lop my head off. But we shall play for touches. The first to draw blood shall lose all his points."

"As you wish," said Edmund, his tone just dry enough to elicit a ticking at Aimery's jaw. Satisfied he had hit his mark, Edmund readied himself to begin. Aimery, too, took a waiting stance.

They burst into motion as one. With both hands locked on their hilts, their swords swung and crashed in a lightning flurry of parry and thrust. The first exchange confirmed this fight would be everything Edmund hoped. From the widening of Aimery's eyes, he knew it, too. It was not that each blow was effortless, but that each was supremely right. Edmund's shoulders felt warm and oiled, his legs resilient. He was more than reacting: he was taking the offensive, pushing Aimery back, making him work to gain every inch.

Before the volley had ended, Edmund had touched him twice.

Dimly, he heard their audience exclaiming at the speed of their display.

"Guard your left," Aimery panted, reaching through the opening Edmund had left. The light touch to his arm might as well have been a slap. Edmund had hit his brother harder than that. He knew Aimery could have as well.

"Guard *your* left," he retorted, whacking the flat of his blade into Aimery's leg.

Aimery staggered at the force of it, then rolled and caught Edmund from behind with a buffet across his shoulders. This, too, was not as powerful as Edmund knew it could have been.

"Fight me," Edmund said, swinging around to catch a descending strike. "Or be damned to you."

Furious, he backed his brother across the yard, sparks jumping off the blades at the vigor with which they clashed.

"Edmund," Aimery grunted, meeting and turning each attack. "Do not . . . be . . . an idiot."

His boot lashed out to catch Edmund in the chest. The kick lifted Edmund off his feet. He slammed onto his back but found his breath was still his own. He had not even lost his grip on his sword. He leapt up again and engaged. "Now that," he said, "is a bit more like it."

There was no more talking then, no more bloody goddamn instructions. Eyes slitted with caution, Aimery saved his energy for the fight. Back and forth the battle swayed, the advantage shifting narrowly between. Edmund lost track of how many points each of them had, nor would he have cared. All that mattered was this glorious equality. He felt as if everything he had ever learned about swordplay was coming together in his head and flowing out to his limbs. For once, *for once,* the anger he always fought with was not futile. He was strong. He was fearless. He was at last the lord.

Aimery nearly disarmed him with a quick twist of his blade.

Now, Edmund thought, merely grinning at his stinging wrist. Now I have him where I want.

He knew the opening would appear before it did. Edmund knew his brother's style. Aimery dropped his guard a fraction to try the trick again. He often repeated a move to give his students a chance to correct their mistakes. Instead of blocking, Edmund thrust. The point of his blade, honed to hair-splitting sharpness, slid through the mail above Aimery's thigh like a knife through butter. Edmund only meant to prick him, but suddenly Aimery's sword was poised at his throat and Aimery unbalanced in his attempt to jerk it away. His loss of footing affected Edmund's and everything went sickeningly wrong. Without his wishing it, without his being remotely able to stop, his blade was sliding too far. His own stumbling weight was pushing it in.

Horror filled him as he felt his brother's muscles give before it, as the tip of his sword met the hard resistance of bone. Edmund yanked free as soon as he was able, but blood sprayed hotly out. The wound was a bad one. Aimery fell with a scream of pain Edmund had not thought he could make.

"No," Edmund moaned, casting the sword aside as he dropped to his knees by his brother. "I did not mean it, Aimery. On my oath, I did not mean it."

Aimery could only pant.

The page ran up with Edmund's towel. It smelled peculiar as Edmund shook it open, like roses steeped in oil. A cry came from far above them, but Edmund paid it no heed. He pressed the wadded cloth against the gouge in Aimery's thigh, all his weight behind it, muttering prayers he did not even know he said.

"It burns," Aimery hissed, clutching at his hand.

Edmund would not let him pull it off. "I have to try to stop the bleeding."

Aimery seemed to realize this, for he left off his struggle and instead rocked back and forth. "Oh, Jesus," he breathed. "Oh, Jesus and Mary."

Edmund called for a tourniquet. One of the older soldiers rushed over with one before the words were out. As they bound Aimery's thigh together, Edmund caught a flash of Robin's ghost-white face.

"It is well," he said hoarsely to his son. "I think we caught the bleeding in time."

"It does look to be stopping, my lord," agreed the guard. "You must not have cut him as deeply as I thought."

Edmund shuddered at the words and touched Aimery's face. An icy film of sweat mantled his cheek, but beneath the hint of green, his color was returning.

"I am sorry," Edmund whispered. "You must believe I did not intend it."

"I am better," said Aimery, his eyes closed against the pain. "Dizzy." He gasped as if his breath was spent. "Leg is numb now."

"That is normal," said the guard to Edmund. "Though it will hurt like the devil's pitchfork soon enough."

Aimery surprised them with a feeble chuckle. "Lost your points," he said with half a smile. "You cut me first."

"So I did." Edmund's hands were shaking as badly as his voice. "So I damn well did."

His body burned with a flush of shame, and he feared he might be sick with relief. Though his brother was the one who had been injured, Edmund felt as if he himself had been snatched from death.

AS three guards and Edmund carried him on a swaying pallet, Aimery experienced an eerie kinship to his father. Less than a handspan separated the location of their wounds. They were even on the same side. Unlike the old lord of Bridesmere, however, Aimery knew that his cut was healing. Beneath the ache, beneath the tingling numbness that came and went, his flesh pulled and prickled as if tiny hands were trying to knit the edges together.

This was his legacy from Gillian's bite, the sharing of her *upyr* power. He was grateful, though it unnerved him. Whether he willed it or not, he was not quite the human he had been before.

Claris caught up with the grim procession as it reached the entrance to his tower. Though Aimery's head swam in and out of clear awareness, he realized she was trying—almost hysterically—to remove the tourniquet that bound his thigh.

"It is dirty," she pleaded. "Dirty! The wound must be redressed."

She followed them all the way up the stairs repeating this plaint in increasingly frantic tones.

"We will remove it when we are sure the bleeding has stopped," Edmund said with surprising patience when they were finally able to set him down on his bed.

Aimery did not hear her response because every scrap of his attention was taken up in finding and holding Gillian's gaze. Awake despite the hour, she stood anxiously by the wall, drawn back from the crowd and wrapped against the sun in her long black cloak. Her face was far too white within the hood. He wanted to tell her to put on her glamour but dared not speak. Fortunately, she either divined his thoughts or recognized the danger herself, because her glow faded from sight.

"I must see to him," Claris was insisting when Aimery turned back. "You have to let me help."

She was straining wildly against her husband's arm. Aimery did not want her aid; helping him would only feed her delusions. He knew, though, that her skill at healing should be respected.

"Release her," he said tiredly. "I can feel the bleeding has stopped."

"Thank you," Claris huffed in exasperation.

Freed from Edmund's hold, she sliced through the tourniquet without delay, then removed the towel by its corners. The manner in which she did this was almost mincing, as though she were disgusted by his blood—a strange reaction, Aimery thought, in one who treated most of the castle's hurts. Flinging the toweling into the fire, she called for new-boiled water to rinse the wound.

Aimery fainted at some point before she finished, falling into a blackness as shocking as it was brief. He had never fainted in his life. He could not help thinking it was an omen of lost control.

GILLIAN rushed to Aimery's side as soon as Lord Edmund's wife finally, grudgingly, and at her husband's firm insistence, left them alone.

He was propped against the bolster, pale and sweaty and clearly in pain. Gillian was so worried for him, her dislike for Claris seemed unimportant. He had swooned, for goodness sake— big, strapping male though he was. Compared to that, all that mattered was seeing him well.

"Oh, Aimery," she said, unable to find better words.

"I shall recover," he rasped as she stroked his feverish brow. "I could feel myself healing almost as soon as I was struck. I think I am lucky people did not realize how deeply I was wounded, else I should have to play as dead as Princess."

"Your brother should have been more careful!"

Aimery shook his head. "He did not mean to do it, and it was as much my fault as his. I almost cut him myself. He must have borrowed some of Nim Wei's strength, just as I borrowed yours. I should have seen it at once and remembered he has no experience holding back."

"He is jealous of you," Gillian insisted. "He wanted to best you. He hoped to use his advantage unfairly."

"Perhaps," Aimery admitted, "but he certainly did not wish to kill me."

"He is fortunate he did not!" she cried and sniffed back a tear.

Aimery's expression was soft as he stroked the curve of bone beneath her eye. "I know you better than that. You would not exact vengeance for an accident."

"I would be tempted," Gillian growled, which made him smile.

"You are a little wolf," he said, "just as your Lucius claimed."

She crawled into bed beside him, fighting back another spate of tears. She embraced him as gently as she could. To her relief, he seemed to relax.

"I wished I dared take your blood," she said. "I am afraid it would make you weaker, but perhaps it would help you heal."

"I am alive," he said drowsily, "and the woman I love is with me. That is all the medicine I require."

Seventeen

A rasping voice startled Gillian from her rest. It took a moment for her to recognize it as Aimery's.

"Gillian," he said. "Help."

Immediately she sat up. Night had fallen. Outside, a fierce spring rain spat against the tower's stones. By the flicker of the lightning she could see Aimery's face twisted in pain. The way his chest labored for air inspired a stab of fear.

"What is it, love?" she asked. "What ails you?"

"I hurt," he panted. "All over. My arms. My legs. And I feel as if . . . I cannot breathe. As if I were suffocating. Gillian, I do not think this is normal."

She ran her hands swiftly over his limbs, searching for a wound they might have missed, though she knew that was unlikely. His energy felt strange as she touched him. It was colder, weaker—withdrawn, she would have said, as if his vital power were pulling inward to conserve itself.

When her survey reached his shoulders, he grasped her wrists. "Gillian," he said, "take my blood. Maybe . . . will help."

She searched his eyes, the plea in them, the panic he was trying to fight. A crash of thunder made him jump. Gently she stroked his hair behind his ear, then lowered her mouth to his neck. He sighed as she broke the skin. Even now this brought him pleasure.

"Better," he murmured after a bit, cradling her against him. She could feel his tension draining away. "Already it is better."

Gillian remained uneasy. His blood tasted oddly flowery—not unpleasant, but out of place. When she pulled away from him, her lips were numb. Though the phenomenon soon faded, it disturbed her. Lady Claris had been so insistent that his first bandage had been soiled. Was she correct? Had Aimery's blood somehow been tainted? Was his condition the result of that?

She did not know enough to be sure. She only knew that whatever relief her bite had given him, it had not effected a cure. The light that burned within him was still feeble. *Upyr* sometimes looked like this in sleep, but never humans.

"Thank you," he breathed as his arms fell weakly from her back. He sagged against the pillow, his eyes too heavy to lift. "I do not know . . . what happened."

He was asleep almost before he finished speaking, not quite a swoon but nearly. His pallor was pronounced.

I must find help for him, Gillian thought. I must consult someone who can figure out what is going on.

To her dismay, only one person came to mind.

———

EDMUND knelt on the family's balcony in the chapel, his forehead resting against the beads of his rosary. His hands, clasped together on the wooden railing, were cold as ice. The chill hardly mattered.

His mind was benumbed with worry, too benumbed even to pray. Through the openwork of the wood, he watched the candles burn on the altar below. Pale as cream, their beeswax scent was sweet. Brother Kenelm must have selected them; their quality was the best.

Edmund wished his uncle's protégé were here now. The monk had recited psalms with him for a while, then gone to bed. Edmund had insisted, wanting—or thinking he wanted—to be alone. But surely God would heed a monk as steady and wise as Brother Kenelm. Alas, He had little reason to heed Edmund.

Aimery had looked haggard when Edmund left. He wondered now if he should have stayed. Of course, had he remained, Claris would have as well. Edmund's wife had been more peculiar than usual tonight, more obtrusive, more oblivious to the facts. She would never see how uncomfortable Aimery was in her presence, how everything in him yearned toward the stranger who obviously shared his bed. Edmund supposed Claris could not allow herself to see the truth. She had built most of her dreams upon her dream of Aimery. Should hope be wrested from her, her life would fall apart.

As would Edmund's if Aimery died.

Edmund squeezed his hands until the knuckles cracked. Pray God Aimery would recover. The guilt would be hard enough to live with: knowing that Edmund's hand, and Edmund's sinful pride, had dealt the fatal blow. Far worse would be the emptiness Aimery's passing would leave in his life. Whatever else he felt, Edmund relied on his brother's gift for leading men. Just knowing someone he could trust implicitly was at his side lightened his burdens. And he did trust Aimery, more than he trusted himself. Time and again, his brother had proved his worth.

With a heavy exhalation, Edmund tipped his head back to face the struts of the roof. The irony was that only now—when he might lose his brother—did Edmund discover that his resentment was not as deep as his love.

I should go down to the chapel proper, he thought. Perhaps his prayers would be more effective there.

Before he could put the thought into action, the movement of a shadow caught his eye. The scent that accompanied it, like old leather-bound books, told him who it must be.

Nim Wei had decided to join him.

He rose and turned. Despite the intimacy of their association, he preferred to meet her on his feet. She sat in her minstrel's garb in Claris's blue velvet chair. Though the *upyr* was too small to fill the regal seat, she looked supremely comfortable nonetheless. Her hands were laced on her belly and her faint, feline smile said that whatever she had been doing, she had enjoyed it.

Guessing at her activity required no great deduction. Nim Wei's ivory cheeks bore a flush of pink and her glow was eerily bright. Edmund suspected a few of his people would awaken paler tomorrow morn. He tried not to be jealous of their lot.

"You are worried for your brother," she said in her cool, sweet voice. "You fear that he may die."

Edmund was not fooled by her casual air. He sensed she was watching him very closely. Did she enjoy his pain, he wondered, or was she curious because she no longer felt pain herself?

"Oh, I feel it," she said with a brief intensification of her smile. "It simply does not mean to me what it once did."

"Well, it means something to me." A prick of anger roughened the words. "I do not know how I would go on if I had killed him."

"No?" She quirked one delicate sable brow. "Not even for your people? Not even for your sons?"

"Of course I did not mean that!"

Amused, Nim Wei flashed her palms to settle his temper. "I know you did not mean it. You were simply indulging in a bit of human drama. In any case, it is my strong belief that, should your brother pass into the great beyond, you will find it was no act of yours that sent him there."

"What do you mean? I know my wounding him was an accident, but—"

She cut him off. "I shall say no more until I am certain."

Edmund stared at her, knowing in his bones that she *was* certain, that some purpose of her own kept her from speech. With that same catlike smirk, she straightened the lie of her hose across her knees. She was clothed all in black tonight. By some trick of his vision, her garments seemed to absorb every scrap of light.

"Would you save him?" he blurted out.

Though he had not planned to ask, as soon as he did, he knew the question had been in his mind since Aimery fell.

Nim Wei ceased her fiddling. "I expect his lover is doing all she can for him."

"I meant, would you make him immortal?"

Nim Wei gazed at him, no more than mildly surprised. "You ask that of me," she said, "for your brother, rather than yourself."

"I harbor no illusions about the depth of your attachment to me."

For some reason this made her laugh. "Do you not?" she said softly.

"I know that I am useful to you and that, for the moment, I entertain you. Believe me, I do not expect what we have to last."

"So much pride," she murmured, "and so little comprehension."

"As you wish then," Edmund snapped. "You are madly in love with me and shall feel that way till the end of time. It makes no difference. My brother is a good man. He deserves to live!"

His outburst erased her humor. Her eyes narrowed, glittering like jet beneath her lids. He could tell her mood was cold, but that cold was very like anger.

"Many people deserve to live," she said, "and Fate decrees otherwise. Shall I save them all, or only your brother? And if I save your brother, what cost would you consider right? Your soul? His? Would consigning him to live forever as a creature like myself be a reasonable price for staving off your guilt?"

"You have a soul," he said, his voice worn to a whisper. "I have seen it. I see it now in what you ask."

To his amazement her gaze welled up with tears. She turned

sharply away, shaking her head with rue. "What a fool you make me."

Before he could respond to this murmured exclamation, she hushed him with her hand. Though Edmund heard nothing, her manner was that of a hound catching a scent.

"Auriclus's child is coming," she said. "Your brother's lover. You must not mention your request in front of her. I assure you, she would not approve."

"But why?" Edmund asked, careful to keep the question low. "For that matter, why would she not change him herself?"

"I sincerely doubt she knows how. The power to change belongs to the elders and she is yet a pup. Mind you, she may come around to asking my aid, but not if she is rushed."

Edmund studied the smooth serenity of Nim Wei's face as she gazed unblinking toward the door. Never had she seemed this inhuman. Her thoughts were so focused, she did not even breathe. This is what she wants, he discerned, to put the younger *upyr* in her debt.

Whether Edmund would choose to help was a quandary he could not solve.

⸺⸺⸺

GILLIAN came, as Nim Wei had known she would. The young *upyr*'s mind was too frantic to be shielded. She hurried through the empty hall and up the vaulted steps to Edmund's chamber. With a thought she did not realize was effortless, she spelled his guard to sleep—the same guard Nim Wei had claimed with her bite. The elder shook her head. The girl was a menace and did not even know it. Finding Edmund gone, and Nim Wei nowhere to be seen, Gillian cast about for somewhere else to search.

The family entrance to the chapel must have seemed a lucky guess. Nim Wei knew better. Gillian had tracked the signature scent of Nim Wei's power, just as Nim Wei had tracked hers.

"We are here," Nim Wei said, stepping from the shadows.

Gillian's eyes were wild as she looked from Edmund to her.

Nim Wei noticed she was not drenched from her trip outside. This trick, too, she had performed with ease.

"Aimery is not well," she said, hugging herself as if she were at risk of flying apart. "He is not recovering from his wound."

"Have you taken his blood?"

Nim Wei was careful to remain matter of fact, but when Gillian nodded, Edmund sucked in a breath. Apparently, he thought his brother too noble to enjoy the same pleasures he did.

"And before he was hurt?" she probed even more delicately. "Have you fed from him more than once?"

"Yes," Gillian admitted. "I thought it made him stronger, but now I am unsure. He is experiencing pain and difficulty breathing, for which there seem no cause. Is there some hidden effect to feeding that I should know? I only took a little this time, and his condition seemed to improve. All the same, I could see it was no cure."

Gillian touched her lips, betraying a memory that confirmed at least one of Nim Wei's suspicions. The elder had been gathering evidence in the keep all night: a witness here, a fragment of hearsay there. Gillian's unwitting gesture was nearly the final nail.

Drinking from Edmund's brother had made her mouth go numb.

"Taking more of his blood would serve no purpose," Nim Wei said, "though it would not harm you. This is a poison to which our kind enjoy immunity."

"Poison!" The gasp of dismay came from Gillian and Edmund both.

"So the evidence leads me to believe." Their emotions flickered across Nim Wei's skin like tickling grass, a pleasant sensation, though she did feel a distant sympathy for their pain.

"Monkshood," she elaborated. "The symptoms you describe— numbness, pain in the limbs, shortness of breath—are appropriate to a mixture made from the powdered root. Your lover would be dead already if you had not shared your power."

"But how—?" Edmund broke in, his face as milky pale as one poisoned himself.

"I expect it was administered as a topical application. Mixed in oil, monkshood provides relief to aching joints. But it is quite deadly. Use too much and it is more than capable of killing through the skin."

"An accident then? If it was mismeasured . . ."

Nim Wei pursed her lips with more sobriety than she felt. She enjoyed having an answer others lacked. "No responsible healer would measure such a physick without the greatest care."

"Then it was meant to kill," Edmund concluded, the pieces of the puzzle gathering reluctantly behind his eyes. "Mayhap someone put it on my sword. But, no, that cannot be. No one could know I would cut him. We wore protection. And who would make a target of my brother? Claris has the knowledge, but even if she knew about Gillian, she would not hurt him. Her perhaps, but not him. I think the poison must have been meant for me, and if it was meant for me, it would not have been on my sword."

He stopped speaking altogether to clutch his head. Nim Wei hid a smile as she observed the progress of his thoughts. My clever monkey, she thought. My clever, handsome monkey.

"My towel!" he exclaimed, his triumph at the solution momentarily blotting out his horror. "Claris must have put the unguent on my toweling, on the inside of the fold, where it would not harm the page. I would have shaken it out and dried my face on it when we finished. No one uses those cloths but me. My crest is sewn into them. And it smelled of her, like attar of roses. That cry I heard before I stanched Aimery's wound must have been hers. Lord save us." He pressed his temples harder as he moaned. "I have killed him twice!"

"Hardly," said Nim Wei. "We are not certain this is what happened. More to the point, if you were the intended target, why should you assume someone else's guilt?"

Still reeling, Edmund sank to the arm of his lady's chair. "I cannot believe it," he murmured. "Willful she may be, but she is not vi-

olent. She never even spanks the boys. Discovering you and I together must have pushed her over the edge."

Nim Wei examined the alabaster ovals of her nails. "Not to
prick your pride, my love, but I suspect her decision had more to do
with discovering your handsome brother had an amour. With you
out of the picture, she would have the freedom she thought she
needed to win him back."

Gillian flinched at Edmund's startled glance. "She did walk in
on us the other evening, and seemed none too happy to find me in
Aimery's arms. But Aimery insisted her only danger was her sharp
tongue."

"Poor Lady Claris," Nim Wei said with a reproachful cluck.
"No one remembered the female is the deadlier of the species—and
never mind the woman scorned."

For her part, Nim Wei could almost admire Edmund's wife for
being so bold and sly; stupid as well, of course, but she was only a
human.

"There must be something we can do to help him," Gillian implored. "Perhaps I could give him my blood."

Her "we" pleased the elder greatly, though she was careful to
give no sign. "Humans do not have the stomach for ingesting
blood," she said. "And I mean that literally. Drinking yours would
just make him sicker. No. I know of no remedy but the change.
From the symptoms you describe, the poison has gone too deep for
other measures—though your friend may linger for a while. I should
not be surprised if he failed to survive the night. Your powers lessen
at dawn, you know. So will the power you shared with him."

Her equanimity stupefied the young *upyr*.

"How can you be so cold?" she demanded once she had found
her voice. "Have you no humanity left at all?"

"Very little, as it happens." Nim Wei put her hand on Gillian's
arm. The girl was trembling. When she tried to shake her off,
Nim Wei held fast. "Come now, would you really prefer that I dis-

semble? This decision is important. I do you honor by being frank."

"I cannot ask you to do it." Gillian's declaration held a mix of misery and defiance. "He would hate being changed by you."

"Possibly. And possibly he would hate you for arranging it. He would, however, be alive."

"I refuse to believe that is the only way."

"Search my thoughts if you doubt my words."

"You are prepared for me now. You could hide anything you wish."

Nim Wei shrugged. "As you like—though the sands fly through the hourglass as we speak. Of course, if you fear facing the truth . . ."

Gillian's hands drew into fists. "I fear nothing except the man I love losing what makes him good."

"Then bid him adieu, my dear, for soon he shall lose all."

She had gone too far. Gillian's fist struck Nim Wei's jaw before the elder saw her move. The impact sent her reeling against the rail, splintering the wood and nearly toppling her over backward. Neither the strength nor the surprise of the attack should have been attainable. More troubling, it seemed to have taken nothing out of the young *upyr*.

"He will not die," Gillian said in a growl that sent alarming shivers down Nim Wei's spine. Gillian's energy had swelled so wildly, it filled the air like stinging bees. "He will not die and you shall not change him. As for you—" She turned to Edmund with equal fire. "If she tries to touch him and you allow it, you shall mourn the day you met us both."

Edmund was too paralyzed to answer, though he did not cower.

"Well," he said once Gillian had stormed away, "what a marvel of diplomacy that was." Despite the dryness of his tone, he was far from calm. "Did you mean what you said? Will my brother die tonight?"

"That is in the hands of Fate," she answered—the truth, if not quite all of it. It was in the hands of Fate until Gillian chose to put it in hers: tonight, tomorrow, whenever Aimery's borrowed strength ran out.

Edmund could scoff at her methods all he liked. Despite the girl's resistance, Nim Wei saw cause for hope. Gillian had not accepted her invitation to read her thoughts. She must have believed Nim Wei was telling the truth, and dreaded knowing for sure. From belief came trust and from trust a bond. In this instance, harsh words had won more than sweet.

But Edmund was upset by them, and that she had not wished.

"I must speak to my wife," he said resignedly. "I need to know if what you guessed was true."

"Now that interrogation I would be happy to assist." She grinned at the sudden worry in Edmund's eyes. "Strictly in an advisory capacity. I doubt pain shall be required to break her. At least, not very much. And, yes, I shall remember she is the mother of your children."

Edmund wagged his head. He did not appear reassured.

⁂

AIMERY seemed confused by Gillian's explanations.

"I will return," she said for the second time. "You must hold on until I come back with help. I will travel night and day. Princess and I will fly as hard as we can."

"Princess?" Sweat beaded his brow as he strove to focus. "No one is supposed to see her."

"No one shall. I will not change until I leave the grounds." She kissed his forehead, wishing she could press her own vitality through his skin. "You must give me your promise, love, that you will be strong while I am away."

"Not sure I can," he said, his movements restless. "Will try."

"Trying is not good enough!"

Her cry widened his eyes. "I only make promises I can keep," he said, his scar creasing slightly with a crooked smile.

"Then promise! Promise or be damned!" She flung herself against him at his gasping laugh. "I love you, Aimery. I do not want to live without you."

"People do," he said softly. "All the time. Lose what they love. Feel bad. Then one day, they find . . . they can be happy again. You . . . taught me that. You . . . made me happy. You are strong enough to live without me."

She pulled back from his patting hand, tears choking her voice. "I have nothing," she said. It was not a bid for pity, but an admission. "No one who needs me. No one who knows me. In all my life, you were the only one who loved me for who I am. You, of all people, understand how rare that is. Maybe I am strong enough to live without you, but know this, Aimery Fitz Clare: If you make me do it, you might as well send me to hell."

His gaze glittered back at her, finally clear. Even now, seeing him so weak, she could scarcely believe a day might come when those beautiful eyes would not meet hers.

"You humble me," he said, the words simple and quiet. "I do not know what to say."

"Say you will fight. Say you will cling to life with everything you have, with everything you are. This is the battle, Aimery. This is the one that counts."

He caught his breath at this invocation of his warrior self. "I promise," he said solemnly. "On my love for you, I give my oath. If . . . your Auriclus is willing to change me, I will let him."

She kissed him once more, gentle this time and tender. That Aimery loved her enough to take this chance felt like a miracle. If honor were all surviving took, she knew that he would live. Sadly, honor would not suffice. Gillian would have to make sacrifices of her own. She did not begrudge them. She would trade everything she cherished for him to live, every shred of freedom, every ounce of strength. He closed his eyes as she drew away. She whispered for him to sleep.

Then, with the taste of him on her lips, she left to do what she must.

———⟨⟨⟩⟩———

WITH Brother Kenelm to serve as witness, Edmund and Nim Wei confronted Claris. They sent her ladies from the chamber, despite her loud affront. How dare he bring his leman here, she demanded, and in the presence of a man of God?

Fortunately for Claris, she was dressed. Layers of silk in shades of peach draped her curving form. Like the gown, all that surrounded her was rich: the hangings on her bed, the tapestries on her walls, the touches of gilding on her ceiling beams. None of these symbols of her dignity would help her now. Their suspicions were correct. Edmund knew that for a fact the moment he saw her eyes.

True to her promise, Nim Wei did not touch her. She did not have to. Her speech was weapon enough.

In spite of her resentment, Claris was as fascinated by the *upyr* as a mouse by a crouching cat.

"You have killed the man you love," Nim Wei said, each word a gentle blow. "Without a miracle he will die. What purpose do secrets serve when hope is gone? All you have is confession. No honor but that remains. He will go to heaven, Claris. Do you want to go to hell?"

Claris tried to resist her, to deny what she had done, but her tormentor was too tenacious.

"Did you dig up the monkshood yourself?" she pressed. "Those pretty lavender bells? Did you grind the root in your pestle and mix it with your perfume? You must have been dreaming of the magic those flowers could do since the day you found them in the forest. Freedom, Claris. To be with the man you loved.

"He was the guardian of your sons, was he not? Once your husband was dead, the two of you could take over. You would not lose a thing. What woman would not understand that lure? What a shame that you killed your love instead, that you will never see him again. Murderers go to hell, Claris. Only penitents are redeemed."

Claris confessed in the end, with storms of tears like the ones that fell in sheets outside. In the process, she heaped the lion's share of the blame upon Edmund. He was the one who had spoiled her plan. He was the one who should have died.

He had ruined everything, just like always.

He felt no anger at her accusations, merely a leaden grief. Even she did not appear to believe her justifications. For once Claris understood she had done wrong. Of course, how long that understanding would last he could not venture to say.

When they had what they needed, he left Claris to Brother Kenelm, glad the other man was there. Edmund dared not leave his wife alone, not on her own account and not on that of their future child. This time, he would not underestimate her desperation. Whether Aimery lived or not, her dream had died. The man she adored would know she had tried to poison his brother. Edmund wondered if, for her, that was the worst punishment of all.

"I will watch her," said Brother Kenelm as they left. "She will rest easier now that she has unburdened her sins."

Edmund was far from certain of that, nor did he much care. He nodded, though, and shut the door. He could not seem to move then, only stand on the landing staring at the curling tips of his shoes.

"You pity her," said Nim Wei.

"She committed her crime for love."

"Which she could not resist feeling because your brother is such a saint?" Her voice dripped sarcasm and amusement. "Edmund, think. Was your wife really drawn to Aimery's nobility, or was it perhaps the killer in him that spoke to her all along?"

"He is not a killer, he is a soldier."

"Would your wife understand the difference? Life can be difficult for mortal women. Who can blame them for secretly wishing men's ruthlessness for themselves?"

Edmund struggled to comprehend what she was saying. "Would you think better of me if I scorned her?"

"No, indeed." She stroked the wave of hair that fell across his cheek. "The world holds little enough compassion. It can weaken, true, but 'tis a precious commodity."

"Precious."

"Quite," she said, "for one does not have to be an angel to feel it. The worst of sinners can be ennobled by its touch."

"Like me."

She smiled, her beauty sharp enough to stab. "Like you, my sweet, though you are not half the sinner you think. If you felt the sympathy I feel for your wife, I doubt you could have brought yourself to treat her as I did. Your pity stays your hand. Mine is an inconvenience I ignore. I am a killer, Edmund, and have no desire to change. It would behoove you to remember that."

He did not know whether to believe her, whether his judgment could be trusted when she was near.

"Only you can answer that," she said, "and only time will tell us what you conclude."

<hr />

"I must go," Edmund said. "I should check on Aimery for myself."

With the pad of her thumb, Nim Wei brushed the shadow beneath his eye. "I will see you later then."

She knew he was tempted to ask her to accompany him on the visit, but his loyalties were already swaying against her. He did not understand the rules she played by, did not trust her with his precious brother—did not want to be seen with her, come to that. She was the dread Nim Wei, the evil *upyr*.

He was ashamed to care for her at all.

So be it, she thought, refusing to acknowledge the constriction in her throat. Better he should be wary. Besides, she had business of her own to see to. Gathering her decision, she spun and tapped on the lady of Bridesmere's door.

As she expected, the monk opened it a crack.

"You," he said, his fingers whitening on the wood. No doubt he had been hoping she would not return. From the pinch between his brows, he was wondering whether she knew that he had killed Damiano, and if she knew, what punishment she might impose.

"Yes, I," she agreed with a deceptively pleasant smile. "I wish to see Lady Claris."

"Lady Claris is somewhat agitated at present. I think it best she be left alone."

Nim Wei could see her "agitation" over Kenelm's shoulder. Edmund's wife was pacing her chamber, her hands twisting together, her lips moving with muttered arguments. The process of convincing herself her every action had been just was obviously under way—and engrossing enough to keep her from wondering who was at the door. Whatever shadow of remorse Lady Claris had suffered would soon be gone.

"Brother Kenelm," said Nim Wei. "You and I both know that woman will not rest until she avenges herself upon her husband and all he loves. If she is not mad, she is very close. Poison will be the least of what she resorts to."

Brother Kenelm lifted his chin. "She will be guarded."

"And who will guard the child who is not born?" Nim Wei persisted. "It is as much a prisoner as she. I know I would not lay odds on how long she will want to carry Lord Edmund's seed."

Brother Kenelm's lips grew even thinner with indecision.

"She is a member of my flock."

"As Damiano was a member of mine."

A trickle of sweat ran from Kenelm's temple to his jaw, but to his credit he did not blanch.

"Yes," she said, sliding her fingers over his where they wrapped the door. "I am aware you are the one who killed him. Knowing Damiano, and his sometimes overzealous pursuit of his ambitions, I suspect you were simply trying to shield your abbot. The fact remains, however, that he belonged to me. I made him. The right to determine his fate was mine."

Brother Kenelm's mouth was hanging open. He shut it and swallowed hard. Thoughts moved like the shadows of a candle behind his eyes. His mental discipline was sufficient to keep her from reading him, but she could guess at his ruminations well enough. She had met men like him before. He had more principles than Damiano, but for the right incentive he could be bought.

The chance to redeem himself with his superior seemed a likely price.

"Your abbot would not want you to defy me," she said. "He would rather the possibility for alliance remain intact."

Brother Kenelm looked at his feet. "What—" he croaked, then cleared his throat. "What will you do to her?"

"Bite her," Nim Wei answered with a tiny smile.

"Lord Edmund would not like that."

Nim Wei shrugged with more insouciance than she felt. "Her mind is a tangle," she said. "I cannot put her under my thrall without stealing blood. Once I have done so, I can ensure the safety of everyone around her, including her unborn child."

"And the effect will last?"

"I am not queen of the *upyr* for nothing, Brother Kenelm. My influence will last for years." With a suggestiveness that made him blush, she stroked the valleys between his knuckles. "Surely your abbot would want Lord Edmund, his cherished nephew, protected well."

The monk sighed in resignation. "You are worse than Damiano," he said as he stepped aside from the door.

Nim Wei noted the tinge of admiration behind his words.

Eighteen

GILLIAN flew for countless hours through the rain, north and west, over river and hamlet and wood, letting Princess transform her memories of the outward journey into something like a homing sense.

At first, despite her anxiety, the freedom to fly so far with no whistle to call her back was deeply enjoyable. After a brace or so of hours, however, the trip became a battle between her will and her fatigue. She did not know how much time Aimery had. To her relief, the rain diminished to a drizzle. The sun rose through its misty curtain, then set, and still she resisted the urge to rest. She rode the winds when they blew with her and fought them when they did not.

If she faltered, Princess took up the burden of flight. Gillian felt no words from the falcon when this happened, merely a sense of being buoyed by a friend—a friend very different from herself, but a friend.

Their love for Aimery united them. The falcon might not understand the complexity of the situation, but she knew this effort was for him.

The stars were beginning to fade by the time they reached the cliff in the forest that hid the cave. Gillian circled, pinions spread, immortal body pushed to its limit, searching for signs of the pack. She had left the clouds behind her. This was hunting weather, diamond clear and cool. Ulric would not lead his pack members home until he must.

A long ululation shivered through her falcon ears, not true wolf but *upyr*. Gillian tracked the howl to a clearing where a stag lay slain on bloodied ground. Four huge wolves drank from its wounds. The fifth, the more excitable Stephen, had paused in his feasting to sing.

The sight of him, of them all, was like an arrow to her breast. Once she had shared in this. Once a hunt had been the pinnacle of her life.

Ulric looked up as she circled lower, his muzzle dark, his wolf eyes flashing yellow behind their gold. She felt trapped in his gaze—as if it were a chain. The effect increased when he shifted form. What a man he was: naked, lithe, an *upyr* who wore his power like a second skin.

Her heart, already struggling, pounded harder. Ulric recognized her. Ulric knew she had come home.

Whether from exhaustion or from his tug on her former self, she changed before she could land, plummeting the last few feet to hit the ground in an awkward sprawl. The impact drove what air was left from her lungs.

She lay there, struggling to breathe, while all around her *upyr* shimmered into human shape: pretty Ingrith, sturdy Helewis, even Lucius had joined the hunt.

"Well, well," said Gytha with remembered scorn. "Looks like our Little One has flown home."

Gillian tried to hide her annoyance at the nickname. She imagined her rival for Ulric's attentions had been happy to have her gone. Had the two grown closer in her absence? The thought caused a pang she was surprised to find she could feel.

If they had formed a bond, it was not a strong one. Ulric ignored the other woman to help Gillian to her feet. Her legs trembled as she rose. She was so tired, she could not magically shed the dirt. Ulric's gaze took in the evidence of her toil. Unused to being naked, his perusal made her blush. When he was finished, he did not smile but took her chin in his hand and searched her eyes.

"Gillian," he said, just that, in a wistful tone.

Only then, with her heart belonging to another, did she understand that the pack leader truly loved her.

"I need your help," she said because she did not want to mislead him and because she might not have an extra minute to spare.

His eyes darkened at her brusqueness, the pupils swallowing their ring of gold. The meal he had eaten allowed his face to flush. "Help?" he said. "Let me show you how I shall help."

He used his grip on her jaw to force a kiss against her mouth. Gillian was too shocked to struggle. His teeth, lengthened since he had touched her, cut her lip. With a throaty moan, he lapped at the blood.

"Ulric," said a voice of chilly warning. Lucius had decided to intervene.

Hearing the older *upyr*, Ulric broke free. Gillian could not say who was more surprised: her, Ulric, or Lucius himself. Lucius had never been one to care what the rest of the pack was doing. Then again, maybe his decision to help her escape had given him a proprietary interest in her well-being.

Recovering, Ulric licked his mouth clean. He was breathing deeply, aroused, and in no way trying to hide it. His eyes were locked on Gillian's face. "Do not worry," he said, "I shall not rape her."

"No," Gillian agreed, "you shall not."

She held his gaze, knowing this for a test of wills more wolf than human. She felt ragged, a muddy pup to his sleek king. *Not pup,* said Princess. *Empress of Air.* The words bolstered her nerve. Ulric's nostrils flared, taking in her determination, scenting the strength she had gained while she was gone.

"You truly are a queen," he whispered, "the queen I always dreamt."

"I come for help," she repeated, "which I hope you will give in the name of friendship."

His finger trailed down her neck to the pulse that beat at its base. She knew its rhythm was unsteady, as Ulric would surely note. "Are you my friend?" he mused. "You are not acting like one. Perhaps I should demand a proof."

"If you help me, we can discuss whatever proof you like."

He stared at her as if measuring the sincerity of each separate word. "Leave us," he ordered the others.

Only Lucius hesitated before obeying.

—⟨⟨⟨⟨⟨ ⟩⟩⟩⟩⟩—

GILLIAN had come prepared for a difficult negotiation and Ulric's terms did not surprise her. She had hurt him: by leaving, by asking him to aid the man who had supplanted him in her bed. She understood his need to make her pay, though she was not looking forward to meeting his demands. They would cost her, both in pride and independence. All the same, she gave thanks he was not insisting on even more.

No price was too high to save Aimery's life.

To her relief, Ulric told her he could contact Auriclus very quickly. There was an ancient crystal, hidden deep inside the cave, by which their thoughts could join. Gillian assumed it was the equivalent of Nim Wei's mirrors.

"He will help your friend," Ulric assured her. "Auriclus knows he is in my debt."

Gillian did not ask what manner of debt it was. In truth, she was too tired to care. "Very well," she said. "We have an agreement."

He embraced her then, gently, caressingly, letting her know how much he had missed the simple contact of her skin. He offered his blood and she accepted. Nothing else would as quickly restore her strength. Feelings moved inside her while she fed—affection, desire, gratitude, a sadness like a heart crying out in pain. Except for the last, the feelings were ghosts of what they had been. The intimacy of feeding, profound though it was, could not reach her core.

Only when he tried to make her touch him did she resist. His expression tightened, but he let her pull away.

She would not cede an inch more than she must.

"Later," he said softly, "when it is done."

For the first time since her homecoming, she bowed her head.

"When it is done," she agreed. "You will have the opportunity to convince me."

<hr />

TO Gillian's astonishment, Lucius had not given up his objections.

"You must not do this," he said to Ulric as they reached the foot of the cliff. "This barter you plan is wrong." The silver-haired *upyr* blocked their path up the wall—or he blocked Ulric's; if Gillian chose, she could fly.

"Have you taken over the pack then?" Ulric asked with an edge of threat. "Is that why you eavesdrop on my thoughts without my leave? Is that why you seek to rule me?"

"Rule yourself, Ulric. Gillian's heart is not yours to command. You are asking for unhappiness if you proceed. For both of you."

Ulric bristled, but Lucius faced him without fear. Behind him, the wall of weathered stone echoed the gray of his eyes. Veins of gentler blue enlivened his iris, but nothing else about him was soft. The last of the starlight limned lean, hard muscles layered perfectly on his frame. He barely seemed to breathe, he was so calm.

Gillian had never seen Lucius challenge their leader directly—though he often went his own way. Ulric had always allowed this. Out of tolerance, she had thought, but maybe it was caution. She recalled the book she had seen in Brother Kenelm's memory, the thick parchment volume that called him Lucius the White. Once upon a time, he had been an *upyr* to merit special mention. *I allowed myself to forget,* Lucius had said the night she left the pack. Was he finally beginning to remember, and reclaim, the power he had possessed?

If he was, he would not do it now. Muttering under his breath, he stepped aside to let them pass. Though his interference had been unwelcome, Gillian had to admit some part of her felt let down.

"Never mind him," said Ulric, gripping her arm. "We have an elder to summon before dawn."

EDMUND haunted his brother's bedside, watching him slip in and out of fretful awareness. A day had passed, then two, with no sign of Gillian's return. They propped him on a mound of pillows to help him breathe. The fall of night seemed to ease his symptoms, as if Aimery's strength were indeed linked to the *upyr's*.

That Nim Wei had been right hardly eased his mind. He feared she would be right about the rest as well. Aimery would die unless she changed him, and Edmund could not foresee his brother accepting that.

Sir John, his seneschal, came to check on Aimery, and to attempt to conduct some of the business Edmund had left undone. Edmund answered his queries with half his attention. "I trust you," he said, and Sir John went away.

Robin was harder to put off, so Edmund did not try. He let his youngest son scramble onto his lap, then held him while they kept vigil. The boy was quiet, and Edmund took surprising comfort in his warmth. Though he was too young to stay for long, he always kissed Edmund before he left, a quick, shy press of lips to his increasingly stubbled jaw. "I love you, Father," he would whisper, and Edmund would smooth his hair.

Claris he did not wish to see at all, even if—by all accounts—she had been unusually docile in recent days. She was confined to her chamber under guard. Though Edmund was aware Aimery's illness must cause her pain, he did not consider letting her visit. She did not know it yet, but as soon as she bore their child, he intended to send her away. He would engage a wet nurse. Come to that, he would mother the babe himself rather than leave it to Claris. She could return to her family or join a convent; Edmund did not care which. Though he was not vengeful, he worried he might become so if she remained.

His sons did not need to see him war with their mother.

"Always loved you," came a mumble from the bed. "You are his father. Robin is just afraid you do not love him."

Edmund's gaze went to the window. The inclement weather had rumbled off, leaving the sky awash in amber and blue and green. Against this backdrop, clouds like scraps of carded wool glowed pink. Sunset had arrived. Aimery might be lucid now for a while.

Knowing he might not get another chance to say what he must, Edmund scooted closer on the step beside Aimery's bed. "I am sorry," he said, taking his brother's pallid hand. "If my behavior had not pushed Claris to the edge, if my envy had not led me to try to best you in a fight, none of this would have happened."

Aimery returned his clasp with a twitch of too-cold fingers. "You are not to blame for Claris's choices. As to that, I made choices of my own."

"Not like I did." Edmund had to swallow before going on. "We have never spoken of this, but I think it is time we do. That day at Poitiers—"

"No." Aimery rolled his head against the pillows. "That is water under the mill."

"It is not," Edmund insisted. "Sometimes I think everything I am, everything we are, began that day. I was terrified, you know, even before we left the ship. The *chevauchée* I could stand because, awful as it was, there never was much danger to us. But battle . . . It was all I could do not to piss my braies.

"When you rallied the archers to help Audley halt the French advance, I could cheerfully have killed you. We were safe where we were, more or less. We had orders to keep our position. Our ranks were diminished from the last attack. No one would have faulted us for remaining.

"I still remember your words, so unpretentious and unadorned. 'We do not have to be heroes,' you said. 'We only have to help turn the tide. Who is with me?' you said. 'Who wants to be done with this fight today?' And they followed you, a boy of just fifteen. Simple Welshmen and peasants, with their bows and their knives against armored knights.

"A handful and I were all who stayed. I told myself someone had to hold the rise. I told myself we could not all hare off like madmen. But as I watched you hack your way through the thick of it, as I watched you take lives and save them with equal coolness, as I watched you join those who captured the enemy's king, my heart grew black. I knew there was only one reason I stood where I did.

"I was a coward. And you were not. I resented you until I was sick with it because you were—because you are—a braver man than I. Worse, I am not the only one who knows it. Half of Bridesmere saw me fall short. Even if they do not speak of it to my face, I know what some of them are thinking. I love you, Aimery, as much as I have hated you, but I cannot swear, not truly, that some dark part of me did not want my sword to go where it did."

Tears rolled down his face by the time he finished, and Edmund did not hide them. It was Aimery who reached up to brush them aside.

"Brother," he said softly, "how you torture yourself for being human! Will you not give yourself credit for the good you have done? For treating me with respect despite your feelings? For letting me share your family and your home? Maybe you held back that day, but you did not run. That is what a true coward would have done. Those men who were there, those soldiers you believe are judging you, probably know the truth better than you do. Most men fear death, Edmund. Most men are more like you than me.

"I do not know why, for me, battle holds little terror. I suspect it is an accident of my birth, like my height or the color of my eyes. Maybe I do have berserker's blood. In any case, if you must put me on a pedestal, at least do so for something I had to learn."

Aimery's breath sighed out as if this speech had tired him. When he continued, it was with a wry, self-mocking smile. "As long as we are trading confessions, you should hear mine. I, too, have drunk envy's bitter draught. Have you not guessed how much it pleases me that some people think I would rule better in your place? So much I can scarcely admit it to myself. It is my consolation for being the second son. And it is not even true. You are the ruler Bridesmere needs. You steer her through the waters of a world I do not hope to grasp, a world that runs by trade as much as by swords. Do you honestly believe I could think like a merchant? You are lord here, not by birth but by merit. If you were not, someone would have usurped your place long ago. Soldiers can be hired. Your gifts are rarer than that."

Edmund let his brow fall to Aimery's hand. He felt shaken and emptied out, not convinced precisely but infinitely more at peace. "Saints above," he said, "what a pair."

Aimery laughed but his nightly surge of strength was clearly spent. His breath grew shallower, his face more pale. Edmund felt such a wrench he hardly knew how to bear it.

"Please let Nim Wei change you," he begged. "She is not as evil as your Gillian thinks."

Aimery's eyelids fluttered as if opening them were a trial. "Would you let her change you," he rasped, "if you thought it would make the darkest part of you destroy the light?"

He drifted off before his brother could answer.

"God help me," he whispered to no one but himself. "God help me, I do not know."

AURICLUS arrived at the cave within minutes of nightfall the following evening. Because Gillian had succumbed to exhausted sleep, Ulric was obliged to shake her awake. She lay alone in the wall niche in his room, just as she had when she collapsed the previous dawn. Nonetheless, she examined the furs that were piled around her. The imprint of Ulric's body flattened the bearskin nearest the edge.

The pack leader's mouth tightened with annoyance. "It is my bed. Would you have me sleep on the floor?"

She did not answer, merely raked her curls back and sat up. She was glad she had found her old clothing in Ulric's chest. The idea that he had spent the day cuddled up to her naked flesh was too disquieting to entertain.

Aimery's were the only arms that should protect or invade her rest.

With a grimace, she pushed away the thought. She had different realities to treat with now. "Where is he?" she asked.

Ulric knew she meant Auriclus. "He is in the fountain chamber. He wishes to speak to you alone."

"Then I shall go," said Gillian.

Though she felt Ulric's eyes on her as she went, she refused to share her nervousness with him.

Whatever she expected, it was not the stranger who stood by the ancient, bubbling well. Lit by the strange blue radiance of the water, his hair was dark and shaggy, his eyes a measuring squint. His skin was, of all things, toasted golden by the sun. His clothes, an assortment of peasant's rags, looked as if they had been dragged through a desert. He did not resemble an *upyr,* much less the king of them all.

"Cairo," he said, which he must have thought was an explanation. With an impatient wave of his hand, he magicked away the dirt, sandy puffs of it scurrying down the undyed cloth as if they were being chased. This, and the distinctive mellowness of his voice, jarred her memory. This was Auriclus, after all, the *upyr* who had changed her, who had hauled her the length of England in a week.

With a flush of embarrassment, she realized she had put another face on him in her mind, the face of her human father. Now he put his hands on his hips. His gaze traveled over her like a shopkeeper taking stock.

"You look well," he said. "Ulric took good care of you."

It should have been a question. Instead, he was patting his own back. Gillian's anger rose toward her throat.

"Ulric would take good care of anyone," she said stiffly.

"But better care of you." His hands closed on her shoulders and his smile lent warmth to his distant eyes. Gillian fought not to let that warmth tug at her heart.

"Would you have come were you not in debt to him?" she blurted out.

Auriclus wound one of her curls around his finger. "That question is irrelevant. Without Ulric, you would not have known how to reach me."

"But would you have done it for my sake? Would you have saved the man I love for me?"

He released the curl to cup her cheek in his cool, smooth hand. "I will *consider* saving the man you love. If I do it, it will be because of him, because of who he is. Only his nature can decide me. And that is as it should be, Gillian. Each prospective child must be judged on his or her own."

Her anger bled away. His response might not satisfy her pride, but he was right. She wondered if this was how Nim Wei felt when her demands were refused.

Auriclus must have picked up the thought. "You are your own person," he said. "You should not compare yourself to her."

This was hardly the same as declaring Gillian immune to Nim Wei's faults. Shaking her head, she laughed quietly to herself. However good or bad she had ended up, she should have been beyond her need for this man's approval.

"Are you ready to depart?" she said to the elder's inquiring glance. "I would like to be on our way."

"Yes," he said with just a hint of surprise.

Perhaps she deceived herself, but in his answer she also thought she heard respect.

Nineteen

THE *upyr* came in the dead of night to whisper her seductions, more like a dream of dangerous beauty than a woman of flesh and blood. Aimery did not know when his brother left, but Nim Wei found him alone. She held his bed hangings back so she could stand above him, her fingers luminous on the brocade.

"You know you cannot last much longer," she said with fatal sweetness. "Everyone can see it. Death has you in her claws."

He felt those claws as she spoke, cold and hard, pushing a bit of panic into his chest. During the day, when he was weakest, he might have succumbed to her suggestion. Now he found the stubbornness to resist.

"You are Death," he said.

Her black hair hissed when she shook her head. "I am Life, long life, with the woman you love by your side." The back of one cool finger traced his scar. "I know you must have thought: What can this perfect creature see in me? But imagine if you were as flawless as Gillian, if you were as strong and quick. That is the gift I bring."

Her face was an oval of white floating in the darkness, her eyes like polished obsidian within the glow.

"She made me promise," he said. "I told her I would hold fast."

"Hold fast until you die, you mean? Your beloved is not here. She cannot come quickly enough to save you. Do you want to leave her behind the way her father did, the way Auriclus leaves every child he sires?" When he lifted his hands to cover his ears, Nim Wei pulled them down. Nighttime or no, he lacked the strength to stop her. "What difference does it make who changes you," she demanded, "as long as you survive? I thought you loved her, Aimery. I thought you were the one who cared."

"I care enough to give her the man I am, as opposed to the monster you would make me."

"Nonsense." The *upyr* laughed, though he sensed his argument had annoyed her. "I am no more a monster than your lover. A killer perhaps, but most of the men you know would admit to that. Come. I know you must be weary. Let me help. Invite me to change you and all your pain will cease."

She was working some kind of magic with her words, increasing his pain, adding to the weight of his aching limbs. Or maybe his mind was playing tricks. Gillian had said her bite would protect him.

"Stop it," he ordered, just in case, and Nim Wei's eyes widened in surprise.

Disgusted as much by his weakness as by her, Aimery pushed off the covers and sat up. The *upyr* took a quick step back, as if she thought he meant to attack her. The response amused him. He was lucky he had strength to stand.

That was when the pieces added up. Nim Wei was afraid of Gillian and, through her, afraid of him. With anyone else, she would have done what she chose without hesitation. In truth, she would not have cared if he lived or died. She asked his permission because she feared Gillian's reaction if she did not. Because Gillian loved him. Because Gillian had lent him her power. Maybe Nim Wei thought he could rally enough to harm her.

"What are you doing?" she demanded as he swung, grinning and wobbly, to the floor.

"Chamber pot," he said, which shut her up quite nicely.

Her silence felt like a triumph, as did standing on his feet. He had been lying in that bed too long. He had forgotten how much his plain old human body could still do. *Maybe I can hold on,* he thought, *and if I cannot, at least I can die like a man.* He would not give Gillian cause for shame.

As he finished his business, Nim Wei moved toward the window. She opened the shutters and looked out. Her air of attention captured his.

"Who has come?" he asked, but she simply held up her hand.

Aimery tried to listen as closely. Though he heard nothing, he noted a curious thickening in the air, a pulse of what he could only describe as power. The phenomenon seemed distant but immense, like a storm building across a plain. Different threads twined through the tension. They touched his awareness as scents: trees lashed by rain, lightning, earth soaked down to mud. Taken alone, and in common measure, none was cause for alarm. Taken like this, Aimery's scalp crawled with sensation and the back of his neck drew tight. He fumbled into a shirt and hose. By the time a howl split the silence, his dagger was in his hand.

Gillian's pack had come to Bridesmere. Aimery lurched to the door with that knowledge clear in his mind. He did not know how he would do it, but he had to be certain Gillian was safe.

"You do not have to go out there," Nim Wei said with obvious exasperation. "You do not have to turn to *him*."

Since she did not physically restrain him, he ignored her.

As long as he held the wall, he found he could manage the tower stairs. To his surprise, Nim Wei followed him down. Perhaps she could not resist facing her old foe. He noticed she remained a few steps behind. Given his invalid's progress, she could not have been hoping he would protect her. He suspected that, whatever threat was gathering, she meant him to face it first.

His apprehension did not lift when he got outside. Though the weather had been clear all day, mist now cloaked the castle grounds. Moonlit curls of it rose from the dew-decked grass. The sight was beautiful but eerie, the silver tendrils seeming to sniff the air. Unnerved by the muffled silence and the sense of being watched, Aimery led the way to the gate. Halfway there the first body tripped him. Shaking, he struggled to his feet. To his horror this obstruction was not the last. As if the fog held some dire enchantment, every guard they passed was sound asleep. Green recruits and veterans alike appeared to have crumpled where they stood. Their fall should have made a sound, but it had not. They were not even snoring. Aimery touched a few to assure himself that they breathed.

"Auriclus," Nim Wei whispered, the name a mingling of fear and awe.

If she was afraid, Aimery knew he ought to be as well. Could a being who exercised such power really be a safer choice than Nim Wei? Were it not for his vow to Gillian, Aimery might have turned back from finding out.

His skin was bathed in sweat by the time they reached the portcullis that barred the main gate.

Beyond the protective ditch where the mist began to thin, and within the curving walls of the barbican, three men waited in perfect, inhuman stillness. Gillian stood with them, dressed in a gown she must have stowed in the woods before she left. Though Aimery's heart leapt at the sight of her, he was taken aback by the presence of so small a force. That these few accounted for all the sleepers made him wish for his sword. Never mind he was too weak to wield it; it would have made for a better show.

He took mixed comfort in the fact that only one of the men wore clothes. At least he knew the naked ones were unarmed.

The man in the peasant garb was not the tallest of them, nor the strongest in build. The blond who had his arm around Gillian's shoulder was both more robust and fairer of face, and the silver-haired one was more elegant. Though their proximity to Gillian irked him, Aimery spared them but a glance. Unlike the others, the clothed one's skin bore no pearlescent glow. Either he was good at glamours like Gillian, or felt no need to show off. He was, however, completely arresting. By some trick of vision, despite the darkness and the distance, the moss green color of his eyes flared bright. For a second, when his gaze met Aimery's, the younger man could not breathe.

He knew this *upyr* had to be Auriclus.

Fear and doubt nudged him again. Could Aimery be trusted with even a shadow of this man's power?

"We can come in if you like," said the famous elder. "Or if it is more convenient, you may come out."

His voice was so rich, so good and wise and kingly, Aimery nearly fell to his knees. With an effort, he reminded himself these manners were mere formality in a being who could spell a castle to sleep. Better, he thought, to meet the titan on his feet.

"I will come out," he said just as politely. "I do not want to disturb the keep."

Nim Wei had to help him raise the gate; he had not strength enough on his own. She did not protest his choice, merely shook her head. Accepting her aid was strange, feeling—even briefly—that she might mean him well. With a grimace, he pushed the thought away. Gillian had chosen Auriclus and he admired who she had become. If she had equal faith in Aimery, he owed her an open mind.

His resolve was steadier than his knees as he crossed the drawbridge to meet her sire. He had promised to let this creature transform him, but until this moment the enormity of that decision had not sunken in.

Maybe he will refuse me, he thought. Maybe he will take one look and change his mind.

And maybe you will change yours, he thought.

The prospect made him uneasy, though he saw no point in denying it. Breathing harder, he stepped onto the trampled grass. He expected Gillian to run to him, but she did not. Perhaps she, too, had doubts about what would come. *I love you,* he thought at her. *Whatever happens, remember that.*

GILLIAN knew her immobility perplexed him but, as it was, she could barely bring herself to meet his eyes. Now that she saw

Aimery, in the weak but courageous flesh, her contract with Ulric seemed wrong. She should have bargained harder, should have demanded he do the boon for love.

After all Aimery had been through, he was not going to like this. As if Ulric sensed her second thoughts, his arm tightened around her back. He had no intention of letting her greet the man she loved. Gillian fought her inclination to shake free. It was too late to change their arrangement. She had given her word. Aimery would discover the truth soon enough. Hiding it now was cowardly.

Instead, she turned her attention to her sire. Everything depended on his judgment of Aimery's worth. Not one to quail, Aimery faced the elder with his head held high. His face was pale as parchment, his feet braced wide. He swayed slightly as he stood. She would not have been surprised if force of will were all that kept him from toppling over. Despite this disadvantage, she had the distinct impression that he was judging her maker. The suspicion made her proud, but also afraid.

She was uncertain how Auriclus would take it.

"You are Aimery," Auriclus said in the way that made every syllable sound important. "I hear you want to be one of us."

"I want to live," Aimery confirmed, "but I am willing to die if that seems best." His gaze flickered to Gillian and then returned. "There is someone I would regret leaving behind."

"Our path is not an easy one," Auriclus intoned. "I cannot promise you will always be glad."

"Ballocks," Nim Wei spat. She had stepped up beside Aimery to steady his elbow, a kindness for which Gillian was tempted to thank her. "If you hated our path so much, you would have gotten off it long ago. Honestly, Auriclus, you do not even want this one. Why must you interfere?"

Auriclus pulled himself straighter but, as always, his voice was calm. "Two of my children requested that 'interference.'"

Nim Wei curled her lip. "Yes, and I am sure you would be leaping to help 'your children' were it not me they stood against."

"I care for all who—"

"Tell your nursery tales to someone else, *Father*. You care about looking noble. You care about paying back the *upyr* on whose doorstep you like to dump your chosen ones. But Ulric only called you because he wants to blackmail Gillian into his bed. How noble is that, I ask? How honorable a reason to give this human eternity?"

"And your motivations are honorable? To shift the balance of power by putting your mark on the human my child loves? Tell me, daughter, how long before you use him to steal my secrets? Before you try to poison them both against me?"

Nim Wei tossed her hair behind her back. "I am what I am," she said. "I pretend to nothing else."

"Do you not? I am prepared to be judged by the character of my children. Can you say the same?"

The two elders were nose to nose. It was hard to imagine Auriclus glaring, but his expression was precious close. The air buzzed with tiny stings of power. They seemed to have forgotten Aimery's existence.

He, however, had heard every telling word. Gillian bit her lip as he narrowed his eyes at the warring pair, then crossed the mist-veiled slope to her. Every step was halting, but he prevailed. Jaw hard, he stared at Ulric's hold on her shoulder, then at her.

Gillian could have crawled underground.

"I wonder that I even need to confirm this," he said with a tartness that made her wince, "but on the remote chance that I am mistaken, I shall ask. You agreed to lie with this man, your former lover, in return for Auriclus making me an *upyr*."

"No!" said Gillian.

"No?"

His skepticism hurt, but she squared her shoulders. "I would have agreed to it if I had to, but I did not. I promised only to stay with him, to keep him company for a year and not have contact with you."

"I see." He squeezed the bridge of his nose. "Only for a year."

His face had darkened like a storm. Gillian felt a stab of worry that he would spend his strength on this. "I am sure I should not be upset. What is a piffling year to an immortal being? For that matter, what is love? It must wear thin after a century or two. Really, I should be grateful you gave me the time you did."

"No," she protested, reaching for him with one beseeching hand. "I do love you. I always shall. Ulric did not want to help us. This was the only way I could enlist his aid."

"And quite a sacrifice!" Aimery shot his rival a bitter glance. "Since you dislike him so much you have slept with him for years already."

Without turning her head, Gillian knew Ulric was smirking. Disgusted, she peeled his hand from her arm. "How can you believe I would lie with him just like that?" she said. "After what we shared. I told you how I felt about Ulric and that it was in the past. I want you to live. I want to know you are in the world even if you never forgive me. Maybe you think this proves my love is weak—certainly Ulric is counting on that—but I know my love is strong. One year or a hundred will make no difference to my heart. You will always be the man I love."

Aimery closed his eyes. "I cannot look at this the way you do. That you can even stand to be near him . . . That you would give him the right to keep us apart . . ."

While Gillian tried to compose an answer, Ulric spoke into the pause. "Maybe," he said in a soft, sly tone, "you are afraid she would be reluctant to return to your arms from mine."

Aimery gave the pack leader no warning; he simply opened his eyes and leapt. Even with a warning, Ulric might not have moved. Aimery could barely stand and here he was attacking an *upyr*. Ulric blocked him easily but Aimery struggled on—out of anger or pride or who knew what basic male need. Unfortunately, whatever drove him could not give him the strength to win.

"Stop," Gillian ordered, trying to catch their wrestling arms. "Both of you stop and think."

Neither man acted as if he heard. With a grunt of triumph, Ulric locked Aimery's head beneath his arm. Aimery's face went red at the pressure. Even worse, Ulric looked maddened enough to twist it off. Auriclus might have taught the pack not to harm humans, but Gillian was not sure she trusted that lesson now. Ulric's lip was curled back in a distinctively wolfish snarl. His incisors were sharp as knives.

"Help me!" Gillian implored the others, knowing she could not subdue the pack leader alone.

"They must find their own way," said Auriclus.

"Do not look at me," was Nim Wei's amused dismissal. "He is not my wolf."

To her dismay, Lucius also seemed entertained. "Wait," he said, lifting one finger as if testing the wind. "The fight is not over yet."

Aghast, Gillian moved to grab them both herself when Aimery dipped his shoulder and caught the *upyr*'s ankle with his heel. Taken by surprise, Ulric crashed back. Gillian scarcely had time to gasp before Aimery's dagger pricked Ulric's throat.

"You shall not touch her," he hissed through gritted teeth. "She belongs with me."

There, in one small word, lay the difference between the men. Aimery believed Gillian belonged *with* him; Ulric demanded she belong *to*. While she doubted she would ever wrap Aimery around her finger, she knew with him she would have more adventures than she could alone. He would encourage her. He would support without trying to command.

If she lost him, she would never know the best she could be.

His hand shook as the point of his blade whitened Ulric's skin. The pack leader blinked at him in amazement, not frightened—for he could throw Aimery off in a heartbeat—but certainly impressed.

"You really do love her," he said, as if violence were the only proof he understood.

Aimery must have recognized the futility of his actions because he stumbled off his prize.

"Be damned to you both," he said, his breath coming in sobs, "if you think this bargain of yours has no cost."

Gillian watched Aimery's anger drain like water from a cracking dam. He fell to his knees and dropped the dagger. She would have gone to him if she could have moved. *Be damned to you both*, he had said. Did she deserve the curse? Had she been wrong to offer Ulric the remotest chance of winning her back? Was Aimery's view of the matter the one that counted most?

She did not see Lucius move, not even as a blur, but when she blinked he stood a foot from where Aimery had sunk to the ground. In no measurable time at all, he had moved at least four body lengths. *Upyr* could move swiftly, but not like this. Gillian shivered in surprise.

"What on earth?" muttered Auriclus and Nim Wei, for once in accord.

Lucius acted as if he had done nothing out of the way. He gazed consideringly at the fallen man, who could not know his little demonstration was unexpected. "If you truly loved her," Lucius said, "you would forgive her no matter what."

"Forgiving . . . not the problem," Aimery gasped. "Could not . . . forget." He lifted his eyes to hers, pleading for understanding. "Could you forget . . . if our positions were reversed?"

Gillian pressed her hands to her lips. If he promised to spend a year with Claris, or Gytha, would it not cross her mind that something might happen? Could she truly forget?

"I would try," she whispered, then dropped to the grass beside him. "I think . . . I believe I *would* trust you, and I know you can trust me. But I am sorry. I should have consulted you first. I thought this would be better than asking Nim Wei to change you. I knew that was a risk you were loathe to take."

"Is better," he conceded, and pulled her into his arms. His cheek rested on her head. "Maybe the best we can do."

She hated the defeat she heard in his tone. "Please have faith in my love," she begged. "And please have faith in yours. You are strong enough to get through this. In the end, we will be together and you will still be the man you are. Surely nothing matters more than that."

He stroked her curls with a quavering hand. "You are right," he said. "We will take the chance we are given and be grateful."

For some reason, this surrender made Lucius sigh out one of his own. "Damnation," he said to the misty air. "I thought at least one of you would prove too childish. But I see I must tell you what you have earned the right to know. Gillian can change you herself."

"No," said Nim Wei, a brush of hollowed sound.

"She would not dare!" exclaimed Auriclus.

Aimery merely gaped.

"Yes." Lucius's grimace of annoyance was at odds with his usual cool demeanor. "When it comes to transforming humans, inborn strength means as much as age. Gillian has that, probably more than is good for a being so young." He met Aimery's astonished stare. "You will steady each other, I think. Otherwise, I would keep this knowledge to myself."

"You should keep it to yourself," Auriclus fumed. "Though gods know how you have it. The secret of the change is a grave responsibility. How can one this young be ready for the burden?"

"Ready or not, the power is hers," Lucius said softly. "Even I could not take it away, only keep her in ignorance of what it can do."

He appeared not to notice Auriclus's wrath, no more than he had noticed Ulric's before. The greatest of them all, the *upyr* who made Nim Wei quail, might have been a gnat buzzing in the distance. Gillian could conceive of only one reason for Lucius to possess this assurance. She looked into his eyes and, for the space of a breath, felt as if she were falling. He was old, older than anything she could imagine.

"You are an elder," she breathed. "That is how you know this."

"Yes," Lucius admitted. He cocked his head at Auriclus and Nim Wei. "They were unaware of my origins. They assumed an earlier elder had made me, one of the last who gave themselves to the fire. I let them assume it, and then I let myself."

"But now you are remembering."

"It appears I cannot avoid it. Ever since you joined the pack and began asking your endless questions, my mind has been waking up. I cannot fight it anymore. I have begun to care about the mess those two are trying to make of our world. You taking your place as their equal will at least give them something new to squabble about."

"Squabble!" said Auriclus, but Gillian barely heard.

Lucius said she could take her place as Auriclus and Nim Wei's equal. Surely he could not mean that. Hugging Aimery's waist, she looked instinctively for his reaction. He smiled at her and shrugged, seeming to understand how overwhelmed she was, if not how afraid.

Why not? said his expression. *Why not you as well as them?* Reasons why not swarmed in her mind, but she could not utter a one. She had wanted power, had wanted safety, and now it looked as if both had been hers all along. Could she really claim to be sorry? Was she not, in her heart, secretly glad?

"I do not know how to change a mortal," she confessed, unable to prevent herself from sounding lost. "No one ever taught me."

Lucius crouched before her, his stone-gray eyes surprisingly warm. "No one taught you how to take your familiar."

She sensed he was giving her the secret, telling her the process was the same. She did not feel him search her, but he nodded at the silent guess.

"It cannot be that simple," she said.

"But it is. When the power of an elder fills an open heart, the change is as easy as falling in love."

"Ha," barked Nim Wei.

Lucius smiled but did not turn. "She has loved," he said to Gillian. "That is why she hates so well."

Nim Wei made some noise—disgust, denial. It rolled off Gillian's back like so much water. A part of her knew this was extraordinary: that she was able to ignore her nemesis and her sire.

Maybe later Gillian would remember her old caution. For now she felt drunk with freedom and hope.

"Will you help me?" she asked her ally.

Lucius patted her shoulder. "If I help you, you will never know how strong you are. Trust your instincts. Then you will be beholden to no one, not even me."

"I do owe Auriclus something," she said, sneaking a look in his direction. The elder's expression was proud and cool. Gillian suspected he was still insulted at having been accused of squabbling.

Catching her thought, Lucius smiled. "You owe it to him to live the life he gave you with honor. It is up to you, however, to decide what honor means."

Aimery interrupted with a little cough. "Much as I am enjoying this discussion," he said, "it might be wise to get me inside—not that I am in danger of expiring this very moment."

"Aimery!" Gillian cried in guilty alarm.

"Indeed," said Lucius, moving to help him up.

One last protest stopped them before they left.

"Wait," said Ulric. He sounded lost, as if he could not believe the way events had turned out. "I need to talk to Gillian."

"Oh, Lord." Gillian sighed, but she was torn.

"I will look out for Aimery," Lucius offered. "You may speak to the pack leader if you wish."

"Yes," Aimery said. "If I were in his shoes, I would want to say good-bye."

Ulric muttered a curse that Gillian ignored. *I love you,* she mouthed to Aimery. *I know,* he mouthed back and grinned.

When she turned, with the glow of that acknowledgment in her face, she saw the pack leader stood apart from the others. Three strides took her to him. His throat worked a moment before he spoke. "Are you sure about this, Gillian? That you want to stay with this man? He is not even a lord."

"I love him," she said. "My life was good before I met him, but with him it is a gift. He fits who I am."

A muscle tightened in Ulric's jaw. His gaze fell to the grass. "Once you change him, are you planning on bringing him to the cave?"

"No." She touched his arm, a tentative brush of contact. She could not comfort him and she knew better than to try. "I would not do that to you. Aimery and I will find a home of our own."

He blew his breath out in a bitter laugh. "I am not certain which is worse: to see you again or not to." His voice lowered and roughened. "I believed we had a chance."

"I know you did." It seemed cruel to say any more. They had had a chance, just not a chance for what she shared with Aimery. "I should go."

"Yes," he said, and looked up one last time. His golden eyes shimmered in the dark. "Be happy, Gillian. If ever you need my aid, know you can ask."

"Thank you," she said, though for his sake, she hoped she would never have to.

Twenty

THE one with the silver hair carried Aimery back to his tower. Though Lucius had evaded Gillian's request for help, he was helping Aimery now. Strength flowed into Aimery's body everywhere the *upyr* touched, steadying his flagging will, making him feel less like one huge ache.

They moved so swiftly, the others were left behind.

Aimery knew they must look ridiculous: this slight man carrying the large with no more effort than if he were a child. Aimery would have walked had he been able, but his fight with the pack leader had exhausted him. Thankfully—if alarmingly—no one was awake to see. The household lay as they had when Aimery left.

Lucius hummed sympathetically as Aimery craned his neck to check on the sleepers. "Auriclus always did have a gift for controlling minds. The fog was mine. Much more artistic, I think."

His manner was so ordinary—if this word could be applied to an immortal being—not to mention so approachable that Aimery found the nerve to voice one of the questions that had been preying on his mind. "What about his clothes?"

"His clothes? Oh, you mean because Auriclus was dressed and we were not. He did not travel in his wolf form. He disembodied himself, clothes and all, then popped up here just as we arrived."

"But how could he do that?"

Lucius gave a little puff as he began climbing the stairs, though the purpose seemed more to focus his strength than because he was out of breath.

"No idea," he said. "Many of us transform into spirit to change our forms, but to actually send ourselves to a particular place when we have no body . . . I suppose that is one of the secrets I have forgotten. Or perhaps I never knew. We are not all born with the same gifts."

"Will Auriclus try to stop Gillian from claiming her power?"

"I doubt it," Lucius assured him. "You heard what he said about you and Ulric: 'They must find their own way.' Bit irresponsible, if you ask me, but I expect he will let her use whatever skills she can stumble onto."

"And Nim Wei?"

"That one is too cautious to interfere. She will not move until she sees which way the wind is blowing. By that time, with luck, Gillian will be secure."

Aimery had run out of air to ask any more. Neither spoke again until Lucius laid him on his bed, a bed he was growing heartily sick of. He promised himself he would burn it for kindling once he was well.

For the first time in a while, it looked as if he would be able to keep his word.

The *upyr* shook his head at the tangled covers, or perhaps at his pathetic state, then turned toward the door. Though Lucius had been nothing but kind to Aimery, he must have had some look on his face that warned the other *upyr* they best not stay. They retreated with amusing haste, like children who feared a scold. Only Gillian entered the room.

Aimery was about to greet her when Auriclus turned back. It appeared to take an effort. The elder grabbed onto the door frame as if some force were trying to blow him back. "It is not too late," he said to Gillian with a grimace. "I can still change your lover for you."

"No," she said quietly. "I think it is time I become responsible for myself. But I shall not forget what you and Ulric taught me. Those rules that seem good, Aimery and I will follow."

Though Auriclus sighed at this, he departed.

Lucius took his leave by holding Gillian's face between his hands and kissing her forehead. "Do not be afraid," he said and tapped her chest. "Everything you need to know is in here."

This did not seem like much in the way of guidance, but Gillian nodded.

She walked to the bed, sat on the mattress and took his hand. "I am sorry," she said, "for trying to make decisions that affect your life without consulting you."

Aimery squeezed her fingers. Her apology encouraged him to make his own. "I would have done the same," he admitted, "if I thought it was the only way to save you. And I should have trusted you to be true. You have shared your secrets with me, and accepted mine. On the other hand, I am very happy to be spared the sight of you in that arrogant bastard's arms."

"He is not really . . . at least, he is not completely an arrogant bastard. Some of his behavior he cannot help because of the nature of his wolf. A pack leader is not meant to take others' wishes into account. He is only meant to rule."

Aimery traced her hair around her brow. He knew how much she would have hated being ruled. "I realize it cost you something to go back to him, even if you do not find him repellent."

"It could have cost me everything I wanted before I met you."

"And now that you have met me, what do you want?"

Her eyes were wide and brilliant, like polished aquamarines. They sparkled as if she might be close to tears. "I still want what I did before: to learn, to see the world, to be independent. But I want to share my pleasure in those things with you, and I also want you to share your pleasures with me. Whatever you hope to accomplish, I want to help you attain. I want us to be a team."

"A team," he repeated, strangely warmed by the word.

She nodded with an enthusiasm that reminded him of their first conversation in this room. "Yes. I do not want to be a queen or a prize. I want to be a partner."

"Princess might have something to say about your not being a queen."

This inspired a flash of humor. "Well, maybe I would like that just a little. I cannot help my nature, either." Her grin faded as she rubbed a spot above her eyebrow. "It is so odd to think that I can change you. That is, if you still want me to." She held her breath, obviously determined to do what she believed was right, and just as obviously hoping she would not have to.

Aimery laughed. "Of course I want you to. How could I wish to leave this world when you are in it?"

"You are not afraid anymore of what turning *upyr* will do to you?"

"Oddly enough, no." He touched her cheek. "Meeting your fellow *upyr* made me realize how much they are like humans, very powerful humans, but still as good and bad, as wise and foolish as anyone else. When I think of Auriclus's face after Lucius accused him of squabbling—! If he can handle this responsibility, so can I.

And I think your friend, Lucius, is right. We will steady each other, keep each other true to what we want to be. I would be honored to share a bit of your nature."

A hint of color washed her cheek, a reaction he found inordinately endearing. He was glad he could flatter her, though he knew she deserved every word.

"We will have to leave Bridesmere once you are changed," she said.

"I know, and I will miss my home, but perhaps it is time to move on. My brother and I reached an understanding while you were gone. Who knows how long it would last if I remained?"

As they shared a crooked smile, a wave of gratitude flooded through him. No one could deserve this good fortune. He could only cherish it with all his might.

"You must open your heart," she instructed almost shyly, her hand cupped gently over his chest.

He covered her fingers with his own. "With you," he said, "my heart is never closed."

The last of her doubt left her at his touch. Lucius had said the power was in her, but it was Aimery's faith that made her believe. She knew how to do this, how to let go of her separate being, how to enter a reality where all living things were one. Like smoke in a breeze, she allowed her barriers to dissolve. This time there was no shock, just a sense of coming home. This was what they all were deep inside. Stars and wishes. A glimmer of self-awareness. An emptiness filled with a sea of peace.

Be with me, she thought to Aimery's mind. *See what lies beyond.*

He came like an otter sliding down a bank. He was beautiful in that other, truer place: a shower of golden sparks, a song like an angel's sigh. He smelled of pepper and honey, she of lilacs. Their star selves moved together in the void and became something greater still. Two halves. One whole. They had rocked in this sea before. She remembered, though she could not count the span.

My other heart, he thought, *the one whose spirit was born with mine.*

And then there was no "I." There was only them, lost in the world behind the world. She sensed other beings, each like a color or a bit of music. Alien, and yet the same. One by one they passed like giant ships, communicating, she thought, but not with words. Princess seemed to understand them better than she.

Good, the falcon trilled with satisfaction. *Big happy good.*

Gillian did not know how long they floated, but it was Aimery who called them back.

We cannot stay here, he said with a sadness that mysteriously did not hurt. *This is not where we belong. Not now. Not for a long time yet.*

No, she agreed, *not for a long time yet.*

Twenty-one

WHEN Aimery saw Gillian turn to stars, he was too caught up in wonder to be afraid. This is what people are, he thought. Everything else is illusion.

Afterward, the experience felt like a dream, but he knew he would never forget it. He could not say the place had been heaven and yet he could not say it was not. Being there, sensing those form-less creatures, humbled him in an oddly reassuring way. Someone is watching out for us, he thought, someone greater than anyone will ever ask me to be.

The world beyond the world had heroes of its own.

His return to everyday reality was startling. He came to himself with a jolt, as if he had dropped the last few inches to the bed. His skin felt like it was being stuck all over with tiny burrs—too full of life somehow, too full of energy and well-being. Even as he thought this, the glittery version of Gillian pulled out tingling from his flesh. Her body was as transparent as a ghost. When she smiled, she turned solid again, just as she had been before. She even sat where she sat before. The only difference was that her gown now lay beneath her.

She touched his face with admiring hands. "You are so pretty," she said.

He looked down at himself, wondering what she could mean. His skin was glowing. When she had separated their bodies, she must have left some of her starry essence behind.

Struck dumb, he lifted his hands and turned them back and forth. The tiny scratches and marks he always collected in his work had disappeared. His skin was pale but not the pale of an ailing man. Gold tinged its whiteness, like a pot of the richest cream. He was like her now. After all their worry, he was like her.

"You did it," he said and his voice was different, too: clearer, stronger, closer to a minstrel's expressive tones. He laughed, tempted to test if he could sing.

Her eyes gleamed in response. "I suppose I need not ask you how you feel."

"I feel wonderful," he said and leapt out of the bed. Without even trying, he landed halfway across the room. Wanting to be sure he had not imagined the effect, he jumped and touched the ceiling. His old scarred knee did not even creak.

"This is just the beginning," she said at his expression of amazed delight. "Imagine if you turn out to be as strong an *upyr* as you were a human."

"I want to try everything," he declared, almost bursting with excitement. The feeling was unlike him. He attempted to rein it in and be serious. "We should test our limits, one by one, as if we were new recruits. We should discover where each of our talents lie. Maybe mine does lie in my muscles, but we should know for sure."

"Oh, quite," Gillian agreed, eyes twinkling despite her sober tone. "I cannot believe I had not thought to do so before."

"It is important. We must know how much we dare."

When she laughed at his insistence, her happiness ran through him in a bubbling stream. "You know," she said, "you are allowed to enjoy yourself a little first."

He had to sit. His head was spinning with marvels. He dropped cross-legged where he was on the bare, cold stone. Even that was a pleasure as his nerves took in details they never could have before.

"You," he said, "are lovelier than I dreamt."

With his new *upyr* eyes, he saw that her glow had colors, delicate veils of green and rose. He gazed at her, entranced, while the rose grew deeper and turned to red. The color pulsed at her breasts and throat, at her belly and between her thighs. When he realized what this might mean, his body flashed hot as coal.

Gillian rubbed one finger across her lips, obviously hiding a smile. "So," she said, "care to see what else is more enjoyable as an *upyr*?"

The question inspired a forceful throbbing in his loins. The surge of lust was so powerful, he dared not move. His fingers dug into his knees as he fought his compulsion to ravage her where she sat. If he had worried about being too rough before, how much more was there to fear now that he possessed this unnatural strength? His very skin was itching to drive inside her.

"Perhaps you need encouragement," she suggested with a husky laugh. She trailed her hand down the inner curve of her breast, then up the pale slope to her nipple. Her flesh tightened there, and furled, like a cinnamon colored rosebud.

Aimery swallowed before he moved, but when he moved it was quick as lightning. His hands found her lissome waist, his mouth the peak of her breast. He was kneeling between her legs on the lowest step of the bed. His erection surged like living stone, and his new instincts urged him to bite the flesh he sucked. A stinging in his gums signaled the rapid lengthening of his teeth—yet more evidence of arousal. How did other *upyr* bear this? Why did they ever leave their beds? Helpless to resist, he scraped his incisors across her skin. To his delight, her scent grew musky and dark.

"Yes." She sighed, her fingers pushing through his hair. "Taste me. Taste my life."

He gave in even as he swore he would not. Waves of dizzying pleasure swept through his soul. Her silky skin, her warmth, the sweetness of her blood drowned him with sensations he could not name. It was an orgasm of the mouth, an intimacy deeper than sex. Her emotions rolled through him as if they were his own: gladness and desire, tenderness and grateful awe. Since the night he had discovered her by his bed, she had wanted him to understand what this pleasure was.

She moaned and he released her.

"Take it back," he whispered, baring his throat. "Take your blood back from me."

Her pupils nearly swallowed her eyes. Her hand stroked the mark he had made on her breast as if she liked the reminder. She leaned forward and wet her lips. His body tensed with anticipation. She touched his neck.

Her mouth was petal soft, her teeth a piercing fire. He almost climaxed just from her bite. His erection jumped and stretched while she draped him in her sable curls. She made an art of feeding, a slow, sensual pull, a lapping of her tongue, a shivering drag of fingers up and down his back. Every touch awakened new sets of nerves. He was quivering with sensitivity by the time she let him go with a drunken laugh.

"You taste the same as you did before," she said, "like the best wine in the world." Her hand slipped down his belly to find his sex. He gasped as one smooth fingernail traced a vein. "This, however, may be different. I think you have grown, love, or at least grown more responsive."

He could not speak through her caresses. Her strokes and squeezes seemed to lengthen him in his skin. She pulled cries from him even as she pulled ecstasy from his flesh. When she cupped his balls, his thoughts unraveled. With a groan of need, he rose and lifted her from the bed.

Whatever changes she might have noticed, she showed no fear. She gripped his shoulders with her silken arms, his hips with her strong, smooth thighs. They kissed as if only this could save them. Her breasts flattened against his chest and his cock pressed her abdomen. It was not nearly enough to ease his need. The heat of her sex demanded he join their bodies. He carried her with long, impatient strides, not even knowing what he sought.

And then he found it. He entered her just as the wall met her writhing back. Deep he thrust, hard, filling her with his cock. She clung to him like a glove. The ache was unbelievable, the relief of being inside her. Both his hands gripped her bottom while his lips pulled back for a growl. This, *this* was what he craved. Gillian sighed with satisfaction even as her hips begged him for more. He drew back and drove in again. Gillian gave in to abandon. Her arms flung outward. Her head tipped back.

"More," she said. "Faster. Pound me, Aimery. Pound me into the wall."

He was half afraid to do it. He licked her throat, her lips. He ground his molars and wondered if he were going mad. Then, because he *would* go mad if he did not, he gave her what she asked. Chips of plaster split off at the barrage and a crack whined through a stone. His body burned, his hands. She gasped, a warning, a promise. He pushed deeper, finding a spot no one but he would ever reach. The secret touch flung her over the edge. Her body shuddered with climax, milking him so violently, so deliciously, his knees gave way.

She did not seem to mind the fall.

"Again," she demanded, her heels thrusting her hips up from the floor.

He could not get enough, could not give enough. That he had not yet come seemed both torture and cause for amazement. How could one body contain such bliss? He drew her wrists over her head and pumped with demonic force. When his orgasm finally burst, the pulsing stabs of sensation were almost too much to bear. She rolled him beneath her with their hands still linked, nipping her way down his body, each sipping bite renewing his lust. When she wrapped her tongue around his shaft, he had to choke back a scream.

Again he came and again he wanted her even more. He crawled after her while she laughed, dragging her back by the ankles, not letting her reach the bed. Like animals they coupled with her on her hands and knees and him behind her, his palm cupping her breast, his mouth panting fire against her perspiring neck. His second hand caressed her mound of Venus until he found the tiny pennant of her desire. Beneath his fingers it was diamond hard. He stroked it, squeezed it, teased it to desperation as he sent himself deep and deliberate into her core. Suddenly, speed was not what he wanted. The tip of him rubbed and held against her womb.

"Aimery," she gasped, "why are you slowing down?"

"I am savoring this," he said, groaning as her body clutched him. "Savoring you."

She was heat wriggling around him, wet and slick and strong. He thrust and felt how her passage stretched, how she nearly could not take all he had.

"You were made for me," he whispered against her nape. "Made to take me." She quivered, almost at her pleasure. He captured her nipple between two fingers and a thumb. "Shall I tease you here, love? Shall I pinch you when you come?"

Her answer was a whimper. A subtle pulsing began between his brows, a delicate mental tap. *Feel,* said her voice inside his head. *Feel with me.* As he had when they drank from each other, he experienced a doubling of sensation. He was both entered and entering, touching as well as touched. The weight of his chest was an unexpected comfort, the sweat of his skin a call to lust. He sensed the tightening spiral of his nerves and the excitement it raised in her.

His climax loomed, immense, building from a flutter to a groaning pull swelling in his balls. The feelings rose until his throat was too tight even to cry out. She did it for him, hoarsely, and the world dissolved in a pool of gold. He shot and shot until he was spent.

The intensity of his pleasure robbed him of strength. After some minutes, he became aware he was on the floor flat on his back. Gillian snuggled atop him, one hand sweeping idly up and down his side.

"Bed next time," she said.

"Next time?" His tone inadvertently betrayed his horror. She had wrung him so dry, he might need an immortal lifetime to recover.

Gillian laughed and kissed his jaw. Her hand wandered lower to gather up his shaft. He gasped as her thumb found a nerve at the base he had thought for certain was dead. A moment later, the pad of her forefinger dug into something agonizingly sweet behind his scrotum. Had the spot been there before, or had turning *upyr* brought it into being? Aimery did not know, and could hardly care. As she expertly worked both points, he thickened and began to squirm.

"You wait," she teased, "soon enough you will beg."

Since he could not doubt her, he scooped her up and laid her on his bed, stroking her thighs apart with his hands. Her body arched in invitation. He slid into her softness with a lengthy sigh.

"Very well." She surrendered, her movements perfectly timed to his. "No begging tonight."

NIM Wei would never have found Auriclus on the ramparts had she not been able to trace his scent. She remembered how exotic that had seemed when she was human: a man who smelled not just like a forest, but like the forest of a foreign land.

Of course, more than his foreignness had drawn her. She had also desired his power. What poor village sorceress would not want that?

Now he stood in kingly isolation, gazing out across the shadowed land. He had allowed the household to awaken, but wove a glamour that kept him from being seen. Guards patrolled within a foot of him and never guessed he was there. She alone could breach his illusion.

Of course, he could also breach hers.

"It has been a long time," he said without turning.

Nim Wei did not respond. It was enough to stand beside him, to put her elbow next to his on the wall. This interlude between skirmishes was as close to a truce as they got. She watched the sheep sleeping in the grass under the eye of their keeper, a boy so drowsy his mind scarcely held more than those of his woolly charges.

One of Auriclus's fingers nudged her hand. "That human of yours guards his possessions well."

"He is not my human."

"But you would like him to be." Auriclus looked at her, a brief, sidling glance.

"What I would like him to be," she said carefully, "is none of your concern."

"He has responsibilities."

"That never stopped you from living as you please."

"Would it kill you to consider that I actually think out what I do?"

"Whether you have convinced yourself your actions are well thought out hardly matters to those you abandon."

"I did not abandon you," he said softly. "We would have killed each other if I stayed."

Tears she rarely shed burned in her eyes. She waved her hand to signify they did not matter. History, she told herself. We are both what we want to be. At any rate, she had not come here to speak of that.

"Did you know Gillian was that powerful when you changed her?"

Auriclus shrugged. "I knew her spirit was strong."

"And Lucius? Did you know he was an elder?"

At this he snorted out a breath. "You saw my reaction. Did I look as if I knew?"

Nim Wei weighed the likelihood of his candor. Know-it-all that he was, he probably loathed admitting he had not guessed.

"What are you going to do now that you know?" she asked.

"Do?" His tone was disbelieving. "I will do what any sensible *upyr* should when he is outflanked. I will respect his privacy. You might consider doing the same. If you poke that nest, more than hornets may fly out."

His tone was fondly amused, as if she were a child. But he was a child if he thought she could not smell his fear. How it must shake him to have not one but three rivals to his power! If she were not shaken herself, she would have been filled with glee.

"Gillian will leave her lover's memory intact," she said in challenge. "When it is over, her child will know how to perform the change."

"Knowing how is not important. This Aimery lacks her inborn skill—for now at least. In a century or two, we can worry about him."

"Oh, 'we' can worry," she said. "I marvel that you know the word."

Auriclus turned to her, the faintest of smiles curving his lips. Nim Wei did not smile back. He still infuriated her, but less than he had. Maybe her recent experiences had matured her, or maybe seeing him taken down a notch had calmed some of her spite. Whatever the reason, with the challenges of the future spread out before her, the passing of her anger seemed a blessing.

<hr />

"I heard you were better!" shouted a boyish voice coming up the stairs. "The dairymaid saw your shadow in the window. I heard, I heard, I heard!"

Robin slammed through the door and skidded across the stones while Gillian and Aimery struggled out of sleep. Aimery felt as muzzy as if he had spent the night in drink. Only a strenuous effort forced him awake. This, he supposed, was one of the drawbacks to being *upyr,* that daylight—and sunshine—were no longer their proper sphere. He had not anticipated how inconvenient that might be. Frowning to himself, he shaded his eyes to make his nephew out.

"Oh," said the boy, realizing his mistake. "I thought . . ." His words trailed away and his eyes grew wide. "Uncle Aimery?"

"Yes," Aimery said in thickly graveled tones. "What is it?"

Robin's jaw fell. "Uncle Aimery?" he repeated, even higher. "What—What happened to your face?"

Aimery touched it and found a disconcerting smoothness. His skin no longer pulled or hurt. Gillian had said he was pretty, but he had not thought . . . His scar was gone. How in Hades was he going to explain this?

"Come here, Robin," Gillian said, showing more presence of mind than Aimery could muster. With the sheet tucked beneath her arms, she patted the bed.

Robin came, shuffling a bit and darting unsure glances at his uncle along the way. Finally he stood next to Gillian while she stroked his hair. "I wager you can guess what happened," she said.

Robin fidgeted and gnawed his lip. "You made him what you are. Because he was dying."

"Partly because of that and partly because I love him and did not want to remain alone."

Robin sighed gustily, the sound a blend of child and adult. "He looks different. Is he going to have to hide now like Princess?"

Rather than answer, Gillian lifted him off the floor and tucked him between herself and Aimery. The boy snuggled into her hold as if he were far younger than eight. "I do not want you to leave," he said, the plaint muffled by her shoulder.

"I know." She met Aimery's eyes over his head.

Aimery felt as helpless as she looked. He rubbed Robin's back in gentle passes, taking in the miracle of his life as he never had before: his pulse beating through his palm, his sweaty little-boy smell, the delicate strength of his growing bones.

"We will come back to visit," he said, "when it seems safe or when you need us. You can think of us as your protectors."

Without warning, Robin let Gillian go and burrowed into Aimery's chest instead. "Take me with you," he demanded. "Make me magic, too."

Aimery did not know he had the words until he pressed his lips to Robin's hair. "Do not imagine this is easy," he said. "Because Gillian changed me, I must say good-bye to everything I know. I am happy to be alive, and thankful for the chance to spend my life with the woman I love but, believe me, I shall miss what I leave behind. My friends. My family. You. I shall never have a son, Robin, never know the pride of raising a boy like you. I do not want you to miss that, nor the rest of your childhood. Besides which"—here he tousled Robin's locks—"your father would be sad if I took you away."

"Would not," Robin insisted, his hands making fists against Aimery's ribs.

"No? I must have dreamt him holding you in his lap beside my bed, just as I must have dreamt the emotion I saw in his eyes. He loves you, Robin. You and your brother are his heart."

Robin pushed back to knuckle his reddened eyes. After a moment, he pulled himself together. "I suppose Father will need cheering up," he said resignedly, "once you are gone."

"Undoubtedly," Aimery agreed.

"And someone will have to look after your birds."

"Quite true, though my assistants can do the boring bits."

"All right then," said Robin with the air of one who has sealed a difficult bargain. "But I shall not share your secret with Thomas. He is a toad-head since he has been fostering out. He does not deserve to know."

"We leave that decision to you and your father's good judgment," Aimery said. "In any case, Thomas might not believe you."

"No." Robin looked thoughtful. "He might not."

The idea that he might be wiser than his older brother appeared to please him. He rested against Aimery's shoulder to enjoy it, then turned to Gillian and kissed her cheek.

"Good-bye, Princess," he whispered through her forehead. He clambered over her blanketed legs to reach the floor. At the edge of the bed he faced them both. His boyish dignity squeezed Aimery's heart. "I must tell Father I am staying."

"Tell him quietly," Gillian advised, "and possibly consider knocking."

Robin wrinkled his nose and nodded.

Speech being beyond him, Aimery waved.

"He does need me," Robin said, "especially with Mother locked in her room. But you must not forget to come back."

"I shall not forget," Aimery assured him.

His nephew's grin of leave-taking speared him like a ray of sun. Seeing it, Aimery suspected Robin would get over this parting sooner than he.

AIMERY'S shoulders tensed as Edmund came out from behind the loaded worktable in his chamber. His hair was mussed, his fingers stained with ink. A branch of candles had burned down half their wax while Edmund caught up on his neglected work. He leaned his hips against the table's edge. He looked tired, but not as tired as he had when Aimery was sick.

He was smiling as he perused his brother up and down. "I see Robin's report was no exaggeration. She has changed you, and you are prettier than I."

"I am sure that depends on whom you ask."

Edmund hummed with dry amusement, his legs crossed at the ankle, his fingers drumming the desk. "The transformation is quite extraordinary. No more scar. No tiny lines."

"I have a few yet. Around my eyes."

"Nonetheless, even without the glow, you are almost a different man. I wonder that you recognize your own reflection."

"The first sight of my face was a shock. Look, Edmund." He pressed his lips between his teeth. "I know I cannot stay at Bridesmere. Gillian's gift for illusion still escapes me, and even if I could work during the day, it would cause a furor if people saw me as I am now."

"A furor, yes, but with your reputation they would probably decide it was an act of God. We could start a pilgrimage site where you were healed and build poor Brother Kenelm a nice, big church."

"I do not believe he would enjoy that. He strikes me as a man who prefers to move behind the scenes."

"Yes." Edmund smudged a cinder into the flagstone with his shoe, his expression flickering with private thoughts. More than ever, he reminded Aimery of their father. Something had changed inside him—a decision, an attitude—which altered the very aspect of his face.

Aimery was not the only one who had undergone a transformation. Maybe almost losing him had touched Edmund more than he thought.

"Are you happy?" Edmund asked, looking up at last.

"Yes," said Aimery. "There are things I shall miss, but I never imagined I could be this satisfied with my life."

"Then I am happy for you."

A silence fell which neither brother knew how to breach. Finally Aimery cleared his throat. "Old Wat can assume my duties until you find a replacement."

"I fear your replacement does not exist, but we shall do our best to march on." The dryness of his tone was habit. A new hint of gentleness lay beneath.

"You may explain my disappearance however you like," Aimery offered.

"I think I shall say your lover took you to the holy land to seek a cure. Then you may come for visits, as you promised Robin."

"I would like that."

Without warning, Edmund laughed, his eyes filling with tears. "Listen to us," he said. "One would think we were friends."

Aimery put his hand on Edmund's shoulder. "We are," he said, "and maybe we always were."

⚬

FROM the darkness of the castle's yard, Nim Wei stared up at Edmund's window, half her mind turned inward, half caught up in watching him and his brother by candlelight.

She was thinking of Lucius, unable to get his revelation out of her mind. She had crossed his path once or twice and had paid him little heed. His power was not obvious. With no apparent ambition, he had faded into the background of Ulric's pack.

But he was an elder. How old? she wondered with a flare of interest. Twice Auriclus's age? More? What might be hidden in his gradually waking mind, and how could she convince him to let her in? No answer to her questions existed yet. She would have to wait and see what developed, just as she would have to wait to sort out this seemingly pointless trip.

Despite her efforts, she had not stopped the balance of power from shifting, had not wooed Gillian to her side. She felt as much a pawn of the Fates as Edmund's foolish wife: thinking she was the center of her world, telling herself she controlled the power of life and death. At most she was an afterthought. Her absence, once achieved, would only inspire relief.

High above her, Aimery put his hand on his brother's shoulder. Edmund bowed his head and laughed.

How poignant, she thought. The siblings reconcile before they part. But her cynicism had no heat. In truth, she envied their ability to engage in this ritual of forgiveness. Slung over her back, Nim Wei carried a pack with her minstrel's clothes and her harp. She had no intention of saying good-bye.

She had read the dreams that bloomed in her lover's heart, and

they had nothing to do with her. Edmund wanted to be a better father to his sons, a better leader to his people. From what she could
tell, he did not begrudge Aimery his change. Edmund might miss
his brother, but Nim Wei suspected his departure would finally free
the lord of Bridesmere to be himself—the burden of resentment
lifted once and for all.

She also suspected she could have seduced him away from his
good intentions. She marveled that she did not. If she wanted to
keep an eye on Gillian and her partner, that seemed the way.

Perhaps she loved Edmund after all.

I shall return, she warned his shadow, when you have lived your
human life and proved, or disproved, what you are. Then we will
see what you choose.

Auriclus had already left, without a word as was his way. Ulric,
too, was gone, though that was more understandable. Following in
their footsteps, Nim Wei shouldered her pack and turned away.

She would leave this place far behind her before the dawn.

Twenty-two

THEY made a ragtag group gathered quietly at the edge of the
wood beyond Bridesmere's fields. Aimery wore hawking
clothes and Gillian a plain brown tunic filched from a page. Edmund carried Robin on his hip, with the boy drooping sleepily on
his shoulder. Following some source of information known only to
himself, Brother Kenelm had accompanied them. To Gillian's surprise, Lucius was there as well. The silver-haired *upyr* was the sole
reminder of her earlier parting from the pack.

Pricked by memories, Gillian squeezed Aimery's hand. He was the brightest difference in this departure. This time she knew what lay ahead of her would be good.

Edmund's manner as he said farewell was awkward but endearing—half stiff, half sentimental. Then again, Gillian thought with a private grin, the baron of Bridesmere might have been stiff because his brother was running off with a commoner—and not only that, but a commoner raised by wolves.

The three of them had shared one private meal together, during which Edmund had politely probed her background. Knowing Aimery trusted him and intended to maintain their ties, she had answered most of what he asked. The result had been raised eyebrows from Edmund, a bit of bristling from Aimery and—when Edmund grew overwhelmed—the chance to sample a very nice Tuscan wine. "Wolves," he had murmured, absently topping up her goblet, "and secret cabals scattered in cities across the world . . . What experiences you shall have! I must say, though, the way you run things does seem rather irregular. No established leaders. No real system of laws."

"Edmund," Aimery had cautioned at his brother's censorious tone, but Gillian took no offense. How could she when Edmund's concern for Aimery was so clear?

"Do you have everything you need?" he asked now, for the second time.

"We do," Aimery assured him. "Apart from that bulging sack of bullion you gave me, we shall be traveling light."

"That coin is no more than you deserve."

"I am teasing," Aimery said. "I am sure it will come in handy."

Aimery's brother tugged the front of his fine blue doublet, a nervous gesture he probably was unaware of. "I am sorry I did not get to know you better," he said to Gillian.

She smiled because he was trying to mean it. "We shall meet again," she said, her hand reaching out to stroke Robin's hair. "I do not think I could resist. Being here has reminded me what life among humans is."

"Rivalry and betrayal?" Edmund suggested wryly.

"Passion and hope," Gillian corrected and leaned up to kiss his cheek.

His arm came around her more strongly than she expected. "Take care of him," he said. "Love him as well as you can."

She stepped back, her answer in her eyes, and let Aimery take her place. She closed her ears to their exchange, allowing the brothers their privacy. When they finished, Brother Kenelm cleared his throat. His black robes flapped in the midnight breeze.

"I thought this might be useful," he said, and handed Gillian a parchment scroll. "It is a list of contacts, churchmen and others, located here and on the Continent, who would be willing to help you should you have need. I do not say the help would be without cost, but you could trust them not to betray you."

Gillian had to think before she spoke. "You take a risk giving me this," she said after a moment, "not only on your own behalf but on that of these men. Their names cannot be common knowledge."

Brother Kenelm held her gaze. "I do not believe you want to make an enemy of the church."

"Maybe not, but I am far from convinced I want her for a friend!" Despite how fervently she meant the words, she laughed and took the scroll. "Thank you," she said, careful to promise nothing in return.

She might secretly feel sympathy for the monk, might even trust him more than most, but allying her interests with his was going too far. Given a choice, she preferred not to make herself and Aimery the means by which Brother Kenelm won back his abbot's good grace.

"It is a gift," he said softly, reading her reservations, "in return for the life I took. I do not ask any recompense."

He seemed to mean it; at least, he seemed to mean it then. Before she could explain or apologize, Aimery put his arm around her shoulders.

"Thank you," he said firmly, an echo of her first response.

He was supporting her, she realized, encouraging her to trust her instincts about the monk. She had said she wanted a partner, but for the first time, she understood what that meant. They would make decisions together, would stand up to danger—or adventure—as a pair.

Gratitude welled inside her, ineffably sweet and rare. She nodded to Brother Kenelm and said no more.

When her gaze fell on Lucius, his eyes gleamed with approval. "I have no gift," he said, spreading his graceful hands, "only an invitation. I thought, perhaps, after you take your year in the wild to hone your powers, you might want to join me in Rome."

"Rome?" said Aimery with a start.

"Yes," Lucius confirmed. "A fascinating city, or it was when I last knew it. Even without *il Papa* in residence, it should be seething with all sorts of people. Quite the spot for an *upyr* who wishes to study humanity."

"I have heard the country thereabouts is beautiful," Aimery mused.

Lucius nodded in agreement. "The Campagna is beautiful. And the ruins. And the wine, women, and song—not that you would be interested in all of that. Our kind had a community there, I believe. I should like to discover if it remains."

"So would I," said Aimery. "I want to understand more about what Gillian and I have become."

"Now that I think of it," Lucius added with a smile that told Gillian he had been thinking for quite some time. "There is always a need for responsible leaders among the *upyr,* and nowhere as much as Rome, I suspect, since Nim Wei avoids it like the plague. I imagine you want a break from such things, but I would not be surprised to find you in charge of something before long."

"Me? But—" Aimery looked at Gillian, the pull of his emotions visible in his face. He wanted responsibility, needed it, in fact, but how could he claim it when he was the youngest of them all?

"No child of Gillian's could be weak," Lucius said. "Besides, for all her mental strength, she would not be ruthless enough for this task—fair enough, no doubt, but not ruthless. An *upyr* lord must be willing to collect and inflict bruises. Boldness and moral surety can often win over age. If you have a vision of how you think *upyr* ought to live . . ."

"And you would not want to rule them yourself?"

"Not I," said Lucius with an exaggerated shudder. "Like your Gillian, I have always been more of an explorer. But I press you out of turn. This is something you may think about, no?"

"Something you may think about *seriously*," Edmund put in, clearly still appalled by her description of her people's anarchic ways.

Aimery shook himself—as if in reminder that this discussion was theoretical. Despite this, Gillian knew the challenge Lucius described had fired his imagination. To lead a city of immortal beings, to devise a system of law by which all could live—what could test his abilities more than that? Gillian could almost hear Aimery and his brother arguing their way enjoyably through that. She would have kissed Lucius had she not been familiar with his reserve. He had given Aimery back a dream.

Her love drew himself to his full height. "We shall think on everything you said, and shall anticipate seeing you again in Rome."

Lucius gave him a small but courtly bow. "I shall look forward to your visit."

One last hug and kiss for Robin signaled it was time to go.

" 'Luck," said Robin, as his father caressed his cheek.

Without a word, Aimery and Gillian reached for each others' hands. As they walked into the forest, the air felt rich as velvet against their skin. The trees closed around them in a soft green veil.

It was wonderfully peaceful—even luxurious—to be alone, their clasped hands lightly swinging, their legs striding in easy tandem along the path. This was their particular world and now they

had it to share. Gillian had not known she was tense until she felt
her body go fluid with relaxation. Here were no listening ears, no
confining walls, just the freedom to be with the man she loved.

The prospect of exploring that intrigued her more than exploring Rome.

"I can hear your heart," Aimery said.

His beautiful, unmarked face lit up with joy, as if this were his
best discovery yet. Gillian reached to touch the place where his scar
had been. For an instant she could see it outlined in a seam of brilliant light. That old wound was a part of him, as her human life
was a part of her. Her triumphs, her mistakes, and all those choices
she would never know for certain how to judge, had led her to him.
Because of this, she could not regret a one.

"Can you hear the love that makes it beat?" she asked, certain
he would say yes.

An owl hooted in the distance as he smiled. "I can," he said.
"Can you hear my love singing back?"

She closed her eyes and stood very still, the darkness wrapping
her in peace. The leaves whispered and the crickets chirped and a
brook gurgled over a fall of stone. Then, as if Aimery's feelings
were sap rising through a tree, she heard the underlying notes, not
with her ears but with her whole being. The melody was the sweetest she had known, one that both comforted and called tears.

This was love, as human as a heartbeat, as heavenly as the stars.
It awed her that it was for her.

His arms came around her to pull her close.

"Yes," she murmured against his chest. "That is the music I always wanted to hear."

Luisa's Desire

For Robert and Lana.
May your worlds always meet in love.

One

Tibet, 1600

THE sun filled the air with diamond knives, its merciless brilliance shooting spires of brightness off the ice-locked Himalayan peaks. Beneath, on the precipitous path that circled the tallest mountain, Luisa del Fiore huddled deeper into her mink-lined hood. Black sheathed her from head to toe: her kidskin gloves, her yakhide boots, even the veil that draped her face was black as ink. Despite these precautions, the effect of the sun was barely muffled. This was Tibet, the roof of the world, and far closer to heaven than a child of midnight ought to go.

The sun was a drug to her kind, a pleasure beyond compare. Like all drugs, however, too large a dose could kill. Indeed, she would not have risked this journey had her need not been so great.

Unaware of her predicament, Dorje, her cheerful native guide, beckoned her forward on the trail. The mere thought of the drop to his right was enough to make her dizzy. The fall might not kill her, but even an *upyr* could break her bones.

"Come," he urged. "Only little way more."

He spoke the pidgin Chinese they used to communicate, the language of the traders to whom he sold yak butter and from whom he bought bricks of tea. A nomadic herdsman, Dorje was one of six whose pilgrimage to this lamasery she had joined. She knew she was lucky to have fallen in with them even though, had she been alone, she could have traveled in the sunless safety of the night.

Getting lost was not safe, of course, no more than freezing to death, a hazard to which she had not known she was vulnerable. Her first night in the mountains had taught her that hard truth.

Thankfully, on the second night, she'd stumbled into Dorje's camp. He and his companions had offered her the foulest tea she'd ever pretended to drink and welcomed her to their fire. When she divulged her destination, they volunteered to guide her. Never mind she was a stranger, and a foreigner, and very outlandishly garbed. Never mind she posed a danger they could not begin to understand. They had heard that the *gompa*—the lamasery—at Shisharovar was holy. Anyone who helped her would gain merit from the trip.

At the moment, Luisa cared more for her next step than she cared for merit. Her exhaustion seemed a living thing, like one of the demons Dorje told tales of around the fire. She had no words for her hunger. She had not fed since she'd left the ship. She had not dared. It was not discovery she feared, nor others' violence against herself. Instead she feared she would feed until she slew these people who had saved her.

This was the crux of her dilemma, that she might kill when she had no wish to. Lately the urge had been getting stronger. She genuinely loved her life. The challenge of doing business among the humans kept her engaged. But fill, and only for a little while. When she had begun to drink from criminals—just in case she lost control—she knew she could not trust herself anymore.

She was not the hand of justice. Better to starve than to act as if she were.

As much as she believed in her choice, she could have wept for the intensity of her hunger. To drink . . . to be strong again . . .

But strength was the object of her journey: true strength, not the strength that came from theft.

Ahead of her, Dorje's crude felt boots punched holes in the snow she strove to follow. Like his fellows, he seemed to notice neither the cold nor the thinness of the air. Luisa felt both, her feet leaden, her blood-starved veins like overstretched wires of brass. She had not thought a mortal could be so strong. Forging steadily before her, Dorje seemed as tough as the grumbling yaks they had left in the spring green valley far below.

When she lagged, he laughed and urged her onward like a father exhorting a child to walk. She felt a child, so sunaddled she could scarcely stand. All around her the light was slow, sure poison, a wine of gold and blue, a scent as sweet and fragile as mountain flowers. It had been days now, weeks mayhap, that this deadly radiance had been seeping through her clothes. Drunk with it, she clung to reason by a thread.

Sleep, the sunshine whispered. *Pull off your cloak and bask in my golden rays. Be one with the beauty of the waking world.*

Luisa cursed and grit her teeth. She knew she must not listen. The waking world was not her rightful sphere.

They came to a turning. Dorje pointed higher and ahead.

"See," he said. "Lamas here!"

As she rounded the scarp, the path widened into a table of land as flat as if it had been carved. Beyond this small plateau the mountain rose again, craggy and sharp, a final heavenward thrust of stone. Shisharovar nestled at its base. The lamasery was bigger than she had expected, many floors of white-limed walls and narrow, defensive windows. Lines of prayer flags fluttered against the sky. *The jewel is in the lotus,* she deciphered, the sum of what Tibetan she could read. A flash of silver drew her eye to men standing on the roof, tall brown men in flowing russet robes. She squinted. They held what appeared to be long trumpets. The low bleating the instruments made a moment later confirmed the guess.

"*Oé!*" Dorje exclaimed. With a sigh of resignation, he and his companions dropped their packs. "Lamas pray now. We wait."

He gestured for her to sit but she could not. Within those walls lay darkness and warmth and quite possibly an end to her travails. She was walking before she even knew she meant to, crossing the trampled snow like a woman in a trance.

"Wait!" Dorje cried. "No can go. Lama here very holy. Very big power. Luisa make *naljorpa* angry. Luisa be sorry."

He had her arm and was trying to drag her back. Anger rising, she spun around. Dorje's jaw dropped. Her hood had fallen with the movement and the light shone clearly through her veil. She caught a glimpse of how she looked through his eyes: pale, porcelain skin and hair as gold as new-minted florins. Her expression was startled, even innocent. But she was too perfect, her eyes too vividly green, her mouth too carnally red.

Beauty like hers was dangerous.

His interest shimmered in the air between them. A sound filled her head: his heart pumping harder with desire, forcing the life-giving fluid through it, forcing his sex to rise. For a moment she felt faint. Blood, she thought, seeing it, tasting it. She closed her eyes at the power of her hunger—not just for food but to destroy.

She didn't realize she had moved. When her eyes snapped open, her hand was wrapped behind his neck, already pulling him into biting range. Her gums were stinging where her teeth had broken through. She shook herself, then shook him.

He seemed not to notice the unfeminine force with which she did it.

"You go," she said, sternly, huskily. "You no stop me."

He stared at her, still under the spell of her foreign beauty. He licked his lips and she knew she'd done the same. Her mouth was watering, her eyeteeth razor sharp.

"You go," she repeated. "Me no want hurt you."

He grinned at that, as if he did not believe she could. "Haha," he laughed with a Tibetan's unpredictable humor. "No wonder you wear veil. You show face, you get too many husband!"

Her own laugh was weak but it allowed her to uncurl her fingers from his neck. His countrymen, she had learned, were polyandrists.

"Yes," she agreed. "Me no want too many husband."

She backed away, gesturing him to stay. He looked worried but this time he did not try to stop her. Perhaps he judged her a match for the terrible *naljorpa*, whatever in Creation that was. Steps led to the lamasery entrance, stone beneath the snow. She climbed them—one dozen, two . . . her eyes holding Dorje in his place.

At last she reached the top. Two large rings hung from the iron that bound the double door. Wincing at the bite of the frozen metal, she set her heels on the step and pulled. The hinges groaned. The door was too heavy for human hands, but impatience prevented her from pretending she could not move it. She was going in. Nothing, not prayers, not fears, not even her failing strength, was going to stop her now.

With a last grunt of effort, she heaved it open and slipped inside.

The shadows folded around her like a blessing, smoky and sweet and warm. Butter lamps, the ubiquitous Tibetan illumination, flickered on various altars along the walls. She had entered a towering hall, its roof supported by heavy columns, its walls hung with banners of colored silk. Through clouds of incense she made out the hazy forms of many Buddhas praying, teaching, and looking much like those she had encountered in Calcutta.

A group of monks, young and old, were crossing the passage as she came in—presumably headed to their worship. As one, they turned to gape. Luisa did not care. She was too elated to be inside. Her head was pounding, sun drunk still, but at least it did not ache. Giddy with relief, she threw back her veil and grinned.

It was a mistake she would not have made had her mind been clear.

Two of the monks cried out and the larger of them rushed her. She barely had time to brace before his weight crashed her over into the floor.

"*Towo!*" he cried as she struggled to free herself. "*Tsem shes tsem!*"

Luisa realized she must have bared her fangs. He had taken her for a demon.

"I pilgrim," she protested in her limited Tibetan. "I come pray."

Unimpressed, the monk took her head in both hands and smashed it against the floor. He must have been very strong. Like the crackle of early winter ice, she felt a tiny fracture in her skull.

The break healed almost as soon as it formed but, however ineffec-
tive, the injury snapped her control. Instinct took over, the remorseless drive for survival that marked her kind.

Taking his head in the same splay-fingered grip, she stunned the
monk by coshing his brow against her own. Then, before he could
recover, before she herself could think better of it, she rolled him
beneath her and drove her teeth through the wind-roughened skin
of his neck.

His blood filled her mouth, hot, rich, a feast for her starving
veins. Her head cleared at the first swallow. The second was just for
greed. But she had to stop. She could not kill within arm's reach of
her goal. When he moaned, she shoved off him and got up.

She might not be sated but she was sane.

"I am not a demon," she said, even as she drew her fine Spanish
glove across her mouth. "Not *towo*."

The monk who had attacked her was on his knees, too shaken
to rise. "No," he agreed, his eyes wide and locked to hers. "You are
not a demon."

He sounded almost normal, almost, but she knew her bite had
thralled him. He was hers to command, for an hour or a day,
though she could not see what good that would do. The rest of the
monks had closed around her, many of them as big as the one she'd
bitten. She knew she could not overpower them all.

"I have come to learn your ways," she said, switching to her
more fluent Mandarin. Pray God, someone here would speak it. "I
beg the favor of studying with your abbot." Silence met her plea as
she turned from one implacable visage to the next. "Look." Careful
to move slowly, she reached into the folds of her fur-lined cloak. "I
bring a gift for him, for Geshe Rinpoche, the holy lama of
Shisharovar."

She held out her offering, wrapped as Dorje had advised in a
white silk scarf. A rustle moved through the crowd, which suddenly
parted to reveal another monk.

Everything seemed to hush as he approached—breath, heart,

thought—as if the world itself had stopped turning on its axis. Even the terrible emptiness inside her stilled. Sun-drunk nonsense, she scoffed, but the sensation did not fade.

Here was a man to weaken knees.

Though young, the monk carried himself like a leader: upright, assured, with the grace of a creature whose body is completely in his control. He must be the lama she had come to see. His head had been shaved but not recently and new growth bristled out in a glossy brush. He looked healthy, smelled healthy. Helpless to quell the reaction, her pulse beat faster in her throat.

Swallowing, she tried not to stare at the way his stride moved the drapery of his deep red robe. Lifting her gaze did not help. The long, toga-like wrap bared one beautifully molded arm. As she watched, his hand settled on the shoulder of the kneeling monk. Without looking away from her, the lama gave the monk an order. Luisa could not suppress a shiver. His voice was as deep as the rumbling trumpets on the roof.

Whatever the lama's authority, Luisa knew her victim could not obey until she released her mental hold. She stepped forward to do so. Unfortunately, watching a woman wipe blood from her mouth did not elicit trust. The lama barked a word and extended his second hand.

As soon as he did, something pushed her belly, something she could not see. It felt like a wall not precisely of wind, but not unlike. Under its influence, she slid backward, slowly at first, then gathering speed, her heels dragging on the stone, her arms wheeling for balance until she hit the plastered wall. The force of the collision drove the air from her lungs. Beside her, on a lighted altar, a heap of barley spilled from an offering bowl.

Luisa could barely contain a gasp. In all her years she'd never seen anyone perform such magic, neither *upyr* nor human. This, it seemed, was the power of a terrible *naljorpa*. She should have been frightened but her skin was tingling strongly with excitement. She could learn from this man. She could finally achieve her goal.

Pinned to the wall by the lama's mysterious force, she watched him help the other monk to his feet. Her victim left the hall with no more than a reluctant glance in her direction. Amazing, she thought. No one but she should have been able to direct him in any way.

The lama continued his approach. Her body tensed, half with wariness and half with anticipation. Oh, she could happily have tied this one to her bed. He was staring directly at her, into her. The effect was eerie but oddly sensual, as if his gaze were touching places she had not known she had. His eyes themselves were lovely, the fold beneath slightly broader than the delicate one above. They did not slant so much as narrow at the ends.

When he stopped a foot away from her, she received another shock. In the light from the butter lamps' floating wicks she saw that his eyes were gentian blue. The back of her neck prickled. This man, this Tibetan sorcerer, had European blood.

His gaze dropped to the package she clutched before her breast.

"You should kneel when you offer that," he said.

She blinked at him. "You speak English."

His expression did not change. "As do you."

He must have assumed from her appearance that she would, a natural assumption and one that should not have unnerved her after all she'd seen him do. Nonetheless, she was unnerved. Though she was more gifted at putting thoughts *into* people's heads than taking them out, she was not accustomed to finding anyone such a blank.

If the lama was unnerved, he did not show it. He was close to her, the tiny spikes of his lashes shadowing his angled cheeks. Luisa was tall but he was taller, tall for any race, even hers. A warm soft scent rose from his robes, incense and yak butter and something sweeter: the scent that was his essence. She wanted to drag it into her lungs but knew she could not afford to, not now and maybe never. Already her attraction to him was stronger than she liked.

"You drank that man's blood," he said, "and you clouded his mind. If you are not a demon, what manner of creature are you?"

"I could ask you the same."

His lips twitched with what might have been a smile. Then, as if this lapse were somehow shameful, he sobered and stepped back. Luisa sensed she was losing ground.

"Forgive me," she said, doing her best to hide her consternation. "I did not mean to hurt that man. His attack surprised me. And I am not familiar with your customs." Dropping to her knees, she bowed her head and held her guest gift up before her. "Please, holy lama, accept this humble token of my esteem."

Someone giggled, a boy from the sound of it, quickly hushed.

"I am not Geshe Rinpoche," said the man with an edge of stiffness, "nor a holy lama. I am, however, honored to be the precious one's student. I will bring him to you when the service ends. If your request is sincere, I am sure he will honor it."

She was not certain, but his final statement seemed to hold a hint of drollness. The possibility did not reassure her. Nor was she happy when he led her down a corridor to a little room. A set of iron chains hung from the raw stone wall. Luisa took one look and wanted to run away. Instead, she let her escort guide her to them. What sort of monastery kept such devices so close to hand? The room wasn't even a dungeon! It had an ornate tea table and an extra cushion for a guest.

"You do not need to do this," she said, fighting panic as he closed the manacles around her sleeves. "I am not a threat."

The glance he shot her was sardonic. She had to admit he had cause to doubt her. But did he know iron was the only metal she could not break? Or had she simply imagined he had seen straight to her core? Either way, she could not fight. She needed these people's help. She could not afford to hurt them.

But then he bent and chained her ankles like her wrists. His soft bristled hair brushed the front of her thigh, an inadvertent intimacy she was sure. Despite the sensual distraction, her panic rose.

"I do not like being restrained," she said. She meant it to be a warning, but her voice shook, betraying her sincerity more clearly than she wished.

He seemed to hear it. He straightened and stared at her with his extraordinary eyes. His pupils gleamed like ink, large in the dimness, or perhaps he also was aroused. Her beauty was not, after all, of the common run. Given his show of control, she was surprised when he cupped her cheek. His palm was warm, his fingers calloused. The comfort they brought made her want to clench her jaw. Too easily she could imagine those careful fingers between her legs. She frowned to herself. His pull was as dangerous as her instinct to fight the chains.

As if he, too, mistrusted the contact, his touch fell away. A second later, so did his gaze.

"It is not a long service," he said without his previous irony. "As soon as it is over, I will bring my teacher here."

His *teacher*, she thought, rolling the back of her head against the stone. If a mere student could do what he did, what did she need to fear from the man who'd taught him?

Two

S O," said the abbot, his Mandarin even more elegant than hers, "Martin says you are interested in our ways."

Geshe Rinpoche was older than his pupil and, at first glance, less imposing. He was shorter, for one thing, with a peasant's solidity and bright black eyes that seemed an inch away from a smile. His robe was humble and the only badge of office he wore was the yellow stole around his neck. Martin stood guard at his side, stern and protective. His teacher, by contrast, did not behave as if she posed a threat.

And perhaps she didn't. Perhaps the magic Geshe Rinpoche commanded turned her own into the useless huffing of the wind. It was a strange possibility, one she had not faced since her first encounters with her kind. True, the smattering of *upyr* at Queen Elizabeth's court were more experienced than Luisa, but none of those backstabbers could take her without a fight—and certainly not by force of mind!

Knowing she must tread carefully, she bowed her head before she spoke. "I have heard much of Shisharovar, your holiness, and of your awe-inspiring power."

"Indeed," said the abbot. "How flattering."

"Perhaps you would allow me to introduce myself?" When she ventured to look up, a grin had creased the old lama's face, the lines fanning merrily outward from his eyes. He spread his hands in permission. Luisa composed herself. "Thank you, your holiness. My name is Luisa del Fiore and I am a prosperous Florentine merchant. My business takes me all over the world and also brings the world to me."

"You travel all over the world? A woman alone?"

"Usually I have companions but sometimes I go alone, sometimes in disguise as a man. It depends on the prejudices of those with whom I deal, and on which appearance will tend to my best advantage."

"Your skill at subterfuge must be great," said the abbot with a wry enjoyment that warned her not to underestimate his wit. "But surely you are not here to trade."

"No, your holiness. I am here because of a trader I met, one who traveled these regions long ago. His name was John Moore and he was rescued by your lamas when a snowstorm caught him in the pass. He remained some months and witnessed many wonders, one of which was a monk who had himself walled in a cave where he survived for three whole weeks on water and meditation. When he emerged, he was as strong as the day he'd left. That monk was, I believe, yourself."

For some reason, the abbot glanced at his student, then at her. "You come here to learn to fast? All this way, to learn a trick any hermit can perform?"

"Self-denial is one of the paths to enlightenment, is it not? I believe in learning from the best."

He furrowed his brow at her. The intensity of his concentration caught her unprepared. His gaze was even keener than his student's. It lapped at her skin like water, crawling over and under until the hairs on her arms stood up in waves. She gasped, abruptly unable to catch her breath. Then, with no more warning than he'd given when he began, the abbot released her.

"You have a strange energy," he said in a musing tone. "I see from the disposition of your subtle bodies that your thoughts and desires are very much concerned with your physical being. Our medical lamas claim such attachment leads to illness and yet your material self is very strong. I have never met a demon of your description, much less one who would enter a holy place. I confess, though, I cannot imagine what you are."

He waited then, a picture of Oriental patience. More than anything he seemed curious. No one who suspected she was not human had ever reacted in this way. Then again, in this country, demons and ghosts were treated as little more than inconvenient neighbors. Tibetans bought an amulet or a spell and continued on their way. Luisa sensed that even if she admitted to being a monster, this holy man would not condemn her.

Of course, a failure to condemn was not the same as giving aid.

At a loss, she looked to Martin. He was watching her just as calmly. She wondered if his composure were a pretense or if, like his teacher, he was prepared to accept her as she was.

"We can see this request is important to you," Martin said. "We would be interested to know why."

Luisa hesitated. Could she tell them? Should she? Would they help her if she did not? She fisted her hands within the iron shackles. The slow, draining chill pulled at her through her clothes. The metal would not kill her unless someone thrust it through her heart. Eventually, though, it would weaken her enough to be killed. By sunlight. Or fire. Or the severing of her spine. She supposed she could take her choice.

As if sensing her fears, the abbot lifted a key from a ring on the belt that tied his robe.

"No," she said before he could use it. "Let me answer before you decide to free me." Uncurling her fingers, she forced herself to relax. "I was born as human as you. One hundred twenty years ago, on the fortieth anniversary of my birth, my master changed me to the creature I am today. He was the descendant of an ancient race who came from a distant star. They lived in peace here once, until a few took to killing humans. We . . . feed off them, you see. It is the only sustenance we can take." She straightened her shoulders. "I am what the people of Russia call *upyr*, a blood-drinker, an immortal."

"An immortal." The abbot's head was cocked birdlike to the side. He seemed not so much shocked as fascinated. "An immortal who is neither ghost nor god. An immortal in human form." Suddenly he laughed. "You know, we of Tibet aspire to leave the world of illusion behind. To us, this earth is a kind of hell—a schoolroom, if you will—where we are repeatedly reborn in order to perfect our true, nonmaterial being. You, Luisa del Fiore, seem to have enrolled for a very long term!"

His humor discomposed her. "I do not wish to give up my life," she said, wanting to be clear. "I simply wish to live more ethically. I wish to live without drinking blood."

"Ah," said the abbot, "now I begin to see. You must realize that may not be possible."

"Yes, your holiness, but surely if anyone can teach me it is you."

"Perhaps." His dark eyes narrowed in consideration. "I will have to meditate carefully before I act. It will not be easy to instruct you, who have not been raised in our system, and it may not be wise to try. We shall see." He turned to Martin, his expression warming with a father's fondness. "I leave it to you to make our visitor comfortable. Perhaps she would like a quiet room in the old east wing."

Martin looked as if he longed to forgo this duty, but he bowed instead, his steepled hands moving smoothly from brow to throat to heart. "As you wish, rinpoche."

From his tone, Luisa gathered "rinpoche" was as much a term of honor as a name.

To her relief, Martin unshackled her and led her in a new direction down the stony, torchlit hall. Apart from instructing her to follow and shooting her the occasional measuring glance, he did not speak. Luisa was no stranger to solitude, but for some reason his taciturnity frayed her nerves. They climbed a set of ancient stairs.

"Have you taken a vow of silence?" she asked.

"No," was his short, basso response.

"Might I ask then why your abbot keeps a set of chains in his reception chamber?"

"They are for interrogating criminals. The neighboring villages sometimes bring their accused here. My teacher reads their auras to see if they speak true."

"Their auras."

"The aura is a second body. It is a match for the physical body, inhabiting the same space and extending slightly beyond it, but composed of life force instead of matter. The life force of the earth is what a hermit survives on while he fasts."

Luisa considered this as they turned down another corridor, apparently uninhabited and lit by narrow windows. The slits were open to the icy air. A dusting of snow swirled in eddies along the floor. She pulled her cloak closer but Martin, like Dorje, did not seem to mind the cold.

She thought longingly of her palazzo, so marvelously snug after living out her mortal life with wind whistling through unglazed windows, a wind that had too often blown her nothing better than the stink of her husband's fish. Resistance to the cold, she sometimes thought, was worth the price of turning *upyr* by itself.

Not that her homeland had ever seen cold like this. This was beyond even the winter she'd spent at sea with Sir Francis Drake.

Ahead of her, Martin pushed open a heavy door and held it for her to enter. Irked by his seeming indifference, she paused on the threshold, not touching him but close enough to mark the subtle pulsing of his heat. To her gratification, a trace of color crept up his neck. So. Monk or not, he was not immune to her appeal. The discovery restored a portion of her confidence.

"I felt you touch my aura before," she said. "You were trying to look inside me like your teacher."

"Yes," he admitted. She thought he would say no more, but then his mouth quirked slightly to the left. "Studying someone's aura is not like a boy peeking under a woman's skirts, if that is what you were thinking."

Whatever riposte she might have made was lost when his gaze settled onto hers. Her spine tingled strongly. Again she had that sense of time held in suspension. She must have imagined the hint of teasing. He seemed the most serious man in the world.

How beautiful he is, she thought. How utterly male and comely. The admiration itself was pleasurable, though she knew it would not satisfy her long. Luisa was a creature who reveled in possession: a painting, a book, a perfect length of brocaded silk. Like her countrymen, she knew an object gained value by being owned: real value. In Italy, as in the rest of Renaissance Europe, a man was judged by what he had. Appearance was power. Illusion became reality. Luisa had survived and thrived by knowing that.

"You are big for a woman," commented the object of her lust.

She choked on a startled laugh. "Not much for flattery, are you?"

He did her the grace of flushing. "I meant you are tall. And you are stronger than our females. You fought that monk as if you were a man."

She was not sure how to respond. It didn't seem wise to confess her strength had been at its lowest ebb. But Martin did not expect an answer. Without asking permission, he pushed her hood back to her shoulders. As if pulled by an unknown force, his hand slid into her golden waves. He seemed as bewitched as she.

"I have never seen a woman with hair like yours. It does not even tangle." His fingers spread gently behind her ear, his thumb stroking the shadowed contours of her cheek. "Your skin is as smooth as satin. Are all *upyr* like you?"

His touch sent a heated shiver to her sex. She had to clear her throat before she could speak. "In some ways. When we are changed, we become what we would have been had we achieved our full potential. Our perfect age. Our perfect height and weight. As a mortal, I was plain and dull."

And bruised, often as not—first by her husband and then, more sadly, by her sons. She shook off the memory with a frown. That life was over. In any case, she had darker sins on her conscience than any that stained those of the foolish brutes who, for better or worse, had been her mortal family.

They were dead now, those strapping boys. Sometimes she regretted her failure to save them from their father's sway. Sometimes she was grateful they were gone. She could pray for them if she wished, and forgive the blows they had no more power to strike.

Martin was watching her face as if he could follow the passage of her thoughts. When he spoke, though, he did not ask about her former life. "Why do your kind 'change' humans? Can they not have children of their own?"

She shook her head. "My master believed the sun kills *upyr* seed. But we have compensations. We are strong, as you said, and can influence human thought. I have heard some *upyr* are able to take the form of beasts, though I have not seen it done."

"How many of you are there?"

"That is difficult to say. Many of the old ones died by human vengeance. Some simply grew tired. It is not easy to make new *upyr*. And we are wary of one another. Territorial. I knew of a dozen in London and heard there were similar circles in Paris and Seville. At least one more *upyr* lived in Florence, but we rarely did more than nod in passing. He was different, that one, dangerous. I suspect he was an elder."

"An elder?"

"One of the old ones who knows how to perform the change. My master claimed there were only two—himself and his student, Nim Wei—but I think he may have been wrong."

His thumb smoothed the orbit around her eye. "And you do not age once you are made?"

She shook her head. "Not physically."

He leaned so close she thought he meant to examine her cell by cell. Knowing her passivity would increase his trust, she allowed him the inquisition. Remaining still was not easy. His scent curled around her while his breath brushed her mouth like velvet. An inch would have brought them to a kiss.

She made a sound she had not intended, soft and hungry in her throat.

At once he pulled away. "Forgive me," he said, reluctantly drawing his hand out of her hair. He rubbed it across his chest as if it itched. "I have been rude."

"Some would say a creature like me deserves no better."

"Some lie. All living beings deserve respect."

She could see he meant it. Dazed for more reasons than she could name, she obeyed his gesture to step inside. The room was small: a stone floor, a low, beamed ceiling. One arrow-slit window overlooked a snowy courtyard. The only furniture was an unlit altar and a pile of squared-off dusty cushions. Luisa assumed these were what she'd sleep on.

"I will bring blankets," Martin said, "and a brazier."

She smiled at him. "That would be kind. I think I must have been changed to suit the climate of my birth. I can stand more cold than most, but we do not have these extremes at home." A burst of childish laughter drew her to the window. A group of boys were engaged in a kicking game with a ball. The shadows were long now, the sun sinking swiftly behind the peaks. After all she had been through, the lingering light did not affect her much.

"I hope the *chelas* will not bother you," Martin said. "They like to play there between their lessons."

"*Chelas?*"

"That is what we call young boys. Older students are *trapas*."

"And you?" She turned to find him a step behind her.

His gaze remained on the scene outside. "I am also *trapa*. I have not been here very long. A year only. There were . . . reasons I could not join the lamasery as a boy. But someday I hope to be *gelong*." If she had not been watching closely, she would have missed his tiny scowl. "*Gelong* is a special ordination. My teacher will tell me when I am ready."

"You seem quite advanced to me. Your powers—"

He waved her words away with his hand. "Having power is not the same as being holy."

"Certainly not in my case," she said with a coaxing smile.

Martin did not return it. "I have been a monk before," he said. "That is why my progress has been swift."

"Before?"

"In previous lives." He glanced at her, weighing her response to this exotic claim. "My memories drew me back to this place, to my teacher. He has never failed to guide me, even at my most stubborn. Always he took me in."

Devotion rang in his voice. As if he heard it himself, and judged it unsuitable for display, he pulled himself straighter and stepped away. "Unless you have further need of me, I will take my leave."

She inclined her head. "I await your teacher's convenience."

He paused beneath the lintel of the door. "If I bolt this, will it keep you in?"

She could not restrain a laugh. No one else would have expected her to be honest. "Probably not, but I pose no immediate danger to your colleagues."

"I can bring food," he offered. "Tea."

"And I could pretend to drink it, but it would not sustain me."

She watched him take this in, his thoughtfulness an echo of his teacher.

"Will you become ill if you do not eat?" he asked.

"There is time before that happens."

"But you will not be comfortable."

"No," she agreed, "I will not be comfortable."

He nodded at this. She sensed he also heard what she had not said: that she was more likely to take what she needed by force than to allow herself to grow much weaker. At any rate, she would try. From what she had seen of him, the outcome of a confrontation between them would not be sure.

Only when he pulled the door shut behind him did she remember where she'd first seen eyes his shade of blue.

"CLEARLY," said Geshe Rinpoche, "the trader she met was your father. You must admit the coincidence is striking, as if Fate were taking a hand in bringing you together."

Martin grimaced. That John Moore had drawn the woman here was hardly a point in her favor. A curse, more like, if she proved as unworthy of trust as he. Martin touched the pale jade horse that stood on the table by his teacher's window. The carving was a gift from the Mongol khan, a thanks for an herbal healing. Nestled on a scarf beside it, the woman's offering curled like a snake. It was a *mala*, a Tibetan rosary, a string of one hundred eight shining emerald beads.

Apparently she had not lied about being a prosperous merchant.

"I saw no sign she lied at all," said his teacher, "though there was much she hid."

His comment did not surprise Martin. He and his guide were so attuned Geshe Rinpoche could often read his mind. He, of course, would not presume to read his teacher's.

"Haha," laughed Geshe Rinpoche, "now I am presumptuous!"

Martin turned, face hot, but his embarrassment faded in the waves of warmth he felt from his friend.

"Yes, *friend*," Geshe agreed, "for, as I have told you, you and I have shared many lives—lives in which *I* was not always the teacher." He beamed up at Martin from the floor, still seated in the attitude of meditation, his legs crossed, his hands curled easily around his knees. After a moment, his smile softened into a look of deep compassion. "I know you are troubled. I would be surprised if you were not. After all, this woman is a living reminder that half of you belongs in another world."

"None of me belongs anywhere but here," Martin declared. "This is the country of my heart!"

Shamed by the passionate outburst, he hung his head.

"The wise man feels neither attachment nor aversion," reminded his master with the patience for which he was renowned.

"I'm sorry, rinpoche. You know I am trying to follow the Path."

His teacher released a quiet sigh. "Yes, I know you are trying. Too hard maybe. There are things I have seen in your future . . . But that is a talk for another day. You will choose your own way, as everyone does. For now you need only know that I have decided to help this woman. Tomorrow we will consult the medical lama. If our pilgrim is as earnest as she claims, I think we may accomplish much."

" 'We,' rinpoche?"

His teacher's eyes held more than a hint of mirth. "Yes, 'we.' My meditation has told me you must help!"

Three

T HE medical lama was a tall storklike man, as gauntly ascetic as Martin and the abbot were robust. He reminded Luisa of scientists she had known, truth seekers who burned for nothing but uncovering hidden things. She did not fear her nature would disgust him, only that at some point he would want to cut her open and look inside.

They had gathered—she, Martin, the medical lama, and the abbot—in Geshe Rinpoche's surprisingly comfortable quarters. They'd come soon after midnight, not for Luisa's sake but because midnight was when the lamasery's day began. Every so often the chant of the morning service drifted up from the floors below. Distant as it was, the sound could not compete with the rapid-fire barrage of the medical lama's questions.

Once he had taken her pulse at various places on her body, he interrogated her about her diet, her sleep habits, her strengths and weaknesses alike. Naturally, Luisa was reluctant to discuss the latter. She understood, though, that she must enter into this process wholly. As Geshe Rinpoche said: a doctor could not diagnose half a patient. All must be known or the treatment would not suit.

After an hour of this, the medical lama was so excited he was pacing back and forth across the colorful woven rug. "And you say you can consume food, but not digest it?"

"Yes."

"But wine you can imbibe, as well as filtered juice and tea."

"I cannot drink Tibetan tea," she clarified with an automatic wrinkling of her nose. "The yak butter and soda disagree with me."

The medical lama stopped to press his hands before his mouth. "Yes. Those additions are too coarse, too material. Blood is food a human has transformed for you and wine is sunlight on which the fruit has done the work. Are you certain you do not remember how you were changed into what you are?"

"Quite certain," she said. "The procedure is wiped from our memory as soon as it is done. Only the elders possess the secret and I'm afraid it is a power they do not choose to share. I do not even know how many of them exist. Two, according to my master, but I often thought he told me less than he knew. However great or small their number, they are shadow figures who rarely walk among their broods."

"Pity," said the lama as if their presence would present no more than a chance for intriguing study. Luisa was beginning to see that nothing in this world or any other could cow these Tibetan monks. The medical lama pondered the ceiling, then turned to the holy abbot. "I must study her *tsakhor*. Please instruct her to undress."

"*Scusi?*" said Luisa with a mixture of amusement and affront. She might not be a fount of modesty, but once upon a time she had been. Even now she drew the line at standing naked before three men—at least, three men she did not intend to bed. That Martin's presence inspired the most discomfort, she chose not to examine.

To her relief, the abbot intervened. "*Tsakhor* are wheels of force within your subtle body. Examining them will tell Lama Songpan how your inner *mandala* channels energy. Your clothing would interfere with the emanations."

"If I understood more than two words of that," Luisa said, "I might be convinced."

Martin frowned at her as the medical lama threw up his hands. Calm as ever, the abbot smiled. "You must forgive us," he said. "We do not think of nudity as you do. To us the body is simply the vehicle of the soul. But perhaps you have something simple beneath those clothes? An undergarment that would preserve your privacy?"

"I am wearing a smock," Luisa conceded, suddenly feeling

foolish. These were men of science, not a science she understood but that did not make them satyrs in search of thrills. Nor, given her history, was she in any position to throw stones. With a shrug at her own illogic, she doffed her fur-lined cloak. Her Turkish-style tunic and trousers spurred no comment, since they were more familiar to her watchers than the ruff and farthingale she would have worn at home.

Hiding her discomposure under her briskest manner, she stepped from the embroidered trousers and undid the tunic's pearl-studded buttons. The sleeveless shift she wore beneath fell past her hips, a cobweb silk woven by her own *bottega*, the best cloth-working shop in all of Florence. The silk was fine enough to pull through a woman's ring, as soft and shimmering as smoke. For all the shield it provided, she might as well have removed it. She kept it, though, perversely determined to maintain at least a pretense of maidenly reserve—not that Martin was likely to be fooled.

She stopped disrobing once she'd peeled off her long black gloves. Feeling the cold now, she handed them to Lama Songpan, who exclaimed in wonderment as he turned them back and forth.

"Not a crease," he marveled. "Not a single sign of wear. Her garments are as fresh as if she never had put them on."

The abbot hummed and rubbed his chin. Only Martin seemed to view her barely clothed body as more than a scientific object. He had crossed his arms as she undressed and, while his face remained impassive, his knuckles were nearly white. Knowing his gaze was on her abruptly heightened her awareness of her flesh.

Yes, she thought, you know I am a woman. A draft stirred her hair behind her back and a shiver swept her breasts. She felt a tightening at their tips as if they had been pinched by gentle fingers. Martin's eyes met hers, hot now, and not the least bit monkish. She remembered carvings she had seen in India's northern temples: gods with thick, rearing phalluses, their consorts small of waist and round of breast. Phantom hands seemed to grip her around the ribs, lifting her, impaling her even as she hung splay-legged in the air.

It was not a position with which she was familiar. Then she knew. These memories were not hers. Martin wanted her. He was imagining how she'd feel. Tiny beads of sweat dotted his brow.

Perhaps he did not, after all, prefer a woman to be a maid.

She smiled at him and he immediately turned away—not, however, before she had seen the flush that tinged his ears.

"I will light the brazier," he said. "She is cold."

Lama Songpan, of course, had missed this little drama. "Hm," he said, circling her slowly on the rug. "In the average person, the earth's energy is continually being tapped for the replenishment of the aura. The process is as automatic as the beating of the heart. But her aura's barriers to penetration are very strong. I suspect this must serve some protective function, for she is virtually cut off from these natural forces. Her heart *tsakhor* in particular is quite guarded."

"You say she is virtually cut off," repeated the abbot, "but not completely?"

The medical lama crouched and laid the tips of three bony fingers on her feet. "I sense a small draw. Very small. Under normal circumstances not enough to sustain a child."

"She must be taught to increase it," said the abbot.

Lama Songpan rose creakily erect. "Perhaps. I do not know if she can." He shrugged. "I would recommend a cautious attempt. Otherwise, I do not know what to suggest."

"Very well," said the abbot. "Thank you for your advice."

His subordinate bowed and retreated, leaving the three of them alone.

The sound of Martin stoking the brazier seemed very loud.

Geshe Rinpoche turned to watch his student. From the look on his face, Luisa could only assume the abbot didn't expect *her* to be watching *him*. For once, his expression was not that of an indulgent teacher. It was considering, rather, almost cool, as if Martin were a racehorse he meant to bet on.

An instant later she thought she must have imagined it because he smiled at Martin just as fondly as before. "Come away from there," he said, a hint of laughter in the words. "If you keep that up, our guest will think we mean to roast her."

Martin straightened so quickly he nearly dropped the poker. "I'm sorry, rinpoche. I—"

"Sh." His teacher patted the air with open hands. "It is all right. Everything is well."

To Luisa's surprise, she caught a hint of her own gift in the lama's voice. He was putting calm into Martin's head, calm that was not really there. Given the expression she had caught a glimpse of, she couldn't help wondering what his motives were.

But maybe she'd grown too cynical. The love the abbot felt for his student lit more than his eyes. Luisa was not easily deceived. She doubted she could have misread that.

"Come," said Geshe Rinpoche, waving Martin closer. "I want you to show our guest how to pull up energy from the earth."

"Me?" Martin's reluctance was emblazoned on his face.

The abbot chuckled. "It is only a request, Martin. You may refuse. But she is drawn to you," he said, proving he had seen their exchange, "as you are to her. This sympathy will make teaching her easier. I will stay, though, if you feel yourself in need of a chaperone."

The implication that he intended to leave startled Martin and Luisa both. Did the abbot's trust run so deep? Or was this meant as a test of his student's self-command? Either way, Luisa was not certain she approved. She drew herself straighter, only to find that Martin had done the same.

"It shall be as you wish," he said, his chin raised up with pride.

This pricked her temper in a different way. Martin himself wished to be alone with her. He simply did not want to admit it.

⸻

MARTIN tightened his jaw against further lapses of control. He might have succeeded had he not recalled those long black gloves peeling down her shapely arms. They were foreign, those gloves, Western, a symbol of everything he'd turned his back on.

Just as his father had turned his back on him.

The gloves' removal should not have inflamed him, should not have dried his mouth or thickened the restless organ between his legs. They should not have aroused him even more than the sight of her skin shining through her filmy shift. As to that, he should not have cared if she did resemble a goddess in a temple, her breasts impossibly buoyant, her belly a creamy curve. The body was simply a vehicle for experiencing earthly life. It was nothing to worship, nothing to lust over until one ached in every part.

But her beauty shattered his efforts to stay aloof. She was a lake at sunset, a mountain touched with gold. Her skin glowed in the lamplight and her hair . . . her hair made him clench his hands and break into a sweat. She smelled of violets and he wondered if all her kind shared this not-quite-human scent. But all her kind did not matter. Only she did. He wanted to burrow against her and breathe her in. She made him forget what he meant his life to be. For that alone he would have kept his distance.

That is, he would have if Geshe Rinpoche had not left them by themselves.

"Well," purred his tempter, "why don't you show me how it's done?"

You know how it is done, he thought, far better than I.

"You seem to know what goes where," she said with a satiny smile and a pointed glance at his loins.

The insinuation hardened him even further, his shock at odds with his arousal. She must have seen the pictures in his mind, the union of god and goddess in the flesh.

It seemed a travesty that this woman could read him as easily as his guide.

"You were thinking very hard," she explained, her amusement gentler than it might have been. "Perhaps you were too distracted to shield your mind. I will stop listening if you prefer."

"No." He squared his shoulders. "Shielding my thoughts will not erase them. And you will learn better if you put no walls between us."

"As you wish," she said.

Her lashes fell in acknowledgment, then rose. Despite his reluctance, he could not look away. Her eyes were a rich, pure green, the color of innocence and nature, of drives both simple and complex. He forced himself to meet their unspoken promise. Whatever her experience in the sexual arena, he was her equal in many others. More to the point, he had faced lust down before. He was a man, after all, not a rock.

"Here." He took her hand, slipping it under his upper robe. "Keep your palm pressed lightly above my heart."

Her pupils dilated at the contact and the softest of flushes stained her cheeks. She licked her lips. The tip of her tongue was small and sharp. In spite of his resolve, he was not prepared for the strength of his reaction. His penis jerked upward, just once but hard, as if her tongue had wet its tip. Without warning, he became aware of the steady throb of an artery in his neck.

Her fingernails pricked his skin like a kitten's claws.

"Your chest is very hard," she said huskily, then shook her head with impatience.

The gesture reminded him she was hungry; that to her a man was more than a partner for her bed. What would it be like, he wondered, to gratify all those needs at once?

"Focus on your hand," he instructed, striving to keep both their attention where it belonged. "You must concentrate on the energy swirling above my skin. It will feel like the currents of a lake in which you are submersed while very still, or perhaps like a sort of tingle. I am going to meditate, to draw on the life force of the earth. You should feel the flow change. If you are able, I want you to follow the current down."

He closed his eyes and began to breathe, to slow his heart and calm the heated rushing of his blood. The touch of her hand was

oddly pleasant, light now and quiet, with none of the twitches un-
trained people tended to betray. Without being told, she matched
her breathing to his own. In and hold. Out and rest. He slipped
quickly into the state he sought, enjoying for a moment the familiar
sensation of weightless peace. He was more than Martin now, and
less. He was, at least in part, the simple spirit Martin hid.

Before his sense of self could dissolve completely, he drew up a
skein of force, slowly, letting Luisa see how it was done, letting her
feel the gradual brightening of the spinning *tsakhor* above his heart.

There, he said, sensing he did not need to speak aloud, *now I
shall send the energy through the channels of my subtle body.*

She shivered as he began. "Oh," she whispered, "I feel it."

She stepped instinctively closer, her thighs and belly brushing
the woven folds of his robe. It seemed natural to wrap her lightly in
his arms, to slide his hand into the small of her silk-draped back. Her
temple nestled easily beside his jaw. Though he had witnessed the act
of love, he had never held a woman. She was soft, a yielding pleasure
to the touch. His arousal returned as calmly as a dream. The energy
he had drawn from the earth fed its intensity, though its progress
seemed honey slow. Hungry for more, he nuzzled her shell-like ear.

"Follow," he murmured, "follow where I go."

Her body pressed his, her free hand raking languorously up his
skull. Sparks seemed to rustle through the shortness of his hair. She
had been cool but now she warmed, reminding him this was no ordinary woman. No doubt her flesh followed strange rules of its
own. When she rose onto her toes, the tips of her breasts matched
his. The change in position made a place for his erection between
her thighs. His skin tightened, his organ struggling against its own
pounding weight. He longed to press her more closely, longed to
slip his ache inside her hidden warmth. Even through their clothes
he could feel her softness.

But this was not where his mind was supposed to go. He forced
it back to the demonstration. "Do you see?" he said. "Do you feel
the current flow?"

She shuddered as if she, too, had to pull herself from the brink. "I see," she said, "but I don't see how."

He tried to explain, in word and deed, but could not make her comprehend. Control she had in overflowing measure. She could regulate her breathing and her pulse as well as the most masterful yogin. What she could not do was change her state of mind. Nor could he feed energy into her himself. When he tried, it flowed around her aura like a stream of water around an egg. She seemed, as far as he could tell, utterly impermeable.

"I'm sorry," she said. "I simply do not understand."

He drew breath to try again, then let his hold fall away. Luisa stepped back as he did. They stared at each other. At once, he missed her body's warmth. As if she felt the same, she hugged her upper arms. Her breasts swelled into the neckline of her shift, beautiful in a different way now that his trance had begun to fade. His too-worldly organ pounded in complaint.

"I am sorry," he said. "Perhaps my concentration was not complete."

Her laugh was low and sweet. "If your concentration had been complete, I would have been insulted."

He could not resist smiling back, at least for a moment. "I will consult my guide. He may have another idea."

"We could try this again."

Her eyes sparkled with teasing like a glacier in the sun. He knew better than to meet their temptation long. Touching her, and having her touch him—for however laudable a purpose—had strengthened her carnal tug. He knew how it felt to hold her, and he wanted that feeling again.

"I should escort you to your room," he said. "Dawn is near. I know you will want to sleep."

"Yes." Her gaze dropped to the floor.

"Is something wrong?"

She looked up, her smile wry but gentle. "No. I was debating whether to invite you to join me. I have heard that some of your monks . . ." Her voice trailed off at the stiffening of his shoulders. "But not you, I take it. Please forgive me for being forward."

"It is nothing," he said, wanting to sound casual but knowing he did not. "The vow I wish to take would preclude me from experiencing sexual pleasures."

"And in return you would gain what?" Her gaze was curious. His fell to the carmine fullness of her mouth, then slid away.

"A deeper spirituality. A chance to reach nirvana." He caught the question in her eyes. "Nirvana means enlightenment, a knowledge of oneness with the universe, a freedom from the cycle of rebirth."

"Like our concept of heaven?"

"Something like," he said, though from what he knew of Christianity the differences were great. No harps played in a Buddhist's heaven. No one lazed about or sang in heavenly choirs. And no sinner went to hell. Hell was here. Hell was earth. If one learned one's lessons well, one could advance to a higher plane and continue one's progress there.

To his surprise, a very human grin flashed across her face. "You don't want to tell me what you are thinking," she said. "You're afraid you will offend me." With a spontaneity that made his throat tighten, she squeezed his upper arm. "You must not worry. I may not be pious but my faith is firm. A matter of faith, I suppose you'd say, since—despite some people's claim that I am a creature of the devil—I have never met him, no more than I've met God. My beliefs require no proof, nor do I fear to hear others speak of theirs, even at the risk they will change my mind."

Martin blinked at her. His teacher would have approved of her attitude. "In that case, I shall tell you what you wish."

"Good," she said, and strode jauntily toward her folded clothes.

Watching her bottom jiggle was a pleasure he could not bring himself to forgo.

MARTIN and his guide stood shoulder to shoulder on the lamasery roof, gazing out toward the soft green haze of the nearest valley. Soon spring would bring herds of *gowa* to graze on the growing grass; herds of pilgrims, too, though not so many as trekked to the holier shrine at Kangrinpoche. He found himself glad they were not here yet. They would have been a distraction from Luisa.

She interests me, he thought, facing the truth as he had been trained. She pulls not just at my body but at my mind.

What would it be like to see history unfold in a single incarnation? To love the material world so deeply one never wished to leave? Martin shook his head. Luisa claimed faith in a higher power, but she did not experience its reality even as much as the youngest *chela*. She could not touch the truth behind the illusion. All things were one and yet Luisa seemed alone: separate from both her God and her fellow beings. She should have been miserable. He could not understand why she was not.

No doubt he would have pondered the matter longer if his teacher had not spoken.

"Do you remember," he said, "when your family first came to Shisharovar?"

"I shall never forget it. I ran straight up the stairs and tried to kick two monks out of 'my' room."

The abbot's eyes crinkled at the corners. "You were quite adamant for an eight-year-old."

"But it was all so clear to me. This was where I belonged."

"Yes," said his guide, "it must have seemed so. I admit, I felt the tug of it myself: to keep my old friend by my side. It is comforting to find again what you have lost, almost as comforting as finding what you have forgotten you ever had."

Martin wondered what the abbot was getting at, but his placid profile gave no clue. He felt his forehead pleat together. "I know sixteen years was a long time to stay away, but I could not have remained here then, not when it meant abandoning my mother. My father leaving before my birth was bad enough. I could not betray her, too."

The abbot patted his rumpled sleeve. "I did not mean to imply your choice was wrong. You had a lifetime in this monastery, more than one. To mindlessly repeat what one has done before can hardly be considered progress."

"But I belong here now," Martin said. To his dismay, his voice made the words a question.

The abbot smiled. "I do not doubt we are all where we're meant to be. Speaking of which"—his teacher shot him a sidelong glance—"what do you think of your new student?"

Martin's hands were clasped on the stony ledge. He stared at them, amazed they did not bear the silky imprint of her curves. "I regret I could not help her."

"We have only begun. No one could expect the first attempt to succeed. And I am certain you did your best."

Had he, Martin wondered, or had he allowed the clamoring of his body to drown out a better, quieter guidance? "I am not certain—" he began.

The abbot broke in. "She is settled in her room?"

"Yes," he said, though he was perturbed by the interruption. "I brought her blankets as the sun was rising. When she took them, she stumbled and nearly fell. I think she is weaker than she is used to. I sat with her for a while, to ensure she was well, but I do not think she knew I was there. She slept strangely, like a fakir on a bed of nails. Her body was stiff and cold to touch. I did not see her breathe more than twice in a quarter hour."

He did not add that her appearance had unsettled him, more statue than corpse but disturbing all the same. For a moment, he had feared she died in truth. But then her chest had risen with a shallow inhalation. The relief he'd felt had not been logical, no more than his gentle stroking of her hair. That contact could have comforted only him.

"She seemed . . . vulnerable," he said, the confession as troubling as the memory.

"Indeed," mused his guide, "if one wished to destroy such creatures, clearly their rest would be the time to try."

"Sir!" Martin was shocked beyond holding his tongue. Among Buddhists, the taking of life, any life, was a powerful prohibition.

His teacher raised his brows. "I am not proposing we murder our guest, only that we prepare for any eventuality."

His tone was eminently reasonable. Martin schooled his pulse to a steadier rate. "Forgive me. I know you will do everything possible to prevent such a necessity from arising."

He did not understand the small, satisfied smile with which the abbot turned back to the view. He seemed almost smug as he spoke again. "I have thought of something else," he said, "a meditation that might bring down her walls. We can drug some wine to induce the proper mental state. It will be dangerous, of course. Inexperienced as she is, she might get lost in the visions the herbs produce."

"Most likely she *will* get lost," Martin said, aghast. "Even trained monks sometimes mistake a vision for reality. Such a thing could break her mind!"

"Not if she has a guide."

Martin caught his breath. He sensed his teacher was not proposing to fill that role himself. "No," he said, before he could think better of it. "Rinpoche, please do not ask that of me. That kind of journey is too intimate. I would—She is already—"

The abbot cocked his head at him. "I know your response to her is strong, perhaps as strong as your first response to Shisharovar?"

"My reaction to her has nothing in common with that. Nothing! I have no memories of her. None!"

"One does not need a memory for there to be a karmic link. Dread can be as much a sign of connection as love. In any case, I know you have not forgotten the importance of facing fears."

Martin's head could scarcely hang any lower. "No, rinpoche."

"Good. Because I am asking you to help our guest face hers. Fear is invariably the barrier to achievement. Once she overcomes it, I suspect we will progress."

Martin had no doubt of that, but to what they would progress he dared not imagine.

Four

D ESPITE the abbot's sponsorship, Luisa's presence unsettled the other inhabitants of the lamasery. Because of this, her tiny, isolated cell was transformed into a chamber for meditation. She was given a robe to wear, a simple wrap of woven cloth. Pots of incense were carried in and a *thangka*, or banner of painted silk, was hung across one wall. The image was grim to say the least: a fire-enshrouded demon with a necklace of severed heads.

"That is Hayagriva," Martin said, "the deity of awakened energy. Those figures he is trampling represent the concepts of self and personality, both illusions of the earthly world. Illusion, of course, is the source of all human suffering."

Luisa hummed in response and tried to blank her face. When Martin explained the purpose of this exercise, she had acknowledged the importance of facing one's deepest fears. She could not, however, imagine wanting to lose one's sense of self. She had spent her human life as little more than a beast of burden: unseen and unheard, almost too beaten down to think. Even after she was changed, her master had to bully her into learning. *You need a strong mind*, he'd said, *to face the dangers of the world. You, my little peasant, will bow to no one else's child.*

However dubious that claim, she relished being someone now,

someone who could read and reflect and affect not just her own future but that of others. If her identity was an illusion, she was not sure she wished to know.

Behind her, Martin chuckled. "I'm sorry," he said when she turned around. "If you could see your expression . . . The self we seek to lose is only the self that is not true. Yes, we believe all beings are part of a greater whole, but within each is an essence that is unique."

Luisa suspected their concept of uniqueness differed. Rather than debate him, she walked her fingertips up his arm. "You know," she said silkily, "you have a beautiful smile. You would cut quite a swath if I brought you back with me to Florence."

Martin's eyes widened. Clearly his experience with flirtation was very small. She looked forward to seeing him blush, but a quiet dignity fell over his face instead. He bowed from the waist. "I thank you for your words," he said. "I am sure you meant to honor me."

To her amazement, heat prickled over her cheeks. His politeness shamed her. They both knew her intent had been not to honor but to tease.

"I do honor you," she said, meaning it sincerely. "I have to remind myself how earnest you are, and that there is no show in you. You are different from other churchmen I have known."

"As you are different from other Europeans I have known— and not just because of what you are." His smile returned, bringing a gleam of admiration to his eyes. The admiration seemed for her both as a person and a woman.

Uncomfortable with the pleasure this inspired, she turned her eyes to the wine into which he was mixing herbs. The cup that held the brew was skillfully worked silver studded with turquoise and coral stones. The merchant in her wondered if the monks had similar creations she might buy. But better, mayhap, not to ask about that now.

"I am not certain this will work," she warned. "*Upyr* tend to resist the effect of drugs."

"These are not ordinary drugs. My teacher prepared these herbs himself."

Well, she thought, her humor recovering: if his *teacher* had prepared them, naturally they would not fail!

With a little bow, he handed her the cup and watched her drink it down. The taste was peculiar, heavy, with an oily bitterness overlaid. Whatever Geshe Rinpoche had concocted, it was strong. Still, she felt nothing as Martin led her to the cushion-bed and helped her to lie down.

"You should relax," he said, lowering himself to the floor beside her. She turned her head to watch his descent, awed again by his grace. His legs seemed to fold naturally beneath him and his spine bore a straightness an emperor would envy. His face was unearthly in its calm. That one so young should have such self-possession, she could only marvel.

He touched her cheek with the back of one curled finger. "It may be a while before the medicine takes effect. Why don't you breathe with me, as you did before?"

As she took his advice, a hush settled around her, and a dangerously seductive comfort. In they drew the incense-laden air; out they blew the breath of life. To soothe her, Martin trailed the tips of three fingers along the naked inside of her arm. She doubted he would have done this if he'd known the pleasure *upyr* took in touch—and no touch more than that of humans. Her kind loved the stroke of mortal hands almost as much as loving it made them wary. To crave a thing was to give it power. But perhaps God meant the need to humble them. Perhaps she was foolish to try to pull her own fate free.

Just as she might have been foolish to trust these lamas and their herbs.

"I'm afraid I do not feel anything," she confessed, "apart from apprehension. I wish you would talk to me while we wait."

"What would you like to talk about?"

"Would you tell me how you came to be a monk?"

His smile was as gentle as his touch. "You could say it was karma. I was conceived here, as you may have guessed."

She nodded. "Your father was the English trader who was stranded in the pass. I do not suppose you knew him well."

Martin's only sign of emotion was a subtle tightening of his lips. "He did not remain here long enough to meet his son, though he knew he was going to have one."

"When I spoke with him in London," she said carefully, not certain he wished to hear, "he seemed the sort of man no one can hold. A restless soul. A foreign fever had spoilt his health and his sight was not what it had been. I think he resented getting older because he could only talk about his adventures. I cannot be sure—his was not an easy mind to read—but I think, underneath, he regretted the human ties he left behind."

"I assume he did not regret them enough to mention me and my mother."

"No," she admitted, "though when he spoke of Tibet, his eyes were warm." Martin pulled a face and she left the sensitive topic behind. "Tell me about your mother. She must have been special."

At once his expression softened. Luisa did not need her powers to know he loved her.

"She was a woman of Kham," he said, "a member of a traveling performance troupe. The Khampa have a reputation for being beautiful and fierce, and my mother was no exception. She once broke a man's nose because he kicked a dog. One punch and he was down. But her voice was like birds warbling in the spring. With her brothers and cousins she would sing and dance and do acrobatic feats on horseback. I remember going from place to place, riding in front of her in the saddle and feeling luckier than any prince. My mother was completely fearless. She always kept me safe."

Which suggested there had been something to keep him safe from. "It cannot have been easy growing up between two cultures," she said, thinking of children she had known, of how cruel they could be to anyone who was different.

The curve of her thoughts caught a piece of memory: Martin as a boy backed into an alley by half a dozen ill-fed youths. Clods of dirt bounced off his lifted arms while tears of fury rolled down his cheeks. How dare they say such things about his mother! She loved him better than all their mothers put together, *was* better than them all.

The violence of his anger shamed the boy he was. He would have hurt those children if he could, even knowing he was much luckier than they.

She broke the link, not wanting to betray what she had seen.

"I was loved," he said, "and I always knew that someday I would live here. From my first glimpse of Shisharovar on the peak, it was my beacon, the place where I knew I would find a home. When my mother died in a fall a year ago, I returned."

The memory seemed to leave no mark on his face but Luisa saw beneath the calm recital. He claimed his mother kept him safe and yet it was he who felt compelled to remain with her, delaying his dream until she could not need him anymore. How great an outcast had she been because of her choice of lovers? She had given Martin an English name. That suggested there had been more between her and his father than an affair. When John Moore went back to England, he must have cut a painful wound.

"You are very loyal," she said.

His robe rustled softly with his shrug. "It is not hard to be loyal to those you love, nor to return to a cherished home."

Luisa's breath escaped in a snort. "I have known people who could barely be loyal to themselves."

"That is their loss," he said as if what he'd done were a common thing. He seemed not to know how rare his integrity was.

Feeling oddly off balance, she covered his stroking hand. "Do you really believe you lived before?"

"I have dreamed of events from other incarnations and later had them confirmed. I have recognized possessions I used to own and people whose paths crossed mine. Of course"—his gaze met hers with banked amusement—"I do not expect you to take this on my word. As you said: faith is a matter of faith. There can be no proof for those who wish to doubt. But tell me of you. I am curious to hear of the man who made you, the *upyr* elder."

"You mean Auriclus." Luisa laughed quietly in remembrance. "My master was tall and dark. Sinfully handsome. The perfect lure for a fisherman's work-worn wife. He had a face like a tragedian, as weary and sad as if he had taken the weight of the world upon his shoulders, as if compassion for every suffering creature suffused his breast. Our kind are good at illusion. Even now I don't know if his face spoke true."

"Did he seek you out?"

"In a way. But I noticed him before he noticed me. It was just past sunset in Florence. The sky was the color of lemons, the clouds like shreds of cotton dipped in blood. He was leaning on the quay, wrapped in his somber cloak, watching the scattered traffic on the Arno. I remember wondering what a fine man like him must think of those rivermen, with their talk and their swagger and their garish clothes. Looking back, he was probably judging which one would make the better meal. That day, though, I felt lower than I ever had. I was less than the boatmen, less than their whores, less than the pink-eyed goat who gave us milk.

"Auriclus must have heard my thoughts because he turned to me, not smiling, just staring as if I were a puzzle he wanted to work out. His attention shamed me so badly I scurried away as quickly as I could, but I saw him the next day at the well, and again the following evening as I left the *mercato*. I had a pomegranate in my basket, a treat I would have to hide when I got home. He blocked my way, then took the fruit to draw it to his nose. His expression when he inhaled was like a man in the throes of climax. When he spoke his voice was as husky as if he'd had one. It made me shiver to hear it, as much as did his words. He told me I smelled better than the fruit, as sweet and clean as summer grass. It was the first compliment anyone had ever paid me.

He had me for the price of it, so cheaply was I willing to sell my soul.

"Only later did I learn he was not supposed to choose me. He had a rival, a student to whom he had ceded the world's great cities to avert a war. I was an experiment to him, an attempt to create a child who would be a bridge between their broods."

"Did it work?"

"I do not know. Oddly enough, I have never met another child he made. I suspect he would say he failed. I may have begun as a peasant but in the end I succumbed to civilization's lure."

"Did he change you that first day?"

She rolled her head in negation against the cushion. "No. But I dreamed of him after our meeting, erotic dreams that made me long for sleep. I was scrubbing the wash and imagining his kiss when I tore my husband's best shirt, the only one that had no mend. I hardly minded when Giulio came into the courtyard to beat me. I had a secret, you see, a hopeless fantasy that made me strong.

"And then it was not hopeless because Auriclus appeared, my dark avenging angel. One sweep of his arm tossed my husband against the wall. He plucked me up and away before I could think to resist. He said he wanted to fan the spark in my eyes to life. Said I deserved to be showered with jewels and draped in silk. I knew he must be a madman but I let him do as he wished because his words were food to me and because, by that point, I did not care what it might cost. My children were grown. I had nothing left to lose."

"Your husband had beaten you before."

"Yes," she said calmly. "To his mind, I was no different from a dog who had misbehaved."

To her surprise, this—rather than her confession of adultery—roused Martin's ire. "He should not have done that. That is not the proper way between man and wife."

Luisa spread her hands. "My husband suffered for his abuse, though he knew it not. I could have been more to him than I was.

But that was long ago. Another life, as you would say." Her mouth curved in a grin. "Now I do not even wish him to roast in hell."

"You are wise to let your resentment go," Martin said. "Strong emotion can bind people together for many incarnations. Perhaps you will not have to meet him on earth again."

Luisa began to laugh, the idea striking her as funny. What would her husband say if he saw her now? Probably fall to his knees and pray. *Get thee behind me, spawn of Satan . . . but please seduce me before you go!*

The room rocked sideways with her laughter. Her head was so light she thought it might float away.

Martin smiled at her hilarity. "Yes," he said, "the herbs have begun their work. Just remember, you must focus your mind on what you fear."

But her mind was beyond her control, cut loose from its moorings like an oarless boat swept down a river. A landscape of images rolled by on the bank. The day her father sold her to her husband to clear a debt. The dirty clay of the hovel floor. One of her sons a wriggling bundle at her breast. So sweet they'd been, a tiny ray of love in her loveless life . . . until they'd grown into smaller versions of their father.

She'd tried to prevent it—how she'd tried!—but their world, or perhaps their natures, stopped their ears to the pleadings of a woman. Kindness was weakness to them; respect the reward for brutish force. She watched her youngest steal a toy from a neighbor's child. When she paddled his bottom, her husband beat her. *Let him learn,* he had roared, *how to live in a heartless world.* Her cheek stung from the blow, a tooth spit bloody into her hand. Suddenly, with the muddled logic of a dream, Auriclus held her close with his face in her golden hair, her only beauty that remained.

Come to me, he'd crooned. *Let me bring you to life again.*

His bite had all the tenderness of death, lancing the stored-up bitterness from her soul. She was nothing then, only pleasure, clinging to his shoulders until the rising, throbbing silence swept her under, into oblivion and forgetting. When she woke she was alive as she never had been before. Strong, healthy, beautiful. So beautiful. Without merit or justice, the power of attraction was simply hers.

For that alone she would have adored him, but her master had not let her. *Little Luisa,* he'd teased, *adore what you can be, not what you think I am.* Sometimes she thought he was sorry he'd made her. He would watch her at her books or her correspondence as if he could not fathom who she was. *Clever little monkey,* he'd call her then, though he might as well have said *clever monster.*

Fourteen years later he was gone, driven out of Florence—so he claimed—by the rise of one infamous book-burning monk. Savonarola had seduced the masses, taught them to hate their bodies and their minds. *I will kill him,* her sire explained. *If I do not leave, I will spray his maddened blood across the square.*

Auriclus did not care that his abandonment broke her heart, that she had a growing business she could not leave. But at least he taught her not to kill. *Charm the humans,* he always said. *Charm them and set them free.*

But it was not the humans who tested her adherence to his rule. That honor went to the *upyr* she met on a trip to London. Until she surprised them hunting for sailors by the docks, she had not known her kind were there. She guessed at once that Auriclus had not made them. They had a sleeker look than he, a darker, more urbane smell.

Mindful of his warnings about Nim Wei's brood, she had approached them with all the diplomacy she possessed. Staying away had not been an option. She longed too fiercely for the company of her kind. Perhaps they could teach her what she sensed her master had neglected. Sadly, far from teaching her, the English circle met her overtures with hostility, calling her *spy* and forcing her into situations where, had she been less strong and quick, she easily might have died.

Only when they discovered her skill at commerce did they begin to warm. Money they respected, money and ambition.

Ironically, finding them made her lonelier than ever: feeling so separate from those she should have been most like. Auriclus cared for humans. These *upyr* saw them only as animals to exploit.

In defiance, she gathered a mortal harem, three youths flush with manhood who vied for the privilege of fulfilling her every need. That was the beginning of her love affair with humans. She chose them for what they could teach her, about life or business or the mysteries of the spirit. Minstrels succumbed to her, adventurers and dukes. To her delight, her business grew by leaps and bounds. She never thralled the humans with whom she dealt; that did not seem fair play. Even so, her conquests at the court of Suleiman were productive, winning her trading rights few could boast. If cleverness failed, she did not scruple to use her immortal body as her coin. Sometimes it bought her influence, other times merely pleasure.

She remembered the pleasure now: hands, kisses, the passion-tensed curves of sweat-streaked skin. Men driven to madness by desire. Gasping. Trembling. Nearly bursting with their lust. *Take me,* they'd plead as she slid her tongue along their veins. *Take anything you want.*

Someone gripped her jaw and turned her face to his. Martin. Beautiful, noble Martin.

"Luisa," he said, his voice commanding, "this is not the way to face your fears."

His eyes burned like the center of a flame. She reached for him, her hand falling limply against his chest. "I want you more," she whispered, the truth freed by the drug. "More than any man I have known."

His gaze went black. She saw him swallow, his Adam's apple moving strongly in his throat. Never mind his oath. Part of him wanted to bed her now.

"Luisa," he said, "remember why you are here."

She sighed like the melancholy finish of a tale. Then she did as he advised.

⌐⌐⌐⌐ ⫷⫸ ⌐⌐⌐⌐

THE drug was meant to let him into her mind, but what he found there shocked him. The things she had done with those men, those many men, were beyond what he imagined. He knew, naturally, what the procreative act entailed. Growing up as he had, in communal tents and inns, the basic facts had been his from an early age. The more esoteric were part of his education since coming to Shisharovar. After all, the union of male and female essences had spiritual meaning, too.

What he hadn't known was the sheer physical joy one could take in sensual exploration. He had been there with her, had felt her body vibrate with longing and her teeth itch teasingly in their sheaths. He'd wanted to be those men, touching her, tasting her, forging thickly into her sex. One pair of hands was not enough. He wanted to be them all.

And the places she had traveled! Stormy seas. Opulent palaces. Even England, so wet and dreary compared to the sunny sparkle of Tibet, possessed an appeal he could not deny. What, he wondered, were those curious platelike collars women wore around their necks? For what reason did they hang those fancy curtains on their beds? Velvets he'd seen, and lustrous embroidered silks, the exotic, nested backdrop to her play.

She was almost childlike in her love of her possessions, though he could not deny a discriminating mind lay behind her greed. Here in Tibet, a painting was an act of worship; no artist would sign his name. In her homeland, Luisa had gleefully added luster to the name of scores. Da Vinci, Michelangelo, Ghirlandaio, and Titian: her patronage had helped them all.

In truth, her life was a foreign jewel. The more he turned it, the more the facets shone. He reminded himself these were temporal pleasures that would soon pass away. The key to Luisa's freedom lay far from such glittering bits of stone.

When she told him she wanted him, though, more than she had wanted any man, the admission struck a resounding triumph in his soul, momentarily drowning out truths he knew.

She lured him because of what she was, not in spite of it.

He needed all his strength to pull them back to the path. "Luisa," he said, "remember why you are here."

His words took swift effect. A flash cut across his vision like the blade of a Mongol butcher's knife. He saw her dream self. She held a baby to her breast—her son—warm and plump. Dread closed around him. Her lips brushed the infant's milky neck. Sweet neck. Soft neck. She tipped the wobbling head back in her palm. Her gaze locked to the tiny pulse. Her baby. Her sweet, warm, sleepy baby. Her hunger rose like a mournful wail, like a sin she could not name.

This was her fear, the monster lurking in her shadows.

"No," she whispered in his mind and in the room.

She set the child on the floor where it gurgled at her wide-eyed, waving its dimpled arms. She had not touched it. She would not touch it, not even in a dream.

"Luisa," he said, knowing this darkness had to be faced.

She shook her head and backed away. *No*, she said, no sound to it. Then she turned on her heel and ran.

He called after her, warning her she'd get lost. She was not familiar with the geography of dreams: how fantasy and fear could parade as truth. To his dismay, she did not heed him. She ran up a narrow and odorous city street, carts in her way, horses, men in tight-fitting hose. She shoved past them, shouting, "Make way! Make way!" They bowed down to her beauty with sweeps of feathered hats. Ignoring them, she flung open a wooden door.

Her harem waited inside the richly appointed room, the same three youths he had seen before. They were old now, walking skeletons with skin, their hands reaching ghoulishly from lace and velvet sleeves. "Don't let us die," they beseeched. "Make us what you are."

She covered her eyes and moaned. She did not know how to change them. She was powerless to help.

The emptiness inside her yawned like a pit.

And then she grabbed them, one by one, drinking them dry. When their bodies fell to the Turkish carpet they were young again, not so young as when they'd graced her bed but strong men still. She had made a terrible mistake. She had killed them in their prime. She had been too hungry, too rash, too loathe to see them age and die. She stumbled to her knees.

This had to be a nightmare. It made no sense for her to have done this. She thought she heard Martin say *Yes, these are only phantoms* but there was blood on her hands. Sins enough to make an angel weep. Her hands were red. Her mouth.

She gripped the gate that rose before her and pulled herself to her feet. The bars were strong. Immovable even to her. They glowed with opalescence as if they'd been carved of pearl. Martin felt her relax, her head dropping back in tired surrender.

Yes, she thought, I am dead now and they must let me in.

But the gate did not open. The wind blew through it and the sun shone on it but no one came to see.

"Speak to me," she demanded, clenching the pearly bars. "Tell me if I am damned."

The air stirred behind her. Luisa spun. A man stood on the path in a dusty robe. He was tall and bearded, gaunt but strong. His eyes looked out from soulful hollows, their expression too beautiful to bear. Martin sensed Luisa knew who he was.

"Answer me," she said in a choking voice. "If I'm damned, I want to know."

The man said nothing, only stared at her sadly. Despite his humble garb, a golden shimmer bathed his skin. He reminded Martin of a bodhisattva, a wise old soul come to earth again.

"I want the ability to choose how I live," she said. "I want my free will freed."

You chose, said the man. *You chose when you let your master make you what you are.*

With that, the man disappeared, and the gate, leaving nothing but grass and sun as far as the eye could see.

"I *am* damned then," she said.

She waited in the silence, empty of everything but despair. Tiny, starlike daisies waved in the gentle breeze. They did not care. No one cared but her. She thrust back her shoulders and firmed her jaw. If she was damned, so be it. She still had herself to answer to. She would live what life she had as she saw fit. If it ended, she would pay the price without demur. Her God had rejected her. Perhaps He had a right to. But from now on, her heart and mind were the only judges she would heed.

Something changed with her decision. Martin felt it. The silence was ringing, the air brightening as if the sun were rising yet again. Each blade of grass glowed like a gem. Luisa's edges were dissolving. The barrier that had guarded her heart for seeming ages had been destroyed. Energy burst from the earth in a golden flood. The sweetness as it rushed inside her was indescribable, a heady mix of light and love and—

And then the link between Luisa and Martin snapped.

Thrust from her vision, Martin gasped. Here, in the material world, Luisa's body began convulsing. Martin could scarcely hold her shoulders down. She had succeeded in tapping the auric resources of the earth. Now energy poured into her unchecked, energy she obviously was not meant to have. To Martin's finely honed senses the flow seemed an angry, caustic river. With every second, the violence of her struggles heightened. Tendons stood out on her neck. Her hands curled into claws.

"Luisa!" he cried, pulling her to his breast.

He could not connect their minds. The energy was a torrent that swept his attempts aside.

The door crashed open. Geshe Rinpoche had been alerted by

his distress. "Speak to her," he panted, robe askew. "You must reach into her vision with your voice."

"But how can she hear?"

"Those in trances still hear those they love," said his teacher. "You must have faith."

Martin could not refuse to try. "Luisa," he said, rocking her gently in his arms, "what you are doing is not safe. I know it feels lovely in your dream. I know it feels as if your angels had at last welcomed you home. But if you do not come back, your physical self will die. You said you did not want that. You said you loved your life."

His throat choked up but he forced himself to speak. "I do not wish to lose you, Luisa. I wish . . . I wish to get to know you on this plane, in this life. Please do not make me wait. Please come back to me now."

With an abruptness that shocked him, her convulsions stopped. Her body relaxed, then went completely still.

He could not help but fear she died.

"Lay her down," instructed his teacher.

Reluctantly Martin did so. She was gaunt, her beauty burned thin, her skin as white and chill as snow. She looked even less human than when she slept.

The abbot knelt by her other side. "Luisa," he said commandingly, and laid both hands atop her heart. Martin knew he was trying to use his healing powers.

For one long, dark moment, nothing happened. She is gone, he thought, even as his mind groaned in denial. Then, like a person saved from drowning, she drew a ragged breath. Martin nearly collapsed in relief. Her eyelids fluttered. She licked her lips. "What— What happened?"

Though she looked at Martin, the abbot answered. "I misjudged, I'm afraid. That energy was poison to you. You must not try to take it again."

"Poison . . ." A slow, shining tear rolled down her cheek.

Martin knew what she was thinking: that all that love was not for her. She did not understand her vision had been a creation of her mind. No holy messenger had rejected her. No gates of heaven had been closed.

Throat tight, he brushed her tear away. "Luisa, the things you saw were just a dream. Your god, if he exists and if he is the source of what we call the energy of the earth, gives this bounty equally to saint and sinner. I do not know why you could not drink, but it is no judgment against your soul, merely an experiment that went awry—as if I were to eat a horse's hay."

She smiled but the attempt was weak. "Tired," she murmured, her eyes drifting shut. "Need to sleep."

Martin and his teacher watched her draw a score of breaths. Then, their thoughts in accord, they stepped quietly away.

The abbot rubbed his chin. "This troubles me," he said. "We have left her weaker than before. Even if I found another method to attempt, I am not sure she could withstand it. I am not even sure she would survive a journey home. She must feed, Martin, in the manner of her kind."

"We cannot ask any of the monks to let her drink."

"No," the abbot agreed, "we cannot."

Martin's heart thumped in his chest. He knew what the abbot was asking and he knew he could refuse. If he did not offer up his blood, Martin had no doubt his guide would volunteer. Even if it killed him, Geshe Rinpoche would do it. That was the kind of man his teacher was.

"She will put me in her thrall," Martin said, the rasp of words not quite a protest.

His teacher's gaze was steady. "I believe you are strong enough to resist her."

If I *want* to resist her, Martin thought, far from certain that he did. He remembered Luisa's harem, the slide of her slim, pale hands along straining skin. How easy it would be, how tempting, to make her *upyr* magic his excuse for giving in.

Then a flash of intuition struck. "This is a test," he said. "You want to know if I am worthy to take my vow."

His teacher neither confirmed nor denied the guess. He put his hand on Martin's arm. "You must decide soon," he said. "I do not think our visitor has much time."

Five

MARTIN'S strong arms lifted her from the cushions and eased her onto his lap. Even that small motion made the room spin around her head. She moaned against the musty sweetness of his robes, smelling incense and skin and an acrid touch of fear.

She thought the fear must be for her.

"Shh," he soothed. One hand stroked the pale gold curtain of her hair while the other cradled her back. He pressed her mouth to his neck. "Drink."

The word made her jerk with longing. She drew back from temptation and stared.

His gaze evaded hers. "I know you've been trying not to, but you are weak."

"Martin . . ."

"I know you will not hurt me." The words were fierce. "Just . . ."

"Just?"

"Please do not make me do things I would not wish."

Then she understood. Smiling softly, she flattened her palm against his smoothly shaven cheek. His skin was so warm it seemed to burn, its color rich against the whiteness of her hand. His eyes glittered in the dimness, wavering between trust and doubt. "Martin, when blood is offered freely an *upyr* does not, cannot, suborn her victim's will."

"She cannot?"

She combed his bristled hair around his ear. "No."

"Will you take very much?"

Luisa shuddered, aroused—or frightened—by a lingering fragment of her dream. "Enough to make you weak. But only for a while. When you recover you will be stronger than before, more resistant to harm or illness. The effect does not last forever: a week, possibly longer."

"No wonder those men—" He closed his mouth and flushed. "Forgive me. I did not mean to suggest you had no other charms."

"Were you thinking I took my harem against their will?"

"Well, I am sure you did not have to force them into your bed."

She laughed beneath her breath. "Thank you for that, though my scruples have not always been so fine. In this instance, I assure you their thrall was no more than any healthy young male might feel when an attractive woman offers him a sexual adventure. I may have added a few compulsions, of course, to ensure they did not speak of me where they should not."

"I imagine they were easier to control because they were young."

She saw he meant this as an observation and not an insult, but she squirmed beneath it nonetheless. "How uncomfortably perceptive you are! Yes, older men—or for that matter, younger men with strength of mind—are difficult to influence without the added coercion of a bite. As the years passed, I found I did not like to use that means."

"Friendship can be lonely when it is forced, or when it is not with an equal."

Tears sprang to her eyes at his understanding. Since her brush with death, Luisa had felt strangely vulnerable, not in body but in spirit—as if her heart had in truth been opened by her dream. His simple statement reached into the raw place, putting into words the yearning of many years.

"I have been lonely," she admitted. "That is why your . . . consideration for me means the world."

He smiled, an unexpectedly boyish grin. Seeing it, she was happy despite the danger to them both—not to mention to the achievement of her desire. Assurances aside, stopping before she hurt him would not be easy. Too much time had passed since she last fed and there were too many ways she found him appealing. With one nail she traced the strong blue thread that marked his neck. Her throat tightened. "Maybe I should not do this."

"My master says you must feed." Though Martin's expression was stubborn, worry lay beneath: worry and an intriguing glimmer of guilt. A muscle bunched in his jaw. "I want you to," he said, his innate honesty forcing the gruff admission. "I am curious to know how it feels."

She could not control the quickening of her pulse. So. He was curious. She skated her fingers down his vein and wet her lips. "It hurts for a moment, for the penetration." She lifted her eyes to his. "After that, it is erotic. Taking blood is the most intimate act a child of midnight can perform."

"More intimate than sex?"

His voice was husky. A quick, sharp sting told her her teeth had sharpened to feeding length. "More intimate than sex," she agreed, "though drawing what we need from another's veins awakens that desire as well."

"You will refrain from indulging it, though, won't you?"

"You may not want me to. Humans find the act exciting, too."

"I have faced attraction before. I am not afraid."

But he should have been. Martin could not guess how strong the urge to join could be, a frenzy of lust that sometimes hours of bed play could not sate.

"My resolve is strong," he said, sensing her hesitance. "I do not fear to put it to the test."

Her smile, gentle as it was, must have been too knowing. His eyes narrowed and he yanked the wrap of his robe halfway down his front. Her smile froze as her body heated. His muscles were tight and flat, their edges chiseled, their development perfectly balanced from sternum to shoulder cap. His chest hair was sparser than a European's, sheer dark swirls that clung to his flawless olive skin. His nipples were flushed and delicately erect. Yearning to pinch them, she curled her nails into her palms.

"Drink," he ordered in a tone that brooked no denial.

She had not the willpower to resist. With a moan she pressed her mouth to his neck, open, breathing heat and soul-deep need. His grip tightened on her shoulders but he did not push away. She licked him, dragging her tongue up the beating vein until a shiver swept his frame. He was hers now. She set her teeth against him and bit down.

Blood flowed, filling her mouth with power and life and will as strong as sugared ginger to her tongue. Here was vigor. Here was hot male strength. Enthralled by his taste, she drew on him, wrapping her arms with grateful fervor around his back. Oh, it was good to be close, better than good. Martin seemed to agree. Gasping her name, he slid his hand down her arching spine. She knew he was losing control but she could not hold back. She pushed even tighter to his chest. Her breasts flattened beneath her robe, her nipples as hard as his. When she writhed against him, he murmured what sounded like a prayer.

It was almost all she wanted, this evidence of his desire. Strength rushed into her with each swallow. She wanted to take him inside her, every throbbing, rigid inch. Desperate to touch his skin, she pushed her hand under his robe. The small of his back was smooth and dewed with sweat. She gripped his narrow buttock. His moan was even sweeter than his blood. Greed swamped her: to have him, to drink him down. Her heart pounded violently in alarm. With a groan of reluctance, she tore her mouth away.

"No," he said, a hiss that drew her eyes to his. His pupils were shining jet within rings of azure flame. She could tell he was dazed but not as deeply as most humans would have been. His protest was not the effect of any thrall. She had not taken anything he did not freely give. As if to assure her of this, he cupped her blood-flushed cheek.

"Let me make you strong. You haven't taken half of what I can offer. Here." He pressed her palm to his breast, his voice sinking to a growl. "Bite me here. Slowly. I want you to make it last."

A rush of moisture squeezed from the tender hollow between her legs. "Slowly," she repeated, the word shaking on her lips.

He nodded, shyness in it, but pride as well. His chin lifted in silent challenge. He did not care how others did this. He was asking for what he wished, drawing the veil from secrets most lovers hid. She thought she had never been so moved by someone's trust. She knew she could not refuse. "Just a little more," she agreed, then flashed a grin. "By sips."

She bit him slowly this time, letting him savor the dull cold sting of breaking skin. From what she had seen of his country, not to mention the discipline of the monks, she was not surprised he would welcome a little pain. It was a test to him, a hurdle to rise above. True to her expectations, he shuddered with enjoyment as her tongue swept his tightened nipple. Knowing he liked this, she suckled him as she drank. His breath came more harshly and his muscles tensed. His aura pricked like fire where it touched hers.

But she wanted to offer him more than this. She moved her second hand to the bend between his torso and his thigh. He flinched but did not withdraw. Slowly, giving him time to stop her, she shifted her caress to the rigid swelling where his erection pushed out his robe. Its crown bumped against his belly, its long thick ridge an invitation to measure how much he'd fill. A plenitude, she decided, her body softening deep inside. He was already too hard to get any harder. She could tell from the way his shaft resisted her gentle squeeze. He sighed at the pressure as if he'd been waiting an eternity to feel it. Taking this as permission, she slipped her hand beneath the cloth and held him bare.

⸺⸺⸺

THE shock of Luisa's touch was not one for which he could have prepared. Her warmth, her strength, her devastating knowledge of male desire combined to set his nerves ablaze. His body tightened in every muscle, then melted with delight. He knew he ought to stop her; no man could resist this temptation long. Instead he closed his eyes and let his head drop on his neck. She was rubbing his aching length, her fingers tightening and releasing in a rhythm that made him wonder just how long such pleasure could be borne.

In all his life he had barely touched himself. Now those years of denied sensations seemed to squeeze together into the present, into those burning inches of stiffened flesh. Waves of rapture rolled through him, surging then ebbing, only to gather higher than before. He knew if she did not stop he would unravel like the sexual novice that he was.

But she had no mercy for his fears. Shifting in his lap, she began to draw on his organ with both hands. The strength of her hold pulled him outward from his body, his testicles drawn up, his tip seeming to burn and prickle each time her fingers tugged its rim. He was going to explode. He was going to burst like a Chinese rocket. Sweat ran into his eyes as he fought the desperate urge. The sounds he made were hardly human.

He had thought he knew desire; had believed he felt it when the young girls and the widows tried to lure him into their tents. They had smiled for him and tossed their braided hair. They had wagged their hips and let him see them with other men. To them, he was a challenge or a game: the handsome half Khampa who wanted to be a monk. Once or twice he had been tempted but never like this, never with more than his body.

This was a lust to sear the soul.

He cried out as she left his breast, and again as she found his mouth. Oh, the taste of her, the feel! She had to lead the kiss, his astonished, enchanting first. It was a mating, he realized, of lips and teeth and tongue. Sensation multiplied as they parried, wetly, sweetly. He tasted a hint of copper, then only her. Her incisors were sharp but they did not cut him.

So lost was he in pleasure that his body jerked at an unexpected touch. She had curled her thumb over the swollen crest of his erection, pressing the tiny slit as if to block his impending end. The move made him excruciatingly aware of the pressure that was building in his scrotum. An uncontrollable tremor seized his limbs.

"Touch me," she gasped against his cheek. "Put your hand between my legs."

Heart thumping wildly, he fumbled through sleek warm folds and tangled curls. This was a woman's *yoni*. This was a lover's prize. Her liquid welcome was a wonder as deep as any he had found through meditation. He had called forth her arousal. *He* had. He slid two fingers through the constriction at her gate and moaned at her forceful clasp. She was soft inside, as soft as the lotus flower most venerated by the sutras. To his gratified relief, her *madanachatra* did indeed project like a plantain root from the upper petals of her sex.

Burnishing the tiny organ with his thumb, he drew his fingers in and out. The sound of her wetness made him swell even fuller with excitement. Her hand gentled on his shaft, but it did not help. His skin was as sensitive as if its nerves had been multiplied by ten. He was not sure he could bear this painful pleasure a second more.

"Your *kama-salila* is very generous," he said through gritted teeth, struggling to distract himself with words.

She laughed, a beguiling, throaty sound, and pushed her sheath up his hand. "I hope that is a good thing."

"It is recommended that the woman be wet in order for the man's organ to slide easily in the narrow—"

She cut him off with a kiss. He could not think at all then, except to wish most heartily that his penis and not his fingers were clasped inside her fragrant depths. As if she knew, her hand tightened on the sensitive ring beneath his crest.

"Move with me," she said. "Pretend that we are joined."

He did as she directed, tightening his hindquarters to push himself through her hold. Without even trying they began to breathe together, gasping in tandem, tensing in tandem, as the end he craved and wished would last forever rumbled like an avalanche into view.

It was a panic in him, to make it last, to engrave the moment in his mind. He showered her face with kisses, a gesture he could not withhold.

"Sweet Luisa," he said, her name a cry for things he'd lost so long ago their only trace was a tangled hurt. He nuzzled her swollen nipple, drawing it with her robe between his teeth.

"Take it," she said, tearing the wool away with her other hand. "Take what you want." She arched up to him and gave him what he longed for. The tip of her breast was softer than silk against his tongue. She moaned as he sucked and the sound was flames licking through his skin.

The final rise was more intense than he had dreamed a man could feel. He hung on a cutting wire, its promise of imminent fall sublime. To plummet, to give in . . . But wrong as the physical pleasure was, it was not enough. His body demanded more. Union. Penetration. He had no mind then; he only had desire.

With a curse of resignation, he wrenched his mouth away.

"I cannot pretend," he said harshly, drawing his fingers from her sweetly clinging sex. "I belong inside you."

"No. Don't relinquish your vow for me." Her hand pressed his fingers back to her softness and her mouth opened on his neck. He was dizzy, confused. Her tongue trembled briefly on his skin. "Now. Come with me now."

She did not even have to bite him. Energy rushed up through his feet, a flood of unstoppable golden-white. He felt the barrier around her aura give, swirling and blending into his. She caught her breath, but not in pain. He had a second to wonder at her reaction and then his climax burst like a never-ending fountain. One instant his shaft was pure, burning steel, the next a convulsing instrument of bliss. His groan echoed through the little chamber, as strange to his ears as this ecstasy was to his body. Again the tight, squeezing shock lanced through him, again, again, a release so deep it seemed to rake his soul.

He did not realize she had joined him until the last flickering pull of her sheath tugged at his hand.

She wriggled as it faded and relaxed against him, her mouth curled, her cheeks rosy, her eyes glowing like emeralds fringed with gold. He could not contain a flush of pride at her satisfaction. His head was light but strangely clear. Already his weakness was fading. Then he looked down at the much diminished organ she still held in her hand. She was petting it as if she relished its sticky softness. So much for pride, he thought.

It seemed important to acknowledge what she had done.

"I must thank you," he said. "I would have taken you if you had not stopped me."

She batted her lashes and dragged one sticky finger across her tongue. The gesture nearly put him in a trance.

"Maybe I did save you," she said playfully. "And maybe you would have found your strength."

He shook his head to clear it. "You should not give me more credit than I deserve."

Her eyes hooded as if she were embarrassed to have been caught doing him a kindness. "I know you are not used to facing urges of that strength. It seemed unfair to let you do something you would regret. Especially when I still need your help."

Martin did not believe her explanation, though he chose to pretend he did. "I do not know what else I can try. Unless . . ." He pushed up from her, recalling the way her aura had momentarily seemed to welcome his. He knew orgasm called up a special energy from the earth, an energy transmuted by the nature of the connection between the partners.

All of which had been academic up till now. But if Luisa could utilize that special force, without ill effect, it could prove an alternate source of sustenance. Lost in thought, he rubbed the sides of his mouth, remembering too late that her scent clung to his fingers. To his embarrassment, his organ twitched and began to lengthen.

"Unless what?" she prompted.

He shook his head and rose, shaking his robe down as he did. The *chuba*'s fall was not as straight as it should have been. Frowning, he shoved his arms back in the sleeves. Apparently one encounter would not sate this new appetite. "It is only a thought," he said. "I do not wish to raise false hopes."

"Or anything else," she said, with a pointed glance toward the tenting wool.

Responding with dignity was a challenge but he managed as best he could. "The sun will rise soon," he said. "I am sure you want to rest."

He left her lolling on the cushions, more beautiful than a goddess, more nettlesome than a fly. He did not tell her he went to consult his guide; indeed, he hardly wished to admit to himself what he planned to do. Fairness, however, demanded he speak to the abbot immediately.

If Martin's theory had the slightest chance of being true, Geshe Rinpoche would know.

HE found his teacher in the storeroom with the steward. They had pulled two dusty cushions together and sat, hunched and cross-legged, before a fat horizontal book. The single window cast a dawn gray light over their heads. Accounting, said their serious faces, is not a business for the faint of heart. Certainly it was not a small business. The consumption of barley, tea, butter, and other staples by nearly two hundred souls had to be closely tracked. Moreover, Shisharovar did not live by pilgrims' gifts alone. The lamasery was famed for its expertly fashioned religious objects— prayer wheels, butter lamps, *malas*—both in silver and in brass. Like most of the brothers, Martin had taken part in the various stages of production, though his gift was not that of a craftsman.

No, he thought sourly, his gift was the one he had so recently put at risk. His mind was strong; it could focus like a sunbeam through a lens of glass. Such a mind was meant to serve his country and his faith. If he let his carnal urges steal the upper hand, he would waste the very talent that gave him worth.

Or so he might have said before. Chewing his lip, he stared at his felt-topped boots. Luisa also had a right to expect his aid. If he failed to put his gift at her service, when he might be her only chance, would not the omission taint any good he might do later on? She had given much to come here, to learn to live a better life, and she had done so with no one to set her a good example. From what he had seen, the one who made her barely deserved the name of teacher. Certainly he was no beloved guide like Geshe Rinpoche. Martin admired her for forging her own morals, strange as he might find them, in a less than moral world. She deserved a chance to achieve her dream.

Just as he was about to clear his throat, the abbot looked up from the accounts.

"Ah, Martin," he said, with the smile that never failed to warm his pupil's heart, "we are finished here. Please come in."

"You are *not* finished," Martin said, reading the steward's startled look.

The abbot laughed. "Well, we are surely in need of tea. Do have a break, Myingmar. I will send the *chela* for you when Martin and I are done."

The steward bowed and left, his obvious eagerness at the prospect of nourishment drawing another smile from Martin's guide. The boy who had been sleeping in the corner scurried off to get them a pot and then Martin and his teacher were alone.

The abbot cocked one wispy brow in his direction. "I must say, you look none the worse for wear. I trust your sacrifice was not too onerous."

"I am well," Martin admitted. He took the cushion the steward had just left. As Luisa promised, his body hummed with vigor. He felt both relaxed and refreshed, his spine loose, his concentration crystal clear. Which did not mean what he had done deserved reward.

"You have a confession," guessed the abbot.

Only a day ago, Martin would have hung his head in shame. An impulse he did not understand kept it upright now. "Of a sort," he said. "Mostly I am here because I require advice."

He explained his theory that the power lovers drew from sex might be changed enough for Luisa to imbibe. Direct sunlight would burn but, as the ripening of a grape transformed its rays to healthful wine, so might lovemaking transform the forces of the earth—if Luisa had a partner who knew how to channel them.

"I felt her aura give," he said, "just as it did during her vision. I admit, the amount of energy that entered was small, but it did not seem to harm her. If what I suspect is true, this could serve as an alternate form of sustenance, perhaps even a replacement for drinking blood. Once she experiences the process in its entirety, she should be able to repeat it."

"An intriguing notion." The abbot tapped his inkstained quill against the low, scratched surface of the desk. "But I do not think we can ask another man to try this. Even assuming she would accept a substitute, she might enspell him. Do you know, we had to barricade Brother Dhondrup in his cell? He kept begging us to let him serve her. Said he lived to be her slave." Brother Dhondrup was the monk Luisa had bitten on her arrival. Martin thought he had saved him from the brunt of her influence, but apparently her pull was stronger than he had known.

"He has not yet recovered?" he asked as he tried to tamp down his unease.

"He is beginning to, though I suspect her beauty dazzled him as much as her *upyr* power. She is not a woman a man could easily forget."

"No," Martin conceded, aware of the abbot's watchful gaze. Geshe Rinpoche was searching him, though for what he did not know. With an emotion akin to dismay, he realized Luisa's beauty was not what called to him most strongly now. She had become a person to him, her outer appearance not nearly as alluring as her inner fire. He thought of jewels again, of all those facets shining in the night.

When he looked outward, the abbot's attention was still on him. "If your theory is to be tested," he said, "you are the only one who can try."

Martin felt as if his guide had kicked him in the belly. Did Geshe Rinpoche place so low a value on his student's continued progress on the Path? Never mind his *gelong* vow, didn't he care that Luisa had the potential to tempt Martin far away? If her only attraction were carnal pleasure, Martin thought he might have fought. But she also offered adventure and mystery and, most persuasive of all, the chance to share an affection whose appeal he had just begun to savor.

Amazing as it seemed, Luisa *liked* him.

Didn't his guide understand how powerful that was to one who had rarely felt accepted? Or did some other motivation lay behind his actions, some agenda Martin was too slow to comprehend?

"Come," the abbot chided gently, "you cannot mean to say you expected, or even wanted, me to assign another lama to this task."

Martin knew his teacher spoke the truth. The thought of anyone else touching Luisa, knowing Luisa's innermost essence, was intensely repellent. "Of course not," he said, then huffed out a harried breath. "But I thought you might at least try to discourage me."

"When have I stood between you and an important choice?"

Martin had to admit he never had and yet his guide seemed oddly eager for him to risk his calling. That was what he could not understand, what seemed a betrayal of their bond.

Before he could find the words to explain, the abbot clasped Martin's upper arms. The growing light picked out the wind-worn lines around his eyes, eyes that shone as black as water in a cave. Martin knew his teacher's face better than he knew his own, but in that moment he might as well have been a stranger.

"Are you so certain," said the abbot, "that this course will lead you from the road you were meant to take? Maybe if you taste what you are proposing to give up, your sacrifice will have more meaning. Or maybe you will decide you don't want to be celibate after all. You know our sect does not require it, just as you know many yogins have taken lovers. Your spiritual progress need not be hampered unless you let it."

But I fear I will let it, Martin wanted to cry. I fear I will trade everything for her.

This, however, was not the abbot's problem.

"You must meditate," he said. "The answer will come."

The suggestion was clearly a dismissal. Martin rose, and bowed, and withdrew toward the door on less than steady legs. He would do as his guide advised. He would meditate. He only wished an answer existed that would be wholly good.

His teacher halted him at the threshold. "Your heart," he said, "is not your weakest organ. You should trust it, old friend. Through many lives it has not misled you."

Martin's throat was too thick to speak but he nodded in acknowledgment.

The abbot, it seemed, already knew what he wanted his choice to be.

Six

LUISA rose from her bed shortly after sunset. Though the butter lamps had burned out, the light of the stars was enough for her *upyr* eyes. Catlike, she stretched her arms and spine. She had enjoyed her first sound sleep since arriving in Tibet. Her first meal, as well, not to mention her first good—

But her mind stopped short of calling what she had shared with Martin her first good tupping. Their encounter had been more rewarding than she expected, if also less than she desired.

Frowning, she straightened her robe and ran her fingers through her waist-length hair. No more than this was required to keep her tidy. What Martin called her aura kept her person and her clothes in immaculate condition—though she had never lost her fondness for a lengthy soak. She would treat herself to one, she vowed, the minute she got home.

But thoughts of Firenze made her restless. Swinging her cloak around her shoulders, she headed for the door. Apparently the nervous monk who stood outside was there for her protection: he let her pass without a word.

Not wishing to disturb anyone else, she turned her steps down the abandoned corridor. The stiff yakhide soles of her boots made shushing sweeps through the eddies of frosted snow. Beneath its powdering the stones were cracked. Had this wing been new when Martin first lived in Shisharovar? Had he wandered down this hall as she did? Had his mind been filled with different dreams?

She smiled at the ease with which she had accepted his beliefs.

But how could she not? Since turning *upyr* she had seen more marvels than she could count.

A narrow stairway led her upward, so dark even she had to feel her way by touch. The sound of air whistling drew her higher. Finally, after shouldering a heavy door aside, she reached the roof. Her breath caught at the vista that stretched before her: range upon range of rugged snowcapped mountains, their peaks milky and effulgent, their shadows streaks of sapphire ink. In every direction the towering crags marched over the horizon, as if their bulk filled all the world. The sky above them was the purest black she'd ever seen. Against its backdrop the stars seemed not like diamonds but pinprick holes through which the light of some higher sphere was breaking through.

God is here, they seemed to say, a greater god than humans can conceive.

Luisa felt simultaneously dwarfed and exhilarated. How can I exist? she thought. How can any creature? Why would God need more than the beauty of this night?

She stepped through the shallow drifted snow, past gilded, onion-peaked structures that rose from blocks of stone. From pedestal to peak the things were twice her height and strung one to another with lines of wind-torn prayer flags. They exuded an eerie vibration as she passed. Were these the reliquaries her native guide had called *chortens*: containers for the possessions, and occasionally the remains, of holy abbots? Dorje had claimed the bodies were boiled in yak butter and salted to preserve them. The practice seemed bizarre, but who was she to judge? Whatever lay inside them, the structures must be some sort of shrine. They reminded her of churches she had known. The lamas' beliefs had not quite let their contents die.

Reaching the wall at the perimeter of the roof, she crossed her arms atop the ledge. As she did, images of her sire came to her mind. What, she wondered, would Auriclus make of her present quest? For that matter, who would she be if he had not left her? If he had taught her more of his secrets, would her powers now be so great these lamas would be in awe of her? Would she even care about a thing like not living off stolen blood?

Martin would care, she thought, then shook her head at how easily the monk filled her awareness. Her own father she barely recalled, so completely had her master's shadow subsumed his. But even Auriclus could not obscure the shadow Martin threw.

Ever since he had withdrawn from her cell the night before, she had sensed him teetering on the cusp of a decision, one that would affect not just her mission but whatever chance they had of being more than a petitioner and her guide.

Troubled, she joined her hands in an attitude of prayer. I want that too much, she thought. I want everything from him too much. She closed her eyes, then opened them to the sky. The truth was as undeniable as the stars. She loved him. For the second time in her long *upyr* life, and perhaps for the first time that was real, Luisa del Fiore was in love.

She had not anticipated this development. How could she? Martin was no father figure like Auriclus. Nor was he a hedonist, despite having shown himself ready enough for pleasure the night before. He had a better heart than she did, and probably a stronger mind. God knew his soul was purer and yet, when she was with him, when she looked into his incomparable gentian eyes, she felt not diminished but complete.

He had never judged her. In truth, she could tell that he admired her.

Which was all the more reason she must not cause his fall.

Let him go, she thought, tightening her jaw against the blooming pain. Stop tempting him and you'll have earned your freedom from the blood. She could make it a bargain with the angels. Surely one good deed was not too much to ask.

And if the good deed gained her nothing, what then?

Luisa forced her muscles to relax. She stared at the mountains, their ceaseless winds blowing the hem of her mink-lined cloak against her thighs. As if in sympathy, her robe twisted around her ankles. Fur and wool, luxury and necessity—and her mind unable to say at the moment which was which. Blithely she had spoken of wishing to live more ethically, a half-truth at best, designed to impress the people whose help she begged. Much more important had been her desire to depend entirely on herself. To need a human for its blood, even a human she could suborn, was to be vulnerable. But now she needed much more than blood.

With a skin-chilling shock, she saw her quest had come to mean less to her than one man's good opinion.

Then she laughed, sharp and bitter, her breath clouding thickly in the air. Even now she hedged the truth. She wanted more than Martin's good opinion. She wanted his well-being.

⚬⚬⚬

FROM his interview with the abbot Martin had gone straight to his private chamber, where he turned at once to light his altar's lamps. Now a cone of his finest Indian incense smoldered sweetly in a dish. He had bathed and stretched and said his customary prayers. He had prostrated himself and fixed his inner vision on a point. Or he had tried to.

His body wanted nothing to do with prayer. His body wanted only to wallow in the memory of Luisa's touch. His phallus throbbed with readiness, hard and heavy and full, demanding union, demanding her.

His guide had claimed his heart was not his weakest organ. What, Martin wondered, would he have said of his cock?

His desires were at war with each other. He wanted to be the man of his own ambitions: a steadfast servant of his faith. Being recognized for his spiritual achievements was admittedly attractive, but more than that he wished to be true at heart.

Of course, he also wished to be the person who saved Luisa.

How else could he ensure that she remembered him? Not in

bed. Too many men more skilled than he had gone before him. But this only he could do. A hundred years from now his image would brand her heart.

Sighing, he unfolded his body from the floor.

He had no business with her heart. Their likely paths in life could not have been more divergent. Except—

He brought both fists to his mouth and pressed them hard against his teeth.

Except his heart had business with her.

In spite of everything, he and Luisa were kindred spirits. Both were strong of mind, both concerned with a longer stretch of time than most lives could hold. Certainly both were trying to balance the promptings of the body against those of the soul.

Nor were those the only parallels. Luisa had twice been betrayed by the men who sired her: the first marrying her to a brute, the second simply leaving. To Martin's mind, neither abandonment was deserved. Whatever her flaws, his life was immeasurably richer for having met her. Auriclus had missed out. And so had Martin's father. Luisa had taught him that by proving how easy to love one imperfect soul could be.

His eyes went hot with the sting of truth. He did not simply admire Luisa's beauty or her spirit or her decadent Western mind. He loved her as any man loved a woman. He loved her as he loved the peace of meditation and the mountains in the spring. He loved her as the boyhood friends he'd never had. He loved her as he loved his cherished guide.

He also loved her as herself, in a manner unlike any other. He, who had never thought to love at all, loved her with all his being.

The discovery floored him. It was a miracle, a raw, exciting terror. He tottered under it like a two-year-old, neither knowing nor caring if the abbot had been right about there being a karmic bond between them. Whether they had shared a thousand lives or none could not have mattered less.

He loved her.

Stumbling to the door, he leaned his brow against its time-worn wood. He could not ignore this emotion. He had to sum it into his accounts.

Not here, though, not in his solitary monkish cell. He needed . . .

He did not know what he needed but he strode into the hall to find it, letting his instincts be his guide. The decision was there before him. He had only to clear his mind.

MARTIN was waiting in her cell when she returned. The sight of him made her heart sink to her belly. He sat tailor-fashion on the floor, in the position his people called the lotus, so still he might have been a statue. His string of wooden prayer beads was wrapped around one hand, their surface smooth as stone from many tellings. Gone was his agitation of the night before: his arousal, his embarrassment, anything that marked him a man of flesh. His absolute, effortless peace filled the room the way a stream of water fills a cup. Luisa inhaled without thinking, as if she could draw his serenity into herself. All she did was underscore the differences between them. Self-denial and contemplation were the essence of his world. She did not see how it would ever mesh with hers.

As if he'd known the moment she entered, his eyelids slowly rose. "I am glad you are here," he said, in his deep, heartbreaking voice. "I have something to show you."

He set down his beads and extended his hand to her, though she knew he needed no help to rise. His hold was warm, its illusion of camaraderie intense. He did not drop her hand even after he reached his feet. With a gentle smile, he led her to the cell beside her own.

She had assumed the space was empty, and maybe it had been. Now, however, it glowed with warmth. Butter lamps ringed the room and someone had softened the floor with a rich Pashmina carpet. The walls resembled a sultan's tent, draped in hangings of painted silk. Far happier than the banner of Hayagriva, these *thangkas* depicted various Buddhas and their consorts, each gracefully straddling the lap of her protector. The colors were bright and pure, the execution of the figures marvelously adept. Decorative as they were, she did not notice at first how explicitly they were joined.

But none of this was as suggestive as the pile of cushions on the floor. No dust marred them, no fading or frays of age. All red, all shining silk damask, they could not be the prop for anything but a seduction.

"No," she said, turning to her companion. "Martin, I don't think we should do this."

If anything, his manner grew calmer. "It is my wish," he said, his beautiful eyes like stars, "and possibly your need. Last night, at the moment we gave each other pleasure, I felt your barrier begin to fall. You opened your aura to mine and the flow of power did not harm you. Because of this, I believe you may be able to live off the energy lovers share. But there is only one way to find out."

"No," she said again. "Your vow . . ."

"I have not yet taken it."

"In your heart, you have." The scope of what he offered stunned her. She ran her fingers through her hair, distressed to the point where she knew she'd become disheveled. "Martin, I am honored. Truly, I am. But this is not a sacrifice I can accept. Perhaps I could make this experiment with someone else."

He frowned at her, his expression abruptly cool. "You are welcome to try, but I doubt you will see the same results, especially since—despite your many lovers—you never saw them before. Those men did not have my mental training. Nor, I think, did your soul view them as equals. Once you have experienced the process of exchanging energy in full, then perhaps your body will know the trick of repeating it with another."

"You are jealous," she said with a flattered laugh.

Martin drew himself up. "If I am jealous, it is no one's business but my own. I do not wish you to be a killer, not even against your will. If I were able to help and did not, any death you caused would be on my hands."

"I am responsible for myself! The minute I took what Auriclus offered that was true. Even if no one but you could aid me, I could not let you do this. You were born to be a monk."

"Was I?" he said. "I have lived as a monk before, taken my vows, followed a path no woman shared. Perhaps it is time to walk another way. Perhaps my spirit shall not progress until I do."

Luisa tossed her hair in exasperation. "How could someone like me help you progress? No. I am not going to let you risk everything just to keep me from drinking blood!"

He covered his face and shook his head, the gesture at odds with his usual self-control. When he dropped his hands, his eyes swam with emotion, part rueful laughter, part something deeper than she could read. "You underestimate the strength of your character—and overestimate mine. I am afraid more lies behind my offer than concern for you and your future meals."

"More?" she said warily.

"Much more," he admitted, his seriousness belied by a spark of humor in his eye. "There is my shamefully eager body, which remembers too well the pleasure of your touch. There is my teacher, who seems to think I should taste what I'm giving up. And let us not forget my curiosity. To know the full fruits of passion is an enticement no holy man should discount."

Luisa fiddled with the edge of her heavy cloak. Though she had no right to ask, she could not hold her next question inside. "Are those *all* the reasons you want to help?"

"No," he said, a laugh in it, but his amusement soon fell away. He looked sad then, as if his years truly were as great as hers. "No. There is one more reason. I am not sure you will want to hear it but, in truth, it is the only one that counts." He took her hand from the button it had been twisting and pressed it to his steadily thudding heart. Her own was fluttering with dread, with hope, with so many feelings she could not sort them out. "Luisa." He laughed again, an ironic puff of air. "How many times you must have heard this! I wonder if you will even understand what it means. I love you, Luisa. I love you and wish to give you the one gift no one but I can offer. I wish to free you. I wish to give you your heart's desire."

"You love me?" She knew she must sound astounded. She was astounded. Her heart felt as if it had been taken out and put in backward. "I—I—" She swallowed and willed her throat to work. "I love you, too."

He blinked, twice, and then his smile spread like honey across his face, slow and broad and, at the last, completely blinding. "Well," he said, "of all the answers I prepared for, I did not think of this."

"I have not—That is, I do not believe I have ever—"

"You are stammering," he said, and this also seemed to charm him. His arms found their way around her waist.

"I am trying to say I have never felt this way before. Not in a hundred sixty years."

He laughed. "I have not felt this way in a hundred sixty life-times."

"Martin." She struck his shoulder in gentle scold. "You cannot possibly remember so far back."

"Perhaps not," he conceded, his gaze falling heatedly to her mouth, "but it feels true."

She waited for him to kiss her, poised between expectation and impatience. He caught his lip in his teeth, and licked it, and finally lowered his mouth to hers. Their softness melded together like two parts of a whole. This time he needed no instruction. Deeper and wetter his kisses sank while he cradled her head and cupped her bottom in his hand. Yes, she thought, meeting the sweet intrusion of his tongue. Oh, yes, this was what she needed. His arousal pressed her hip, thickly eager and sun warm. If her bones hadn't been melting, she would have climbed him. Happily, one of his thighs found a home between her own. She rolled herself up it and clutched his muscled shoulders, moaning as his teeth lightly scored her neck.

"Luisa," he murmured, the sound a soft caress, "let us share what lovers know."

Her answer was a groan he had no trouble understanding. With endearingly awkward ardor, he divested her of her clothes. Her cloak fell with a thump, then her robe. He nearly tripped over both trying to wrestle his arms out of his sleeves.

The stumble was forgotten in an instant. His naked body was spectacular: long, lean, as graceful as any artist's masterwork. More graceful, really, because it was alive. His erection jerked and throbbed, its blood-dark thickness luring her to her knees.

"No," he gasped as her mouth engulfed the silky crest, as his hips cocked forward in spite of his denial. He tasted of salt and lust, his pulse so quick she could not count it. "Luisa, stop." He was laughing but he meant it. With one final purse-lipped pull she set him free.

"Up," he urged, and pulled her to her feet.

Her hands went immediately to his chest, stroking, exploring. His skin was smooth, his hair a rasping warmth. She followed the line of it to his navel and twirled the tip of one finger just inside. His eyes went dark. With her touch still on him, he turned to toss her fur-lined cloak across the bed. Incense wafted as the garment settled neatly, mink side up.

She was behind him now, behind his beautiful tapering back. She pressed her breasts against it and kissed his nape. The dip of his shoulder invited her cheek to rest and she could not restrain a sigh. The comfort of holding him was stronger than shade at noon. He was so solid, so marvelously aroused. His body hummed silently with excitement. To her, his control was as alluring as his need. Wound tight with anticipation, she looked beyond him to the waiting cloak-draped cushions.

"You," she said, "want to see me on that fur."

He shuddered as her hands smoothed downward toward his groin. "Yes."

"Legs spread . . . sex wet . . ."

"I will spread your legs," he offered, then hesitated. "If you would allow it."

Her nails drew another shudder as they ruffled his pubic curls. "Yes," she said, "I believe I would."

She pulled away and circled him, hands trailing, gaze locked hungrily on his face. A muscle in his side twitched as she strafed it. He could not quite keep his attention on her eyes. Her naked body was clearly a distraction: her breasts, her belly, her pale and rounded thighs.

Look your fill, she thought with a secret smile as she lowered herself to the bed. Never had she been so grateful for her beauty. It was a gift she gave him, a gift that—pray God—would please them both. Especially him, though. She felt young again beneath his reverent gaze, every nerve and sinew born anew. Her back settled to the cushions. With knees bent and pressed together, she reached up for his hands.

"Come," she said, "make a place for yourself where you belong."

His face darkened at her invitation, the blood rising up his chest and neck. He did not speak but knelt as if in supplication at her feet. His palms settled on her knees, their dampness just as erotic as their warmth. Gently, slowly, he pushed her legs apart until her golden triangle was bared to view.

He exhaled then, long and hushed, and slid his fingers up her thighs.

"You are a flower," he breathed, spreading her folds with such delicacy she had to strain to feel the touch. "I would paint you, if I could, and gaze at you every day."

His words and his gleaming, avid eyes robbed her of speech. Called forth by his admiration, a trickle of fluid slipped from her sex. As his thumb traced its downward course, his mouth fell open, then closed when he swallowed hard.

She wanted to laugh but she did not, no more than she told him what to do. These discoveries were his to make, his to learn on his own. With a mixture of confidence and shyness, he shifted between her legs. He was intent now, his breathing shallow, his pulse racing visibly in his throat.

Hush, love, she thought, her hands stroking down his back. Your body knows what to do. Indeed, his instinct led him better than he knew. His hips settled into the cradle of hers as if a lodestone drew them down. With heart-stopping accuracy, the tip of him probed her then pressed inside. His breath caught, held. He was testing the feel of her, taking in that first luscious clasp. She knew her softness pulled him, knew he wanted more. He pressed deeper, surer, his vision glazed, his senses tuned to that miraculous inner glide. He hilted with a sigh.

"Ah," he said, a sound of enchanted wonder. "Ah, Luisa, that is so *good*."

She laughed and hugged him with all her limbs. His hips ground back at her but it wasn't long before he complained.

"You must not hold me so tightly," he said. "I am certain I should move more vigorously in and out."

She let him do as he wished, loving his fits and starts and gasps.

"No," he said, after a rather amusing failure to find a working rhythm. "I need—"

With a strength that impressed her, he secured her against him, then tipped back and crossed his legs. The movement brought her over his lap, her thighs to either side of him, her sex pressed snugly onto his. His erection thumped inside her as if it approved the change. She could not help noting that their position echoed the sacred pictures on the walls.

"There," he said, happily flexing deeper with his hips, "now you are my consort."

"May your consort move?"

His eyes twinkled. "I should be grateful, for my hands would be free to touch you as you deserve."

He must have thought she deserved a lot. He caressed her as she rose and fell: her back, her haunches, her belly and hard-tipped breasts. His touch was like a drug. Her skin began to hum at the sweeping strokes. She would have purred if she'd had the means. His mouth glided up her neck and found her ear. The rush of his breath made her sheath tighten on his shaft. His fullness was exquisite, his living, vital pulse. His hands fell to her waist. He gripped her, half guiding, half greedy, then rested his forehead against hers.

"Let down your walls," he whispered. "I want to touch your soul."

Letting him in was as easy as drawing breath. Between one thrust and the next, her barriers simply fell. He was inside her then, as if her heart had always been his home. She could see with his eyes, feel with his body. His love was a sea that buoyed her in boundless warmth, deep, unstinting, as amazing as it was sure. No emptiness could survive it. This was her salvation, no matter what came to her in the end. She was loved and she could love, a blessing greater than any for which she'd dared to pray.

Their auras flickered together, shimmers of green and blue, ribbons of red and gold. Martin groaned and thrust so hard he lifted her from his lap. She could feel his swelling rise to climax, or maybe she felt her own. Sensation blurred, doubled, as if he were joining with her in truth, as if their bodies had lost their separate forms.

A hallucination, she thought. Real or not, the intermingling was delicious. Her body became her sex, yielding, giving, being taken in every cell.

And then she remembered.

This was how she had changed. This was how Auriclus had made her an *upyr*.

Exultation rose like new spring wine. She could make Martin

what she was. She did not have to lose him, did not have to watch him age and die.

But—said the last sane corner of her mind.

But—said the first selfless corner of her heart.

If she made him what she was, she shared not just her gifts but also her burdens. He might have chosen to love her but he had not chosen that.

Her awareness expanded, then stilled. Colors pulsed in the hush like veils spun out of gems. She felt his attention, and his question, as if it were her own.

"We must stop," she said, or maybe only thought. "I cannot steal your future."

"And if my future lies with you?"

She wanted to believe so badly, the ache of it rang through her bones.

"Luisa," he said, his thought-voice as rich as velvet spice. "In all my lives, I have lost and found more treasures than I can count. But none of them, none, ever meant as much to me as you. There is no nirvana without you. There is only an empty night."

She searched him for the truth, though she knew he could not lie. What if he came to be sorry? What if she dragged him down?

"We will drag each other up," he promised. "Together we will be twice as strong."

"This is your choice? Truly?"

"I did not know how much I wanted this until I looked into my heart. I will not be sorry, Luisa. And I am not afraid."

All that he was infused the declaration: his pride, his courage, his curious, questing mind. It seemed impossible to fathom and yet she saw that loving her had made him stronger. Gone was his bitterness at his father, gone his fear that he never would belong. Because she loved him, all of him, he knew he belonged and always had. He did not need to renounce either West or East. Instead, all the world could be his home.

"Change me," he said, "and I will share the world with you."

⟶⟨⟨⟨⟨⦿⟩⟩⟩⟩⟵

A shower of stars burst within him, diamond cool and bright. His body disappeared, no boundaries, no limits, just sparks spread far and wide. I am the world, he thought, but a heartbeat later he slammed back in.

He was all body then, all tautly focused nerve and flesh. His phallus tightened. His throat burned with a swallowed scream. Luisa tugged at him, outside, inside. She was so wet, so warm. Sweat sprang from his pores, the pleasure like a cramp. When it swelled his cry broke free. He could not stop it, could not stop any of it. He came so strongly he almost turned inside out.

When Luisa arched, he came again.

And then a peace like none he'd ever known spread outward from his sex. It was purely a peace of the body but its power coursed sweet and deep. For the first time in his life, he knew what it was to be flawlessly in balance, every bone and muscle, every particle of being. Sighing at the liquid, golden feel, he toppled with her in his arms onto the bed. Apparently her strength had not abandoned her. She leaned over him, smiling, her hair hanging around them like new-washed silk. She seemed an angel to him, a *dakini* of the highest grade.

Angel or not, she traced the shape of his face with the tip of her longest finger. "You hardly look different," she mused, then laughed deep in her throat. "You must have been nearly perfect as you were."

The compliment pleased him, though it seemed vain to admit.

"I am sleepy," he confessed, watching her through pleasantly drowsy eyes. "If I let myself go under, will I forget what you have done?"

She smoothed his brow beneath her thumb. "I am not sure but I do not think so. Auriclus never taught me to blank a mind. Not that it matters. I would not alter your memory. I trust you with my secrets more than I trust myself."

This compliment he accepted without shame. "I shall strive," he said huskily, "to be worthy of your esteem."

HE woke to a subtle twang inside his body. *Sunset.* It was almost a taste, like water from a spring: sweet, pure, the darkling dawn of his new day. At some point, he and Luisa had rolled out of bed onto the carpet. Despite the fading light, his vision was crystal clear. Different. Changed. I am *upyr* now, he thought. I am a foreign being. The recognition inspired exhilaration instead of fear. Maybe tomorrow would bring regret. For tonight he was simply glad.

He shifted, oddly at home in his altered form. The nerves in his back were alive to every strand of Kashmir wool. Luisa, bless her, lay sleeping across his chest. She was warm even now, or possibly he'd grown cooler. Her skin still felt like burnished silk. Desire overwhelmed him, sharper and harder than before. If this was what *upyr* felt, he did not know how she had held off. Too impatient to wake her, he rolled her under his body and thrust inside.

"Mm," she said, and cocked her calf around his hip. "I like an early riser."

The act was easier now, more natural. The rhythm came without duress. His arms were tireless, his thighs like tempered steel. And the pleasure . . . that was a roaring flood. When he threw back his head in climax her nails left approving half-moon pricks against his skin. Sadly, they had healed by the time she climbed atop and began to ride. He would have liked to bear her mark, just as the sages promised in the sutras. That one small disappointment, however, could not allay his joy.

As if she sensed this, she smiled through her flaxen hair. "You are not hungry," she said, wonder growing in her eyes.

Martin gripped her waist. "Only for you," he said, and thrust as deeply as he could. "From now on only for you."

"SHALL I come with you?" she asked. She stood before him, her head lowered, her hands resting lightly on his breast. She was the picture of the wife he had not known he wanted.

"No," he said, "I have delayed this long enough."

She smiled at that, a secretive curling of her mouth. Since sunset they had put everything off but love. On the floor. Against the wall. Standing. Sitting. Twice they had even done it head to toe.

He had liked that. He thought it was a thing a god would do.

"I do not care what you say," he grumbled even as his body stirred again. "This incessant desire for coupling cannot be normal."

Her hands flowed seductively across his shoulders. "I did not say it was normal, I said it was natural. You were a healthy young man. Now you are a healthy *upyr*. Given your history, how could you not have numerous unmet urges to fulfill?"

"But I am turning into a fiend!"

She looked at him, her eyes round with concern. "Is that what you think? That I made you a fiend?"

"No, my love, no." He kissed her alabaster forehead. "I am merely feeling guilty for enjoying this so much. Or, rather, I am feeling guilty for not feeling guilty enough."

Her face lit up, as sunny as daybreak. "You called me your love."

He laughed. "You are my love. And now I must go, before you convince me I cannot."

She nuzzled the hollow beneath his throat. "Are you certain you don't want me to talk to the abbot with you?"

"I am," he said. "This task is mine alone to perform."

He was sorry to leave her despite his words. Her warmth had kept his anxiety at bay. Yes, his teacher had expected him to share the act of coition with their guest. He could not, however, have expected Martin to turn *upyr*.

Hands fisted determinedly at his sides, he strode through the lower hall. He stopped when two monks shrank in horror from his path. Only then did he realize how swiftly he had been moving, huge inhuman bounds that ate the distance.

"I am practicing a new power," he growled at the wide-eyed monks.

The men exchanged a wary look. Obviously this feat was more than they expected even from Shisharovar's best *naljorpa*.

I shall have to go, he thought. I do not fit in here now.

The knowledge hurt but not as much as he feared. Even if Luisa had lived close, he would have been ready to leave. The wider world was calling. Perhaps it had been all along.

He closed his eyes and let the new awareness find a home. When he opened them, his teacher stood before him. The glow that lit his aura told Martin he had come from the midnight prayer.

"Rinpoche," he said, bringing his hands together for his bow.

"Martin," responded the abbot, "I see you have achieved all that I hoped."

Martin gaped at him. The abbot's eyes crinkled in amusement.

"Come." He took Martin's arm. "I think this calls for a cup of tea."

He led him to a small reception chamber, the same room in which Luisa had been chained. A pot waited on a table with two brown cushions pulled to its side. When his teacher poured a cup of pure gold Indian brew, Martin knew he had seen the truth. Luisa could not drink Tibetan tea, and neither now could he.

"How could you know?" he demanded. "And why are you not upset?"

"You have your gifts," said the abbot, "and I have mine."

"But—"

"I saw it," he said, "in a vision the day she came. You were gleaming in the moonlight white as stone. 'She is mine,' you said. 'She is the one for whom I have blindly waited all these years.' Oh,

I knew my vision of the future was a chance and not a surety, and that it would be wrong to push, but I hoped . . ."

"You hoped!" Twice now his teacher had used that word. Martin was so flustered he had to put down his cup. "Rinpoche, I know I have come to view what happened as a blessing, but how could you hope? This change can only take me far away."

"That," said the abbot, blowing firmly across his tea, "is precisely what I hoped." To Martin's astonishment, his teacher's eyes welled up with tears. "Old friend, if you had seen the shadow I have seen hanging over our little country, you would know we will need every friend that we can make. You are no longer my charge, and I cannot give you orders, but I am not too proud to plead. Be our emissary, Martin, not to preach but to share our ways, to teach the world that Tibet is a treasure that must be saved." With heartfelt strength, he gripped Martin's icy hands. "It is a work of many years, but I know you will have them now."

A tremor swept Martin's newly sensitive *upyr* nerves. What sort of shadow could cause his guide to plead?

"Do not ask," said the abbot, one hand raised as if to fend off a blow. "We may yet find a way to turn this tragedy aside. Still"—he ventured a brilliant smile—"what country does not need friends?"

"It would be my honor," Martin said through his thickened throat, "to make them on your behalf."

He rose then before emotion could shame them both. An errant thought stopped him at the door. "What would you have done if I had not let her change me?"

The abbot's grin was impish. "I could lie," he said, "and say I would have asked your Luisa to change me. Alas, even if she would have, I fear you would see through my deceit. I have always aspired to win free of this earthly plane. You are the brave one, Martin. With all my heart, I bid you joy in your life to come."

"Thank you," Martin said, and hid his smile as he turned away. For all the abbot's wisdom, Martin knew he could not conceive how much happiness one life could hold.

Seven

WITH her hunger taken care of—and so enjoyably—the voyage back to Florence was far more comfortable than the voyage out. Just the same, Luisa was not sorry to be home, especially since she had come home with him. Home, home, home, to her stately fortress on the Arno, with her view of the Duomo and her courtyard and her private cellar of fine French wine—each pleasure doubled by being shared. Even sunset, she discovered, possessed a deeper charm. A glimmer of scarlet still blooded her windows' mullioned diamond panes. She had had her blessed soak and was now being dressed for her first dinner since their return.

Martin lounged against the bedpost to watch the maids prepare her. Outwardly amused, the gleam in his eye bespoke arousal. To him, her Western clothes were like a whiff of she-cat to a tom. His nostrils flared as her whale-bone stays encased her smock, followed by the hip-widening cage of the farthingale. As her skirts were eased down the frame, he had to shift one ankle over the other. The way her breasts over-swelled the bodice made his gaze shoot aqua fire. When the maids began pinning jewels onto her slashed and embroidered sleeves, however, he could not restrain a laugh.

"Behold the glittering idol," he said, spreading his arms in a gesture he had been practicing for a week. The pose was convincingly Florentine. "Tell me, milady, is there an inch of that gown that does not bristle with lace and bows and a sultan's ransom in precious stones?"

"Pray God there is not!" she huffed, surprising the younger

maid into a laugh. Both girls curtsied when she dismissed them, leaving her alone with her new spouse.

Unaccountably nervous, she adjusted her open ruff. With a small, quirked smile and a careful foot, Martin stepped into the circle of her skirts. In waves of emerald silk they spread around the giltwood stool on which she sat. As if to make certain she was real, he touched her powdered cheek. The cosmetic pinked her skin, a requirement for one so fair when mixing with mortal guests.

"My attire is part of doing business," she explained. "People do not believe you are successful unless you put on a show, and unless they believe you are successful, they will not help you to be more so."

"Is that what you want, to be more successful?"

Heart overflowing, she kissed his hand. "How I love you. When you ask a question, you never act as if you will judge the answer. I enjoy my success, yes. I worked hard for it. It is also a kind of safety. The Inquisition cast a shadow, you know, not as long in Florence as elsewhere, but such dark days I shall not soon forget. Besides"—she flashed a smile—"someone must fund the ventures of men whose stockings are full of holes."

"Is that what you do?"

"Among other things. I am not one lone woman anymore, I am a net of enterprise. My success supports that of others and that, too, warms my pride."

"And these partners do not know what you are?"

"No. Only my lawyer and his venerable father know. The Vasari are a proud Florentine family, back from when the great *casate* built towers to defend against being assassinated by their rivals. Old and young Piero understand loyalty—and discretion. I shall have to start silvering my hair, though, soon enough." She touched the youthful coils that supported her velvet cap. "After a time, I shall go into seclusion, perhaps even leave the country. Then, once I pass quietly away, I can return as some far-flung niece and heir."

Martin rubbed his nose. "It seems complicated."

"It is inconvenient," she admitted, "but necessary, and considerate in its way. If people do not know for certain why you are odd, they are content to have you be so."

"As long as you are successful."

Luisa smiled at his quickness. "Precisely."

"I have much to learn," he said, and plopped down on their bed. The feather bolster fluffed around his hips but could not detract from his dignity, no more than could his foreign clothes.

Much as Martin enjoyed her dress, he had been shocked by the fashions for men: their expense, their colors, their—to him—immodesty. But "I do not mind," he had assured her. "I cannot make friends for Tibet unless people see me as one of them. It is only, well, to wear this garb in public . . ."

Since he was determined to try, she had steered his disappointed tailor to the less flamboyant products of his trade. Now a pair of snug black venetians, sans padding, hugged Martin's well-formed thighs. The ice blue doublet displayed his shoulders to perfection and the blazing white neck ruff, small though it was, enhanced the still-warm color of his skin.

Despite his discomfort, his regal bearing and natural talent for mimicry carried off the style. With his hair growing out, his wonderful Asian face almost seemed Italian.

"You have learned so much already," she said. "I hope you do not think—"

He shook his head, hearing the words before she spoke. "I do not think you expect it of me. In truth, I find I must work hard to discover what you desire."

"As if you could not guess!"

His blue eyes darkened with amusement. "Yes, there are many things I can guess, but since most would require being shut up in this bedchamber . . ." His grin turned wolfish, but his gaze as always was sincere. "I am learning because I want to, my love. I wish to move smoothly in your world. Once I can, I will decide what I want to do." He laughed, the sound both deep and happy. "I cannot imagine what I shall be. A builder of ships? A lawyer?"

"Oh, not a lawyer, love."

He leaned in to nip her ear. "Then perhaps a famous sculptor. Shall you sponsor me, *donna*, if I model my creations on your form?"

"Our guests . . ." she murmured as his palm slipped down her pearl-decked bodice to her waist.

"Let them wait," he growled, beginning to gather her undergown. "Then they will savor you as I do."

His mouth breathed heat across her bosom, stirring the longing that never ebbed very far. Her teeth sharpened, then the peaks of her breasts. How lovely it was to feel this hunger without fear, to know it would be matched and met. Her hands seemed to drift of their own volition up his thighs. She found the extravagant swelling at their apex, the hardness of his desire.

With a moan of impatience, he pierced her neck.

"Oh, my," she sighed at the throbbing pleasure of his bite. "By all means, let them wait!"